Alan Plater was born in Jarrow in 1935 and was brought up in Hull before training as an architect in Newcastle. He has been a full-time writer since 1961, with over two hundred assorted credits in radio, television, theatre and films. His illustrious television career began with a string of single plays as well as contributions to the pioneering *Z Cars* series. In more recent years his work has included *The Barchester Chronicles*, *The Beiderbecke Trilogy*, *Fortunes of War* and *A Very British Coup* – accumulating awards from BAFTA, the Broadcasting Press Guild and the Royal Television Society. His first film for the big screen was *The Virgin and the Gypsy*, from D. H. Lawrence's novel, while his distinguished work in the theatre includes *Close the Coalhouse Door*, written with Alex Glasgow and Sid Chaplin, a key work in the development of British political drama. His most recent television film, *Selected Exits*, based on the autobiography of Gwyn Thomas, was shown on BBC2 on Christmas Day, 1993; he is currently working on a six-part series of *Oliver's Travels* for BBC1.

Alan Plater was made a Doctor of Letters by the University of Hull in 1985 and now lives in London with his wife Shirley. When he remembers where he left his spare time, he spends it hanging around jazz clubs, willing Hull City to show some form and trying to be a useful President of the Writers' Guild of Great Britain.

For Tom Courtenay

ALAN PLATER

Oliver's Travels

WARNER BOOKS

A *Warner* Book

First published in Great Britain in 1994
by Little, Brown and Company
This edition published in 1995 by Warner Books

Copyright © Alan Plater, 1994

The moral right of the author has been asserted.

A CIP catalogue record for this book is
available from the British Library.

ISBN 0 7515 1037 8

Printed in England by Clays Ltd, St Ives plc

Warner Books
A Division of
Little, Brown and Company (UK)
Brettenham House
Lancaster Place
London WC2E 7EN

1

The End of a Beautiful Friendship

The New University of the Rhondda Valley was not a lovely place. It had not been lovely in 1944 when first built to house Italian prisoners of war. Nor had it been transformed to loveliness when the Italians went home and the Nissen huts and air-raid shelters, without benefit of paint, became a teacher training college in the first dawn of Clement Attlee's social democratic paradise. And it was not lovely now.

Oliver never worried about it.

'Oxford has dreaming spires,' he would tell his students. 'We have brooding shacks. It doesn't make the dreams any better, or any worse. Jesus Christ, D. H. Lawrence, Charlie Chaplin and Billie Holiday were all children of the shacks.'

Oliver never worried about anything. Twenty years of teaching comparative religion had left him with a profound faith in very little, though he found chaos theory a very beguiling notion. The idea that a butterfly flapping its wings in a tributary of the Amazon could eventually result in the closure of a steelworks in Port Talbot seemed as persuasive a doctrine as most variations of world theology. He had taken to telling his students:

'Disregard the universal. Pursue the trivial, preferably side-ways. The truth isn't on the main road. It's more likely to be on a side-street, or in an alleyway round the back.'

His students, apart from an occasional stray American or fun-damentalist, generally ignored him. Comparative religion was a peripheral option dangling from the main curriculum by a cob-web. Oliver was aware of this too, and rejoiced in the fact. Most of the world's ills, it seemed to him, were caused by men who believed themselves important doing things they believed to be important: on a good day it always ended in tears, on a bad day in global destruction. Oliver was not a man to start a war or pro-voke pestilence: his icons were the makers of music, the tellers of tales, the clowns and the balladeers, and all who celebrated life's footnotes, appendices and afterthoughts.

As he was driving on to the campus, Oliver stopped between the twin watch-towers where armed soldiers had once stood guard to deter Italians from escape attempts: a totally pointless precaution, even though many of the prisoners had relatives in Swansea, Cardiff and Newport. They had other preoccupations, like survival.

Today the watch-towers stood guard over a sign-writer, work-ing diligently with paint and brush. Oliver decided to watch: sign-writing, after all, was a peaceful trade. Given a sufficiently harmless text, it could well qualify for an annual subsidy from the Society of Friends.

Oliver was also intrigued by the word the man was painting: 'POLYVERSITY'.

'Polyversity? Is that a word?'

'Hardly ever. Look more closely,' said the sign-writer, a large local man, known in his village as Goronwy Grace the Lower Case, an act of homage to a great Welsh writer.

Oliver looked more closely. What he saw was:

POLYVERSITY

'POLY' was written in faded grey letters, 'VERSITY' in a brand of newly regurgitated green that could have been a designer's con-cept or a special offer at the neighbourhood DIY complex.

'I understand,' said Oliver. 'You're changing the word "Polytechnic" to the word "University".'

The sign-writer nodded.

'Behold! The New University of the Rhondda Valley! It'll look more convincing in Welsh, of course.'

Oliver, a Northern Englishman in origin and therefore a Celt, was unworried by the racial challenge, but fascinated by the work in progress.

'It seems to me that you are working backwards. If you were working forwards, the word would be . . . "unitechnic".'

'It helps to assess the spacing, see, if you work backwards. You don't see it as writing, you see it as a beautiful composition. Like a fugue or a sonata or a try by Barry John. Space and elegant proportion.'

'And a touch of nobility?' Oliver suggested.

'I might as well give the sign-writing a touch of nobility. In view of the fact that the whole university notion is terminal bollocks.'

'Is that your honest opinion?' said Oliver, impressed. 'As a man with a fine sense of proportion? The notion is bollocks?'

'Sublime lunacy, impressive even by Whitehall standards. When I was a small boy this place was a prisoner-of-war camp. We used to stand beside the perimeter fence listening to the Italians singing Verdi arias. It was their way of compensating for pasta deficiency. That's what it was fifty years ago. A prisoner-of-war camp. What does it look like now?'

'A prisoner-of-war camp?'

'Precisely. All it requires is a Kommandant and an escape committee.'

'Thank you for reminding me,' said Oliver.

'What about?'

'I'm late for an appointment with Mein Führer.'

Oliver drove off, deeper into the campus.

'Another English lunatic,' said the sign-writer, as he concentrated on transforming a grey 'POLY' into a green 'UNI' with a touch of nobility and a hint of subversion.

*

Driving across the campus, Oliver was aware of semantic tides flooding in on every shore. 'CANTEEN' had become 'SENIOR COMMON ROOM', 'TABLE TENNIS' had become 'SPORTS COMPLEX', 'LIBRARY' had become 'INFORMATION RESOURCE AND RETRIEVAL CENTRE'. All the new names had spaces beneath them to accommodate their Welsh equivalents, pending, Oliver assumed, decisions by the sign-writer about the finer nuances of translation.

He parked outside the Admin Building, known to the students as Cell Block H. It was a predominantly brick structure in the cavalier style favoured by the Ministry of Defence in the 1940s, secure against aerial bombardment but short on gaiety.

Outside the main door was a large, freshly painted parking bay marked 'VICE-CHANCELLOR'. Oliver checked with his foot to see whether the paint was still wet. It was.

He left a single footprint – like Man Friday, he realized – in the corridor leading to the Vice-Chancellor's office. In those modest days when the institution was content to be a teacher training college and, by and by, a polytechnic, he and his colleagues had lived gently and painlessly through a succession of Principals. Oliver used to tell them: 'We are a docile and co-operative community and like to keep our Principals intact.' Meeting a Vice-Chancellor would be a new and exciting experience; he had read about them in books and newspapers, seen them interviewed on television but, to the best of his recollection, had never met one face to face.

A brand-new door confronted him. It had a simulated walnut plastic veneer, and a name-plate in designer lettering reading 'T. H. MOODY, VICE-CHANCELLOR'. There was an empty space poised to receive a logo.

Oliver knocked at the door.

'Come in.'

Oliver did as he was told.

Moody was not what he had expected. The Vice-Chancellor of his imagination combined the finest elements of Albert Einstein, Duke Ellington, Bertrand Russell and Leo Tolstoy: the wisdom of all the ages, tempered with mischief. Moody possessed neither of these attributes. He was probably forty years old but looked like a sixteen-year-old television executive. He wore visible stress symptoms, suit trousers, red braces and a blue striped shirt unbuttoned at the cuffs to give easier access to his computer keyboard.

'Good morning. Oliver, isn't it?' he said, without looking up from the printout spilling out of his machine.

'That's very impressive, Mr Moody,' said Oliver.

'Sorry?'

'One small sherry party and you know all our names. Not only that, you recognized me without looking at me. Amazing sensitivity.'

'I don't know people's names. I don't remember people's faces. I'm just very good at accessing information.'

He indicated one of the many computer screens scattered meaningfully around his office: on it was a list of his morning appointments.

'Well,' said Oliver, with a shrug, 'accessing information . . . it's almost the same as remembering things, isn't it?'

Oliver, who believed in good manners, was relieved that his absence from the sherry party had gone unnoticed. He had used the back of the invitation to write down something interesting about jet aircraft, fastened the card to the refrigerator door with his magnetic frog and forgotten to go to the party.

'Be with you in a minute,' said Moody. His face and body language clearly said, I am under pressure and that is the proper condition of mankind.

Oliver looked around the office. He hadn't been in the room since 1973, for a discussion with the then Principal, a Bradford man, on the moral and ethical implications of Yorkshire allowing non-natives to play cricket for the county. At that time, the walls had told the history of the room, like ancient cave paintings. There had been a map of Europe, with arrows along the south coast of England, showing the Allies poised for invasion; a faded copy of the Beveridge Report; a set of Thomas Bewick prints; and framed photographs of the young Brian Close and Raymond Illingworth.

All these had gone, in the spirit of the 1990s. The walls were now lined with simulated cork. Enormous graphs, diagrams and projections clung to the walls, without visible means of support, as a background to the array of computers. Oliver glimpsed phrases like 'PROACTIVE MANAGEMENT INTERFLOW' and 'SYN-ERGETIC INTERFACE'. He realized the Vice-Chancellor was a man who thought himself important, and therefore likely to do important things. He reflected that, although they were little more than half a generation apart, they were separated by a culture gap that made the Grand Canyon seem like a cat scratch.

'I haven't been out of the office for a week. Things going well out there on campus?' asked Moody.

'Fine. Your parking space is very impressive and almost dry.'

'Excellent!' said the Vice-Chancellor.

Oliver assumed his pleasure related to the progress of the park-ing arrangements; obviously it would be helpful to the cause of scholarship if the cars were to interface and interact in a mean-ingful context.

'Well, what I always say is, if you get the parking right, all you have to do is work outwards and everything else will follow,' he said.

Moody crossed to his desk, sat down purposefully and read from the latest batch of computer printout: this was the true source of his delight.

'Oliver. Humanities Department. And your speciality is . . . comparative religion?'

'Yes. I originally planned to bowl off-spinners for England and play a cool jazz tenor saxophone. A true Renaissance man. But somehow I drifted. As one does.'

Moody gave no sign of having heard any of this.

'And you've been here over twenty years?'

Oliver was still drifting.

'Do you realize, Vice-Chancellor, you share a name with a fine jazz tenor saxophone player? Moody. James Moody. He worked for many years with Dizzy Gillespie.'

'My name isn't James,' Moody said sharply. His breed of man hated deviations from the designated agenda.

'I do realize that,' said Oliver. 'You would hardly have the initials "T. H." if your name were James. Do forgive me. I have a weakness for trivial footnotes and asides. Some people think it's my only distinguishing feature.'

'Since you've worked here over twenty years, you'll qualify for our maximum redundancy payment,' Moody said brightly, in accordance with the business school manual. Be positive at all times, but especially when conveying negative information.

'Excellent,' said Oliver, delighted that the interview had gone so well. He was half-way to the door when he realized he had mistaken brightness for goodness.

'Excuse me, Vice-Chancellor,' he said, 'but when you say redundancy payment, do I take you to mean . . . redundancy payment?'

'Yes.'

'There is no room for comparative religion in your philosophy?'

'It doesn't sit comfortably in any of our teaching modules. Cost-effect-wise.'

Oliver walked back towards the desk. As he did so, Moody stood up and crossed to another of his keyboards, eager to access fresh and yet more challenging information.

'I thought a module was a shiny bubble floating through space, bringing little green men from Mars. Apparently not. May I look at my information?'

Oliver warily fingered the printout relating to his case.

'Of course. I believe in open government.'

Oliver browsed openly through his career record. He found it difficult to believe that one small adventure could fill so much space, while at the same time omitting everything of interest. To be sure, there were dates in abundance and curriculum details he had long forgotten. But where were the jokes? Where were the lateral thoughts and trivial perceptions? Where was the accumulated daftness of a lifetime? He may not have given his students a true philosophical direction but he had deflected several of them half a degree to port or starboard by introducing them to the life and work of W. C. Fields, W. G. Grace, W. S. Gilbert or

W. A. Mozart. They had little superficial relationship to comparative religion but, as Oliver always said: 'It depends what you believe in.'

None of this was stored in the computer memory; therefore, it had never existed. Only one item caught his attention.

'On the final page, there's an asterisk beside my name. Is that good?'

'I hope so. It means my wife will be calling on you to discuss your leaving present.'

'Will you be passing the hat around the common room?'

'Absolutely not. We believe a compulsory levy is much less invidious.'

'And probably more cost-effective?' suggested Oliver.

'That's what our researches indicated,' said the Vice-Chancellor, with the granite confidence of a man who believed that feasibility studies told the truth.

'And if you could clear your desk and study . . .' he added, as Oliver reached the door.

'By the end of the week?'

'By the end of the afternoon.'

In the corridor Oliver met Boswell, an elderly classicist with a taste for fine old port, Donald McGill postcards and Gregorian chant.

'Good morning, Oliver.'

'Good morning, Mr Boswell. I wish you an asterisk.'

'What?'

Oliver's department building was a Nissen hut on what was now the western perimeter of the campus. Until a year ago he had been able to look out on to the student playing field, but this had been sold to a house builder who had dug trenches, laid foundations and gone bankrupt the day his workers reached the level of damp-proof course. The field now looked like an archaeological site in mint condition.

The inside of the hut formed the lecture room. Oliver's study was a boarded-off section at one end. He opened the door to find a young woman called Tricia sitting at his desk. She looked ten years old so was probably twenty. She wore blue jeans and a T-shirt with a picture of Bob Marley and the word 'WICKED!' She was working, inevitably, at a computer. Give her a fountain-pen, thought Oliver, and she'll ask for the instruction manual.

'Hi,' she said.

'Hi,' said Oliver, keen to prove he was amiably disposed towards the Now generation.

'You must be Oliver.'

'Oliver with an asterisk. I've been ordered to clear my desk and study but . . .'

'I took the liberty of doing it for you.'

In a corner of the room beside the door was a variegated pyramid: cardboard boxes, topped with black plastic garbage bags, topped with Oliver's old portable typewriter.

'Thank you,' said Oliver, genuinely grateful. The job would have taken him weeks.

'I needed to start work.'

'I see. What is your work? Would I be likely to understand?'

'I'm the Euro-Semiotics Research Fellow.'

'My congratulations. But I don't understand.'

'I'm doing research.'

'Into what?'

'Into the cost-effectiveness and relative methodologies of market research.'

'I see. And who is or are Euro-Semiotics? Is that what you said? Euro-Semiotics?'

'Euro-Semiotics PLC. They're my sponsors.'

'What do they do?'

'They're a market research company.'

Oliver weighed his thoughts and words very carefully; a passionate need to understand ran deep in his psyche, beneath the stratum marked trivia.

'Let me get this clear,' he said. 'You're being sponsored by a market research company to do market research into market research?'

'Yes.'

'And thereby work out which is the best kind of market research?'

'There's no such thing as the best. We don't make value judgements.'

'It sounds very like comparative religion.'

Paradoxically, her research programme made total sense to
Oliver. It was completely devoid of any practical meaning or
purpose. Nobody's life would be improved. She would spend ten
years examining a thousand alternative strategies. She would conclude that they were all much of a muchness and that the best
plan was for each person to select one that matched the music of
the inner soul. Scholarship had prospered since the Middle Ages
on this basis.

A thought flitted across Oliver's mind: he might have done a
sponsorship deal with Gideon Bibles PLC and saved his job.
While he was pondering this, the telephone rang.

'Hi,' said Tricia, then handed him the receiver.

'It's for you.'

'Hi,' said Oliver.

It was the Vice-Chancellor's wife, ringing to make an appointment to discuss his leaving present.

'You'd be most welcome to come to my house,' said Oliver.
'Indeed, why don't we take tea this very afternoon?'

Tricia's face and body language said: how long, O Lord, how
long will this conversation go on? She found out.

'I live at Number 3, Allchurch Avenue. Allchurch. Named
after Ivor Allchurch, a famous footballer who played for Swansea
City, formerly Swansea Town, later for Newcastle United and
throughout, with great distinction, for Wales. Though it might
be named after his lesser-known brother, Leonard. But almost
certainly Ivor. Shall we say three o'clock? Traditional kick-off
time?'

He completed the arrangements and hung up the receiver.

'And now, I imagine, you'd like me and my chattels out of
your way so you can pursue your research.'

'I was promised immediate access . . .'

'Of course.'

He crossed to his pyramid of possessions and picked up the
typewriter, an old Imperial portable. It had been Oliver's twenty-

first birthday present from his parents. His father had bought it in a pub, from a Hull docker.

'Imagine,' said Oliver. 'Once upon a time typewriters were made in England.'

'Imagine typewriters,' said Tricia.

The sign-writer had finished his work. It read 'UNIVERSITY OF THE RHONDDA VALLEY – PRIFYSGOL CWM RHONDDA'.

A team of consultants from the City of London had recommended omitting the word 'NEW', which carried overtones of impermanence and opportunism. The same team had suggested the regurgitant green paint and a logo based on the concept of a leek reading a book or, according to sceptics, a book reading a leek. This advice had cost £85,000. According to the Vice-Chancellor, it was good value. The same firm was responsible for a leading Cabinet Minister's haircuts.

Oliver stopped his car as he was leaving the campus.

'Oh, what a piece of sign-writing.'

'Thank you,' said Goronwy Grace, with a half-turn of the head, then a full turn as he saw the plastic sacks and cardboard boxes in Oliver's car.

'Another one for the gold watch, is it?'

'Yes. But you should be kept busy. Do you have a word in the Welsh language for module?'

'Module?'

'Higher education is coming in modules from now on. You'll be painting the word everywhere.'

'But what is it?'

'I thought it was a capsule bringing little green men from another planet.'

The sign-writer relaxed.

'That's all right then. I mean, they took over years ago, didn't they?'

'Yes. I think perhaps they did,' said Oliver, and headed for home.

*

Oliver's home had begun life as a miner's cottage in the nineteenth century, when pitmen were comrades, capitalists were hyenas and forelocks were touched only at gunpoint with the arrival of the militia. At its peak, the cottage had housed a collier, his wife and six children, a disabled father, a strike committee and two whippets. It was ideal for a middle-aged academic living alone.

'Time for reflection,' said Oliver and looked in the mirror.

He saw a fifty-five-year-old face, lean but not hungry, with a full head of hair and a moustache he liked to think was audacious without being aggressive. He had a wide range of facial expressions and could select at will, given a decent incentive, from a range of buttons marked world-weary, soulful, avuncular and life-in-the-old-dog-yet. Since his divorce, he had given the old dog an occasional run around the block, most recently with a pliant librarian, though these days he favoured the brisk and brief trot over the cross-country hike.

But whichever way he looked in the mirror, he saw a man in mid-life crisis. His menopause had been a long time coming. Many of his colleagues, at little more than half his age, were on their third or fourth.

'You have been made redundant. Declared irrelevant to society's needs. Of no further value to the body politic. On the other hand, since what you have been doing was of no great value in the first place, what has been lost? Zero minus zero equals zero. Look on this as your golden opportunity to do all the things you've always wanted to do.'

He frowned, trying to remember the things he had always wanted to do. He could only think of one.

'Aristotle!' he said to the mirror, and the doorbell rang.

The Vice-Chancellor's wife matched the description given to Oliver by Mr Boswell, the elderly classicist, who believed in old-fashioned good manners, whatever the odds against, and had therefore attended the welcoming sherry party.

'I found her a comely woman, patient and reluctantly dutiful, more sensitive and intelligent than her dreadful husband, by a factor of ten times ten. I was impressed by the way she gritted her teeth as her prince of darkness recited, like an ill-trained parrot:

"This is my wife, Norma". If I were she, I would seek political asylum in Tredegar.'

Oliver served tea in his living-room, which had the look of a small branch library: eighty-seven per cent of the wall surface was covered with book-shelves or stacking systems for the storage of records and compact discs. All the items were impeccably filed in alphabetical order, a farewell gift from the pliant librarian.

The one vacant area of wall had a large whiteboard which Oliver used for writing important messages to himself. The Vice-Chancellor's wife was intrigued by a list that ran:

BOEING 747
11,000 BITS
GIRAFFES
1.6 MILLION PEOPLE
SOCKS

She would have liked to ask about it but was obliged to begin with her prepared speech.

'First of all, I have to say, on behalf of the Vice-Chancellor and the University of the Rhondda Valley, how sorry we are that we are losing you.'

'I expected it,' said Oliver, 'from the very first moment.'

'You did?'

'Oh yes. Let me explain.'

Oliver stood up, crossed to the board and picked up a felt-tipped pen.

'A card arrived from your husband, inviting me to meet him at a sherry party. It was signed "T. H. Moody".'

He wrote 'T. H. MOODY' on the board.

'Unfortunately, I mislaid the invitation, in the sense that I used the back of it to write down something urgent about jet aircraft. I later transferred the information to the board here. See? I've written it here. Boeing 747.'

'I've always been fascinated by the Boeing 747 but you haven't explained why you were expecting redundancy.'

'Forgive me. I digress easily. It's very simple. Your husband's name is an anagram of "Thy Doom".'

Oliver illustrated the point on his board:

T. H. MOODY = THY DOOM

'Consequently, when I was summoned to his office this morning I said to myself, Oliver, prepare to meet Thy Doom. And I did.'

'Do you base all your life's decisions on anagrams?'

'I'm an old trivial quiz and cryptic crossword buff. They work every bit as well as the world's great religions. Rather better, as a matter of fact. And there is no known cure for my condition.'

'What about Oliver? Considered as an anagram?'

'Very astute of you to spot that, Mrs Moody.'

'Norma.'

'Quite so. The Vice-Chancellor's wife, Norma. Thank you. You are very gracious.'

Oliver continued with his exposition.

'There is no satisfactory anagram of my name in the English language. However, in French, we have the verb "*voiler*" . . .'

He wrote 'VOILER' on the board.

'This means to veil, cloak or conceal. You could say I am a veiled, cloaked and concealed man.'

'And what would this veiled, cloaked and concealed man like as a leaving present from the University?'

Oliver hesitated, caught a poignant whimper of coquettishness straining at the leash, and smiled.

'In the best of all possible worlds . . . you.'

'This is not the best of all possible worlds. This is the Rhondda Valley.'

Oliver had already picked up the pen.

'When your husband, T. H. Moody . . .'

'Or Thy Doom as he's known to his friends on the campus,' said Norma.

'When he introduced you to people at the sherry party, I am reliably informed by an eminent classicist that he did so with the words: "This is my wife, Norma."'

Oliver wrote 'WIFE NORMA' on the board.

'Another anagram?'

Oliver nodded and completed the equation so that it read:

WIFE NORMA = FIRE WOMAN

The Vice-Chancellor's wife was startled by the revelation and tried to think, very quickly, what a public-spirited woman should do in case of fire. Send for the emergency services or dig around in the attic for that old pair of bellows?

'Fire woman,' said Oliver. 'You give off heat, which is more, alas, than I can say of your husband.'

'Your veil and your cloak are slipping.'

'I know. It happens from time to time. I do try to keep them fastened. More tea?'

He knelt beside her, teapot poised, trying to create a brooding Lawrentian moment. It had worked with the librarian, but that was with the old brown teapot, inherited from his mother. He only used it at weekends. His modern, everyday teapot was high on heat retention, low on eroticism. And wife Norma was made of sterner stuff than the average librarian.

'I am not on offer,' she said decisively, remembering, albeit reluctantly, the lateral career move that had brought her marriage westward from Romford to the Rhondda.

'What *is* on offer?' Oliver asked with good grace, pouring the tea and diluting the tension.

'A set of matching suitcases.'

'Don't tell me. Your husband has done an advantageous deal with Euro-Matching Suitcases PLC?'

'Something of the sort.'

Apart from the name of the firm, Oliver's guess was exactly right. The company was run by one of Moody's old friends from business school. The suitcases were imported from Taiwan and fully guaranteed against everything except usage.

'Well,' said Oliver, 'since he's gone to all that trouble, I shall just have to travel somewhere with my suitcases. Alone.'

'In your Boeing 747?'

'In my what?'

'Your Boeing 747. It's written on your board. I was hoping you would explain it to me. Is it an anagram?'

'No. It's a piece of trivial information. Did you know that if a passenger farts in a Boeing 747 or any equivalent aircraft, no smell is given off? Despite extensive research, the world's leading scientists cannot explain this phenomenon.'

'My fault for asking,' said wife Norma, reflecting that on balance she had probably been right to send for the fire brigade and ignore the teapot.

As Oliver walked her to the car, she asked:

'Were you ever married?'

'Once upon a time.'

'When the world was young?'

'Exceedingly. She left me on Cup Final Day in 1979. Boring old Arsenal from the South beat the gallant lads of Manchester United from the North 3–2 in a pulsating finish. And she wanted me to talk to her.'

'I don't blame her for leaving you.'

'Nor do I. I understand now. I'm feeling the chill of a mid-life crisis. I need the warmth of a good woman.'

'Bullshit.'

'Correct,' said Oliver, as she climbed into her car. Then he started to laugh.

'What is so amusing?'

'I know something very funny about sex. And you'll never know what it is.'

'I'm sure that's my loss.'

He stopped laughing.

'No. Probably not.'

Oliver's leaving presentation was a modest affair, held in the Senior Common Room, one of the better-preserved Nissen huts on the site. As he stood poised to receive his parting gift, Oliver observed that the affair had a fearful, and potentially tearful, symmetry. Two parallel lines stood in wait, one composed of truculent academics, the other of matching suitcases.

The platform party comprised the Vice-Chancellor, whose job was to shake hands with each of the condemned in turn, and wife Norma, in charge of the suitcases. A memo had been circulated to the recipients suggesting that there should be no acceptance speeches, since this would occupy time that could be better exploited in thrusting market endeavours.

'It's a simple transaction,' Moody had said, 'and we mustn't let it turn into an emotional circus like the Oscars or BAFTA.'

As a final gesture of defiance, the academics had agreed amongst themselves that they would all make speeches, the longer and more pedantic the better. Mr Boswell, revealing a hitherto unnoticed radical streak, had prepared an hour-long speech in Latin with quotations from the Greek, beginning with a line of Virgil: '*Monstrum horrendum, informe, ingens, cui lumen ademptum.*' In the Boswell translation, which he had shared with Oliver but nobody else, it ran: 'A horrendous monster, hideous and vast, deprived of sight.'

It was, according to the classicist, an accurate description of the nation's approach to higher education, and he had no intention of translating it for the benefit of the mountebanks and pretenders who had brutalized his beloved Mount Olympus.

'May he live with permanent dread, wondering what I said about him, tantalized by his own ignorance. May he be haunted by demons of uncertainty. May flights of fear and paranoia taunt him to his rest.'

This was still to come. The Vice-Chancellor, already in a state of shock because the ceremony was running two hours behind schedule and the day's flow chart was fatally clogged, shook hands with Oliver, brusquely and without a word. Wife Norma handed over the matching suitcases. Oliver kissed her on the cheek once, twice, three, four times.

'Four kisses?' she said.

'A form of graciousness invented by the great Duke Ellington,' said Oliver. 'One kiss for each cheek.'

Then he turned to the lines of teachers and suitcases.

'May I be the seventh, unless it be the eighth, person to thank the University for this magnificent gift?'

'Ninth,' murmured Norma.

'These splendid matching suitcases symbolize for me the new age of reason sweeping across the campus, the broom handle firmly controlled by the Vice-Chancellor. Verily, a university for the twenty-first century.'

The Vice-Chancellor noted what sounded like a compliment – the first of the day – but was unhappy that it was expressed in terms of garbage disposal. He wondered yet again, as Oliver continued, why human beings never behaved according to the computer projections. It had never been mentioned at business school.

'One or two people, though perhaps not as many as that, have asked me about my plans for the future. They are not a secret. I am going to pack my splendid matching suitcases with a change of clothing, a favourite book, a luxury object, an apple, an orange and a toothbrush, and I am going to set out on a journey in search of Aristotle. I'm sure you will all agree, Aristotle is enough to keep anyone out of mischief.'

Oliver smiled, picked up his suitcases and walked towards the door. There was an appreciative round of applause. He was well liked by his colleagues, though they rarely knew what he was talking about; but that was the norm and nobody minded. Each of them lived and worked in a highly personal goldfish bowl, shaped and refined over several decades of teaching and learning. Each of them accepted responsibility for changing the water.

The code of behaviour dictated that you might peer into other people's bowls in a mood of affectionate curiosity, but you respected the sanctity of their water. Most of the time nobody knew what anybody else was talking about and it was not a problem. It was simply the nature of the universe and anyone who thought differently was a bloody idiot.

The Vice-Chancellor was therefore a bloody idiot. *Quod erat demonstrandum*.

It was in a mood of affectionate curiosity that wife Norma followed Oliver out of the hut as he carried the suitcases to his car.

'Who the hell's Aristotle?' she asked, as he opened the car boot.

The reply came from Goronwy Grace, who was repainting the sign reading 'SENIOR COMMON ROOM'. The consultants had changed their minds about the internal colour-coding and he was covering up the autumnal tomato with a moulting canary yellow.

'Aristotle?' he said. 'Greek philosopher, 384–322 BC. Now deceased.'

'Correct,' said Oliver, 'but I'm not looking for that Aristotle. Mine is contemporary.'

'A philosopher?' said Norma.

'No. A crossword compiler. The best in the business. *The Times*, the *Observer*, the *Guardian* and the *Listener*, rest its soul. We've corresponded for many years.'

'About anagrams?'

'Nothing as simple as that. Generally about the fine grain and subtle nuances of his more cryptic clues. I've always promised I would pay him a visit when the moment arrived.'

'And this is the moment?'

'As Mr McLuhan almost said, the suitcases are the message.'

Through the open window of the Nissen hut they heard Mr Boswell intoning:

'*Forsan et haec olim meminisse iuvabit.*'

He had been speaking for half an hour and was smoothly into his stride, like David Gower in his prime.

'Do you understand that?' Norma asked.

'It's another quotation from Virgil,' said Oliver. 'It means: "Maybe one day we shall be glad to remember even these things."'

'Maybe we shall,' said Norma, with the smiling resignation of a woman married to a career structure.

Oliver shook his head.

'I think this could be the end of a really beautiful friendship.'

2

Assisting the Police with Their Inquiries

A week later, on a Tuesday after lunch, Oliver set out to find Aristotle. He took both suitcases, more as a goodwill gesture than a practical aid to the journey. Neither of them was even half full, but they had a tendency to creak even when empty and caution seemed a sound policy in the matter of weight.

Besides, Aristotle lived in the Brecon Beacons, only an hour's drive away, so it was one of the more modest treks in the history of pilgrimage; but Oliver was, none the less, aglow with the spirit of adventure and a destiny stretching even beyond Brecon. He might well go on to Shrewsbury. He could do as he liked. It could easily be mistaken for freedom.

Driving along the valley road he improvised his own narrative.

'Quite early one afternoon, I set off on my travels.'

He smiled and added:

'Oliver's Travels.'

He realized he was driving out of a campus novel into an Odyssey. It was goodbye Amis, Bradbury and Sharpe; hello, good afternoon and welcome Virgil, Homer and Swift. It could easily be mistaken for progress.

'I left the New University of the Rhondda Valley to darkness and the Vice-Chancellor.'

He slid a cassette into the machine and pressed the Play button. He switched up the volume. The hills were alive with the sound of Lester Young playing his legendary version of 'Lady Be Good' with Count Basie's Kansas City Seven. It could easily be mistaken for happiness.

Five miles away, in a south-easterly direction, the Vice-Chancellor walked up the drive of his executive home, shouting into his mobile telephone.

'Tomorrow just won't do! Today is already too late! It must be done yesterday at the latest!'

He hated the mobile phone, though it was essential to his career profile; but he had yet to discover a way of slamming it down angrily. He had once bitten the aerial in rage, leaving it totally intact, but breaking a front tooth and ending up in the dentist's chair for three hours of root canal work.

He slammed the front door instead, not an astute thing to do in an area famous for mining subsidence. The building trembled, pondered collapse but stood firm. It was one of the few inhabited houses on the estate, a tasteful arrangement of Georgian-style executive homes, built in the mid-1980s by a local thruster on the lookout for a lunch invitation and a knighthood from Mrs Thatcher. He was twenty minutes away from his chosen destiny when he was arrested for cheating on his VAT returns. He was now in prison.

The house had consequently been cheap, and Moody had calculated that if they managed to sell their identical Georgian-style executive home in Romford before the end of the financial year they would be able to pay off the bridging loan and make a profit of fifty pence.

Wife Norma sat reading the *Daily Telegraph* in the executive through-lounge. They took the *Telegraph* and the *Independent* on alternate days, the negotiated settlement of a routine marital spat. She had suggested taking both, but as Moody had pointed out, this would almost immediately consume the anticipated profit on the house transaction. These were keen times on the fiscal frontiers.

Moody hurled his briefcase, his telephone and himself on to the settee, in that order.

'Welcome home, darling.'

'The man should be boiled in oil.'

'Good day at the office?'

'But only after he's been castrated.'

'Forgive me, darling, but whose testicles are we talking about?'

'The sign-writer's.'

'I've only met him once but he seemed very capable. He knew Aristotle's dates.'

'He doesn't know Welsh. Apparently all his translations are wrong. I asked him about it.'

Moody continued, in a bad imitation of Goronwy Grace's accent.

'I'm sorry, boyo, but I don't speak Welsh myself. My brother-in-law told me what to put. He's always been a bit of a mischief-maker, see.'

The Vice-Chancellor should have been aware of a couple of ancient truths about valley culture. Celts have a tendency to distort objective reality when confronted with apparently pure-bred Anglo-Saxons, and use of the word 'boyo' is the call-sign that indicates the speaker is telling lies.

'How bad are the translations? Will anyone notice?'

'We've run them through the computer on the Welsh spell-check facility. Do you know how he's translated "Market Research Department"? In Welsh it reads "Small Building Full of Little Green Men".'

Norma laughed.

'It isn't funny. It's humiliating.'

'Module!' she cried.

'What?'

'The answer's "module". Seven down. In the crossword.'

She wrote in the word and threw down the newspaper in triumph.

'Are you doing the crossword?'

'Yes. And I've just finished it, thanks to your little green men. They travel around in modules. Everybody knows that.'

'Don't be ridiculous. You never do crosswords,' said Moody.

He was cross. He hated any fundamental change in lifestyle that he had not personally initiated and run past a panel of specialist consultants.

'Be very careful,' said Norma, who never responded well to being snapped at. 'You're speaking to Fire Woman. You could get burned.'

He slumped back in the settee and was half-way to the foetal position before he remembered what he had learnt at the Interactive Body Language Workshop. He sat up to attention.

'I feel as if I'm marooned in a sea of madness and subversion.'

'Run it through the computer and you'll find that's probably about right. Never mind. I'll make a nice cup of tea for Thy Doom.'

She got up and walked briskly into the kitchen, doing her impersonation of a housewife.

'Marooned,' said the Vice-Chancellor.

Oliver had found Aristotle's house, an old farm cottage high in the Brecon Beacons. Sheep were grazing in the garden. They were grazing in the cottage too. The roof, doors and windows had apparently all been destroyed by fire. The walls were blackened and weary.

Oliver checked the letter he had received from the great compiler, about six months earlier, when they had first planned the visit. Aristotle had drawn a map and given detailed directions. This was unquestionably the place. There was no other building for miles around.

He called out to the sheep.

'I don't suppose you remember the man who lived here? Aristotle? Eminent compiler of crosswords? Trivial quizzes too, in his spare time?'

The sheep elected a spokesperson.

'Sorry, sunbeam. We're only sheep. What do we know? Grazing, that's what we do. Keep our heads down, mind our own business.'

'Aristotle isn't his real name, of course. I don't know his real name,' said Oliver.

'That's a big help,' said the sheep.

'You're right. That could be a problem. A little like carelessness.'

Oliver realized that his quest might be a little trickier than anticipated. Where was Aristotle? Who had burned down his house and why? The nationalists having a bit of a do? Maybe a fund-raiser? But why pick on a harmless crossword compiler? This was not a holiday home. It was where Aristotle lived all the time, and Oliver had always assumed the man was Welsh anyway.

A deeper question gurgled to the surface. Why had the inner voice told Oliver, at his point of departure that morning, to take *both* matching suitcases? Was it part of a larger, universal scheme of things? Or was it the same old cosmic chaos that ruled the rest of the time?

Clearly he would not find answers to any of these questions hanging around the burnt-out shell of an old farm cottage.

'Thank you for your help,' he said to the sheep.

'You're welcome,' said the spokesperson.

'Stay cool,' said Oliver.

'Baa,' said the sheep.

Oliver drove into downtown Brecon and asked a policeman for directions to the police station. The policeman explained that Oliver was already parked, illegally, outside its front door.

'Forgive me,' said Oliver, 'I hadn't noticed the blue lamp.'

'There isn't a blue lamp.'

'Precisely.'

The duty sergeant opened the report book. He was a large man who looked as if he had been quarried, ready-made, from one of the harsher rock-faces in the principality.

'You want to report a missing person?'

'Yes, please.'

'Name and address?'

'Mine or the missing person's?'

Oliver had never reported anything to the police and was anxious to be procedurally correct.

'Let's start with the missing person's, shall we? Since he or she is the person who is missing.'

'That's the hard one,' said Oliver. 'I don't know him by his real name.'

'I see. You know him by an unreal name?'

'I know him as Aristotle. But that's a pseudonym.'

'Professionally speaking, we prefer to call it an alias. Do you know him by his real address? Or is that false as well?'

'It's a cottage, just off the road to Abergavenny. But I was there earlier this afternoon and it's deserted. It also looks as if there's been a fire.'

'Well, we're great boys for burning down houses, ridding ourselves of the English imperialist yoke. This friend of yours, what does he do when he's at home, bearing in mind he's not at home – otherwise you wouldn't be here telling us so?'

Oliver peered through the foliage of the sentence and spotted what looked like the question.

'He compiles crosswords. He's a near genius. And to the best of my knowledge he's not an English imperialist.'

'Would you like to give me a description of this intellectual giant and political paragon?'

'I'm afraid I can't do that. I've never met him.'

There was a silence. The sergeant reached a decision. He closed his book.

'I think this is a job for Princess Di. If you'd like to follow me.'

The sergeant led Oliver through a door, along a short corridor and into a sparsely furnished interview room. There he left him, with the self-satisfied demeanour of a man dumping an unwanted item at a recycling centre.

The room had concrete walls, a single high window with bars on the outside, a table and two chairs. On the table stood an ashtray, filled three times beyond its capacity, and two plastic cups with residual dregs of a brown liquid that had turned green and was studying a colour chart before deciding what to turn next.

Oliver sat down as far away as possible from the cups and the ashtray.

The door opened and in walked a uniformed policewoman. She was in her forties. She looked cool and resourceful but that might have been the uniform. She also looked veiled, cloaked and a little concealed, but that might have been Oliver's idle fancy.

'The missing person,' she said, pulling the other chair downwind of the cups and ashtray, and sitting down.

'I'm not missing. I'm here,' said Oliver.

'The case of the missing person.'

'Yes.'

She opened her notebook.

'The sergeant gave me the broad outline of your problem . . .'

'Forgive me for interrupting during your official duties, and also for any apparent impertinence, but I cannot help but observe . . . you are not Princess Di.'

'Correct.'

'I thought not.'

'I am WPC Priest.'

'Priest.'

'But my first name is Diane. Calling me Princess Di is what passes in the police force as a joke.'

'I imagine it's a male-dominated peer group.'

'You imagine right.'

'I have great respect for law and order, but I don't think much of the joke.'

'Thank you. I'm delighted to hear it.'

'But Priest is a fascinating coincidence.'

'Is it?'

He felt comfortable in their enforced intimacy, huddled together at one end of the table, keeping the maximum distance between them and the toxic shock waves from the plastic cups. We are united against a common enemy, thought Oliver. I can talk to this policewoman. She may live to regret it, should she decide to listen.

'Until I was made redundant, I used to teach comparative religion at a teacher training college which begat a polytechnic which recently begat a new university, hence my redundancy.'

'I haven't spotted the coincidence.'

'Religion? Priest? Yes?'

'Yes.'

She acknowledged the validity of the coincidence but there was no sign that she was impressed.

'I agree it's not a *major* coincidence but it is moderately charming, don't you think?'

'Are you a religious man?'

He was startled both by the directness of the question and by its content. Nobody had ever asked that question before. Perhaps there was a lapsed Catholic inside that uniform? Or some other old-established faith that shoved guilt into the child as a guarantee against joy in adult life?

'Absolutely not. I have a good working knowledge of all of them. Judaism, Islam, Buddhism, Rastafarianism, Christianity in its fifty-seven lethal varieties. They all seem to end up killing each other. On the whole, it's rather like working on quality control in a chocolate factory.'

'Is it?'

'It's a job I did once, during the summer vacation, when I was a student. It's a long time ago. When there were vacation jobs for students.'

'When there were jobs.'

'I had to stand there with my clipboard and my taste-buds and officially approve the coffee *crèmes* and hazelnut clusters on behalf of the company. But if I wanted a decent meal, real food, proper sustenance, I would go elsewhere. In religion, as in chocolate, I am a non-believer, though I have my gods,' he concluded.

'I'd be failing in my duty if I didn't say . . . name a few names.'

'My gods? Lester Young, Dizzy Gillespie, Charlie Parker, Thelonious Monk.'

'Billie Holiday? Bessie Smith?'

'Unquestionably.'

This was no ordinary policewoman on the beat. She had an ear for the off-beat. She was cool. She had heard the blues at midnight. He even glimpsed the possibility of a beautiful friendship. Maybe he should have packed the old brown teapot.

He continued the litany.

'And we mustn't forget Beethoven, Bach, Brahms and Mozart. William Shakespeare, Oscar Wilde, George Farquhar, Anton

Chekhov. Jimmy James, Sandy Powell, Max Wall, Jack Benny. Charlotte Brontë, George Eliot, Dorothy Parker . . .'

'Aristotle,' she said firmly, tapping her notebook with her pen. Playtime was over. It was back to business.

'Aristotle,' said Oliver.

'I assume you want to find your missing person?'

'Oh yes. He is a god of the highest magnitude and I would very much like to find him.'

He gave her his morsels of information and she recorded them in her notebook.

The duty sergeant quickly concealed his copy of the *Sporting Life* as WPC Priest guided Oliver through the entrance lobby.

'If we discover anything to your advantage, we'll contact you,' she said. 'Are you staying in Brecon?'

'For a couple of days, yes. I'm in meandering mode. I'm at an old coaching inn near the market-place. The Three Tunes.'

'The Three Tuns,' said the sergeant.

'Forgive me. Is it Tuns? I was wearing the wrong glasses when I checked in.'

He paused beside the door for a brief curtain speech.

'Thank you for your help and courtesy. I shall tell all my old radical friends from the campus that they are totally wrong about police harassment and corruption.'

As soon as he had gone, WPC Priest turned on the sergeant.

'You're playing that game again, aren't you?'

'Game? What game?'

'Pass the loony.'

'I'm sorry, girl, you'll have to explain what you mean.'

'Anybody who comes through that door with a loony problem ends up with me. And purely for the record, I am not a girl. I am one hundred per cent woman, ripe and mature.'

'It's all done with the best of intentions, Constable.'

'Keep me out of the way so the big strong men can get on with the proper grown-up police work. Like picking winners.'

She snitched the *Sporting Life* from its hiding place under the report book, rolled it up into a baton and whacked the sergeant over the head.

'That's police brutality,' said the sergeant.

'You ain't seen nothing yet.'

She hurled the newspaper at him, then returned to her office. She would track down Aristotle as quickly as possible. Then she would resume grown-up police work.

Oliver's hotel was an old building, late nineteenth century, but it had never been a coaching inn. It was a converted abattoir but, as Henry Ford and Phineas T. Barnum never quite got around to saying, nobody ever made a buck by messing up heritage with history.

The food was fresh and new, late twentieth century, and Oliver had eaten responsibly, in accordance with his current dietary obsessions. It was the Boswell diet, based on ancient Athenian principles. You only ate what was good for you. To preserve the classical balance, you drank whatever the hell you liked.

He had reached the coffee – heavily caffeinated – and was contemplating a brandy when she walked into the room. She had changed out of her police uniform into casual jacket and trousers. They didn't match, nor did they need to; but they fitted where appropriate. Wow, he thought. Without her glasses she was lovely, and she didn't wear glasses.

'Good evening,' she said, arriving at his table.

'Good evening,' he said, standing up, 'and may I say the obvious thing?'

'Try it.'

'Out of all the phoney coaching inns in all of mid-Wales, you had to walk into this one.'

'Too obvious. Don't say it.'

'All right. I won't.'

They sat down.

'You were right about one thing,' she said. 'The hotel. It *is* called the Three Tunes.'

'Yes. I checked with the management. It *was* called the Three Tuns, but the man who owns the place is a jazz fan. They do very good business here during the Brecon Jazz Festival. You know about the Festival?'

'We help clear away the empties.'

'So he renamed it after his three favourite tunes. "Mood Indigo", "Lover Man" and "Blue Monk". But thank you for telling me. I hope you didn't make a special journey?'

'I made a special journey, but not for that reason.'

'Have you eaten?'

'Yes.'

She had, after a fashion: an M&S chicken casserole, heated on a defective microwave, so it was tepid around the edges, volcanic at its core.

'Have you drunk? Or are you on duty?'

He picked up the wine bottle.

'A little Château de Merthyr Tydfil? Highly recommended by the manufacturers. No additives. Or some coffee? Or both? Or something else?'

'A glass of wine, please,' she said, keen to stem the tidal wave of hospitality.

Oliver took a glass from the next table, poured her some red wine and topped up his own drink.

'Thank you.'

'So why did you make this special journey? To tell me your three favourite tunes?'

'No.'

'Tell me what they are, anyway. I'd be most interested.'

' "Every Time We Say Goodbye", "God Bless the Child" and "Mary from the Dairy".'

'Three beautiful songs, beautifully sung.'

He raised his glass in a silent toast to the beautiful singers of beautiful songs. She raised hers in response. Then she said:

'Do you want to know why I made this special journey?'

'Does there have to be a reason?' said Oliver. He did not say: perhaps you made this special journey so I could gaze more closely upon your face in the voluntary intimacy of a muzak-free dining zone; so I could look into your eyes while wearing my proper glasses and peer into the mystery of a woman whose world-view embraced Ella Fitzgerald and criminal investigation; so I could carry out a preliminary feasibility study, without obligation on either side, into the possibility of a beautiful friendship.

He did not say any of these things. He said:

'Does there have to be a reason?'

And she said:

'No. But there *is* a reason. And since I've come all this way, you're damn well going to hear it.'

There was strength in the woman too: outer and inner strength, he suspected. That could be one lot too many. He liked his women the same as he liked his boiled eggs: firm on the outside, soft and runny in the centre.

'In that case you had better damn well tell me the reason you came here.'

'I've found your friend Aristotle.'

'You have? That's amazing! Where is he?'

'The Orkneys.'

'The Orkneys?'

'They're a group of islands off the north coast of Scotland.'

'Yes. I know what they are and where they are. I'm just very impressed by your speed of action and response.'

'All part of the job, sir,' she said, with an affectionate parody of a George Dixon salute.

Before she could stop him, Oliver ordered a bottle of champagne from the waiter, a congenial youth called Gareth who worked on the Three Tunes reception desk during the day. He was on an ancient retraining scheme designed to massage the unemployment figures. So far the only thing he had learned was that his tuxedo didn't fit. The scheme had been abandoned by Whitehall two years ago, but the news had yet to reach the mid-Wales branch office of the Ministry of Truth.

Opening champagne bottles had not been part of Gareth's training programme. Oliver came to the rescue and chose appropriate glasses from behind the bar.

'Are you trying to get me drunk?' WPC Priest asked.

'Possibly,' said Oliver.

'Good.'

'I like getting drunk,' said Gareth.

Oliver sent him away with a tumbler full of Moët, then turned to his companion.

'This is to celebrate your success. Now that we're alone in the room, perhaps you can tell me how you did it?'

'How I did what?'

'How you tracked down Aristotle. I suppose you have access to the national police computer?'

'I didn't use the national computer.'

She leaned forward, glass in hand, indicating that what she said was for his ears only: burn before listening.

'I telephoned the *Observer*. I asked for the features desk. I said: "You have a famous crossword compiler called Aristotle. Do you know where he lives?" And the person at the other end said: "The Orkneys." They weren't allowed to give the exact address. I timed the call. It took five minutes.'

'Astonishing.'

'It's not in the least astonishing. You could have done it yourself.'

It was a startling suggestion.

'Well, I suppose I could, but . . .'

'But what?'

'It's too obvious. I would never have thought of it. Obviously, if I had thought of it, I would have done it. But I didn't. Because I didn't think of it. I came to you instead. Let me freshen your champagne.'

His consonants were slipping. The word 'freshen' came out like the name of an obscure central European town: perhaps Freschnen, scene of archaic festivals devoted to medieval flag-waving or unperformable works by Bartók.

He raised his glass and spoke slowly, deliberately. He would hang on to the vowels and let the consonants take care of themselves.

'To you. The world's greatest policeman. Policewoman. Policeperson. Thank you, Mrs Priest.'

She was touched by the elegant compliment. It was the first she had received for seven, unless it was eight, years. Elegant compliments had gone the way of rural buses. She might have to wait well into the next century before another one came along.

'Why don't you call me Diane? Not Priest,' she said.

'Diane. Not Priest. As you wish.'

'I inherited the "Mrs" from my ex-marriage. And the "Priest" from my ex-husband. I've just about got rid of both.'

'Diane. Not Priest,' he said, thoughtfully.

'What is it?'

'Nothing.'

But it was not nothing; it was an anagram, lying in wait and ready to pounce.

After they had finished the champagne, he walked her home. She had a grace-and-favour maisonette, courtesy of the constabulary, ten minutes from the town centre.

They were gently pissed but, as Oliver pointed out, if everybody is gently pissed, nobody is pissed but everybody is gentle – it was an underpublicized aspect of Einstein's theory of relativity.

'And I am deeply indebted to you for your help, Diane. You have given me a direction for my life.'

'North.'

'Precisely. Most people spend a lifetime seeking a direction and you have given me one in a day. Not only that but North. There is no better direction. And if I can do anything in return, to help you . . .'

'You? Help me?'

Even under the influence of champagne, it was an unlikely proposition.

'What sort of thing had you in mind?'

Perhaps he could cook.

'Any old unsolved crimes? Things that have baffled your people's finest brains. I could take them off your hands.'

'It's a very generous offer.'

'I've got the whole of tomorrow. It would be a pity to waste it.'

'What sort of crime would you prefer?' she said, humouring him for reasons she was not yet ready to analyse. 'Over the last twelve months we've had a series of arson attacks, a kidnapping, a murder . . .'

'Tell me about the murder,' he said eagerly.

'Your speciality, is it?'

'Goodbye Virgil, Homer and Swift. Hello, good evening and welcome, Allingham, Chandler, Rendell and McBain. Come on. Tell me about it.'

'A farmer called Griffiths was found dead.'

'Murdered in his red barn?'

'Floating face-down in a river.'

'And you're still working on it?'

'Not me personally.'

It was a sore point in a mighty landscape of irritation. She had never worked on the Griffiths murder investigation. The Regional Crime Squad had moved in like wolves on the fold, and she, as usual, had been kept well away, as she was from all major crimes. The station superintendent believed her skills should be focused on what he called female-oriented casework, and what she called the wet and the wimpish: missing cats, dangerous hamsters and, on one occasion, a consignment of hijacked pizza bases.

'That gives me enough to work on,' said Oliver.

'It does?'

'We shall put the guilty party behind bars. Never fear.'

She did not invite him in for coffee. She was out of coffee. She was out of recklessness too. They said good night with a formal handshake.

'Is Oliver your first name or your second name?' she said.

'It could be either.'

'But which?'

'Quite so. Thank you for a lovely evening.'

'I'm not sure what to make of you.'

'Many things have been suggested. From doorstop to hatstand.'

She freed her hand and went into the house.

As he walked back to the Three Tunes he solved the anagram. That was the tough part. Tomorrow he would mosey on down into the 87th Precinct and solve the murder mystery.

3

Predestination

Oliver did not dream about Diane. Instead he reran one of his old favourites. He was at Millmoor, watching a Third Division match between Rotherham United and Bradford City. It was odd because he had no allegiance to either side, but, then, it was a dream. It was a long time ago and the players had centre partings and baggy shorts. At half-time, when the score was 0–0, Oliver went for a cup of hot Bovril and a meat pie. As the whistle blew for the second half he tried to find his way back to terraces, but in vain. Every door was barred and bolted and protected by large dogs. He ran up and down concrete stairways, found himself on the New York subway, on the beach at Skegness, in the physics laboratory at his old school. All the time the cheering from the match grew louder.

I have seen all this before, he decided. Might as well wake up. When he had woken up he thought about Diane. She reminded him of Marjorie. He had fallen in love with Marjorie when they were both in the fifth form. He had proved it by preparing a chart, listing all the women in his life, and giving them marks out of ten in various categories: beauty, sexuality, knowledge of Duke Ellington, Igor Stravinsky, sport and French romantic poetry, mysterious depths to be explored, and likelihood of turning up at the school dance on Friday.

Marjorie had ended up top of the league, an impressive achievement considering that her competitors included Sophia Loren, Ingrid Bergman, Virginia Woolf and June Allyson. It had been a theoretical exercise because Marjorie arrived at the dance with a knuckle-headed sixth former who played in goal for the first eleven and had, in Oliver's view, absorbed all the sensitivity and intellectual rigour of his goalposts.

Diane reminded him of Marjorie because for the first time since he was in the fifth form, he had played the game again, assessing her qualities in comparison with the other women in his life – past, present and fantasy. She had emerged well ahead of the field, with Jean Rhys second, Helen Mirren third and the Vice-Chancellor's wife Norma unplaced.

He concentrated hard, trying to remember what she looked like. He remembered thinking Wow! when she walked into the dining-room, but that was because everybody looks better not wearing uniform. Uniforms diminished the human spirit. People only wore them to give the enemy something to aim at.

He remembered the quality of her face. It had lines and wrinkles that said: we have worked our passage and have a right to be here. Did she have damask cheeks? Or would that be too much of a coincidence? He remembered, through the mist of a pleasing champagne hangover, a dewy complexion, but decided not to tell her she was dewy, in case she thought he was confusing her with Donald Duck's nephew.

The more he tried to focus on fine detail, the more he floundered. Colour of hair? Was it dark brown? With the odd grey streak? Was the grey streak artificially applied or had she earned it the hard way? Colour of eyes? Blue? Brown? Beige? Did people have beige eyes? He checked in his dictionary. It said that beige was 'buff with a slight suffusion of pink'. And buff, it said, was yellow. Well, maybe not beige in that case. It must be tough being a lyric poet. Did Byron, Marvell and Donne take notebooks to bed?

But beige was a clue to his state of mind. Oliver was suffused with pink. He had met a dewy complexioned woman he wanted to cuddle and protect with layers of pink suffusion. Whether she wanted or needed his protection was a decision to be postponed, indefinitely if necessary. It was the only way to deal with decisions. He devoutly hoped there were no goalkeepers in her life.

Oliver got up, bathed, shaved, ordered and ate his two lightly boiled eggs, and enquired into the whereabouts of the nearest library, suffusing pinkness all around.

Diane did not dream about Oliver, but she thought about him. She thought about him when she overslept. She thought: not only do I get handed the loony, but the loony gives me bullshit and champagne and I end up missing breakfast, late for work and hungover. Damn and blast the loony was what Diane thought and positively no dreaming.

Mrs Scott was a librarian of the old school. She had seen the uses of literacy and knew they worked. She had read most of the books in her charge and knew what was in the ones she hadn't read. Several times a day she would grasp the arm of a borrower in the act of touching the latest best seller and guide it towards a more nutritional piece of work.

In her view, audio-cassettes, video-cassettes and floppy discs were fine in their place: in a lead-lined box at the bottom of a disused mine shaft. She had once taken a fresh-faced believer in modern information storage and retrieval to the British Library.

'Read, mark, learn and inwardly digest all the books in there,' she had said, 'then use your modern technology to fill in the gaps. And if you have a minute, let me know what the gaps were.'

She could smell a fellow Luddite at a hundred paces. She spotted Oliver as he was turning the corner at the end of the street.

'I should explain,' said Oliver, punctilious as ever, 'I am not a poll tax payer.'

'Join the club,' said Mrs Scott.

'I beg your pardon. You misunderstand. I have paid an instalment of whatever it is called now. Possibly even the first. But not here. I am not local. I am a wayfaring stranger.'

'A tourist?'

'On my way to the Orkneys.'

'You'd like to borrow an atlas?'

'No. I'd like to see back numbers of your local newspapers. I'm doing a small research project for a friend. It concerns . . .,' he leaned a little closer, ' . . . homicide.'

'You may research whatever you like, wherever you like, providing you fill in a form. I apologize. But it helps with the newly installed bureaucratic nightmare at head office. Mr Kafka's instructions.'

'I understand,' said Oliver.

'All you have to write is your name and address. Invent them if you like. Use your imagination. I don't mind.'

'It isn't a problem. I'm very good at writing my name and address. I could do it when I was four years old. Of course, I've moved house several times since then, but my name has stayed fairly constant.'

The reference section of the library was in a separate room. Oliver browsed through back numbers of the local newspapers, and paused at a headline reading 'BODY IN RIVER'.

He made minimal notes on the back of a menu from the hotel. His attention wandered. There was a magazine display stand nearby, with a pleasing and eccentric selection of publications on show. Without moving from his seat he could see *Jazz Journal*, *Golf Monthly* and the *Fortean Times*.

Soon he moved from his seat and made a few more minimal notes. *Golf Monthly* was of special interest.

After leaving the library, he drove to the scene of the crime. He left his car on an old stone bridge and peered over the parapet down into the river. This was where the body of a local farmer called Griffiths had been found, a year ago: the crime that still baffled the police.

Oliver gazed into the water. There were no clues to be seen. He supposed the water was much the same in depth, quality and pollution as on the night of the murder, but that was of no significance. Griffiths, according to the official account, was already dead when dropped from the bridge. There was no investigative purpose to be served in gazing at the river, Oliver decided, though he enjoyed staring at water. It was a time for lateral vision.

He walked into the village and found the local pub, the Slater's Arms. He glanced across the street and saw the premises of Kelsey Brothers, Plumbers and Glaziers. He made another minimal note on the back of his menu, then went into the pub. The landlord was a dour man, still smarting over the treatment of Owen Glendower.

'Tonic water?' he said, insulted by Oliver's request.

'Yes, please. On the rocks, with a twist of lemon.'

It was a drink favoured by a reformed alcoholic he had known on the campus. Oliver enjoyed its cadences: it sounded like the tough drink of an ex-alcoholic. He could imagine Scott Fitzgerald or Dylan Thomas ordering tonic water on the rocks with a twist of lemon, though not often.

'Driving, are we?' said the landlord.

'Yes.'

'Tourist, are we?'

The questions whipped across the counter like accusations in court, with a presumption of guilt.

'Yes. Passing through. Looking up one or two old friends.'

'Tonic water, on the rocks, with lemon, as requested.' He slid the glass towards Oliver, keeping it at arm's length.

'Though most of my friends seem to have left the area. Heading north.'

'Things change, don't they?'

'Except the one that was murdered.'

'You owe me eighty-five pence.'

Oliver paid with a pound coin. He put the change in a charity box: the Royal National Lifeboat Institution. That was a puzzle. They were a long way inland to be collecting money for lifeboats. Perhaps they needed one to help haul the bodies from the river.

'A man called Griffiths. A farmer.'

'What about him?'

'The man who was murdered. According to the newspapers, this was the last place he was seen alive.'

'Isn't that always the case with dead people?'

'They all drink in this pub?'

'There is always a place where they are last seen alive. Obviously. That is a fact of life.'

'A fact of life about death?'

'Obviously.'

'Obviously,' Oliver agreed.

The landlord disappeared into the cellar. There was no sign that he would ever return. He was probably discussing aspects of gloom with the ghosts of the departed. Oliver finished his drink and left.

Half an hour later he walked purposefully into the police station.

'Good day, sir,' said the desk sergeant, brightly and in accordance with the latest recommendation from the public relations consultants looking into law enforcement officers and their public profiles. Then he recognized Oliver and dimmed his brightness.

'Have you lost someone else?'

'No.'

'I believe we tracked down your Mr Aristotle.'

'Indeed you did. This is a separate issue. I need to speak to WPC Priest.'

'In what connection?'

'I have information to share.'

'What kind of information?'

'Information which could lead to an early arrest.'

The sergeant gave him a look that indicated arresting people was not a matter of priority. Then he remembered his public profile.

'One moment, sir.'

He went through a side door, closing it behind him. Even so, Oliver heard, quite clearly, the triumphant cry:

'It's spot the loony time!'

In the car, driving for the second time that day to the scene of the crime, Diane confirmed the sergeant's diagnosis.

'He's right. You *are* a loony.'

'I've twice been a specialist question-setter for *Mastermind*.'

'Is that right?'

'The life and work of the jazz musician Lester Young. The life and work of the dramatist George Farquhar. Would the BBC entrust such work to a loony?'

'Pass.'

'And I have things to tell you which are best said in seclusion.'

'What sort of things?'

'Two things. One highly professional. One deeply personal. Almost intimate.'

'I see.'

She braced herself for a declaration of everlasting love, expiring after twenty-four hours – a week if it was truly eternal. She had experience of such declarations and had timed them.

'I thought we should deal with the professional matter first.'

She relaxed.

'And you can offer me the sweets later.'

'Sweets?'

He shrugged. He never ate sweets. Mr Boswell said they were bad for your teeth.

They stood on the bridge, looking down into the river.

'A year ago,' said Oliver, 'quite early one morning, just as the sun was rising, the body of a farmer called Griffiths was found . . . down there, floating face-down.'

'I know. I told you that.'

'Cause of death. A blow to the back of the head.'

'That was in the papers.'

'Police inquiries were carried out by Superintendent Butler of the Crime Squad.'

'That was also in the papers. Tell me something I don't know.'

'Come with me.'

He walked her into the main street of the village.

'The previous night Griffiths had been drinking in his local pub. That one.'

He pointed to the Slater's Arms.

'Inquest verdict. Murder by person or persons unknown. And a very boring verdict too, if I may say so.'

'Can you improve on it?'

'Easily. Superintendent Butler's theory was that Griffiths had an argument in the pub which turned into a fight in the car park which rendered him deceased. After which, this unknown psychotic and argumentative stranger drove to the bridge, dropped the body into the water and disappeared without trace. There were no witnesses to any of these highly dramatic events. Not even the landlord of the pub, who, if I read him correctly, has total recall, especially in matters of death and disaster.'

'So tell me what really happened, Holmes.'

'First of all, I followed a false trail. I spotted the plumbers across the road.' He pointed to the premises of Kelsey Brothers, Plumbers and Glaziers, opposite the pub.

'What the hell have plumbers got to do with it?' Diane said, losing patience and wishing she were back at her desk, with the lost pizzas and recalcitrant hamsters.

'My first theory was that Griffiths was murdered in the car park, either by Colonel Mustard or Miss Scarlet, with the lead piping. Plumbers sell lead piping. Elementary, my dear policeperson.'

She had heard enough. He was not just a loony, but certifiable with it.

'Take me back to the office.'

'But then I saw my mistake. I was in the wrong plot.'

'You're on the wrong planet.'

'You should arrest Superintendent Butler of the Crime Squad.'

'What?'

'Come with me.'

She went with him, but only because they were ten miles from the police station and it was too far to walk.

He drove high into the hills, and stopped overlooking the valley; the river was no more than a silver trickle in the afternoon light.

'Over there,' he said. 'The Griffiths farm. It's been in the family for generations.'

'I know.'

'But did you know that somebody was trying to buy his land to make a golf-course?'

'There was a rumour at the time. It didn't seem relevant to the murder. And like I told you, I wasn't on the case.'

'A company called Nineteenth Hole Developments PLC.'

'All right. So somebody wanted to buy his land and he didn't want to sell it? And you want me to arrest Superintendent Butler?'

'Obviously.'

'It is not obvious to me!'

'Obviously, in view of the fact that according to my researches, Superintendent Butler is a major shareholder in Nineteenth Hole Developments PLC. Under his wife's name, of course. You should certainly hold him for questioning, as a major accessory. I doubt whether he wielded the blunt instrument on the night. It was probably a close friend or a hired assassin.'

He placed a gentle, consoling hand on her arm.

'I am very, very sorry.'

'Sorry?'

'It feels like a boring old police corruption plot. Colonel Mustard would have been much more amusing. This way you'll probably unearth wicked property developers and local councillors taking bribes. Terribly clichéd, I'm afraid. I wish I could offer you something more original. Mind you, the lead piping could still be a factor. You could pull in the plumbers for questioning.'

They fell silent for a while. Oliver was deeply concerned that his diagnosis was unoriginal and the stuff of second-rate thrillers and mini-series. Diane was equally concerned that he was, for all practical purposes, spot on. Butler had served for a time with the Met, and she was aware of rumours that he had returned to Wales with some fancy London ways running two furlongs ahead of his salary scale. Homely phrases like 'bent as buggery' and 'don't rock the boat if you're not in it' had filtered through the Woodbine smoke and fried egg fumes of the canteen.

She had brooded uneasily on these doubts and murmurs for months but Oliver had found the heart of the matter within a day. She needed to know his secret.

'How did you work it out?'

'It's obvious.'

'Stop telling me things are obvious when they are not obvious! Like hell is any of it obvious!'

'When I'm confronted with a murder mystery, especially out in the countryside, I always assume the butler did it.'

'You assume it, and then you try to prove it?'

'Exactly. These days they call it lateral thinking. It used to be called imagination. You imagine it, then you try it to see whether it works. It's what Archimedes did with his principle. Or Newton with gravity. Or Charlie Parker with bebop. Or, in this case, me with Superintendent Butler.'

'You are a one hundred per cent guaranteed head case. Crazy to the last slice.'

'It doesn't matter. None of it's very important.'

'You want me to arrest the chief of the Crime Squad as a murder suspect and you tell me it isn't important!'

Again he placed a calming hand on her arm.

'Don't shout at me. Don't be cross. I haven't even got to the personal and intimate bit. That's ten times as interesting and a hundred times more important than murder stories.'

'Has your intimacy always been metric?'

'Wait.'

He drove on a little further to a spot he had chosen earlier, a low stone wall with overhanging trees. It was not quite the secluded bower of his dreams. An overflowing concrete litter bin marked 'THANK YOU FOR KEEPING OUR COUNTRY BEAUTIFUL' marred the perfection; but it was always tricky to find the bower of your dreams at short notice.

They sat down on the low stone wall and he said:

'Do you remember what you said to me at the hotel last night?'

'Yes. I told you Aristotle was in the Orkneys.'

'Not that. I tried to call you Mrs Priest. And you said to me: "Diane, not Priest."'

'Diane, not Priest,' she repeated blankly.

'Those words are a perfect anagram of . . . Predestination.'

He showed her the hotel menu. On the back were the notes made at the library. He opened it. On the à la carte page, between the starters and the fish, he had written:

DIANE NOT PRIEST = PREDESTINATION

'Check it, if you like.'

'I don't do crosswords.'

'Then take my word.'

'What's predestination got to do with us?'

'As I understand it, and without wishing to embarrass you, it means we were sent on this earth to be together.'

'Oh my God.'

'Mind you,' he said, ignoring her appeal to the deity, 'there are one or two things I should warn you about.'

'Like lunacy.'

'No. I am not a lunatic, but I am occasionally a bit of a flirt. I made a tentative approach to the Vice-Chancellor's wife because her name was an anagram of "Fire Woman". Totally unrequited, I might add. But that was a quest for brief and temporary warmth, whereas this is altogether more permanent.'

He looked around, then continued:

'As eternal as these hills.'

'Take me back to the police station.'

'As you wish.'

In the car he said:

'Do you like conundrums?'

'I'm travelling with one.'

'According to the economists, this green and pleasant land we are driving through is apparently more valuable as golf-courses than it is for growing food. Conclusion?'

'The economists don't know from shit. And we'll all starve.'

'Here's the conundrum. I enjoy food. I also enjoy golf. Tricky one, isn't it?'

'I hate sport.'

'That needn't come between us.'

'Stop going on about us! There is no such thing as us! You don't know anything about me. I don't know anything about you.'

'The glory is in the quest. The search. The discovery. As the great Miles Davis once said: if you knew everything that was in my head, you would be me.'

As he dropped her outside the police station, he said:

'Eleven o'clock in the morning?'

'What about it?'

'Outside the hotel. Suitcase packed. I can lend you one if you wish. I have a matching set.'

'I am *not* spending the rest of my life with you. I am *not* coming to the Orkneys with you. I am *not* pursuing some crossword freak who's probably even further round the twist than you. And I am *not* prepared to change the whole of my life because of a bloody anagram!'

'Sleep on it,' he said, calm and reassuring. 'I promise you anagrams make as much sense as any of the world's religions. I know. I've checked them all.'

'Just go away. For ever.'

'If I do that, you will never know.'

She looked at the half-smile, the silent chuckle hanging around the corner of his mouth. She had to admit it. He was clever. He had a well-honed Ancient Mariner routine. No question, he would stoppeth one in three any day of the week, and three in three when match-fit and really trying.

'All right,' she said, 'tell me. What will I never know?'

'The very funny thing I know about sex.'

The desk sergeant was in the middle of an important telephone call as she crossed the lobby.

'Yes, that's it. Crossed and double, each way.'

He hung up.

'How was the loony? Are you still in one piece?'

'I'm not sure. I'll have to go somewhere very quiet and count myself.'

She reached the door of her office, then turned and walked back to the desk.

'A question, Sergeant.'

'We're here to assist the public.'

'I'm not the public. I'm a serving police officer. A respected colleague.'

'I'll make an exception. I'm still prepared to assist.'

'If you heard something serious, possibly incriminating, about a senior officer in the Crime Squad, what would you do?'

'Apply Plan A. Keep my mouth shut.'

It was the answer she had expected. The sergeant had a dream. He was working hard towards early redundancy. He would spend the money on a twelfth share in a racehorse. He would not allow law enforcement to get in the way of his dream.

'Isn't there a Plan B?' she said.

'I never heard of a Plan B. Describe it to me.'

'Double-check the files. Make a couple of phone calls. See whether the story hangs together. If it does, have a word with the chief.'

They looked across the lobby to the door marked 'CHIEF INSPECTOR PINKERTON'. They knew he was in his office. There was American football on BSkyB.

The sergeant shook his head.

'I think my Plan A makes more sense than your Plan B. I've tested it through the ages. It works. It guarantees survival. That is why "A" comes before "B" in the alphabet.'

'Thank you, Sergeant.'

She went to her office and was pleased to find it empty. She needed to double-check the files and make a couple of phone calls.

Oliver was collecting his room key from Gareth when the voice called to him.

'There you are.'

He turned to see the Vice-Chancellor, wrapped up in a large armchair next to the artificial log fire in the lobby of the Three Tunes.

'Yes, here I am,' said Oliver, walking towards him with a friendly outstretched hand. 'What a very pleasant surprise, Vice-Chancellor.'

'No. Not pleasant.'

'No?' said Oliver, in a mood to find the whole world pleasant.

The Vice-Chancellor struggled to stand up.

'It's a bugger, that armchair,' said Gareth. 'Lovely to sit in and have a nap but a bit of a sod to get up out of.'

'Shall I tell you what I'd really like to do?' said Moody, reaching the upright position and ignoring Oliver's hand.

'Yes, please.'

'I'd like to take you outside.'

'Outside? Why? It's cosy in here. Ask Gareth nicely, he'll switch on the log fire.'

'I'd like to take you outside to settle this the old-fashioned way.'

'You mean . . . by fighting?'

Oliver frowned. He had never had a fight in his adult life. There had been one in primary school, when he was six: a dispute over Plasticine. He had lost that one, but his opponent was seven, and she was tough with it.

'I'm sorry, Vice-Chancellor, but I truly cannot accept your proposition. Violence solves nothing and invariably breeds more violence. And you're younger than I am. You're fitter. You jog and play squash. You do circuit-training at the Sports Centre to relieve your executive stress. So it wouldn't be fair, would it?'

'I don't want it to be fair.'

'And for all I know, you might have bought some lead piping from Kelsey Brothers, Plumbers and Glaziers. So why don't we go into the lounge? Gareth will bring us tea and biscuits, and you can tell me what the matter is.'

Oliver walked out of the lobby and into the lounge. The Vice-Chancellor hesitated, then followed.

'Earl Grey?' Gareth called after them, but there was no response. He shrugged. No problem. There was only Earl Grey. Pity about the fight. He enjoyed a good fight.

'You are destroying my marriage,' said the Vice-Chancellor as Oliver rummaged among the biscuits, looking for a chocolate digestive.

'I don't recall touching your marriage. I plead guilty to a little innocent and totally unrequited flirtation but . . .'

'My entire life is now dominated by anagrams, acronyms and word games!'

'Ah!' Oliver began to understand. 'It can easily become an obsession.'

'Let me tell you what happened last night.'

Moody opened his briefcase and hauled out a large, fat

document, typewritten, single-spaced. It had the dimensions of an early draft of *War and Peace* without the compensating grandeur.

'I decided we needed a new committee. These are its terms of reference.'

'New committees, they never come amiss,' said Oliver, conciliatory.

'I told Norma about it. I said: "It's for Departmental Investigation . . . open brackets . . . Vital Organizational Research . . . . stroke . . . Corporate Enterprise . . . close brackets." She said to me . . .'

'That spells "Divorce",' said Oliver and the Vice-Chancellor, finishing the sentence together.

'Is it so obvious?'

'I can see it clearly.'

Oliver wrote it out on the back of a slim volume of undemanding local walks: DI(VOR/CE).

'Perhaps you should be more careful with your committees and their terms of reference.'

'She's phoning her lawyer today.'

'I don't think you can cite an acronym as co-respondent, if that's any consolation.'

'She also says I'm boring.'

There was no reply.

'Do *you* think I'm boring?'

'Sorry. I wasn't paying attention.'

'You do, don't you? You think I'm boring. You agree with her. You've conspired with her, haven't you? Come on. Outside!'

The Vice-Chancellor was out of his seat, fists clenched, poised for pugilism like an old sporting print of Gentleman Jim Corbett.

'I'm much too busy solving your problem to consider the question of whether you are boring. That is a matter between you and your wife. There. That's the solution.'

He handed the Vice-Chancellor the slim volume.

'I'm afraid you'll need a new committee.'

'I'm told they never come amiss,' said the Vice-Chancellor sourly. But he had dropped his fists.

'You must call it an Emergency Task-force Examining Research . . . open brackets . . . New and Liberated Learning of Vital Education . . . close brackets.'

'That is total gobbledegook.'

'I know. It's a committee. I've written it all out on the back of the slim volume.'

The Vice-Chancellor read what Oliver had written: ETER(NALLOVE).

'Eternal love?'

'Your wife will spot it immediately.'

'It's *Alice in Wonderland.* Nothing makes sense.'

'Do you expect things to make sense?' asked Oliver, in a spirit of sincere enquiry.

'Yes.'

'I'm not aware of any cure for that condition, Vice-Chancellor.'

Moody looked at him, then carefully placed the slim volume bearing the answer to his problems into his briefcase. He zipped it up, set the anti-theft alarm and left the hotel.

Oliver finished the chocolate digestives.

'Don't do it,' said the sergeant.

Diane stood outside Chief Inspector Pinkerton's door holding half a dozen case files and her notebook.

'Sometimes,' she said, 'a woman's got to do what a woman's got to do.'

She knocked on the chief's door.

Oliver dined alone. He had asked Gareth to put a bottle of champagne on ice, just in case. It had remained on ice. It was ten past eleven. The dining-room had closed at ten thirty and was deserted. Oliver, as a resident, was permitted to stay in the room, on the strict understanding that he did not ask for more food. He could, if he wished, drink himself into oblivion. That was not part of his plan. His plan was that Diane would join him, without prior arrangement, purely by mystic osmosis. Then they would drink the champagne to celebrate tomorrow's departure into the glory of a new life together.

Gareth wandered in.

'Telephone call for you, sir.'

Oliver leaped up.

'That's exciting, don't you think?'

'No.'

Oliver hurried to the lobby. Obviously Diane was ringing to say she had been delayed. It had probably taken longer than expected to clear her desk. Perhaps she needed one of his matching suitcases. Or maybe a brief discussion about what sort of sandwiches to pack. It was those little intimate details that made for a loving relationship.

The receiver was dangling over the edge of the counter.

'Diane?' he said, picking it up. He soon realized the caller was not Diane.

'Forgive me, my mistake, your voice is much too deep . . .'

The message had nothing to do with loving relationships.

'Are you sure you mean me?'

The rest was silence.

Oliver replaced the receiver, then turned to see Gareth standing close by, keen to discuss a Plan B he had in mind for the champagne, if the woman didn't turn up.

'Does this happen very often?' said Oliver.

'The telephone? Rings all day sometimes. Other days, not. I like it best when it's out of order.'

'What about anonymous calls threatening your customers? Saying get the hell out of town within twenty-four hours or we break your legs?'

Gareth thought hard.

'No, sir. We don't get too many of those.'

'It isn't likely to help the tourist trade in the area.'

Gareth decided to abandon Plan B.

The following morning as the town hall clock struck eleven, Oliver walked from the Three Tunes and loaded his matching suitcases into the boot of the car. He checked his watch against the official municipal time. They were synchronized. On the final stroke of eleven, Diane appeared around a corner, carrying a holdall.

'Good,' said Oliver. 'I thought for a moment you were going to be late.'

'Is that all you have to say?'

'Forgive me.'

He smiled and inclined his head in a respectful bow.

'Good morning, Diane.'

He took the holdall from her and loaded it into the boot. She followed him around the back of the car.

'Because of you, I've been suspended indefinitely and told to leave town.'

'You see? Predestination. I did tell you.' Then, as he closed the boot, he added: 'That's odd. I was told to leave town as well.'

'You were?'

'An anonymous caller. If I don't leave town within twenty-four hours he's going to break my legs.'

'Mine wasn't anonymous. He called himself the Chief Constable.'

When they were seated inside the car, Diane said:

'Do you know the way to the Orkneys?'

'The road to the Isles? Yes. It's more or less due north.'

'You can drop me off in Shrewsbury.'

'Shrewsbury?'

They had driven in silence for over half an hour when Oliver said:

'I'm sorry, but I had hoped that our predestination might have stretched a little beyond Shrewsbury.'

'How far had you in mind?'

'For all eternity. At least. Longer if possible. Besides . . .'

He smiled. She recognized the smile.

'You know something very funny about sex,' she said.

'Yes. I could share it with you now, if you like. Totally without obligation.'

'First things first. I have business to attend to in Shrewsbury.'

'In which case you must go about your business in the town. And I will go about mine.'

'In Shrewsbury?'

'Yes.'

'What business have *you* got in Shrewsbury? You're not a police officer. Not even a suspended police officer.'

'George,' he said.

'George?'

It was his game. He wanted her to ask. She didn't ask. That was her game.

'Good,' she said.

A little further along the road, he said:

'And so it came to pass that, like the great Charlie Chaplin, we left town at the end of one small adventure, and set off in eager pursuit of the next.'

'Is this another game?'

'I expect so.'

'Who's George?'

4

Games People Play

As they approached the outskirts of Shrewsbury, Diane thought: what the hell am I doing in this car? Accepting a lift from a total stranger who claims to have been a lecturer in comparative religion? Who calmly announces to me that we are to spend the rest of our lives together on the basis of an anagram? Who also claims he has been a specialist question-setter for *Mastermind*? And you haven't even checked his credentials. Call yourself a policeperson!

She also thought: he makes me laugh, he hasn't tried to maul me and I do need to go to Shrewsbury. In addition, his moustache is quite amusing and it might, just might, in the fullness of time, be interesting to find out whether it tickles. Purely in the interests of research, you understand.

Then she concluded: you're a silly cow.

For the moment, the policeperson won and she said:

'I think it's time I checked your credentials.'

'Checked my credentials? You're reducing our relationship to the level of a Carry On film.'

She ignored his jest.

'We haven't got a relationship. That's the whole point. I know nothing about you. That's why I need to check your credentials.

For example, you claim you were once a specialist question-setter
for *Mastermind*.'

'Not once. Twice.'

'Prove it.'

'Easy.'

He slammed on the brakes and stopped the car in a rustic lay-
by with municipal overtones.

'It only works with the proper configuration,' said Oliver, guid-
ing her to the low stone wall that formed the perimeter of the site.

'Sit there and pretend it's a black leather chair illuminated by
a single menacing spotlight. Try to look nervous.'

She did as she was told. Oliver sat on the car bonnet, facing her
in a cold, inquisitorial pose.

'Your name?'

'Diane Priest.'

'And your chosen specialist subject?'

'Pass.'

'The life and work of George Farquhar.'

'Whatever you say.'

Oliver steamed into staccato action.

'Diane Priest, you have two minutes on the life and work of
the Restoration dramatist George Farquhar, starting . . . now!
George Farquhar was born in Ireland in 1677. What was his
father's profession?'

'He was a leprechaun.'

'No. He was a clergyman. Farquhar began his theatrical career
as an actor but gave up as a result of what incident?'

'He got drunk at the BAFTA Awards and insulted somebody
royal.'

'No. He accidentally wounded a fellow actor in a duel on-
stage. What is the setting of the first scene of his play *The
Recruiting Officer*?'

'The forest of Arden.'

'No. The market-place in Shrewsbury. In Farquhar's play *The
Beaux' Stratagem* . . .'

Diane stood up.

'All right,' she said.

'I've started so I'll finish,' said Oliver.

'No need. You've proved your point.'

'But you've got seventeen more questions to answer. Stop the clock!'

'I believe you. About *Mastermind*.'

'Let's just play the game for the fun of it.'

'Why? I don't know a thing about George Farquhar.'

'Your answers have been beautiful so far.'

'And all wrong.'

'But I love the way you get them wrong. Such confidence. Such assurance. Such charm.'

'You just love playing games.'

'Of course. Doesn't everybody?'

'As a matter of fact, no, they don't.'

'You mean they think it's all real?'

She ignored his question, opened the car door and got in. Oliver realized playtime was over and it was back to lessons. He joined her in the car. Before switching on the engine he said:

'Now that you've checked and approved my credentials, does that mean we're together for all eternity?'

'Until lunch-time. Now take me to Shrewsbury, please.'

'Start the clock.'

Oliver did two circuits of the roundabout before seeing the exit marked 'Town Centre' that Diane had spotted five minutes earlier. She glanced in the wing mirror and saw that a grey car had also done two circuits and was still behind them.

'Is that car following us?' she said.

'When you say following us, do you mean *French Connection* following us?'

'Yes.'

Oliver checked in his mirror.

'No. I think he's probably just too sensible to overtake in the prevailing traffic conditions.'

Diane was not convinced. The car had been with them, at a cautious professional distance, since they left Brecon. Its colour, a muted metallic grey, was aggressively anonymous. It was the sort of car driven, in her experience, by men wearing suits of muted metallic grey with matching souls and ID cards.

'I still think he's following us.'

'Well, you're the policeperson,' said Oliver, unconcerned.

'I'm not a policeperson. I'm suspended on full pay.'

'Isn't it like riding a bicycle? Once a policeperson, always a policeperson?'

'It could be those people who threatened to break your legs if you didn't leave town.'

'But I've left town. Therefore my legs are totally unthreatened. But if it would make you happy, I could take spectacular evasive action and shake him off.'

'I'd rather you found a place to park near the town centre.'

'That would be my preference too.'

When they had parked the car, they walked into the market square, setting for the opening scene of George Farquhar's famous play, *The Recruiting Officer*. As Oliver pointed out, the kebab house with fax facilities was probably a later addition.

There was no sign of men in metallic-grey suits. Diane spotted a traditional-style park bench, dedicated to the memory of a long-forgotten citizen.

'Sit there and don't move until I come back,' said Diane.

Oliver sat down.

'Where are you going? What are you going to do while I sit down?'

'I'm pursuing a murder inquiry. Why did you think I wanted to come to Shrewsbury?'

'Predestination. Fate decreed we should spend our life together.'

'There's somebody I need to talk to.'

She put on her best police voice.

'Just a few routine questions, sir.'

'You're not allowed to ask routine questions. You've been suspended by the Chief Constable.'

'Perhaps I enjoy riding the bicycle.'

Oliver stood up.

'I could come with you. I could be your partner. I could be Cagney. Or Lacey. Whichever you prefer.'

'Sit down. Do not move. Do not pass "Go". Do not solve any anagrams.'

Oliver sat down.

'Is it all right if I speak to strange men?'

'Only if they're *very* strange.'

It had been a noble street in its prime. The bus stopped at the corner and you could buy a shirt, a crusty loaf, a hot pie and peas, a bag of humbugs, sheet music of Flanagan and Allen's latest hits, and have your boots and bicycle mended.

In the 1980s, courtesy of the economic miracle, it had become a pedestrian precinct with a sculptural featurette. Over a six-month period the bus service was privatized, rationalized and discontinued. Soon, all you could buy was a mortgage, an insurance policy or a photocopy — but you could buy as many as you wanted. They were cheaper by the dozen and the bank would help.

Now it was still a precinct but half-heartedly so, devoid of all passion and purpose. It was used by traffic as a short-cut, by drunks as a lavatory, by the homeless as a dormitory and by social critics as a metaphor. The butchers and bakers had long departed, followed by the merchants and moneylenders. The featurette had been repossessed. Even the pawnbroker was on short time. All you could buy today was the street, but there were no takers.

Diane found the door she was looking for. It had a buzzer, an Entryphone and a vandalized logo. It seemed too frail to bear such weight. She pressed the buzzer as gently as possible.

'Yes? Who is this?'

The man sounded distant and distorted, as if speaking direct from the BBC Sound Archive.

'This is Samantha. I telephoned yesterday,' said Diane, her voice deep and sultry. It was a voice she only used on very special occasions and hardly at all in the last ten years.

'You'd better come in,' said the man from the Sound Archive.

The Entryphone buzzed, like an asthmatic bee waking up after a heavy night on the pollen. Diane pushed open the door. In front of her was a narrow staircase. You might meet anyone at the top of these stairs, she decided: Mr Rochester's mad wife or Norman Bates, with or without his mother.

She walked up the stairs and turned at the landing to find a door that, in context, was in remarkably good shape. Perhaps there was a preservation order on it. It bore the words 'NINE-TEENTH HOLE DEVELOPMENTS PLC' and an unvandalized logo. It had been designed by the same consultants responsible for the visual aids at the New University of the Rhondda Valley. The concept was of a stylized golfer swinging a stylized club. It looked as if the club was swinging the golfer.

Diane made a mental note to tell Oliver about the logo. He was interested in golf. She pushed open the door and walked into a deserted reception area. There was a desk, a chair, a switch-board and a waiting area with a built-in settee and a low coffee table. On the table lay a dead rubber plant and a glossy in-flight magazine, a free gift from a forgotten airline. Diane picked up the magazine. It was dated Spring 1989.

There was no receptionist and nobody waited in the waiting area. It was *Mary Celeste* territory. Another door opened. It led from an adjoining office.

'Samantha?'

It was the voice from the Sound Archive, less distorted, but still with its origins in an alien decade. The man was in his late thirties. He matched the precinct. He wore a suit that was once sharp but now needed stropping and honing, a striped shirt like a television picture when adverse weather conditions distort the signal, and the last surviving pony-tail in the county. He was gal-loping towards a mid-life crisis with the speed of light.

'For the purposes of this exercise, I am Samantha. And you are Mr Rowley?'

'For the purposes of this or any other exercise,' he said, with an attempt at a roguish, entrepreneurial smile. It had been known to work once upon a time, but was rusty with disuse.

He glanced at the empty chair behind the desk.

'It's my secretary's day off.'

'How very convenient.'

'Would you like to come through into my office?'

They sat either side of Rowley's desk. It was arranged to look busy: files, plastic folders, a message pad and an executive toy made out of magnetic nails. Hanging on the walls were large, graphic illustrations of decaying dreams: computer-generated landscapes, in full colour but fading fast: fantastical golf-courses, sports centres and theme parks: magic lands conceived for the warriors of the market-place, where men like Rowley could disport themselves and beat each other over the head with bags of silver and gold. The glory that was greed.

'How can I help you?' he said.

'*I'm* here to help *you*. I believe I said as much on the telephone.'

'Indeed you did. It's my practice to keep a record of all incoming calls.'

He flipped through the message pad. Diane's message seemed to be the only one he had kept on record in the last six months.

'Intimate executive massage to relieve managerial stress? Is that the one?'

'That's the one.'

The sultry voice was well into gear and ready for overdrive. It promised a remedy for much more than managerial stress; it promised redemption for the entire human race. Rowley was feeling better already.

'When do we start?'

'We have to establish the need first. Do you have managerial stress?'

He relapsed immediately.

'My God. You should see the books.'

'I shall need a little more detail than that. So we can make a proper diagnosis. Then we can decide what form of executive massage will best serve your specific managerial needs, Mr Rowley.'

'What sort of detail?'

'Let me try a little guesswork. It isn't your secretary's day off. You can't afford a secretary any more, can you? Check?'

'Check.'

'You and your company never recovered from the slump in property values. Check?'

'Check.'

'In fact, things are so bad you can't even offer me a cup of coffee. Check?'

'Check. Sorry. Wait a minute.'

He stood up.

'I think there's a tea-bag somewhere if you don't mind sharing. It was a special offer.'

He wandered into the reception area, lonely as a rain cloud. Diane heard him opening cupboards and drawers, muttering to himself: 'I hope she didn't take the kettle.'

Oliver was talking to a stranger. The stranger was called Ned, a hairy man, dirty and harmless. People normally walked away from Ned, but Oliver had been told not to move, and he always did as he was told when it was part of a greater destiny ordained by anagram.

'I sit here every day,' said the hairy man.

'It's a very congenial place to sit,' said Oliver.

'How do you know? You never sit here at all. Never seen you here before.'

Oliver realized the man was a regular. He had probably sat on this bench every day since he was young and clean.

'You're quite right,' said Oliver, with proper courtesy. 'I have never sat here before. I'm passing through. On my way to the Orkneys. But I looked across the market square at this bench and thought: that seems a pleasant seat on which to dally.'

The hairy man nodded agreement.

'Me, I dally here every day, dreaming my dreams of Gay Meadow.'

'Gay Meadow?'

'Got you there, haven't I? You don't know what I'm talking about, do you?' There was a hint of challenge in his voice.

'Ah, but I do,' said Oliver, keen to establish his credentials as a traveller and a scholar. 'Gay Meadow. Home ground of Shrewsbury Town Football Club.'

'You're an educated man.'

'I know some of the things that matter. There were seven, the last time I counted.'

But there was no room in the hairy man's philosophy for other people's metaphysics. He had found his theme.

'Shrewsbury Town are famous for having played in both the Third Division North and the Third Division South of the Football League.'

'Really?' said Oliver, who had once known of this sporting distinction but had forgotten that he had once known it. It was good to be reminded, a small and harmless pleasure.

'The senior officials of the Football League, in their wisdom, can't decide where we are. Nobody can decide where we are. Where are we? I'll tell you where we are. Nowhere.'

'Nowhere is often a very good place to be.'

'You're right there, friend. I knew you were an educated man. It shows in your cleanliness and your vowel sounds.'

'Thank you,' said Oliver, who valued appreciation from any source, especially the dirty and the dispossessed. Most of his problems, historically speaking, had originated with the clean and the acquisitive.

Diane looked into the pale-brown shallows of the cup of tea. Should she drink it or send it to Forensics? Then she remembered her suspension.

Rowley sat opposite her. He was boldly drinking a cup of the same tea, a residual twitch of his 1980s bravado.

'Now where were we, Samantha?'

'We were making educated guesses about your managerial stress. First the diagnosis. Then the prognosis. And finally, the healing therapy.'

She raised her cup but was careful not to drink from it.

'Exhibit A. Cup of tea. Made from a free, special offer tea-bag, probably recycled. No milk. No sugar. Conclusion? Your business is in deep trouble. Probably bankrupt but you're too proud to admit it. Check?'

'Check.'

'And last year you tried to build a golf-course in the Brecon area on land owned by a farmer called Griffiths. And Griffiths refused to co-operate? Check?'

'What's this got to do with intimate executive massage?'

'I need to know these things if I'm to give total therapeutic satisfaction, Mr Rowley.'

'Diversifying into golf-courses wasn't my idea.'

'You were just carrying out orders? Check?'

'Check. No. Yes.' His brain was tottering on the brink of free fall. She pushed harder.

'Whose orders? The shareholders' orders? A senior policeman's orders?'

'Our parent company's orders.'

'Your parent company? You were doing what mummy and daddy told you to do? Tell me about mummy and daddy.'

'They're in London. A consortium. Serious money. We were part of the leisure niche in their portfolio.'

'A leisure niche in somebody's portfolio! Is that proper work for a grown man? More important, is that the reason Griffiths ended up face-down in the river?'

He fell silent, took a sip of tea, winced and said:

'You've got nothing to do with executive massage. Check?'

'It's not much of a career for a grown woman.'

'And sure as hell, your name isn't Samantha.'

'Correct. WPC Priest. I'm a policeperson.'

She produced her ID card. He looked at it, then at her.

'Priest,' he said, then repeated: 'Priest. There's something about your name.'

'You're not another one who's into anagrams, are you?'

'No, it isn't that.'

He stood up.

'I had a message about you. You're suspended from duty.'

'A message? Who from? Your parent company? Mummy and daddy? Superintendent Butler of the Crime Squad? The Home Office? MI5?'

He walked to the door.

'Out! And take Samantha with you!' he said, with a brief resurgence of the ruthless, decisive qualities that had once made him briefly rich and then betrayed him.

It was Diane's turn to stand up and cross to the door. Rowley barred her way.

'I should warn you,' she said. 'I've passed my GCSE in karate.'

'You have?'

'A single flick of your pony-tail and I can break your neck. Plus I have a distinction in genital shredding.'

It sounded a pack of lies and it was; but he believed her. For all practical purposes there was nothing of him left to shred. He stood aside.

Diane and Samantha left the premises of Nineteenth Hole Developments PLC. After they had gone, the executive director sat down and wept.

'Do you dream dreams, my friend?' asked the hairy man.

'I do very little else,' said Oliver. 'When we first fell into conversation, I had been dreaming of George Farquhar.'

'George Farquhar?'

'An Irishman.'

'They often are.'

'It's a long time since he was in Shrewsbury, of course.'

'But I remember him,' said the hairy man, with total certainty.

Oliver examined his companion, discreetly, so as not to give offence. How old was he? He could be forty. He could be eighty. If he remembered George Farquhar, 1678–1707, he must be over three hundred. It was unlikely but, in Oliver's world, not totally impossible. Nothing was totally impossible.

'Tell me about him,' said Oliver.

'He used to be in charge of the coracle.'

'The coracle?'

'It's like a little boat, made out of wickerwork and canvas.'

'Yes, I know what a coracle is.'

'At Gay Meadow.'

'The football ground?'

A coracle at a football ground: vindication of Oliver's view that nothing was totally impossible.

'See, the football ground's right beside a river. You're defending a one-goal lead with five minutes to go, what do you do? You play for time. You kick the ball into the river, don't you? And who gets it back again?'

'A man in a coracle?'

'Your friend!' the hairy man said triumphantly.

'George Farquhar?'

'He was definitely called George. I don't recall his second name. It's a long time ago, see.'

'About three hundred years,' said Oliver, now resigned to the fact that they were talking about two different men, both called George.

'It could well be. But I can see him now, in his coracle. What does that teach us?'

'The power of the folk memory?'

The hairy man shook his head. It was, as he always hoped and intended in these park bench debates, the wrong answer.

'The greatest brains in the world can put a man on the moon. But they can't design a computer that'll fetch a football from a river.'

'Computers will never replace the coracle,' said Oliver with what he hoped was appropriate sagacity. It worked. The hairy man smiled with the remnants of his teeth.

'I knew you were an educated man.'

They sat in a contented silence, staring into the middle distance at a universe going to hell, but secure in the knowledge that there would always be men on park benches to keep an affectionate eye on the enveloping gloom. When the human race finally crawled back into primeval slime, they were the men who would cough, spit and say: 'I told you so.'

'Am I intruding?' said Diane.

She had approached the bench from behind and was now leaning forward between them.

'Is this your husband?' said the hairy man.

'Definitely not.'

'You're an educated woman.'

As they walked along the High Street looking for a place to eat sensibly, Diane asked:

'Who was that?'

'An educated man.'

'He didn't half smell.'

'It's often the case with philosophers. They pong, therefore they are. Besides, he sits there every day. It's his bench. He has a right to smell, within his own parish.'

'Huh.'

They ate at a small hotel called the Recruiting Officer. The building dated from the turn of the century, and the brewery had carried out the later improvements on the advice of their marketing consultants and gone to great lengths to make it look Victorian again. There was an imitation log fire in the bar, folk singing every other Thursday, and customers were encouraged to play dominoes.

Oliver stared at his food.

'Is this what we ordered?'

'Yes. It's a vegetarian ploughman's lunch.'

'There can't have been many vegetarian ploughmen in the history of agriculture.'

'Eat it. It's good for you.'

'That's what I feared.'

He pushed the plate aside, though not in a spirit of rejection. He would eat it soon enough. Bread and cheese wouldn't get cold and he had things to say.

'If we're going to spend our lives together, there's something you should know.'

'There's something you should know. I do not iron shirts.'

'I like the taste of cholesterol.'

'And if we're going to spend our lives together, I'd like you to show a little more interest in my work. For example, what was I doing this morning while you were talking to that smelly old man?'

During their walk to the hotel he had given her a full and frank account of his conversation, all the fine grain of the history of Shrewsbury Town, the Football League and a man called George who used to be in charge of the coracle. She had listened, apparently attentive, certainly polite. But was it really fascination? Might she have been thinking of something else? Was it even possible she was bored?

Either way, he needed a good *Guardian* strategy, and quickly.

'It seems to me that what you do in your personal time and space is your business, unless you decide to share it with me.'

'That was a neat bit of footwork.'

'All right. I'm very sorry I didn't ask you what you were doing. What were you doing?'

Suddenly hungry, he nibbled a piece of cheese.

'I was pursuing my murder inquiries.'

'But you're not supposed to. You're suspended. Won't you get into trouble?'

'I'm already in trouble.'

'So who did it? Was it the butler?'

'I don't know yet. But I do know a great deal more about Nineteenth Hole Developments PLC.'

She brought out her notebook, opened it at a significant page and passed it to Oliver, who stared, bemused, at what she had written.

'I don't understand any of this,' he said.

'Nineteenth Hole Developments PLC are part of a huge consortium of companies. That's a list of some of the names.'

'They're ludicrous. There's one here called Worldwide-Transglobal-Universal Communications PLC. They probably call themselves that because they can't think of anything to communicate. But I expect they smell lovely.'

'They have people murdered.'

He returned the notebook, aware that it might contain vital evidence.

'How did you find this out?'

'I went to see a man called Rowley. He's the executive director for this area.'

'Did he smell nice?'

'He gave off a smell of fear and desperation.'

'If he's an executive director, does that mean he gives directions about executions?'

'Pass.'

'And why did he tell you all this?'

'He didn't. I sent him out of the room and went through his filing cabinet.'

Oliver had never realized a policeperson's work was so alive with intrigue and ingenuity, even the policeperson who was his predestined lifetime companion. He needed to know everything, preferably within the next five minutes.

'How do you do that? Do you say: "Please leave the room, I want to go through your filing cabinet?" I can't see that working with the average murderer. Or even a below average murderer.'

'I asked him for a cup of tea.'

'You asked him for a cup of tea?'

'And . . .'

'No, don't tell me. I've worked it out. The kettle was in the other room!'

'Yes.'

'And while he was out of the room making the cup of tea, you searched his filing cabinet. Brilliant.'

'Of course, he didn't know I was a policeperson.'

'You mean . . . you had a cover story?'

'Yes.'

This was the greatest revelation yet. He had met liars by the score but had never met anyone who operated with a genuine cover story. Everything was getting better and better: his chosen companion, his life, his world, the universe, space . . .

'What was your cover story?'

Diane slid into sultry mode, picked up a stick of vegetarian celery, offered it to Oliver's lips, murmuring: 'I told him I was Samantha, specialist in executive massage therapy. I give relief to high-level managerial pressure.'

Oliver felt the warmth. She sounded like Lester Young playing a slow ballad. He nibbled the end of the celery, and said:

'I've had a lot of pressure lately. I was recently made redundant, you know. At a very high level.'

'And you know something very funny about sex.'

'Would you like to know what it is?'

'No, thank you.'

She crunched into the celery. Eroticism left by the nearest exit. She had blown the whistle. Game over.

'I said we'd stay together until lunch-time. This is it. Lunch.'

She was brisk, practical. He hated it. He put on his soulful face. His moustache drooped. He had practised that in a mirror.

'Much ado about nothing? A brief encounter? The end of the affair?'

'We have to be realistic.'

'No, we don't.'

'I need to stay here for a couple of days. Pursue my inquiries. You have to go to the Orkneys. In case you've never looked at a map, we're talking about two different places, hundreds of miles apart.'

He leaned across the table and spoke quietly and passionately, the young D. H. Lawrence.

'But you're the most wonderful woman in the world. You have notebooks and cover stories. And I promise to smell nice at all times.'

Then he leaned back, casual, world-weary but uncorrupted, the mature Raymond Chandler.

'Besides, I too have inquiries to pursue in this town.'

'You? Inquiries? You don't have inquiries.'

'I need to know more about the coracle of Gay Meadow.'

He stood up and walked towards the door leading from the bar into the lobby.

'Where are you going?' Diane asked.

'Onwards into a golden future,' said Oliver.

5

The Man with No Name

Mrs Evans had run the Recruiting Officer for years. She had survived brewery take-overs and mergers, and outsmarted generations of time-and-motion experts with clipboards and management consultants with laptops. She remembered when sales executives were called commercial travellers and truckers were called long-distance lorry drivers. She had chaired the transitions from dominoes to fruit machines to space invaders to karaoke and back to dominoes with sceptical impartiality.

A small, spry woman, she was unmoved by rampaging rugger players or soccer hooligans, disposing of them with a stevedore's vocabulary inherited from her father, and a lightning left hook inherited from her mother. In an act of penance, a bruised lock-forward had written in the visitors' book: 'Memorable hospitality. Don't be fooled by the grey hair. Mrs Evans is as fragile as an ox.'

She took any combination of Mr and Mrs John Smith in her stride, and she could certainly handle Oliver and Diane. One swift glance was enough. Mr John Smith was certain of his role but Mrs John Smith was hedging her bets.

'One room? Two rooms?'

'Well, in an ideal world . . .' said Oliver.

'Two,' said Diane.

'Two,' said Oliver, then explained: 'You see, my companion is married but not to me, whereas I am divorced but not from her.'

'And I'm separated, but not from him.'

'That's pretty straightforward these days,' said Mrs Evans, thinking: they talk too much because they're nervous, but give them time and they'll go quiet, like all the others.

As Oliver signed the visitors' book, he said:

'Perhaps . . . and I don't wish to be brazen about this but . . . perhaps two adjoining rooms with a connecting door? I used to see them in Cary Grant's films.' He looked to Diane for a second opinion.

'A connecting door with a lock,' she said.

Mrs Evans led them up a single flight of stairs and showed them to the adjoining rooms. She gave a brief demonstration of how the connecting door worked.

'It locks from the lady's side, see? I'll give you the key, dear.' She handed the key to Diane.

'Thank you.'

'You're a very sophisticated and understanding woman, Mrs Evans,' said Oliver.

'And you're a bullshit merchant,' said Diane.

'He is, isn't he, dear?'

'Am I?'

'Oh yes. We've had them all staying here,' said Mrs Evans. 'In these adjoining rooms. Captains of industry. Mercantile adventurers. Members of Parliament. The odd Cabinet Minister.'

'With their research assistants?' said Diane.

'Yes. With their research assistants. They always ask for adjoining rooms. It makes it more convenient when they need to discuss their agendas.'

Oliver protested.

'But politicians, they're professional bullshit merchants. I do it for love. I'm an enthusiastic amateur.'

'Don't take it personally, sir, but enthusiastic amateurs are easily the most dangerous.'

'Thank you very much,' said Oliver. 'You're very gracious.'

'QED. Have a nice agenda,' said Mrs Evans, and left.

After they had unpacked, Diane knocked at the connecting door.

'Come in.'

She came in, picked up a chair and placed it in the centre of the room.

'Sit.'

'What?'

'Sit.'

Oliver sat down.

'You're not going to cut my hair. I hate having my hair cut.'

'No, I'm not going to cut your hair.'

'Executive massage therapy?'

'Definitely not.'

She picked up another chair and placed it opposite his. She sat down.

'If it's musical chairs, it'll be a very short game. And we have no music. One of us will have to whistle. Do you know how to whistle?'

She ignored the question.

'I want you to imagine that you're sitting in a black leather chair illuminated by a single, menacing spotlight. Try to look nervous.'

'It's Mastermind, isn't it?'

'It's Mastermind.'

'My favourite game,' said Oliver, delighted. 'Well, almost my favourite. What is your chosen specialist subject?'

'You.'

'How can you answer questions about me? You don't know anything about me.'

'That's why *I'm* asking the questions. That's why *you're* sitting in the black leather chair. Now, you have two minutes, starting from . . . now. Your name is . . .?'

'Oliver.'

'Is that your Christian name or your surname?'

'It could be either. It's part of my mysterious charm.'

'Profession?'

'Lecturer in comparative religion. Now redundant.'

'Birthplace?'

'A native of Yorkshire, with tribal ancestry in the ancient kingdom of Northumbria.'

'Marital status?'

'First confused, later divorced.'

'When?'

'Ten years ago. On a Thursday.'

'Children?'

'No.'

'Reasons for divorce?'

'She alleged I didn't listen when she talked.'

'And was she right?'

'Sorry. Could you repeat the question? I wasn't paying attention.'

'Stop the clock.'

'Did I say something wrong?'

'Don't mess me about,' said Diane. 'This may be a game but don't mistake it for a game. As I explained to Mr Rowley this morning, I have a distinction in genital shredding.'

'All that and executive massage therapy too? What a versatile woman you are.'

'Versatile and resolute. I want honest answers.'

'But it's difficult in two minutes. Especially all that marriage and divorce business. It's very complicated. It began to go wrong on our wedding day. The vicar said: "Do you take this woman to be your lawful wedded wife?" And I said: "Do you mind repeating the question, I was thinking of something else?"'

'And were you?'

'Yes. I was standing at the altar and into my head floated a musical phrase. And I was trying to remember the name of the tune. It was Billie Holiday's "Fine and Mellow" but in the split second it took me to remember, I'd omitted to pay proper attention to the vicar. It could happen to anyone. So I'm very happy for this game to continue but you must try to keep it simple.'

Diane sighed, then said: 'All right. Start the clock. Was your wife right to divorce you?'

'A very good judge. Yea, a Daniel.'

'Is there one good reason why I should even consider spending the rest of my life with you?'

'Yes.'

'What is it?'

'Predestination. It was written in the anagram.'

'Can't you give me a better reason?'

'Yes, but you'll say I'm a bullshit merchant.'

'Try me.'

'Very well. I would like to make me a willow cabin at your gate.'

'Huh?'

'Shakespeare. *Twelfth Night.*'

'Anything else? Apart from building a shed at the bottom of my garden?'

'I'm nice. And kind.'

'Why should I believe you?'

'Take my word. I give generously on flag-days. I pat dogs, excluding Alsatians. I make friends with strangers, even if they smell.'

Oliver checked his watch.

'You've had well over two minutes.'

'My game. My clock.'

'All right. Carry on. I don't mind. I enjoy games.'

She shrugged.

'No more questions. The more you tell me, the less I understand.'

She still needed to know about him, but had run out of steam. There must be a connecting door into his head, but she was trying the wrong key.

'Your mistake is to put your faith in information,' Oliver said kindly.

'Is it?'

'In the words of my good friend Thomas Stearns Eliot: "Where is the Life we have lost in living? Where is the wisdom we have lost in knowledge? Where is the knowledge we have lost in information?"'

They sat in silence, pondering the words of T. S. Eliot. It was probably a new experience for the room.

'Would you like a turn?' asked Diane.

'Doing what?'

'Mastermind. Your chosen specialist subject. Me. Assuming I *am* your chosen specialist subject.'

'You are my chosen specialist subject. Therefore I don't need to ask any questions about you. I *know*.'

'You do?'

'Yes.'

'No questions at all?'

'I already know the answers.'

'I see.'

Again they fell silent, but it was a dangerous silence, a silence that said: 'Don't just sit there, do something.' A questioning silence that said: 'All right, let's do something but what do you suggest?' A mischievous silence that said: 'Well, at the very least find out whether the moustache tickles.' A warning silence that said: 'Hang on a minute, we know damn well this thing is bigger than a moustache.' A tender silence that said: 'Shakespeare was right, make the willow cabin, call unto your soul, give the lad a kiss.'

Then somebody knocked at the door.

'Are you expecting anyone?' said Diane.

'Probably the local vicar, touting for trade.'

'I'm still married, remember.'

'In that case, it's probably the neighbourhood divorce lawyer. I expect Mrs Evans passes the work on to him, for a nominal percentage.'

Oliver called out:

'Could you come back later, please? You're interrupting a tender moment.'

The door opened. A man walked into the room, closing the door quietly behind him. He was tall, of an age with Oliver. Diane noted he wore a metallic-grey suit, impeccably cut with hand-stitched lapels. The tie looked regimental. His hair was cropped close, in accordance with precise orders. He had a layer of authority like an extra skin.

Oliver and Diane stood up.

'Remain seated.'

'But where will you sit?' said Oliver.

'I don't need to sit.'

He seemed to imply that if he needed to sit down, he had other people to do it for him.

Oliver and Diane sat down.

'Are you sure you're in the right room?' said Oliver.

'Oh yes.'

'Shouldn't you identify yourself?' said Diane.

'Yes,' said Oliver. 'I've seen public service announcements about that on television. Don't admit strangers without proof of identity.'

'I don't need to identify myself.'

The voice fell into place: it came from within the Authority Triangle, the non-elected power structure with key points located, approximately, in Whitehall, Sandhurst and a rarely defined place not unlike Cheltenham. It was a voice with echoes of acronyms: MI5, MI6, GCHQ, with a hint of MCC. It was a voice you heard selling top-quality insurance over television commercials on Channel 4.

In matters of identification, the man probably had ID cards under a variety of names, suitable for all occasions, but was never asked to show them to anybody.

Oliver decided not to insist on the ID card, despite the admonitions of the public service announcements. They tended to be about burglars disguised as gas meter readers and this felt like a different situation.

'You wish to remain anonymous. That is your right in a properly constituted secret society. But that being so, are you therefore the man who telephoned me in Brecon, giving no name but threatening to break my legs?'

'We don't play adolescent games of that kind.'

'We?'

'We don't telephone. We don't threaten. We do it.'

'You break legs?'

'If it's appropriate.'

Diane was growing impatient with the men's talk. It was too much like men's talk. Macho Man meets Cute Man. It was like being back at the police station. So she played the muddle-headed woman card.

'Look. Will this take long? We've just checked in and I haven't even started to unpack. We're bound to need extra coat-hangers and . . .'

The man interrupted her in mid-muddle, raising his voice, apparently without any increase in volume. It was an impressive trick.

'I'm here with an instruction. Stop interfering. Stop making waves. Stop asking questions.'

Oliver protested:

'It's very difficult for us not to ask questions. Life can't go on without questions. What time do they serve breakfast here? Is it possible to order a morning newspaper? To be or not to be? That kind of thing.'

'You know precisely what I mean.'

'Could you give us an example? Then we'll know what sort of questions we must beware of.'

'I will give you a precise example. This morning, in the market square, you were asking questions about Farquhar.'

Diane had been bracing herself for cross-examination about her visit to Rowley's office. The stranger's concern about Oliver's Farquhar connection came not so much from left field, but from a totally different stadium.

'So who is he?' asked the man.

'Farquhar?'

'Yes.'

'Either a Restoration playwright with local connections or a man with a coracle who rescues footballs from the river. Though I'm a mite sceptical about the latter possibility. I need to research it a little more.'

'You expect me to believe all that?'

'Of course. Only because it's true.'

'But is my message received and understood?'

Diane intervened, keen to find a foothold in a debate about to be swamped by Restoration drama and Shrewsbury Town Football Club.

'Your message is received and understood,' she said. 'But are you also asking us to keep our noses out of the Griffiths murder inquiry?' She hoped the introduction of the name Griffiths would disconcert the man. She was wrong. He focused, for the first time, on Diane.

'I take that for granted. You are, as I understand it, Mrs Priest, under suspicion. And let me be clear. I am not *asking* the two of you to do anything. I am *telling* you. This is an instruction and I have powers of enforcement.'

He knew her name. That was enough to make her wonder about his powers of enforcement. Judging by the suit and the haircut they were more likely to be hired killers than kindly probation officers. She wanted this man to shut up and leave. She also wanted Oliver to shut up, but he had decided to be helpful.

'Would you like us to leave town as well? That's the normal arrangement, isn't it? Especially in Cary Grant films where he and the girl are staying in adjoining rooms with a connecting door. We'd be happy to leave town. We're planning to go north anyway.'

'Stay here. Where we can keep an eye on you.'

'And if we stay here, is it all right if we go for a walk by the river later on? After we've unpacked and organized the coat-hangers?'

'The river?'

'It's a research project. Into coracles. I mentioned it earlier.'

'It's up to you. Rivers can be very dangerous places.'

He opened the door and left.

Oliver and Diane remained seated, still in their Mastermind positions. It was almost as if they had imagined the visit – not so much a visit as a visitation. The room felt chilly.

'Did we imagine that?' said Diane.

'That's a question. We're not allowed to ask questions.'

'Sorry.'

'But if we're not allowed to ask questions, how can we play Mastermind? How can we play anything?'

'You just asked several questions.'

'Sorry.'

'It's cold in here. Let's go for a walk by the river.'

There were no coracles to be seen on the water, but it was warm and sheltered on the river-bank. Oliver and Diane felt safe and secure as Ratty and Mole.

'I'm sure it's all right if we ask questions, just between the two of us,' said Oliver.

'We are both consenting adults,' said Diane.

'I've never really thought of myself as a consenting adult. It opens up all sorts of possibilities.'

'That man. He gave off a smell.'

'I disagree. I couldn't fault his personal hygiene.'

'Plain clothes. Special Branch. Fraud Squad. That sort of smell.'

'I see. You're speaking professionally.'

'CID, SAS, CIA, MI5, MI6.'

She had counted them in and counted them out of the police station in Brecon. They turned up every couple of years or so, whenever there was a major investigation in the area, considered beyond the intellectual compass of the local constabulary. They travelled by fast car or occasionally by helicopter. Their self-importance arrived twenty-four hours in advance and lingered for weeks after their departure. As far as she could remember, they had only ever solved one case, and that on the basis of a confession thrown out in the High Court five years later.

She had been alarmed by the man visiting their room – Oliver's room, that is – but she was not intimidated by the species. Such men could be lethal; they could also be stupid.

Oliver could see that she was brooding. He needed to know what about.

'All those initials you mentioned . . . do you have any preference? Are any of them especially nice or especially nasty?'

'They've all got their fair share of SS.'

'Gestapo?'

'Shifty sods.'

'Ah. Very like universities. They're full of SS. I think Mr Moody, the Vice-Chancellor, was an SS, but I didn't realize it until afterwards. Heigh-ho.'

'What do you think we should do?'

'Carry on as if nothing has happened.'

'A man breaks into your room . . .'

'He did knock first, give him credit for that.'

'A man breaks into your room and tries to frighten us, and you say carry on as if nothing has happened . . .'

'I've been doing it for years. Carrying on as if nothing has happened. Most of the time nothing *has* happened. Most of the great events that shake the world turn out to be clerical errors in the long run.'

'So your immediate plan of action . . .?'

'Walk around this pretty bend in the river, and hope to see a coracle. Then perhaps we'll take tea. And then . . .'

The policeman stepped out from behind a tree and stood in the middle of the footpath, blocking their way forward. Diane never found out what Oliver planned to do after tea.

He was taller and younger than Oliver, but looked like an old-fashioned policeman: a genuine bobby on the beat, in his mid-forties. Ten years earlier he might well have been good-looking in the bland manner once used to advertise hair cream. The hair had survived intact but now looked as frayed as his nerves.

'Get the hell out of town, can't you?'

Oliver was calm, conciliatory.

'I realize you're speaking with the full power of the law, Constable, but you put us in a very difficult position.'

'Would you like to leave this to me?' said Diane.

But Oliver persisted, the diplomat still, but with a dab of righteous indignation on his side.

'One minute we're being told not to leave town, then within the hour we're told the exact opposite. It's very confusing and we're entitled to an explanation.'

He turned to Diane for a second opinion.

'Shall we ask for proof of identity? He's obviously not a burglar or here to read the gas meter.'

The policeman produced an ID card and held it up for Oliver to read.

'Police Constable Priest,' said Oliver. 'How extraordinary! My predestined companion is called Priest and she's also a police-person. Suspended, of course.'

'It isn't extraordinary,' said Diane.

'It's a bit of a coincidence.'

'No, it isn't. He's my husband.'

'Ah.'

It had been a busy day for revelations. Oliver paused briefly to absorb the latest, then continued:

'But it's still a teeny little bit of a coincidence that we should all be walking by the river at the same time, isn't it? Grant me that.'

'I've been following you for the last half-mile.'

'In which case it isn't a coincidence at all, is it?'

'Not at all.'

'We thought there was a car following us this morning. Was that you? Or a near relation?'

'No.'

'Do you make anonymous telephone calls?'

'No.'

'It wasn't you who threatened to break my legs?'

'No.'

'You don't mind my asking questions?'

'Why should I mind?'

'The other chap was very firm about it. Stop asking questions, he said.'

'Are you really happy with this guy?' said Priest to Diane. Having had the benefit of a closer look, he was profoundly unimpressed. Diane suddenly saw Oliver from her husband's point of view and could see what he meant. She acted like a mature, consenting adult. She hedged.

'I've only known him a couple of days.'

'But it seems longer,' said Oliver. 'Also shorter. The briefest of moments, yet in its way a lifetime.'

'But are you happy?' Priest persisted.

'That *is* the question,' said Oliver, because it was, and they all three knew it. Diane trimmed the hedge a little.

'Not unhappy.'

Oliver was delighted. He was old enough to have been schooled in traditional English grammar and syntax. Whichever way you did the sum, two negatives equalled a positive. Diane was not unhappy. Ergo, she was happy.

'Thank you,' said Oliver, because he was happy too.

'He makes me smile,' she added, sensing the need for a little supporting evidence.

'And I've grown accustomed to her face.'

Priest nodded, accepting defeat in the face of impenetrably cryptic odds.

'That's why I want you both to get the hell out of town.'

'Sorry?' said Diane.

Priest lurched into what sounded like a speech he had prepared earlier, perhaps even years earlier.

'Diane. I want you to be happy. I now realize you can't be happy with me. Because I still love you, I naturally hope you'll find happiness with someone else . . . even . . .'

He hesitated, glanced at Oliver.

'Even him?' said Diane.

'That's all right,' said Oliver, conciliatory. 'People usually underestimate me. Often with good cause.'

'But if you're going to be happy, for God's sake go and do it somewhere else! Don't do it where I might see you! Or I won't be responsible for my actions!'

He turned smartly on his heel and marched away, eyes front, close to tears. Diane called after him.

'So this has nothing to do with the Griffiths murder?'

Without breaking stride, Priest yelled back.

'Stay away from the Griffiths case! Stay away from this area! And stay away from me!'

'We are planning to go to the Orkneys,' said Oliver, by way of comfort, but Priest was already out of earshot and the words died on the wind.

They waited until he was safely out of sight, checked in both directions that nobody else – officially or unofficially uniformed – was following them, then walked slowly on around the gentle bend, though the hysterical policeman had driven all thoughts of coracles from Oliver's mind.

'I didn't know you were married to a policeperson.'

'That's how we met. We joined the force in the same month. He'd been made redundant when the steelworks closed. I'd been made redundant when my mother died.'

'And I'll wager you turned out to be a better policeperson than he did.'

'Yes. He tried to pass his promotion examinations and failed. I tried to fail them so as not to upset him. But I passed. They didn't actually promote me, of course.'

'He seems a very sad man.'

'Yes.'

'Not unhappy is better than sad.'

'Yes.'

Diane stared at the water making its way from the dark hills to the chilly sea. It kept its distance most of the time, but occasionally burst its banks to remind people that it made no distinction between the sad and the not unhappy. The river was cold and impartial. It just kept rolling along and it didn't give a damn.

'May we skip the coracles? I need a cup of tea.'

Mrs Evans brought them tea in a private lounge of the Recruiting Officer that she kept secret from all except customers she liked. It had a real log fire.

'You didn't tell me how popular you were.'

'We're not. Well, I'm not,' said Diane, looking at Oliver. 'Are you?'

'Hardly at all,' said Oliver.

'People keep asking after you. I took the liberty of sending the first one up to your room. He said he was a close personal friend.'

'A total stranger,' said Oliver.

'I'm sorry. But he said he was from the government. Well, he didn't exactly *say* he was, but there was a smell of Whitehall about him. The cheap end.'

'We noticed that,' said Diane.

'And he showed me this card but I couldn't read it without my glasses.'

Mrs Evans poked the fire, poured herself a cup of tea, pulled up a chair and joined them at the table.

'You don't mind if I join you? We're short-staffed. Out of season. You get dry rot in your legs.'

'You're more than welcome,' said Oliver. 'We make friends easily.'

'Who else was asking after us?'

'There was a policeman. He claimed to be your estranged husband.'

'That was my estranged husband.'

'I told him you'd gone for a walk by the river.'

'He found us by the river,' said Oliver.

'Did he jump in? He seemed under a lot of stress.'

'No,' said Oliver, 'we saw him safely return to dry land.'

'We never had stress when we were little, did we?' said Mrs Evans. 'However did we manage?'

'We were too poor,' said Oliver. 'We had to make our own amusement.'

'Who else was asking after us?' said Diane, quickly and urgently, fearing the nostalgia routine would turn into the *Monty Python* parrot sketch and funny *Goon Show* voices. These were among her estranged husband's speciality acts. He thought they were very amusing and expected them to make her laugh. Had she known about these delusions on their wedding day, she would have quoted them as just causes and impediments and gone to the nearest garden centre to buy compost instead. Compost was funnier than her estranged husband.

'There was a skinhead asking after you,' said Mrs Evans.

'A skinhead from Whitehall?' said Oliver.

'He didn't say where he was from. He sounded local. Only a youngster. Eighteen, nineteen. He wasn't a real skinhead. He

had a bit of hair. A spiky bit on the top. He looked like a big
bottle-opener.'

'Mohican?' said Diane.

'Yes, that's what he looked like. The last but one of the
Mohicans.'

'I don't know any Mohicans. Do you?'

Oliver shook his head.

'Only a trendy vicar from Swansea who used to tell my students why Christianity was failing everywhere except Swansea.
But he was about our age.'

Both women looked at him.

'I beg your pardon. My age.'

A telephone rang in the lobby. Mrs Evans took no notice.
Favoured customers were always right and had first option on her
time and attention. Oliver and Diane traded glances but agreed,
silently, that they shouldn't tamper with company policy. It was
probably another anonymous caller waiting to say 'We'll break
your legs if you leave town', or 'We'll break your legs if you
don't leave town', or maybe a politician's research assistant wanting to book the adjoining rooms.

'Do you really want to see all these people?' said Mrs Evans.

'I have nothing against people, in principle,' said Oliver, 'but
no, I don't. Do you want to see all these people?' he asked Diane.

'No.'

'Would you like me to use my system?' said Mrs Evans.

'What is your system?' said Diane.

'Telling lies.'

'It has a pleasing ring to it,' said Oliver.

'I shall need false names for the two of you. The parliamentary
gentlemen who stay here do it as a matter of course.'

It was the sort of challenge Oliver relished.

'That's easy. If anybody asks, my name is Mr Farquhar.
Travelling with my research assistant, Samantha. Can you handle
that?'

'Easily.'

'It's crazy. Total madness,' said Diane.

The telephone stopped ringing.

'Madness is all anyone believes these days. Can you blame them?' said Mrs Evans.

Oliver was deeply impressed by Mrs Evans. She saw, true and straight, what needed to be done and got on with it. She handled life as confidently as she handled the log fires, genuine or otherwise. By comparison, the men he had recently done business with – the Vice-Chancellor, the police sergeant, the man with no name and Diane's estranged husband – seemed to be acting in a variety of second-rate soap operas, and constantly getting their lines wrong. Was this a profound truth about men and women? Were women simply better than men at living? He would ask Diane. She would know.

As she gathered up the empty cups and saucers, Mrs Evans said: 'Was that the telephone?'

'Hardly at all,' said Oliver.

'And will you be eating in the dining-room this evening?'

'Do you recommend it?' said Oliver.

'Definitely not. The chef's gone to a health farm and I'm doing the cooking. I once gave food poisoning to an entire male voice choir. They never made it to the Eisteddfod.'

'What do you recommend?' said Diane.

'There's a nice Italian place just around the corner. They're real Italians. From Wrexham.'

6

A Long Night's Journey into Day

It was dark by the time Oliver and Diane set out on an amiable, meandering walk in search of the Ristorante A. C. Milano (Prop: W. and G. Meredith). Mrs Evans had been quite specific with her directions.

'You can't miss it, it's got pictures of footballers in the window. The Merediths claim to be descended from the great Billy. Have a nice meal. Good evening, Mr Farquhar, good evening, Samantha.'

Though notionally just around the corner, the restaurant was in reality around three corners. As they turned at the second, Diane said:

'Nothing personal, but before you walked into the police station, most things made sense. I didn't like a lot of them but they did make sense. Since I met you, nothing makes sense.'

'Nothing personal,' said Oliver, 'but before I walked into the police station, you were wrong. You only *thought* things made sense.'

'I see. You are the way, the truth and the light?'

'Yes.'

'Except the way doesn't go anywhere?'

'The truth is contradictory.'

'And the light's fused?'

'You see? You do understand.'

There was the distant sound of a fire engine as Oliver continued: 'All I can promise you is confusion and one or two very old jokes.'

'What girl could refuse such an offer?'

'Practically all of them so far. And the ones who didn't refuse – those few, those happy few – all regretted it.'

'And who's Billy Meredith?'

'A legendary Welsh footballer. A winger. He was famous for . . .'

'That's enough,' said Diane.

She had nothing against legends and cherished several of her own, but detailed accounts of the footballing brand had the same effect as her estranged husband's *Goon Show* voices: nausea, vomiting, internal bleeding and a reflex need to destroy the kitchen.

Oliver took the hint. If she did not want to know what Billy Meredith was famous for, that was fine. All the information was on the public record, should she need it at a later date. He would be happy to guide her towards the essential reference books.

They arrived at a street corner. Oliver turned smartly to the left. Diane stopped.

'That's wrong. Next on the right, Mrs Evans said.'

'I'm following the fire engine.'

'I want my supper.'

'But I've always followed fire engines. I've done it since I was a child.'

'When you had to make your own amusement?'

'You see? You do listen. You pretend you don't but you do.'

They followed the noise. By the time they caught up with it, the firemen were at work. The fire was in the precinct visited by Diane earlier in the day. The hoses were directed at broken, upper-storey windows above a boarded-up shop, most recently a kebab house closed by the authorities after a localized but virulent salmonella epidemic. It was now on the market at a bargain price, with a further reduction for lack of customer goodwill.

But the seat of the fire was the first floor: the local headquarters of Nineteenth Hole Developments PLC. Smoke drifted across the precinct. It gave off a smell of corporate avarice and confusion, with maybe a tiny whiff of regret – as if Rowley, the doomed executive in need of massage therapy, now wished he'd done his A levels and become a primary school teacher.

'That's where I went this morning,' said Diane. 'Nineteenth Hole Developments PLC. It's their office.'

'I can understand it. One look at you. Spontaneous combustion.'

'Oliver.'

He smiled. It was the first time during their brief but eternal life together that she had addressed him by name.

'Yes?'

'Shut your face.'

'My pleasure.'

And it was. He stood quietly by, fascinated by her professionalism as she watched the firemen at work. He saw men rushing back and forth, jets of water, flashing lights: fun but meaningless. She looked more deeply and read between the lines. It reminded him of the way he first watched *Waiting for Godot* or the great spin bowlers like Benaud or Laker.

'Probably an insurance job,' she concluded.

Oliver was impressed but baffled.

'Why would an insurance company set a building on fire?'

She was patient with him.

'You set fire to your own building, then you claim the insurance.'

'Isn't that cheating?'

'Yes. The only other question is whether Mr Rowley decided to take to the lifeboats or go down with his ship.'

'Set fire to the place and then stay to fan the flames? That's a little grisly.'

'It happens.'

She was totally matter-of-fact about the possibility. It was another impressive aspect of women. They were strong. They might squeal at the glimpse of a moth, a mouse or a spider, but confront them with a major league horror — an anti-tetanus jab, a blocked lavatory or a case of self-immolation — and they would boldly go on as if nothing had happened.

A large crowd had now gathered. It was too early for serious drinking, the disco was closed for redecoration and there was show-jumping on television.

A policeman with a loud-hailer approached them.

'Move well back everybody, please. There's nothing to see.'

But these were border people with a Celtic majority and there-fore given to protest and disputation. They disagreed with the policeman, in a mood of friendly and creative dissent. Whatever he said, there was lots to see. A fire was interesting in itself. The flames were pretty and, in conjunction with smoke and spray, the visual impact had considerable appeal. J. M. W. Turner would have had his easel and paintbox out in a trice and started an aes-thetic revolution.

Then there were the socio-economic considerations. Here were firemen in regular, full-time employment: men with proper jobs. That was an increasingly rare sight. It could be the first and last chance for many people in the crowd to see such a species, before it went the way of the butcher, the baker and the bus conductor.

And finally there were the narrative implications. Nobody knew what might happen next. A desperate figure might emerge from the upstairs window and perch on the ledge. He might leap down on to a sheet held out by the firemen. There were sev-eral ladders still unused and hoses yet to be uncoiled. Who could tell what heroics lay hiding in the precinct?

The crowd was in no doubt. They agreed unanimously, on a show of hands, that the policeman's proposition was unaccept-able. There was plenty to see, and it beat seven bells out of show-jumping.

The policeman had momentarily lost interest in his duty and in the great public debate. He had recognized Oliver and Diane. They, in their turn, had recognized PC Priest. He lowered the loud-hailer.

'I thought you were leaving town.'

'My friend likes to follow fire engines.'

'And you may argue there's nothing to see,' said Oliver, 'but as you can hear from the reactions of the crowd, several of them demur from that view. Personally I enjoy watching people work, learning about different professional disciplines, that's always interesting . . .'

'Go away and don't stop until you get to the Orkneys.' PC Priest spoke with the same ferocious despair they had heard by the river. His eyes blazed red, some of it reflected from the fire, but not all. During the terminal year of their marriage Diane, urged on by their counsellor, had pleaded with him to get in touch with his true feelings and stop talking like Bluebottle. Now he was in touch with his feelings, with a vengeance, and not a Bluebottle in sight.

He raised the loud-hailer. Vengeance, Diane realized, might be his at any moment and the loud-hailer could be the means of destruction.

'We're going,' she said.

'So in the name of God, go!'

They went, walking briskly from the precinct. After all, officially there was nothing to see. The estranged husband's amplified and distorted voice followed them:

'Please keep back. Clear the street. There's nothing to see and there are buildings that could collapse at any moment.'

That was clearly another contradiction in terms: hardly anybody had ever seen a collapsing building. It was definitely well worth seeing.

The great public debate continued as, a hundred yards away, Oliver and Diane turned into the relative peace of the market square. The traffic-lights changed, a car alarm howled and in a shop window twenty unwatched television sets were half-alive with silent show-jumping; but the rest was tranquillity.

They almost collided with the nameless man from the cheap end of Whitehall. He was making his way to the scene of the fire. Whatever the police said, Whitehall clearly thought there was something to see.

He spoke in a relaxed, friendly fashion, like a regular dog walker greeting a park-keeper.

'Good evening.'

'Good evening,' said Diane.

'Warm for the time of year,' said Oliver.

'As long as you're still safe and well and within reach.'

They went their separate ways.

Mrs Evans had telephoned the Ristorante A. C. Milano and reserved the window table, overlooking the market square, for her influential friends, Mr Farquhar and his research assistant, Samantha.

The restaurant menu reflected the passions of the Meredith family. The pizzas were named after Italian football teams; the pastas after Welsh footballers with Italian connections. Oliver ordered Pizza Juventus and Diane a Pasta John Charles which Oliver said should be called Fettuccine Giovanni Carlo. They drank a bottle of the house white, which Diane said should be called Château D'If.

Over supper they discussed their predicament and the contradictions closing in on all sides.

'My estranged husband has ordered us to leave town.'

'And he's a policeman.'

'But the man with no name who came to our adjoining room says we shouldn't leave town.'

'And he smells of Whitehall.'

'So what do we do? We can't do both. We can't leave town and not leave town.'

'I've been thinking about it.'

Diane was uncertain about the usefulness of such an exercise. Oliver's thoughts tended to zoom off at great velocity and with little sense of direction. There were probably anagrams and cryptic clues galore lurking in the menu and wine list. She was unwilling to stake her immediate future on a rearrangement of the letters that comprised a Pizza Fiorentina or a Pasta Ian Rush, especially in an Italian translation: all those Zs and Is – anything could happen.

'What have you been thinking about?' she said cautiously.

'I think we should disappear.'

'Without the aid of a net?'

But he was serious.

'According to official statistics, there are 1.6 million people in the country who don't exist. They've disappeared from the public record. We can join them. They're probably friendly enough and two more won't make any difference.'

She was puzzled. If all these people were not on the public record, how did the authorities know they were there? What method had Whitehall invented to count the invisible? Was it like those other baffling abstractions that sometimes kept her awake: negative equity, the speed of light, and the pollen count? How could anybody count pollen? Was it a recognized trade? 'What do you do for a living?' 'I count pollen.' 'How many did you count today?' 'Thirty-seven.'

She was tempted. It might have been the second bottle of Château D'If taking its toll but she was tempted. There were clear advantages in being invisible. Presumably you were exempt from paying your income tax and rates, whatever fancy clothes they were currently wearing. On the other hand, you would also lose your democratic right to vote, the right for which generations of brave dissenters had fought and died. But she had voted conscientiously all her adult life and everything seemed to get worse. The harder she voted, the worse it became.

Damn it, she was very tempted. It had been a tough day all round and here was an instant and beguiling solution. Like those sporting volunteers who come up from the audience when invited by the conjuror, they would step into the magic box and, with a crashing chord and a 'Hey presto!', they'd be gone, and the world would stop pestering them.

'I suppose we've taken the first step,' she said.

'Have we?'

For once, she was ahead and slightly to one side of Oliver in her thinking.

'We've got new names. New identities. Mr Farquhar and Samantha.'

'So we're half-way to disappearing already.'

'What happens next?'

'We go to the Orkneys and find Aristotle.'

She had forgotten Aristotle, the enigmatic crossword compiler who had first brought them together. He had disappeared too. Was he one of the mysterious 1.6 million or was he another late starter? If so, it would be good to meet him in the land beyond the magic box. They would have invisibility in common: it would be something to talk about and help break the ice.

Diane topped up their glasses. The second bottle was now empty.

'A toast to disappearance,' she said. They clinked glasses and she added: 'Here's *not* looking at you, kid.'

She was pleased with her joke. So was Oliver. She could tell by the serious look on his face, as he explained the ground rules of their new situation.

'*We* can see each other. It's only other people who can't see us.'

They sipped the wine and looked into each other's eyes. It was a genuine, twenty-four carat intimate moment. There should have been a piano player in the corner with a bluesy Thelonious Monk version of 'As Time Goes By'. But there was no piano player.

Instead, there was a Mohican. He was standing beside their table, looking down on them. They didn't see him arrive. He simply materialized. He matched Mrs Evans's description: he was ninete·n years old and looked like a big bottle-opener. He wore jeans and a Bob Marley T-shirt.

'Can I have a word with you two? I saw you through the window.'

'That must have been just before we disappeared,' said Diane.

'Just before you what?'

'Take no notice. It's a little joke I've been sharing with my friend, Mr Farquhar.'

Pull yourself together, you stupid cow, she thought. Try to show a little dignity, even if you are invisible. Look not upon the wine when it is the house white. She glanced at Oliver, was relieved to see that right now he had a firmer grip on Planet Earth than she did, and left him to it.

'We haven't met, have we?' Oliver said to the Mohican. 'But I think you might have been described to us. Did you call at our hotel this afternoon?'

'Yes.'

'I thought so.'

'Is it all right if I sit down?'

'Why not?' said Oliver. 'We both enjoy it.'

The young man sat down. In close-up his face was older than its biological years, with a quality of despair common to many of his generation. Oliver and Diane had each noticed this in their dealings with young people. At age nineteen they proclaimed either despair or apathy. There was a big hole in the middle where wacky idealism used to live.

'It's about my dad,' said the boy.

'Do we know your father?' Diane asked.

'We don't actually know *you*,' said Oliver. 'It's a great pleasure to have you sharing our table and I'm sorry the bottle seems to be empty but . . .'

'The name's Griffiths.'

'Griffiths?' said Diane, startled. 'So your father was . . .?'

'Murdered. A year ago.'

'I see.'

'And your name?' said Oliver.

'Kevin. And I sort of heard, like the word got around, that you two had been asking questions and such. And I just wanted to say thank you for trying. And watch it.'

Oliver and Diane had sobered up in ten seconds. The romantic daftness had evaporated and suddenly there was no room for piano players.

Kevin looked vulnerable. It was another recurring theme in his generation. Scratch the despair or the apathy and there was vulnerability. The average streetwise nineteen-year-old turned out to be six and in need of a cuddle.

Diane reached out, touched his hand.

'Were you close to your father?'

'Not very. He was a bit of a wimp.'

She withdrew her hand.

'It's like the guy said . . . they fuck you up, your mum and dad. Well they did it to him. I expect I'm the same, but I don't know yet.'

Oliver, wondering how the poet Larkin would have reacted to being quoted in the context of a murder investigation, asked Kevin:

'Could you be a little more specific? About how your father was . . . fucked up by his parents?' He still felt uneasy using the dreaded word in public and in the presence of a woman. He was an old-fashioned man. He blamed his happy childhood. His parents had not fucked him up; they had brought him up, good and proper. He did his best to live with this handicap.

'Basically,' said Kevin, 'it was all that crap about keeping the farm in the family. Dad hated being a farmer. He was frightened of animals, for one thing. Especially the cows. You ever heard of a farmer who's frightened of cows? Well, he was. He should have taken the money when it was on offer and let them build their stupid, rotten golf-course. But even if he was a wimp, I still want to know who murdered him. And the police are no good. They're under orders. Do nothing.'

'And why did you tell us to . . .watch it?' said Oliver.

'Because we're talking heavy-duty villains.'

'In that case we will be very careful to watch it, providing we can find it.'

'I mean, murdering people is wrong, isn't it?'

Oliver nodded.

'Most of the world's great religions say thou shalt not do it. Many of them will kill you to prove the point.'

Diane, stone-cold sober and now a fully reconstructed police-person, already knew Oliver well enough to head him off whenever he strayed into areas of moral philosophy or forgotten footballers.

'What do you do, Kevin, when you're not following us around?' she said firmly, back on the information trail.

'I'm a student.'

'Whereabouts?'

'The University of the Rhondda Valley. First year. Media studies.'

'I might almost have guessed that,' said Oliver.

When they returned to the Recruiting Officer, they played another game of Mastermind. The chairs were still in place and Oliver said it seemed a pity to waste them. Diane asked the questions.

'And your chosen specialist subject?'

'Our golden future.'

'You have two minutes on our golden future, starting . . . now.'

'But there is only one question,' said Oliver, 'and you have to answer it.'

'Do I believe in predestination? That's the one, isn't it?'

'You said you would stay with me until lunch-time. But you stayed with me until supper-time, and then we disappeared, and now you've stayed with me until bedtime.'

'In adjoining rooms, under false names.'

'Parts of the day have been very good.'

Yes, she thought, parts of it have been very good; and parts of it have been alarming. The really alarming part was that the alarming parts would have been much more alarming if Oliver had not been with her. She had grown accustomed to his presence. That really was alarming.

'What happens next?' she said tentatively.

'We set off at first light.'

'Is that all?' She had expected more.

'All my life I've read adventure stories where people set off at first light. But I've never done it.'

'And then?'

'After first light? I don't know. Second light, I expect.'

'But what happens to *us*?'

'Nobody knows. That's why we have the institution called tomorrow. Prediction's impossible. I know that in my blood. My father used to back horses.'

They sat in their Mastermind chairs, alternative world-views facing each other across a canyon. Oliver believed in walking towards the mystery of the second light, eager to be delighted by what lay in wait but prepared to shrug his shoulders if the delights turned out to be dud. Diane believed in sending a reconnaissance party to check out the second light in advance, to count the delights, if any, and make sure they were non-toxic.

She was also still under the influence of her marriage guidance counsellor, a zealot in matters of human relationships. Everything should be talked about, talked over and especially talked through. Talking through was vital. It was the recommended route to your true feelings. Get in touch with your feelings and bingo! – you would inherit the earth.

Oliver had met this phenomenon on the campus, especially among teachers of liberal studies and the social sciences; but there was no room for it in his philosophy. He said it was like digging out the foundations of a building to prove why it had just fallen on your head. He had opted to be a veiled, cloaked and concealed man because humanity needed veils, cloaks and concealment. And if, in the heart of the second light, there came a moment when it was meet and right to drop the veil, remove the cloak and reveal himself, that would be lovely and it would be as inevitable as Granny Smith making her little apples, with no need to talk anything through.

That, though they didn't know it at the time, was the unspoken debate conducted in total silence – the natural form of an unspoken debate – before Diane stood up and crossed the room to the connecting door.

'I'll see you at first light,' she said.

'Thank you. What about second light?'

'I need to have a closer look at it before I decide.'

'You're a sensible woman,' said Oliver, standing up, crossing to the connecting door and holding it open for her with old-fashioned courtesy.

'I need a sensible woman,' he said.

'Don't we all? Good night.'

'Good night.'

She went into her room and closed the door; then, after a tiny hesitation, brief as a butterfly's intake of breath, she locked it. She knew there was no need to do so. Perhaps that was why she did it: a matter of principle so obscure even she had no idea what it was, except it was hers and she was sticking to it.

'I've locked the door,' she said, raising her voice so Oliver could hear.

'I said you were a sensible woman.'

'You could have fooled me,' Diane said, lowering her voice so nobody could hear.

They paid their dues to Mrs Evans, ate kippers for breakfast, then set off, in accordance with their solemn vow, at first light. Oliver was driving. Diane had the map book open on her knee.

'Shall I navigate?' she asked.

'Only if you think it's absolutely necessary.'

'I think it's absolutely necessary if you want to go the right way.'

'Is there a right way?'

'The M6. It goes due north to Scotland.'

'But if we go that way, we miss the Great North Road.'

'Is that important?'

'The Romans thought so. Question. Is it the road that is great or is it the North that is great?'

'Am I supposed to say the North?'

'Yes, please.'

'The North is great.'

Oliver's navigation blended intellectual homage with directional primitivism. Leaving Shrewsbury, he said they should aim the car slightly to the left of the sun, where it was rising in the east. They would be bound to arrive at a useful junction in the Great North Road eventually.

Their compass bearing would be north-by-north-east, an appropriate homage to Alfred Hitchcock, since they were on the run because of their involvement in a murder mystery. A true homage would have been north-by-north-west but that would have taken them into the Irish Sea.

'We all have to pay homage the best way we can,' said Oliver.

'Yes, dear,' said Diane, realizing too late that she sounded like a wife humouring a husband. Oliver seemed not to notice, but that could have been a careful arrangement of his veils and cloaks.

She switched on the radio to see whether there was anything on the local early morning news about the fire in the precinct. There was. The newsreader said there had been a fire in the precinct.

Thank you very much, thought Diane. Wait until we have twenty-four-hour news services on radio and television and then we'll be able to hear things we already know around the clock, day and night.

The newsreader went on to say there had been no casualties and firemen had yet to establish the cause of the blaze. That was more helpful. Diane had little residual affection for Mr Rowley, the stressed executive, and others of his kind, but broiling was an extreme form of social criticism.

As far as the cause of the fire was concerned, she had lost confidence in the analytical ability of the local fire service the day she saw two of their top experts tossing a coin in the charred remains of a Nonconformist chapel.

The fire was the lead story on local radio. After that the news dribbled away down a plug-hole, with gurgles of diminishing importance: the opening of a supermarket by a long-forgotten game show host, the postponement of a gymkhana because of a viral infection among the neighbourhood ponies, and the continuing drama of a midfield player's groin strain.

'Shall we have music?' said Oliver.

'Wherever we go,' said Diane.

As they tacked their way diagonally across England, on B and C roads and old wagon-ways too modest to qualify for a letter, Oliver played a series of tapes. He had carefully designed them, it seemed, as a counterpoint to the strange-sounding places with faraway names that lined their route like an eccentric guard of honour.

Brahms serenaded them as they passed within sight and sound of Blackbrook, Mucklestone and Loggerheads. He gave way to the sublime Billie Holiday as they crossed Saddleworth Moor and glimpsed Upperthong, Netherthong and Holmfirth. Billie sang 'Don't Explain' as Oliver explained to Diane the correct pronunciation of Mytholmroyd and Luddenden Foot, before tumbling sideways into a giggling anecdote about a school trip to Ugglebarnby in North Yorkshire.

They found the Great North Road as Spike Jones and his City Slickers played the *William Tell* overture. Oliver had elaborate tales to tell about the place-names on the signposts. There were legendary figures like Thornton Watlass, the eminent Victorian actor-manager, whose Hamlet still caused hearts to beat faster in Denmark; Patrick Brompton, runner-up in last year's Booker Prize, and hot tip as the next Franz Kafka by critics who had run out of things to say about the last one; Hornby, Hackforth and Fencote, the rapidly expanding law firm; and Little Fencote, of whom so much was expected.

'And did you know,' said Oliver, 'there's a place called Constable Burton in North Yorkshire, and a place called Burton Constable in East Yorkshire?'

'Am I supposed to believe any of this?' said Diane.

'You have the choice. You will always have the choice.'

They had driven through Lancashire and Yorkshire and soon they would be in County Durham: from black pudding to Yorkshire pudding to pease pudding. Diane glanced at the map book as they arrived at Scotch Corner on the Great North Road, known to reconstructed policepersons as the A1. Good. They were on course. His geography and hers coincided.

Then, abruptly and without warning, they divided again. She had settled back in her seat ready for the steady drive north to Darlington, Durham, Newcastle, Hadrian's Wall and Scotland, when Oliver suddenly took a left-hand turn which appeared, to her untutored eye, to lead absolutely nowhere.

'I thought we were staying on the A1.'

'We are. Except when we deviate.'

'I give up,' she said, throwing the map book on to the back seat of the car.

'You must never do that.'

'But . . .'

'I have to show you something.'

'What?'

'Second light.'
He switched off the music.

The street was short, the houses built of brick and the windows
boarded up. Like the main street where Oliver had left the car,
the place was deserted. Oliver counted the houses and stopped at
the fifth.

'This is the one,' he said.

'Sorry?'

'This is where my parents used to live.'

'You're the son of a coalminer?'

Oliver nodded.

'I'm a living, walking stereotype. The working-class boy who
passed his scholarship, was granted some state education and
made good.'

'Is this the house you were born in?'

'All in good time.'

'A collier's son. Will you make me read D. H. Lawrence?'

He smiled affectionately, as if Lawrence was an old school-
mate, which in a way he was.

'Poor old Bert. Travelled the world looking for noble peasants
and they were down the pit in Eastwood all the time. Mind you,
he can give all those Oxbridge chaps three goals start and a good
hiding.'

She was beginning to understand the way his mind wandered.
It was like a bee flitting from flower to flower: from Billie
Holiday to Burton Constable, from Bert Lawrence to Thornton
Watlass, from George Farquhar to Little Fencote. They were
flowers of every shape, size and colour, but they flourished and
bloomed in the same exotic, uncultivated garden.

'Let me show you something else.'

He walked quickly back to the main street. She almost had to
break into a run to catch up. He seemed in a hurry to share this
part of his garden. Or was he in a hurry to get it over? Maybe it
hurt. Families often did.

'Slow down a bit.'

'Sorry.'

At the end of the main street were the stumpy remains of the old colliery buildings. The headstock had been demolished long ago and the authorities had made a token attempt at landscaping before losing interest.

'This is where my father worked. He lost his job in the 1930s. Went south. Found work at a pit in Yorkshire. Lost that job in the 1960s. Then he gave up and died. Corrosion of the lungs. Then my mother gave up and died. Corrosion of the soul.'

'You were born a Yorkshireman?'

'My dream was to open the bowling at Headingley. But the ball hurt my fingers. So I had to settle for comparative religion. It has a lot in common with cricket.'

They walked the bounds of the pit-head, the village's little acre of industrial wasteland, respectfully paying homage, as they would in a great cathedral. The place gave off a smell of coal-dust and broken promises.

'Let me show you something else,' said Oliver as they left the sacred site.

Hepburn Street School had been built in the 1870s as a response to the great Education Act, designed to produce generations of literate workers to sustain the Industrial Revolution and the British Empire. The street was named in honour of Thomas Hepburn, a famous leader of the Durham miners in the nineteenth century.

The school, closed in the 1970s because of a glut of education, then had successive, brief and unsubstantial lives as a bingo hall, a strip club and a DIY superstore. Now it was a boarded-up shell in a boarded-up village. The only boom industry in south-west Durham was boarding up. Euro-Boarders-Up PLC must be making a fortune.

'This is where my parents went to school. Reading, writing and arithmetic. Hepburn Street Primary. Shall I tell you something very interesting about Hepburn Street Primary?'

'What?'

'The last time I counted, there were 412 Old Etonians in the House of Lords. But nobody who attended Hepburn Street Primary.'

'Nobody from my school either.' There were stories to tell about her school but she would save them for the proper time.

'As my friend Shakespeare used to say, is it not strange? Is it not strange and strange?'

They walked back to the car. The main street was as boarded up as the rest of the village. The church, three chapels, the Miners' Institute, the Co-op and the Job Centre: all sightless, brooding on unanswered prayers and visions of glory, all withheld by jealous, invisible gods.

'Do you know about Category D?' said Oliver.

'I imagine it comes after C.'

'It's a town-planning expression. When they started to close the pits in the south-west Durham coalfield, all these villages were placed in Category D.'

'What does it mean?'

'It means the official planning policy is to do absolutely nothing.'

'They seem to have kept their word.'

Diane had never seen a real ghost town. This one was haunted. There were ghosts on every corner and along the main street: ghosts of colliers and their families, marching behind their band and the lodge banner with its portraits of Arthur Cook, Tommy Hepburn and Karl Marx, on their way to Durham for the Big Meeting; and ghosts of other days, and the same band, playing 'Gresford', the miners' hymn, marching in slow procession to commemorate another victim, too small to qualify as a genuine pit disaster with headlines and an appeal fund. Oh yes, there were unforgiving ghosts aplenty in this town.

'Category D,' said Oliver. 'They put my parents into Category D.'

'What about you?'

'I battled my way up to C plus. Almost managed B minus, but I know my place.'

They were at the car when they saw their first human being, though he too could have been a ghost. He was a very old man, walking with a stick, taking his very old whippet for a slow walk. He stopped every few yards to cough and spit. The whippet looked bronchial too. The old man saw them, smiled, touched the peak of his cloth cap, and called across the street in a voice that sounded like an extension of his coughing:

'Wotcheor kiddars! How's your luck?'

Oliver could have explained that the greeting had been handed down the generations by a long-ago Geordie comic called Jimmy Learmouth: the greatest comedian ever seen by J. B. Priestley – he had said so in print, so it must be true.

Instead, Oliver responded as he remembered his father responding.

'Very canny. How's yourself?'

'Canna' grumble, hinny.'

The old man and the whippet coughed their way slowly along the deserted street, making their gentle way towards a dream of a destination, in the absence of any tangible ones. They left Oliver and Diane to wonder at the majesty of a common man, officially marooned in the oblivion of Category D, with a cough that tore at the soles of his feet, who could yet conclude there was no need to grumble. Was it not strange? Was it not strange and strange?

And Oliver said:

'It was when that boy with the bottle-opener haircut was talking to us last night, I realized something. His father and my father were probably killed by the same people. The names change but the principle stays the same.'

'You're not going all political on me, are you? I'm not crazy about capitalist hyenas myself but I am *not* building any barricades. I'm allergic to sawdust.'

'No. Nothing like that.'

If she was allergic to sawdust, he was allergic to revolutionaries. He had met too many on the campus. They were low on laughter and talked things through even more tediously than those who were out of touch with their true feelings. Many of them ended up in the City.

'No,' said Oliver, 'we will go to the Orkneys to seek out Aristotle and no doubt solve your murder mystery along the way. I'm pretty sure it's turning into a boring old establishment conspiracy plot anyway, so it shouldn't take long.'

Then he realized Diane was standing beside him, at the driver's door. She held out her hand for the keys.

'I'll drive.'

'You?'

'I'm a policeperson. I have passed the advanced driving test. Besides, I know where we're going.'

'The Orkneys.'

He gave her the keys.

She drove quickly and safely towards the Great North Road. It was when they joined it that Oliver checked the position of the sun and protested: 'You can't do that!'

'I can't do what?'

'You're going south! You can't go south on the Great North Road!'

'We're not going far. We're just popping over the border into Yorkshire. I want you to meet my father.'

Gulp! thought Oliver. 'Meet my father' was one of the world's most menacing phrases. It was in his *Handbook of Ultimate Dread* along with 'This won't hurt', 'Roger and Stephanie are dying to meet you', and 'Do you ever give talks to youth clubs?' Besides, he had lived through an extended family of in-laws and had never remembered their faces or their birthdays. The only in-law he had liked was now in Parkhurst.

'Is this likely to be a pleasurable experience?' he asked carefully, so as not to give offence.

'First light. Second light. Third light.'

She was beginning to talk like him.

'Yes. I can count. I did arithmetic.'

'If it goes well, I might ask you to tell me that very funny thing you know about sex.'

'I'd forgotten about that,' said Oliver, frowning. 'What does that prove?'

'I can't imagine,' said Diane.

They headed south and the sun was in the wrong place; but Oliver had shared his ghosts with her and they were invisible by mutual consent. The car was filled with a tantalizing possibility that could easily have been mistaken for happiness.

7

A Masonic Ritual

When that he was a tiny little boy, Oliver's mother had taught him: if you don't know, ask. If you don't ask, you'll never find out. He could chart the voyage of his life by the questions asked, and the answers given.

Aged five, in Harry Brown's fish-and-chip shop: 'Is this all the chips you get for sixpence?' Answer: 'Yes.' It was his first lesson in consumer-driven market choice.

Aged fifteen, to his marker while playing in a football match for his grammar school second eleven: 'Why do you keep kicking my ankles?' Answer: 'Shut your fat face.' The fatness remark had caused Oliver intense adolescent anxiety. He took pride in his lean and hungry look. He gazed into the bathroom mirror for weeks until the return match, when he kicked the kid's ankles, and felt better immediately. Sigmund Freud, had he played football for his school second eleven, would have called it the kicking cure.

Aged twenty-five, to a young woman at a dance-hall in Leeds, twenty minutes before it became a disco: 'May I have this waltz?' Answer: 'Suit yourself, but it's a foxtrot.' Later they had married. With the benefit of hindsight, 'Shut your fat face' would have been a more constructive answer, from both points of view.

Aged thirty-five, to a student in his comparative religion foundation course: 'Do you really think the Rolling Stones represent an advance on the black blues singers who inspired them – people like Bessie Smith, Muddy Waters and Big Joe Turner?' Answer: 'Well, like, you know, we're not into, like, value judgements, right? But like, yeah, the Stones, you know, right?'

Aged forty-five, to his wife: 'Can't we talk about it when this record is finished?' Answer: 'Your records never finish.' After that they had communicated via their solicitors. The legal profession, Oliver discovered, was where communication crawled away to die.

In retrospect, asking questions had taught him a great deal, if only that the staple ingredients in the answers were generally frustration, incoherence and rage. That was all right. He was not looking for certainty or comfort. He agreed with Damon Runyon that all life was six-to-five against. But he was the long-term prisoner of his own personality. He had an obsession that passed all understanding, including his own: a passionate need to know everything – from the size, shape and texture of his immediate destiny to the size, shape and texture of the trumpet player on the version of 'Black and Tan Fantasy' recorded by Duke Ellington on 3 November 1927. He knew the trumpet player was Jabbo Smith and he hoped his immediate destiny was unalloyed bliss, but he was prepared to take his chances, at Runyon's odds.

It was therefore inevitable that, driving south on the Great North Road into the fringes of Yorkshire to meet Diane's father, he needed to know the size, shape and texture of the impending patriarch.

'Is he a nice man?' he asked.

'I think so.'

'Is he retired?'

'He's a mason.'

'I don't know any secret handshakes.'

'Not a Freemason. A monumental mason.'

'He's a big man?'

'Strong. Very strong.'

There was a dour, non-committal quality to her responses.

They reminded him of Jack Webb in the old *Dragnet* television series. On balance he decided not to mention this.

'How,' said Oliver, picking his words carefully, 'is this very strong man disposed towards prospective suitors?'

'Blokes who fancy me?'

'I think that's cheapening the quality of our relationship but . . . yes.'

'He is merciless.'

'Thank you for letting me know.'

He said it out of politeness rather than gratitude. He was nervous, sensing an initiative test around the corner, with the hand of his lady as the prize. He had been terrified of initiative tests since primary school, when the boys in Standard 3 started a club you could only join by eating a worm. He had joined the junior section of the public library instead.

He feared Diane's merciless father would require something akin to eating a worm. Would he be expected to draw a sword from a stone? Or give a short recitation of his career prospects and pension provisions? Excalibur might be the better bet.

Diane slipped down the gears with the smoothness of a Johnny Hodges glissando. The car never sounded like that when he drove it. She was turning off the Great North Road. He looked up at the road sign.

'Hutton Conyers!' he said.

'Don't tell me,' said Diane, hearing the exclamation mark in his voice. 'It's a perfect anagram of "I know something very funny about sex and why don't you perform an erotic dance while I try to remember what it was?"'

'It's a famous name.'

'I know. My dad lives there.'

'Apart from that. A famous theatrical name. Jimmy James with Hutton Conyers and Bretton Woods.'

'I haven't the faintest idea what you're talking about. Is it a long story?'

'Not short.'

'Save it for later. We're nearly there.'

The sign outside the yard read: 'DELANEY THE MASON'. It

was impeccably carved in classical Roman lettering on a marble slab built into the dressed-stone boundary wall. The words proclaimed, simply and directly, that this was the man for the job. If John was the designated Baptist, and Edward the recommended Confessor, Delaney was clearly the pedigree Mason, and prepared to say so, in upper-case characters.

They found him at work in the yard, carving the initials RIP on a headstone. He was surrounded by a petrified forest of assorted headstones, neatly packed. It was like a friendly cemetery where pressure of space meant people had to be buried standing up, all cosy-like.

Without looking, he seemed to know his daughter had arrived. He kept his eyes on his work and said: 'Hello, love.'

'Hi, Dad.' Diane kissed him on the cheek. He was an outdoor man in his sixties, seemingly wrought from a piece of his own granite, finely hewn. His accent was predominantly Yorkshire, with residual Irish peering out between the cracks, as if his Celtic ancestors were keeping an eye on him. He glanced at Oliver.

'Who's your funny friend?'

'This is Oliver.'

'Oliver?' said Delaney, continuing work on his serifs. 'Any relation to Vic?'

'Ah!' said Oliver. 'If you remember Vic Oliver, you'll also know why Hutton Conyers is a famous name.'

'It's where I live.'

'Not only that.'

'Do you mean Jimmy James with Hutton Conyers and Bretton Woods?'

'Excellent,' said Oliver.

'Oh God. It'll be football next,' said Diane, under siege yet again from impenetrable historical footnotes, this time in stereo.

Having put the finishing touches to his work, Delaney slipped hammer and chisel into the appropriate pockets of his overalls.

'Come on, son,' he said to Oliver. 'She can make us a cup of tea.'

The affectionate patriarch, master craftsman and time-served chauvinist, led them across the yard towards his workshop, Diane following and Oliver bringing up the rear.

'Tell you what, our Diane. If I'm not careful, I could end up liking this one.'

Oliver was intrigued. Was he supposed to hear this? Probably. Delaney seemed totally uninhibited in manners conversational: it was a well-known Yorkshire characteristic. Was Oliver to assume he had passed part one of the initiative test? And was this because he knew of Vic Oliver and Bretton Woods? Jimmy James as Excalibur? There was a piece of casting for the gods to cherish.

The workshop was clean and well ordered, with wooden racks for tools, a bench with a circular saw, assorted slabs of unworked stone lying in wait for the newly deceased, and half a dozen finished pieces ready for collection by the recently bereaved. The place gave off a smell of useful toil, and not a PLC in sight.

They sat around the bench, drinking their tea from tin mugs that had served long apprenticeships on building sites the length and breadth of the British Isles, but only in the stone-quarrying regions. Delaney regarded steel and concrete as passing whims that would go the way of hula hoops and the Charleston.

He took a sip of his tea, added two more spoonfuls of sugar, then asked Diane: 'So have you got rid of Sexton Blake?'

'The divorce is nearly through. Next month I shall be a free woman.' She pondered the phrase, then added: 'A free woman. Ha ha. Ho ho. On with the fun.'

'And how's that lad of yours. Is he working?'

'Selling hot dogs in Macclesfield.'

'That's not proper work. He's got a degree, hasn't he?'

'Yes. In geology. In Macclesfield there's more call for hot dogs than there is for geology.'

'Excuse me,' said Oliver, puzzled. 'You have a son? With a degree? He must therefore be a grown-up?'

'More or less, bearing in mind he's the male of the species.'

'He's a big lad for his age,' Delaney said approvingly.

Oliver gazed at Diane with calculated adoration.

'Well,' he said, 'if you tell me you have a grown-up son, I have no alternative but to believe you. But as I sit here, looking at you, it seems totally incredible . . .'

'Shut your face,' said Diane.

It was just like old times. Nobody had told him to shut his face since the ankle-hacking footballer.

'Fine,' he said, and shut his face.

'So where did you find this one?' Delaney asked his daughter, as if Oliver were a strange-shaped pebble picked up on the beach at Scarborough.

'He walked into the police station in Brecon. Looking for a missing person. His friend, Aristotle.'

'Oh aye. Any joy?'

Oliver leapt in, keen to regain lost ground in the initiative stakes and shed the status of eccentric pebble. He also wanted to prove his ancient thesis, learned from Duke Ellington, that people love praise and flattery always works if you persist.

'Yes. A great deal of joy. Your daughter, who I now know to be the world's greatest policeperson, traced my friend to the Orkneys. That's where we're going now.'

Diane glanced at him. He corrected himself.

'That's where *I'm* going now. The rest of my destiny is still on the negotiating table.'

'We're also on the run,' said Diane. 'Pursued by mysterious men, and carrying out a murder inquiry, plus I've been suspended from duty.'

The flattery had begun to work. She had referred to them as 'we'. There was reassuring warmth in the first-person plural.

'That sounds all right,' said Delaney, totally unmoved by the catalogue of danger and adventure. 'Let's have more tea.'

He topped up the tin mugs. As he passed Oliver the sugar bag, he asked: 'So did you ever see him?'

'Who?'

'Jimmy James.'

'Yes. In Leeds.'

'A genius.'

The two men drank a toast in sweet tea to Jimmy James, the

greatest comedian of the century. Diane resigned herself to a ninety-minute explanatory lecture later in the day.

'May I ask you something very personal?' Oliver said to Delaney earnestly, as if about to ask for a sight of medical records relating to genetic insanity in the family.

'Certainly,' said Delaney, a man with nothing to hide, except whatever he decided should remain hidden.

'What's your favourite joke?'

Diane apologized immediately.

'I'm sorry about my friend, Dad. He likes asking trivial questions. He's twice been a specialist question-setter for *Mastermind*.'

'If you never ask, you never learn,' said Delaney.

Oliver smiled, vindicated and reassured that after half a century there were still parents in the world who sounded like parents when they talked. Delaney pondered.

'What's my favourite joke? It's a fair question. It deserves a fair answer.'

He fell silent. Diane guessed her father was rerunning, in memory, a litany she had not heard since she left home: music-hall acts, pantomimes, summer shows and taproom yarns; the wireless programmes of his youth -- *It's That Man Again* and *Happidrome*, *Much Binding* and *Ignorance is Bliss*; those ancient films with George Formby and Frank Randle, Sandy Powell and Old Mother Riley, made in Manchester for £2 17s 6d each and occasionally glimpsed on Channel 4 on wet afternoons, though he had seen them in the flea-pits of his courting days.

He hated television: it was all big-heads and lying politicians, he reckoned. Its job was to give out the football scores and racing results and be sure to get the odds right. Jokes were another matter, and too serious for television.

Diane could only remember him laughing at the screen twice: once when the ferret bit Richard Whiteley, and again during *Come Dancing* when some vital buttons came adrift during an exotic formation tango performed by a team from the Midlands. It confirmed all his prejudices about Birmingham.

But when he made his pronouncement, like an Old Testament

prophet delivering a brand-new commandment, she had no idea of its origins.

'My favourite joke. I think it's the one about the horse that liked to sit on eggs.'

'Oh yes, I always enjoy that one,' said Oliver.

Diane was totally bemused. She resigned herself to a second ninety-minute lecture later in the day.

'Any more personal questions?' said Delaney, who had enjoyed the first.

'Yes,' said Oliver. 'What became of Adrian L. Walsh?'

'Adrian L. Walsh?' said Diane. She assumed he was another relic from the outer limits of Oliver's dreamworld: a long-forgotten roller-skating xylophone player, an eccentric goalkeeper, a neglected Restoration dramatist, or possibly a Renaissance man who did a bit of each.

'Him,' said Oliver, and pointed at a brand-new headstone, standing by the door, awaiting collection. It bore the inscription:

ADRIAN L. WALSH

1911–1994

RIP

'What became of him?' said Delaney. 'Well, he died. Obviously. That's why they buried him. Mate of yours?'

'No.'

'Right bastard, from all accounts. A merchant and a money-lender.'

'I didn't mean to pass judgement on the man. It's simply that I couldn't help noticing, Adrian L. Walsh is an anagram of Hadrian's Wall. That's where we're planning . . . I'm planning . . . to stay tonight.'

Diane remained silent, too befuddled with the latest anagram, Jimmy James and the horse that liked to sit on eggs to start complex negotiations about the night's sleeping arrangements.

Delaney stood up, crossed to the headstone and stroked it with affection and admiration.

'I've never bothered much with anagrams myself. Stone, that's what I like. This is made out of Frosterley marble. Quarried on the banks of the River Wear in County Durham. The font in Beverley Minster's made from the same stuff. That's a lovely piece of workmanship you're looking at.'

'Fascinating,' said Oliver.

'Never been told I was fascinating before,' said Delaney with a raised, sceptical eyebrow that indicated he was in no hurry to be called it again.

'I didn't mean it personally. What I mean is . . .I see the world as anagrams and trivial questions. You see it as pieces of stone and fine workmanship.'

'Stone, it's about the only thing that impresses me. That, and stonemasons. Did you say you were heading for the Orkneys?'

'To look for Aristotle,' said Diane, keen to introduce a realistic note into the male-dominated cosmic debate, yet aware as she said it that a quest for a legendary crossword compiler scarcely qualified as hard-edged practicality. She was in danger of ending up as wacky as Oliver, though a segment of her soul said: so what?

'When you get to the islands, have a look at the cathedral in Kirkwall,' said Delaney. 'Built by the same masons that built Durham Cathedral. Good masonry, it lasts for ever.'

He slapped the marble with the flat of his hand, emphasizing the challenge in his words and, Oliver sensed, the expectation of a response. Was this the true initiative test? Oliver decided it was and said, with equal certainty:

'My questions last for ever.'

'Name one,' said Delaney.

'Well, for example, what are we all doing here?'

Delaney shook his head. 'You said trivial questions. There's nothing trivial about that one, sunbeam.'

'Forgive me. I stand corrected.'

'But I can tell you the answer. What we're doing here is waiting for the undertaker and the stonemason. Note the order. See who gets the last word?'

'You didn't tell me your father was a philosopher,' said Oliver to Diane.

'You didn't ask.'

Delaney gave a farewell pat to Adrian L. Walsh's memorial stone, then crossed the workshop to Oliver.

'Now, if you'd like to have a walk around the yard, I need a word with my daughter.'

'Parental advice?'

'I do my best but it always comes out advice. And it always comes out parental.'

Oliver strolled around the yard, admiring Delaney's craftsmanship and relishing the names on the headstones: the people believed by their nearest and dearest to be resting in peace. He hoped they were too.

There was 'ALBERT COOPER, 1902–1994, RIP'. They were good names, both. Albert, a watch-chain, a concert hall, a type of clarinet and co-star, with a lion, of a famous monologue. And Cooper was a good name, derived from the trade of making barrels. Was Albert Cooper a barrel-maker? It must have been hard, demanding work but with a core of tranquil satisfaction. Maybe the tranquillity had enabled Albert to survive for ninety-two years of a destructive century. Oliver hoped so. He sought communion with Albert Cooper: he wished him barrel-making.

While Oliver was communing with Albert, Diane and her father watched through the dusty window of the workshop.

'What do you think of him?' Diane asked.

'Bit of a nutter.'

'But harmless with it, wouldn't you say?'

'Well, he's heard of Jimmy James. I'll grant him that.'

Diane had never heard of Jimmy James and found it hard to grasp why this should be such a weighty element on the scales of judgement, but decided not to let on. It was all part of the mighty agenda marked 'ASK OLIVER ABOUT THIS LATER'. Which also presupposed that Oliver would be around later. There was a funny noise in her head: it was the sound of chickens and eggs chasing each other, trying to decide which came first.

She attempted a brief, clarifying résumé.

'So I'm on the road with a bit of a nutter who's heard of Jimmy James?'

Delaney shrugged his formidable shoulders – there was a lot to shrug.

'These things aren't made in heaven, whatever the book says. Give the lad a couple of turns around the block. Send me a postcard. Let me know what happens.' Delaney glanced at the headstone, then added: 'Funny he should ask about Adrian Walsh.'

'Why?'

'They reckon he was murdered.'

'Really?'

Preoccupied with seeking guidance from her father about the intimate patterns of her life, she had forgotten she was a policeperson. It was good to be reminded. Even a suspended policeperson had a book of rules to work by; but there was no rule book for fathers with daughters who found themselves heading north with a harmless nutter. She felt more secure as a policeperson.

'Tell me about Adrian Walsh,' she said.

Outside in the yard, Oliver gazed at an inscription reading 'JOZEF KOWALCZYK, 1929–1994, RIP'. Kowalczyk was not a traditional Yorkshire name. Very few Yorkshire names ended in -czyk; the favoured suffixes were -clough, -worth or -bottom. To be sure, Jozef was a long way from home. And where was home? Central Europe? Poland perhaps? Or some territory that changed its name on a monthly basis, at the whims of the power brokers and field marshals?

Oliver tried to imagine a life for Jozef Kowalczyk as tranquil as Albert Cooper's but found it difficult. Whatever path Jozef had travelled to his resting place, there was likely to be blood on the trail, to this day.

Sad.

Oliver and Diane left the premises of Delaney the Mason and made their way along the main street towards the car. Diane stopped beside the driver's door, keys in hand. Oliver carried on, walking purposefully.

'Where are you going?' Diane asked.

'It's Thursday,' said Oliver.

'Where are you going? Thursday. That doesn't make sense.'

She caught up with him as he stopped outside a newsagents and he explained.

'Every Thursday Aristotle sets the crossword in the *Guardian*.'

'You're buying a newspaper. Why not just say so?'

'I'm buying it because it's Thursday, not because it's the *Guardian*. It's knowing little things like that about each other that will help us build our relationship. I read that in the *Guardian*. One Thursday.'

The name over the door read: H. W. SMITH.

'Probably a lesser-known brother,' said Oliver.

'Or sister,' said Diane.

'Fifteen-all,' said Oliver, taking a copy of the *Guardian* from the rack and going into the shop. Diane followed. They were the only customers in the shop. A wispy man stood behind the counter: H. W. Smith, a close relative or a trusted friend.

Oliver placed the newspaper on the counter. As he was looking for his money Diane placed a copy of *Viz* on the counter, alongside the paper.

Oliver frowned, perplexed.

Diane smiled and explained:

'We need to know these little things about each other. A friend of mine read it in the *Guardian*. One Thursday.'

'In that case . . .' said Oliver.

He crossed to the freezer cabinet, slid back the lid and took out two frozen Mars bars. In his modest catalogue of secrets, this was the one that caused him most guilt. During his years in South Wales he had bought them from several shops on a rota basis, so no single shopkeeper would detect the nature and intensity of his addiction.

Diane watched him.

'Another little thing you should know about. I believe in going to the dentist for a check-up every six months.'

'Ah.'

Oliver replaced the Mars bars in the freezer cabinet.

Walking to the car he said: 'There are so many of these things I need to know.'

'You and me both.'

'For example, you have a large son with a geology degree. Where did he come from?'

'His mummy's tummy.'

'I realize that but . . .'

Diane interrupted: 'And what about this horse that liked to sit on eggs?'

'Everybody knows about that.'

'I don't.'

Oliver went to the driver's door.

'I'll drive. I know where we're going. We can discuss these things on the way.'

They settled into their seats and Oliver asked Diane the key question: the little thing he needed to know above all the other little things.

'What does your father think of me?'

'He says you're a nutter but harmless with it. And I should give you a couple of turns around the block.'

'That makes me sound like a whippet or a bicycle.'

'But you'll do to be going on with.'

'Thank you. If we're going to be together for all eternity, that's good to know.'

There were two little things Oliver did not know and perhaps he never would. The first little thing was that, by historical standards, Delaney's cautious approval of him was a rave notice, a high-octane, five-star rating. Jimmy James had done the trick. Previous suitors had been ruthlessly assessed and swiftly dismissed, generally with the suggestion: 'Take him to the canal, love, and dump him – you can borrow the truck.' In extreme cases he offered to mix the concrete.

The second little thing was that Diane took notice of her father. That was why she said: 'I'm still not sure about eternity but I'll stay with you till Hadrian's Wall. And all being well, you can tell me that very funny thing you know about sex.'

'I can?' He looked at her. All being well? He had no idea what the all was and what he could do to make sure it stayed well, but, even so, the space between them suddenly glowed with erotic promise and possibility.

'Never mind the dirty talk,' said the man in the back of the car, as he sat up. 'I need to know what you two are doing here.'

'Hell's bells!' Diane almost shrieked, as she turned and recognized the man with no name from the shabby end of Whitehall.

Oliver stayed cool.

'What are we doing here? We're like everybody else. We're waiting for the undertaker and the stonemason, in that order. But remember. The stonemason always has the last word.'

'I told you not to leave town.'

Diane was still shaking, her initial shock now giving way to rage. This man had invaded Oliver's car, which in a very short time had become their car, their very own personal space. He had violated a tiny part of their destiny. God damn it, you shouldn't do that to people's destiny, especially when they're discussing sex. She had a right to be angry.

By comparison, Oliver remained calm but indignant, like a clergyman at a vicarage tea party who has found a caterpillar in his cucumber sandwich.

'You should be ashamed of yourself,' he said.

'Why?' said the man, startled. Shame was a quality rarely discussed in his line of business.

'It's the oldest trick in the book. Hiding in the back of the car, then popping up like Mr Punch. If you're going to pursue us all over the country, telling us not to leave town, you could at least try to be original.'

The man frowned, puzzled. He had been accused of most of the world's deadly sins during his career, but lack of originality was a new one, especially in association with shame. He leaned forward between Oliver and Diane, trying to recapture the midfield initiative.

'You left Shrewsbury. You came here. Why?'

'My friend's father lives here,' said Oliver.

'Oh yes. Pull the other one.'

Diane was beginning to feel better, under the influence of Oliver's soothing irreverence. Restored to full policeperson status and confidence, she decided to grab the horns and see whether they belonged to the right bull.

'All right, then,' she said. 'We came here hoping to solve the mystery of who killed a Welsh farmer called Griffiths. We're unravelling a huge network of criminal conspiracy. Is that better? Is that what you wanted to hear?'

'Yes. That's better.'

Good, thought Diane. It was the right bull.

'But it's not true,' she said. 'My dad lives here. If you turn around and look across the road, you can see his workshop. Delaney the Mason.'

The man craned round to look across the street at Delaney's premises. Diane noticed that he seemed a little confused. That was good. A bit of confusion never came amiss when dealing with the forces of darkness. The important thing was to be the person running the confusion.

'Delaney is your father?'

'Yes. But be careful,' said Oliver. 'He's monumental.'

The man's attention reverted to Oliver and Diane.

'And where are you two going now?'

'We're going to the Orkneys to look for Aristotle,' said Oliver.

'By way of Hadrian's Wall,' said Diane.

Oliver started the car and asked the man: 'Would you like a lift?'

'Are you crazy?' said the man.

'No,' said Diane. 'He's a harmless nutter.'

The man opened the rear door and got out of the car. Before closing the door, he said: 'But don't forget. I'll be watching you two.'

'Enjoy,' said Diane.

They watched him cross the road to Delaney's workshop.

'Shouldn't we warn your father?'

'Didn't you notice? My father can look after himself.'

'Yes. I noticed.'

'Drive north.'

A church clock was striking noon as they left Hutton Conyers, returning to the Great North Road. It was high noon, but higher for some than for others. It was high for Diane, who had made an important discovery.

'Now we know who he is and who he works for.'

'He's a man in a grey suit who works at the shabby end of Whitehall.'

'Wrong. His name's Baxter and he works for Cosmos Security PLC.'

'How do you know that?'

Diane passed Oliver a small business card. On it was written:

COSMOS SECURITY PLC
BAXTER

The company obviously believed that the best publicity was no publicity and that the cryptic would inherit the earth. There was no address and no telephone number, but there was a logo. It symbolized a strong man protecting the world. It looked like a courageous fireman rescuing a grateful melon from a burning building. It also looked like a courageous melon rescuing a grateful fireman from the same building. It took all sorts of firemen and melons to make a designer logo.

'Where did you get this?' Oliver asked.

'I snitched it from his top pocket when he turned round to look at Dad's workshop.'

'And the man with no name has a name. But no initials?'

'Probably a deprived childhood.'

'Well, I can't say I fancy their chances.' He returned the card to Diane.

'Their chances of what?'

'Making the globe secure. And I'm sorry he's called Baxter. It's an honourable name. It's wasted on him. Do you remember Jim Baxter?'

'What was he? A saxophone player?'

'Footballer. Gentleman Jim Baxter, Glasgow Rangers and Scotland. He once sat on the ball in the middle of an international match at Wembley and defied the English to take it away from him.'

It sounded like the first paragraph of a thesis on Celtic mythology and tribal mores as reflected in Association Football. Diane interrupted him quickly.

'I know something else as well.'

'You're very clever. You know all kinds of things. What else do you know?'

'Adrian L. Walsh was murdered.'

'The man on the tombstone?'

'Yes.'

'Perhaps someone took exception to his being an anagram of Hadrian's Wall. It could have been Hadrian.'

'Did you know this man was murdered?' said Baxter.

He was standing beside Adrian L. Walsh's tombstone in Delaney's workshop. The mason was preoccupied, carefully arranging a set of wooden mallets in order of size on his bench, prior to cleaning them. When Diane was a little girl, he used to tell her the story of the Three Bears, using his favourite mallets as the bears, and a broken chisel as Goldilocks who, in his opinion, behaved like an overprivileged, middle-class brat throughout the yarn.

'Cause of death doesn't concern me. My job's to spell their names right and comfort the bereaved with a little bit of beauty. I use this . . .' – Delaney picked up the smallest mallet, known once upon an innocent time as Baby Bear – ' . . . for the delicate bits.'

'You had visitors this morning.'

'I operate an open-door policy. It's a free and democratic workshop. That's how you got in.'

'A man and a woman.'

'People, they sometimes travel in pairs.'

'The woman claims to be your daughter.'

'That's because she's my daughter,' said Delaney, picking up a medium-sized mallet, Mummy Bear, implying he would use it to add emphasis to any discussion about the next generation.

'Your daughter and her friend . . . were they asking questions about Walsh?'

'No. Mostly they were asking questions about Jimmy James, Hutton Conyers and Bretton Woods.'

'Jimmy James? Who's he?'

'If you have to ask, you wouldn't understand if I told you.'

Baxter committed the names to memory. He had a good memory, honed by training and professional experience. He would run a check on them later.

'Did they also ask you about George Farquhar?'

'Never heard of him. Who does he play for?'

'But they did ask you about Adrian Walsh?'

'No, they didn't ask me. It just cropped up. In the course of conversation.'

Delaney performed a brief juggling act with Mummy Bear, throwing it high in the air, catching it by the handle. It was one of Diane's favourite tricks, when she was seven.

'I used this on the headstone. The family wanted Roman lettering. It's like a woman, is this one. Strong but subtle. Beautiful to the touch. Just right for adding the serifs.'

He waited for Baxter to ask him what a serif was. People usually had to ask. But the man was embedded in his own peculiar tramlines and resolved to go to the terminus.

'Do you know how Adrian Walsh was killed?'

'I heard he was standing in the way when the shotgun went off.'

'And do you know why he was killed?'

'He was a merchant and a moneylender and he paid the price, I daresay. It's not a proper job. Any more than yours is, whatever it is you reckon to do.'

'What about your job?' said Baxter, ignoring the jibe.

'I'd rather be building cathedrals than making headstones, if I'm truthful. But there's not much call for cathedrals these days. No, it's honest craftsmanship and I don't hurt anybody.' Delaney picked up the largest mallet on the bench: Big Daddy Bear. He looked up at Baxter and added: 'Unless it's absolutely necessary.'

'Is that a threat?'

'Just making a point. Forty years of working the stone, your arms get strong and you've generally got a big hammer in your hand when you need one. Like this one. I keep it for the heavy-duty work. The big stuff. Pyramids and such. Shut the door as you go out.'

Delaney indicated, as firmly and graciously as any fully paid-up royal majesty, that the audience was at an end. The words emerged in the same gentle Yorkshire monotone as everything else he said, craggy and monolithic. It was impossible for an outsider to differentiate between truth and lies. Ancient grievance and tribal rage haunted every cadence. If the Pennines and the Cleveland Hills had the power of speech, this was the way they would sound.

Baxter was a hard man. He had fought a few good fights and even more dirty fights in his time. He had won the ones that mattered. He was also selective in matters of violence; he only fought necessary fights, those with a discernible purpose. And he could take a hint, especially from a muscular man with a big hammer. He was a moveable force who recognized an irresistible object when he met one.

He crossed to the door, but before leaving tried a parting shot, like a good professional investigator.

'Did your daughter and her friend say where they were going?'

'Yes. Macclesfield.'

'Macclesfield?'

'Yes, Macclesfield. Her son lives in Macclesfield.'

It was another new name to remember and run a check on. Baxter, startled by the sudden flow of apparently helpful information, was encouraged to ask:

'Have you got a phone I could use?'

'Yes, I've got a phone; but no, you can't use it.'

'Why not?'

'I don't like you,' said Delaney.

Baxter left. He shut the door as he went out.

8

The Horse That Liked to Sit on Eggs

According to Baxter's information, Oliver and Diane were going to Macclesfield. He sat in his car, noting this alleged fact along with the names of Jimmy James, Hutton Conyers, Bretton Woods and George Farquhar. He suspected Delaney had fed him a Yorkshire pudding of lies. But he had been in the investigation business for a long time, and he knew that if you turned a lie inside out you often caught a glimpse of the truth. He had a lot to check out.

While Baxter was contemplating a journey to Macclesfield and the possibility of truth in an imperfect world, Oliver's car was heading due north along the A1. Diane had the map spread out on her knee.

'Can we stop off in Durham?' she said.

'You don't mean stop *off*,' said Oliver. 'You mean stop. It's like people who say "scoreline" when they mean "score". And "check out" when they mean "check". And "off of" when they mean "off". Or "of". Not to mention the greengrocer's apostrophe.'

'Yawn,' said Diane.

Oliver ignored the yawn. In matters of grammar and syntax he was implacable.

'You should say: "Please may we stop in Durham?"'

'Please may we stop in Durham?'

'To see the cathedral? Out of respect for your father?'

'No. To call at the police station.'

'We know what time it is.'

'I want to run a check on Adrian L. Walsh. Find out how he died. And I want to run a check on Baxter and Cosmos Security PLC.'

'You're suspended from the police force,' said Oliver. 'You're not allowed to run checks.'

'I'm only suspended on the Welsh computer. I bet the news hasn't reached Durham yet.'

'Shall I tell you a trivial fact?'

'I haven't discovered any way of stopping you,' said Diane, who had begun to enjoy Oliver's trivia but was not quite ready to own up.

'It is a statistical fact that there are more people working for private security organizations in this country than there are in the proper police force. If you ask Cosmos Security PLC for the correct time, they'll send you a bill plus VAT.'

'Is that trivial?'

'You decide. You're the policeperson.'

No, she thought, it isn't trivial. In her experience, people ended up working for security organizations as a last resort, at the end of a long, desperate trail that began with unemployment. It was dressed up, of course, in the fancy but fading clothes of the 1980s. In the good old days of plain English you were called a night-watchman, and you had a big torch and a flask of tea. Today you were called a security operative, given an ill-fitting uniform with a fading logo, paid a pound an hour and you supplied your own torch. If you had any sense you supplied your own dog, too.

The problem was that once you put a man in uniform, however shabby, he was expected to carry out orders, without question. That was how the system operated, whatever the quality of the orders. Grey suits were not exempt. They were generally the most lethal. And there were some very funny people around, giving very funny orders. She wondered who was giving the orders to the grey-suited Mr Baxter of Cosmos Security PLC.

'Baxter,' she said. 'I need to know about Baxter.'

'I'm sure he's one of life's failures,' said Oliver. 'He probably wanted to be a famous concert pianist.'

'So?'

'We should always respect the dignity of failure. It tolls for all of us. By the way, I also know something very interesting about Beethoven.'

'Later.'

'Obviously. This is much more important than Beethoven.'

'What is?'

'Durham.'

Oliver explained that the city of Durham was too noble a place to be sullied by conversation, even about Beethoven. It should be approached quietly and respectfully. Then you came close to the grandest cathedral in the world, presiding over the River Wear as it had for nine hundred years, and respect gave way to primitive awe. In such a place as this, Duke Ellington's comment – 'Too much talk stinks up the place' – became universal truth. People, from subversive anarchists to subservient grovellers, could find God here. Durham provided gods for all seasons and all reasons. Listening to the massed colliery bands playing 'Gresford' in Durham Cathedral on the Miners' Gala Day, you would sure as hell end up believing in something, though it might not give you comfort.

Oliver and Diane parked the car, then walked in silence along Saddler Street and Owengate, across Palace Green, then through Windy Gap which led down to the river. They found a quiet place to sit, sheltered by tall trees, the trees protected in their turn by the might of the cathedral.

Oliver sat down. Diane stood over him. By now he knew the routine when constabulary duties were to be done. 'What are you going to do?' she asked.

'Stay here until you get back,' he said.

'What are you *not* going to do?'

'Wander off in pursuit of the trivial and meaningless.'

'Unless . . .?'

'Unless it is likely to lead to an early arrest.'

'Car keys.'

'Promise you won't be long,' he said as he handed her the car keys.

'Of course I won't be long. You're going to tell me something very funny about sex.'

She walked back along the path. Oliver sat quietly on the bench and thought about sex and the possibility of close encounters of the sweetest kind with Diane. It was only a possibility; he was taking nothing for granted. But still he smiled. Wouldn't you?

Yes.

Baxter was not smiling.

He sat in his car, parked beside an isolated telephone box on a country lane in the no man's land between Yorkshire and County Durham. He had chosen it because it was isolated and he had a taste for isolation.

He had telephoned Cosmos Security PLC's information centre and asked them to run checks on Jimmy James, Hutton Conyers, Bretton Woods and Macclesfield. He suspected they could all be code-names. He had also asked for guidance about his immediate movements. He had given them the number of the telephone box. When they were half-way through a promise to get back to him within ten minutes, his money ran out.

Two hours had passed. After an hour, a farmer had driven by on a tractor, pulling a trailer laden with horse muck. He had shouted to Baxter in a jovial, impenetrable accent. The more Baxter brooded about what the man had shouted, the more the message seemed to be that people had died of exposure, boredom and old age waiting for that particular telephone to ring. Or it could have been a rural observation about the weather, the view or the smell of horse muck. Anything was possible in this God-forsaken wasteland, including hallucination.

There were only two certainties. The telephone had not rung, and Baxter was not smiling.

Sergeant Milburn was smiling. He came from a long line of smilers, and the woman approaching his desk was well worth a beam.

'Good afternoon. My name's WPC Priest of the Mid-Glamorgan Crime Squad,' said Diane.

'WPC Priest? Why that's a canny thing to be, pet. You're a long way from home, mind,' said Milburn, with a genial, approving glance at her ID card.

'I know I'm a long way from home.'

'Well I'm Sergeant Milburn, and I'm here to help bonny lasses like you. What can we do for you, hinny?' he said, still beaming.

Diane remained wary, distrustful of compulsive beamers, especially when they were patronizing with it. Given three pints of lager they often turned into gropers as well.

'I need some information,' she said.

'Oh, man, we've got stacks of information since we got computers. We've got information we haven't even looked at yet. It's there, like, but retrieving it, that's the problem. What sort of information did you fancy, like?'

'Information concerning the murder of a man called Adrian Walsh.'

'Oh aye?' The smile stayed in position, but tilted slightly to starboard, as if struck by an unexpected cross-current.

'Did you know him?' said Diane.

'Well, not personally, like. I don't move in them circles.'

'What circles?'

'Stinking rich.'

'A merchant and a moneylender, I'm told,' said Diane.

'Well, somebody made a scourge of small cords and drove him out of the temple.'

'Except they used a shotgun.'

'Twelve-bore.'

'Any theories?'

'He was doing real estate deals. So I daresay it was a negotiating ploy.'

'May I have ten minutes with your computer?'

'It's in the back room, like.'

Milburn hesitated, as if groping in the back of his head for a half-remembered order from above, then lifted up the flap on the enquiry counter. The smile remained but it was no longer a cheerful,

Wearside welcome. It was more like a habit he was unable to quit.

'Howay, hinny. Let's see what we can access for you. Are you all right with buttons and such like?'

'Brilliant. Lead me to your small back room and you can then resume your normal duties.'

She allowed Milburn to hold the door open for her, but made it clear it was a favour she was doing for him.

Oliver had done as he was told. He had not moved. He had remained seated. He had also completed Aristotle's *Guardian* crossword, which contained several intriguing clues.

It was tranquil by the river. Joggers passed him by at ten-minute intervals. Most of them were sluggish and overweight. They were happy to stop and exchange pleasantries about the weather, points of local interest and the human condition. There were frequent dog walkers, all as docile as their animals. Oliver patted two Labradors, a Dalmatian and an affectionate beast of indeterminate breeding.

On the water eight oarsmen and a cox drifted by in a long thin boat. They seemed out of place. They should have been Ratty, Mole and Badger. Oliver wondered whether they were lost. Or was this the scenic route from Putney to Mortlake?

By the time Diane returned, Oliver had disappeared. She was not pleased. Keeping her voice down, out of deference to the ambience, she said: 'Shit.' Then she heard his voice.

'I haven't gone away. I'm here. Walk towards the sound of my voice.'

She left the path and walked up the slope towards a clump of trees and beyond them found a palisade of old tree trunks sticking out of the ground. The tree trunks formed a lozenge-shaped enclosure. She walked into the enclosure. Oliver sat on a seat formed within the tree trunk at the point of the lozenge.

'Stand at the end opposite to me,' he said, 'and tell me what you see.'

She did as she was told. She saw, carved in relief on the receding trunks, in skilful perspective, a picture of the Last Supper. Oliver sat in the centre.

'A local sculptor made this,' he explained, 'out of dead elm trees. It's the Last Supper.'

'Thank you, I recognize it.'

'Isn't it remarkable? A woman with a Labrador told me the story. Out of Dutch elm disease came forth art. There's a parable there if you care to look.'

'And I see you're playing Jesus Christ.'

'Sorry,' said Oliver, standing up. 'That's a bit pushy.'

Later, they walked along the path up the slope towards the cathedral.

'I love this place,' he said. 'It's full of coincidences.'

'What a surprise.'

'Did you know they kept prisoners of war here? A man with a spaniel told me the story.'

'How is that a coincidence?'

'My old campus, now the University of the Rhondda Valley, started life as an Italian prisoner-of-war camp.'

Now the cathedral loomed over them, a massive threat or an eternal promise, according to taste.

'They kept Italian prisoners of war here?'

'No. Not Italians. Scotsmen. After the Battle of Dunbar in 1650. Cromwell kept four thousand of them here. It was cold so they burned all the wooden bits.'

They paused in the great doorway. It had a door-knocker with a funny face.

'A woman with a Great Dane told me about the door-knocker,' said Oliver, but before he could continue the story, Diane said:

'If we are going to live together for all eternity, I will listen patiently to stories told to you by the dog walkers of County Durham and beyond. But in return, I expect you to take a keen interest in everything I do. I expect you to say: 'How did you get on at the police station, my dear?''

'How did you get on at the police station, my dear?' said Oliver.

'Very well. They gave me lots of information. Feel that.' She handed him her shoulder-bag. He tried it for weight. It contained a furlong of computer printout retrieved from the police computer while the sergeant's back was turned. The bag was heavy. Oliver handed it back.

'Information,' he said flatly.

'You don't seem very impressed.'

'T. S. Eliot says we shouldn't confuse information with understanding.'

'You told me that in Shrewsbury.'

'It still applies. And "T. S. Eliot" is an anagram of "toilets", so he should know.'

The great door opened and thirty-eight Japanese tourists emerged to take photographs of each other on Palace Green before continuing their journey to York, Norwich and Ely.

'And now,' said Oliver, 'I think we should inspect the work of the Durham stonemasons, and pay homage to your father.'

'Thank you,' said Diane.

'Why?'

'For respecting my father.'

They went into the cathedral. It was a coincidence that the organ should start to play and the choir should start to sing at that moment. Not all the proud dog walkers in the world and their assembled beasts could have orchestrated such a moment. The music echoed through the vaults, a mighty celebration of everything that is holy, with a special descant for the prospective lovers of the world and the coalminers and stonemasons who gave them life and a precious heritage.

'Now do you understand why I fill my head with trivia?' said Oliver.

'Why?'

'Because the people who built this place . . . people like your father . . . they thought they knew the answer.'

'They believed God was the answer.'

'That's what they believed.'

'And you don't?'

'No. Do you?'

'No,' said Diane. 'Not the answer.'

'But they were asking a big question,' said Oliver. 'Look at it.

Did you ever see such a big question? It's too big for me. That's why I stick to silly and trivial questions. Fear. Big questions terrify me. But then, I suppose that's why we have the big questions. To frighten us and keep us in our place.'

They walked down the centre aisle. As they approached the altar, the music stopped.

'You're an amazing man,' said Diane.

'You're an amazing woman. Mind you, all people are amazing, if you give them the chance. Mostly we don't give them the chance. That would be much too dangerous.'

'I want to ask big questions.'

'There are no answers.'

'Questions I have to ask *myself*.'

'Always the best kind. Would you like to give me an example?' She turned to face him.

'Questions like . . . will I take this man as my unlawful wedded husband, even as far as Hadrian's Wall?'

'We have to travel further than that. We have to travel well beyond the wall.'

'I know. I said it was a big question.'

'All you have to say is yes.'

'But I don't understand the things you say. You talk about people I've never heard of.'

'By my trivia shall you know me.'

'I need to know your trivia,' said Diane.

Later in the afternoon, walking arm in arm by the river, Oliver gave her a guided tour of his bedrock trivia: his Ten Commandments and Beatitudes of the peripheral and the forgotten. He started with the greatest music-hall comedian of the twentieth century.

'Jimmy James, with Hutton Conyers and Bretton Woods. Jimmy James, a comic genius from Stockton on Tees.'

'Tell me about Hutton Conyers and Bretton Woods.'

'They were the straight men, except they were funny as well, and they weren't always the same men.'

'I'm sorry?'

Oliver explained:

'On the posters and in the programme it always said: Hutton
Conyers and Bretton Woods. But they were just the names of the
characters, like Hamlet or Hedda Gabler. Jimmy James found the
name Hutton Conyers on a signpost on the Great North Road.
And Bretton Woods was a conference the government organized
to rescue the British economy.'

'So Hutton Conyers and Bretton Woods could be anybody?'

'Precisely. Sometimes Jimmy's brother-in-law, or his son, or
Roy Castle, or Eli Woods. They were all brilliant. But Jimmy
made them so. He invented Monty Python but nobody noticed.
Genius is supposed to come from Oxford or Cambridge. Nobody
expects genius to come from Stockton on Tees.'

'Except you.'

'You noticed?'

'You expect to find genius everywhere.'

'Obviously. I found you,' said Oliver.

But all this was later, walking by the river.

Earlier in the afternoon, standing at the altar, Diane had asked a
big question:

'Do you really mean to take this suspended policeperson as
your unlawful and unwedded wife?'

'I have no choice. It's predestination.'

'Even beyond the wall?'

'We need to know what's beyond the wall. That's why we have
walls.'

'What about my trivia?'

'I'm happy to wait for your trivia. But I need to know about
your son.'

And later in the afternoon, walking arm in arm by the river,
Diane told Oliver about her son.

'When I was twenty, I got pregnant. I was an unmarried
mother years before it was fashionable.'

'What about the father?'

'He was already married.'

'I very much hope he wasn't a tired, middle-aged business-man,' said Oliver, who loved life when it imitated art, but drifted into a coma when it resembled an Australian soap opera.

Diane shook her head.

'No. He was a young, energetic motor mechanic.'

'And he's still promising to leave his wife . . .?'

'No. He offered to leave his wife but I wouldn't let him. He offered to pay maintenance but I refused.'

'You emancipated yourself early.'

'Yes.'

'And your ex-husband? That nice policeman who followed us to Shrewsbury . . .?'

'I met him when I joined the force. I told him what I've just told you. I also told him a condition of our marriage was that I could manage without him if necessary. I've always been very good at walking away.'

Oliver smiled.

'I bet he didn't believe you.'

'He didn't.'

'And I bet he does now.'

'He does. And I expect you to believe the same thing.'

'Of course. A condition of our predestination is that either of us may walk away at any point.'

'I hadn't realized that.'

'I understood that from the first day.'

To Oliver it was obvious. A wise, eccentric woman who used to teach economic history with a Chico Marxist bias had once told him, when he was in the cheerless whirlpool of his divorce: 'People shouldn't get married, my dear, unless they are capable of living alone.' He now regarded it as a self-evident truth. He had shared it with several Americans, suggesting they might add it to their Constitution, but mostly they just walked away.

To Diane it was a shock and a delightful revelation. She had read in a dentist's waiting-room that freedom could only be found by way of intimate human relationships. But in her experience, the freedom was a prison cell furnished as a kitchen, with a broken microwave, a fridge that needed defrosting and a male voice chorus endlessly singing: 'What's for tea, Mum?'

'You are an amazing man,' she said to Oliver, with a gentle squeeze of his arm.

'And your son, is he an amazing man?'

'Yes, of course. I'm his mother. He's six feet tall, strong, handsome, intelligent, with a good university degree and unemployed.'

'I thought he was selling hot dogs in Macclesfield?'

'I don't call that employed.'

'I can't comment,' said Oliver. 'I've never been to Macclesfield.'

But all this was later, as they walked by the river.

Earlier in the afternoon, standing at the altar, Oliver had recapitulated on the vows they had solemnly sworn in the sight of the departing choir, two school trips and nine hundred years of accumulated ghosts.

'We've done: "Wilt thou take this man?" and: "Wilt thou take this woman?" What else are we supposed to cover?'

'Forsaking all others?'

'All the others have forsaken me so it isn't really a live issue.'

'Check.'

'How about worldly goods? Some people feel very strongly about worldly goods.'

'I couldn't care less. I left mine at home for my ex-husband. LPs mostly. Pink Floyd, Tubular Bells and that dirty one with Peter Cook and Dudley Moore.'

'Purely for the record, I have a little house in South Wales, full of books and music . . .'

'And a head full of trivial facts, specialist Mastermind questions, anagrams . . .'

' . . . and old jokes. Don't forget the old jokes. With all my merry quips and wheezes I do thee share.'

And later, walking arm in arm by the river, Diane asked him:

'What about the horse?'

'I see no horse.'

'The horse that liked to sit on eggs. My father's favourite joke.'

'Don't you like it?'

'I've never heard it.'

'What sort of a father doesn't share his favourite joke with his daughter?'

He was gently indignant. Inwardly he sensed major betrayal. If we didn't share our jokes with the people we were supposed to love, what hope was there for world peace?

None.

'It was probably my fault,' said Diane. 'There was a time when I thought my parents were boring and stupid and I didn't listen to them.'

'But you've started listening to your father before it's too late. That's good.'

'I know.'

'So listen.'

And Oliver told her the joke.

'Once upon a time there was a farmer who had a horse. His neighbour admired the horse and offered him £10 for it. The farmer thought this was good value so he accepted the offer. However, before they shook hands on the deal, he said to the neighbour: "I should warn you, this is a fine horse, but he has one serious weakness. He likes to sit on eggs. So whatever you do, keep him away from eggs." The neighbour said yes, he would keep the horse away from eggs. So the deal was struck. The neighbour paid the money and took the horse away.'

'It's terrific so far,' Diane said flatly.

'Pay attention. If you don't concentrate you won't get the full flavour.'

'I'm concentrating.' She concentrated as Oliver continued the story.

'A week later the farmer heard loud cries coming from the river. He went down to the river and there was his neighbour, on the horse, in the middle of the river. "He won't move," said the neighbour, "we've been here all morning." "I'm very sorry," said the farmer. "I should have warned you. I told you that he likes to sit on eggs, but I forgot to tell you that he also likes to sit on fish."'

There was a long silence. They continued walking. Then Diane said: 'I see.'

And Oliver said: 'That, in your father's opinion, is the world's greatest joke.'

'And in your opinion?'

He gave long and careful consideration to her question. There was nothing funny about jokes. He took them very seriously. He announced his conclusion with the cavalier jollity of an Old Testament prophet bearing a tablet of stone with a freshly carved spiritual agenda.

'In my opinion? The second greatest.'

She guessed she would live to regret it but had to ask:

'And the greatest?'

'Is about frogs.'

'Frogs?'

'Frogs.'

But all this was later, as they walked by the river.

Earlier in the afternoon, standing at the altar, Oliver had said:

'With my body I thee worship.'

'Thank you.'

'Though it remains more of a philosophical concept at this stage in our developing relationship.'

'Quite so.'

'But because I believe in truth and honesty, I should tell you that your body is rarely far from my thoughts. And all that being so, and duly placed on the record, thereto I plight thee my troth.'

'We had that one at my wedding, too. I never knew what it meant. And I didn't like to ask.'

'I checked in the book when I got home. To plight is to pledge or promise. Your troth is loyalty and fidelity. So it's a pledge of loyalty and fidelity.'

'All right,' said Diane. 'I plight thee my troth.'

'You do?'

'From this day forward.'

'As long as we both shall live?'

'As long as it takes to get to the Orkneys.'

Oliver took her hand and said:

'I will.'

'I will,' said Diane.

It might have been coincidence that the organ started to play at that moment. It might have been a sentimental verger tipping the wink to the keyboard player. Or it might have been all in the mind. But there was an explosion of triumphant organ music as the middle-aged, happy couple walked down the aisle, smiling at imaginary friends and distant cousins.

It might have been coincidence that the bells started to ring as they left the cathedral by the great door. It might have been a newly minted marketing ploy intended to enliven the heritage trail. Or it might have been all in the mind.

But bells were ringing as Oliver and Diane stepped out on to Castle Green and posed for invisible photographers.

'I thought it went rather well,' said Oliver.

'Yes. And didn't the bridesmaids look lovely?'

Then they walked down to the river, arm in arm, to share quips and wheezes, bitter secrets and old regrets; unless that was all in the mind, too.

Dusk was falling across the ancient kingdom of Northumbria as they drove towards Hadrian's Wall, and Diane said:

'Tell me.'

'Tell you what?'

'The very funny thing you know about sex.'

Oliver chuckled, shuffled and made a mess of changing gear. He apologized.

'I'm sorry. But you see, I've been using that line for years. When I first started, it was what we called a chat-up line but we're not allowed to say that any more. Ideologically unsound, I'm told. You're the first woman who ever wanted to know.'

'I may live to pay a terrible price.'

'Do I look like a serpent bearing forbidden fruit?'

She had a good look. He didn't. Aside from the moustache, he looked like a twelve-year-old who had just discovered a more exciting game than conkers.

'Well?' he said. 'Do I?'

'Pass. Just tell me the great secret.'

'All right,' said Oliver. 'The very funny thing I know about sex is this. A woman, naked except for her stockings, is an extremely erotic sight. A man, naked except for his socks, is a totally ludicrous sight.'

Diane pondered, smiled, then laughed loudly: good, honest, dirty, if-you-don't-like-it-you-can-go-to-hell laughter.

Oliver joined in. Their laughter rang out across Northumberland and bounced back off the Cheviots. We're behaving like a couple, thought Diane. Is this what I want?

She decided. Yes. No. Possibly.

9

Why Did We Eat the Frogs?

Baxter woke up as *The Archers* finished on his car radio.

'Blood and sand! Now I'll never know what happened about Nelson Gabriel's parking ticket.'

Then he looked through the windscreen and remembered where he was, on the black border waiting for a telephone call. It was raining: harsh, vindictive northern rain that means to hurt: the rain that aims, quite deliberately, at Headingley cricket ground when Yorkshire need one more wicket to win a Roses match; the rain that wipes out a few Harrogate galas and garden parties, then sweeps up the coast, by way of Bridlington, Filey and Scarborough, just as the kiddies have started to dig their sandcastles. It was a night, Baxter decided, deserving of the Nobel Prize for Bleakness – and here to present it is King Lear, and it's great to see his lovely daughters in the audience tonight.

No question. In this job a man needed a daily fix of Ambridge, and never more than tonight. Then the professionalism – ruthless, according to his CV – returned. Baxter reached over to the back seat where he kept his undercover overcoat, specially designed to look like ten million others. He scrambled into the coat, left the car and, bracing himself against the weather, crossed to the telephone box.

There he raged at the silent receiver.

'Ring, damn you! Speak to me! The name's Baxter. The special operator. The main man. I've run out of small change and I've run out of patience. Don't you remember? You were going to call me back in ten minutes. With instructions. Macclesfield or Hadrian's Wall? You remember what we agreed? Big decision. Heads could roll. Future of the nation at stake. Top priority. We'll get back to you.'

There was no response from the telephone. The wind moved up from force eight to force ten, and no hanging about with nine. The rain was falling almost horizontally. It would probably hit the ground on the outskirts of Peterborough.

Baxter returned to the car, yelling at the night:

'Cosmos Security PLC? I wouldn't trust you with the security of my budgie! And I haven't even got a budgie!'

Inside the car he accepted the inevitable: he would have to use personal initiative. Decisiveness was on his CV along with the ruthless professionalism. Hadrian's Wall or Macclesfield? He felt in his pocket for a coin. Then he remembered. He had no small change.

He opted, decisively, for Plan B. He would open his AA book at random. He would keep on doing so until he opened it at the map containing Hadrian's Wall or Macclesfield. Either of them would be a far, far better place to go to than where he was now. He opened the book. The system worked, at the twenty-third attempt.

Baxter's car disappeared along the road. The northern gloom swallowed it with a cold embrace, like the quicksand enveloping Carver Doone. There might have been a plop but it was drowned out by the wind.

Five minutes later the telephone rang.

The weather was heading from the north: Scotland's revenge for Culloden, the clearances, and the theft of her greatest footballers. In the lee of Hadrian's Wall, Mrs Robson's farmhouse provided shelter from the storm and bed and breakfast on reasonable terms, dogs and children welcome.

Her living-room doubled as the residents' lounge – also, at first glance, as a furniture warehouse. Oliver and Diane sat on the settee, hemmed in by a dining-table and chairs; a television set; a Welsh dresser; two bookcases; three armchairs and a piano; and, cosily, by Mrs Robson. She was a cheerful border Northumbrian with a gentle accent, a husband marooned on an oil rig and a big brown teapot. Mrs Robson had a healthy nose for other people's business. She believed that gossip, like the fruits of the soil, should be in common ownership, but this doctrine came with an unspoken assurance that nothing would ever be used in evidence.

'So are you on your honeymoon, or what?' she asked.

'I suppose, strictly speaking, the answer to that question should be "or what",' Oliver replied.

Diane smiled. She had guessed what he would say. She was getting to know this man, *her* man, if their cathedral vows were as serious and lasting as they felt.

'That can be more fun than the real thing,' said Mrs Robson, pouring the tea.

'But rest assured. This is unquestionably the real thing,' said Oliver.

Diane decided to get the conversation on a less mawkish and sentimental keel before the angel choirs started on their songs of love.

'We're travelling north,' she said, brisk and businesslike, 'on our way to visit a friend in the Orkneys.'

'You're off over the border?'

'Beyond the wall,' said Diane.

'As long as you've got your passports and visas in order. I say that to the Americans that stay. About the passports. Makes them really nervous. I tell them the Roman legions have been mounting extra patrols because of border incursions. I said it to some Japanese tourists; they turned round and went back home to Osaka.'

'I've never been to Osaka,' said Oliver.

'Nor me, pet. I'm told it's a bit like West Hartlepool.'

Mrs Robson laughed and poured herself another cup of tea. Diane realized this was another woman totally at ease with herself, like Mrs Evans, the fearless innkeeper of Shrewsbury. It was a repeating pattern. Was it because they were innkeepers or because they were women?

One guess.

By comparison, the men they had encountered were a hundred-carat mess: from the heavy-hitting Baxter to Rowley, the go-getting executive who wasn't going anywhere or getting anything, to Durham City's beaming police sergeant, whose beam was thinner than the skin on custard, but ten times as sickly. These guys wore their self-images like cheap suits bought carelessly from last year's mail-order catalogue.

Oliver, she realized, was the exception. He was Oliver to the last slice. As if to prove the point he said to Mrs Robson:

'May I ping your middle C?'

'Do you allow him to talk like that to strange women?' said Mrs Robson.

'It's just his little way.'

'In that case, do as you like, pet.'

Oliver leaning back over the settee, reached out to the piano and pinged middle C.

'Better now?' Diane asked.

'Go ahead, give us a tune,' said Mrs Robson. 'We could have a bit singsong.'

'I'm sorry, I don't play the piano. But I do like to ping middle C whenever I get the chance. It's a little homage to Beethoven.' That was the end of Oliver's explanation.

'Beethoven? He was German, wasn't he, Beethoven?' said Mrs Robson.

Oliver nodded and Mrs Robson continued:

'I've had lots of good fun with the Germans that come here. I show them Hadrian's Wall and I say: "Look at that, man, we were first." But they never laugh.'

In the bedroom, Diane laughed. Oliver stood before her, naked except for his socks. He was a totally ludicrous sight. That part of the theory was correct.

Mrs Robson had lit a big log fire, and they had switched off the bedside lamps. The firelight cast tall, shimmering shadows, purpose-made for the higher realms of erotica.

'I'm sorry, but you look totally ludicrous,' said Diane.

'I told you I would. Whereas you . . .'

Diane was naked, except for a pair of black stockings.

'You're very lucky,' said Diane.

'From where I'm standing, that's an understatement, lady,' said Oliver, slipping into Bogart-speak.

'No, I mean lucky that I own a pair of stockings. All women wear tights these days.'

'How did you come by these stockings?'

'Police issue. I sometimes wear them under my tights, for additional warmth. Very good if you're doing an all-night surveillance.'

'An all-night surveillance,' said Oliver. 'That phrase has a sweet ring to it.'

'Well?' said Diane. 'We've agreed you are a totally ludicrous sight. What about me?'

'You are highly erotic,' said Oliver.

'Am I?'

'Oh yes.'

'Thank you.'

No man had ever called her highly erotic. She had endured the familiar catalogue of crap: from 'Get 'em off' to 'Show us your tits' to 'Give us a feel' – invitations she always found easy to resist, to the astonishment of the speakers. But this was different: a serious man about serious business.

'You are a highly erotic sight and I desire you. As you might have observed by my tumescent tendency. Indeed, if I turn slightly to the left, I will probably cast a shadow on the wall.'

He tried it. He was right. He cast a shadow.

'Not unimpressive, as shadows go, wouldn't you say?' said Oliver, in the objective tones of an Oxbridge don analysing an obscure metaphysical footnote.

'I'll let you into a secret,' said Diane. 'It's working for me, too.'

'Is it really? That *is* good news.'

Minutes later, socks and stockings lay in two neat piles on the floor. Oliver and Diane lay in one untidy, infinitely adjustable pile on the bed. Later they would remember the deeds they did that night and the sweet small change of their conversation. It turned out surprisingly numerical; but, then, it was small change.

Oliver said to Diane, in the early stages:

'We must be very honest with each other about what we like.'

'This *is* what I like.'

'I mean in detail. Concerning zones.'

'Zones?'

'And erogenousness.'

'Huh?'

'If I do this, say, here . . .'

'Very good. You're working well.'

'You must tell me, say on a scale from one to ten, whether or not you find it pleasing in terms of erogenousness.'

'You can't even say the word.'

'It's a little difficult with my mouth full.'

'Don't worry. You're scoring well.'

'Thank you,' said Oliver, anxious to please, and keen to explain: 'You see, women have an advantage in that they have more erogenous zones than men. I can't be in all that many places at once.'

Diane discovered one of his zones. It wasn't all that difficult.

'Oh, my word,' said Oliver, 'that's very erogenous. An immediate ten. I might even suggest it would be in both our interests if you slow down a little.'

After that the conversation continued, as far as they could remember – which was hardly at all – along mathematical lines, like an upward graph designed in heaven.

'Three,' said Diane.

'Ten,' said Oliver.

'Five.'

'Ten.'

'Seven.'

'Ten.'

'Nine.'

'Ten.'

'Ten. Ten. Ten.'

And then, in unison 'One hundred and eighty!'

It was a glorious vindication of Oliver's theory about world peace: synchronize your jokes and everything else will follow.

Then they lay in a lovely, sticky, post-coital languor.

'I don't smoke,' said Diane.

'Nor do I. I managed to give up when I was eleven.'

'What do you normally do afterwards?'

'I can't remember.'

'Neither can I.'

'We could listen to the music.'

'I can't hear any music.'

'Listen harder.'

So they listened and they heard Ella singing 'How High the Moon' and Hoagy singing 'My Resistance Is Low': and Nina sang 'I Love You, Porgy' and Louis sang 'Sleepy Time Down South'; and Billie sang 'Fine and Mellow' with a lovely tenor solo by Lester Young. All for them in the dark shadow of Hadrian's Wall.

Then Oliver said:

'Sex always reminds me of *The Battleship Potemkin*.'

'Obviously,' said Diane, who had no idea what he was talking about.

'It's that bit where the captain's giving the orders and there's a caption that says "Fire!" with one exclamation mark, and then there are some more pictures and then another caption that says "Fire!!" with two exclamation marks, and then some more pictures and then a caption that says "Fire!!!" with three exclamation marks. And the guns go off and the revolution starts.'

'I see. It's a film.'

'Made by Eisenstein in 1925.'

'Fascinating,' said Diane, switching on the bedside light and reaching out for her shoulder-bag.

'What are you doing?' Oliver asked.

'Well I know it always says in those short stories in women's magazines: "Afterwards they slept", but I feel wide awake.'

'So do I. Would you like me to tell you about the frogs?'

'I'd like to check that information I collected from the police station in Durham.'

'It is the world's greatest joke, after all.'

Diane opened the bag and hauled out yards of computer print-out. She did her best to arrange it in a practical and logistical order on the bed. She looked like Venus rising from the microtechnology.

'Do you mind?' she said.

'I hope ours will always be a free and democratic bed.'

As Diane started to browse, Oliver said:

'I know a story about information.'

But she was already absorbed in her research, a fully fledged naked policeperson.

'We know the man Griffiths was involved with Nineteenth Hole Developments PLC and he ended up dead.'

'It's an American story.'

'And according to *this*, Adrian Walsh was negotiating with a company called Universal Megamarkets PLC who are part of the same group as Nineteenth Hole Developments PLC. And he also ended up dead.'

'It isn't a joke. It's a serious story. About information. In America.'

'And listen to this . . . Cosmos Security PLC is also part of the same group.'

They realized, simultaneously, what was happening. They were both talking but neither of them was listening. They had both been married and they both recognized the symptoms. They apologized simultaneously.

'I'm sorry.'

Synchronize your apologies and love will flourish.

Discuss.

'You want to tell me a serious story?' said Diane.

'A serious American story.'

'Tell me the serious story and if I like it you can tell me about the frogs.'

'A serious true story. It's about an American who was black-listed by McCarthy during the 1950s. It doesn't matter what for. Thirty years later, he gained access to his own files. The FBI had half a million words about his activities. And exactly fifty per cent of the information was wrong.'

Diane held up the sheets of information and peered over the top at Oliver.

'Are you saying half of this is wrong?'

'If it's official information I should think yes, half of it will be wrong.'

'But half of it will be right.'

'Possibly. But nobody knows which half.'

'I still think murderers should be sent to prison.'

'If they *are* the murderers. But if half the information is wrong, half the time the wrong people go to prison and in ten years time they end up in the High Court getting free pardons from the Crown.'

She suspected Oliver was right, or at least half right. In other circumstances she might have argued the point. In these circumstances, a stout defence of the British judicial system was low on the list of priorities.

'Tell me about the frogs.'

'Are you quite sure?'

'How do I know? Tell me the joke and then I'll tell you whether I'm sure.'

Oliver told her the story.

'Once upon a time there were two Russian peasants called Ivan and Igor. And the area where they lived was visited by a plague of frogs.'

'Frogs?'

'Yes, frogs. And one day Ivan and Igor were out for a walk and Ivan said to Igor: "I bet you five roubles you dare not eat a frog." So Igor picked up a frog and ate it. And Ivan gave Igor five roubles. They walked on for a couple of miles, whereupon Igor said to Ivan: "I bet you five roubles *you* dare not eat a frog." So Ivan picked up a frog and ate it. And Igor gave Ivan five roubles. They walked on for another couple of miles, whereupon Ivan said to Igor: "Why did we eat the frogs?"'

Whereupon Diane looked at Oliver in total silence.

Oliver shrugged.

'I said it was the world's greatest joke. It's bound to take a little time to achieve the full effect.'

'No question about it,' she said. 'Cosmos Security PLC is behind

behind all these murders.' She curled up under the duvet with her
computer printout.

Oliver lay back on his pillow, and stared at the ceiling. After
a while, he murmured:

'If you don't like my American stories or my Russian stories,
would you consider making love again?'

'Now?'

'Not quite immediately but . . .'

'When?'

'Soon. Say . . .within the next three or four weeks.'

Diane rolled the information sheets into a large paper club
shaped like a baseball bat and whacked Oliver with it, gently and
caressingly. It struck him as an amazingly erogenous weapon.
Swords into ploughshares. Information as aphrodisiac. Who
would have believed it?

Oliver did.

This time, afterwards, out of deference to romantic fiction and
exhaustion, they slept. Outside, the rain had stopped, and the
wind had calmed down in sympathy. A full moon shone on
Hadrian's ramparts, another ultimate weapon fallen into point-
lessness, a craggy stop on the heritage trail. It was four o'clock on
a chill morning and all was tranquil.

In the bedroom, the embers of the fire glowed in the darkness
like a childhood memory. It was warm in the bed. Oliver slept
soundly, on his back, arms outstretched. He looked like a teddy
bear. He was breathing out through his mouth. His moustache
rippled as if blown by a benign sea breeze.

Diane stirred, opened her eyes, remembered where she was,
watched Oliver's moustache for a while, smiled and closed her
eyes. Then she opened them again, as she heard a noise outside.
She frowned – her first of the night. Was she dreaming? What
she heard – or *thought* she heard – was the sound of marching
feet. Then, as her eyes opened fully, the sound disappeared. So
she closed her eyes to see what would happen.

She went back to sleep.

*

There was nothing nouvelle about Mrs Robson's cuisine. She believed in hearty breakfasts: bacon, eggs, sausage, fried bread, tomatoes and a few chips. She allowed her customers an element of choice: any combination of ketchup, brown sauce and mustard.

Oliver stared at his meal. It was as big as Birmingham, but smelt better.

'Is there cholesterol in this?' he asked.

'Why of course there is, pet,' said Mrs Robson. 'There's very little else, as a matter of fact. So the Americans tell me.'

She patted Oliver on the shoulder.

'Build up your strength, man. You know it makes sense.'

She seemed to know they'd had a grand night in bed. She could sense these things. It came with the noble peasant kit. She was very happy for them. Life was a sod most of the time and, in her experience, a good time in bed was the best consolation prize on offer.

'Mrs Robson?' Diane said cautiously, knowing she had to ask a daft question.

'Yes, honey,' said Mrs Robson, in the welcoming manner of a woman with a lifetime's experience of daftness.

Diane continued in small, incremental stages, as if crossing a fast-flowing river on irregular stepping-stones.

'Have any of these Americans, or Japanese, or Germans . . . or anybody else for that matter . . . any of the people who've stayed here . . . have any of them ever said to you . . . over their cholesterol in the morning . . . that they heard things in the night?'

'Happens all the time, pet.'

The answer came swiftly, matter-of-fact.

'Really?'

'I didn't hear anything,' said Oliver, sensing exclusion from an adventure.

'What was it? The marching feet?' said Mrs Robson.

'Well . . . yes.'

'Marching feet?' said Oliver.

'It's what people generally hear, when they hear things in the night.'

'Is tnere . . . an explanation?' said Diane, still on the stepping-stones but glimpsing a secure landing somewhere ahead in the mist.

'Two.'

'What are they?'

'The first explanation is that there's some sort of Outward Bound place up the road where they get middle-aged executives doing rock-climbing and route marches and such. Apparently it makes them better at running their PLCs and ruining the country when they get back to the city. Can't see it myself, but some people'll believe anything if it's stupid enough and costs a lot of money.'

'That's a rather boring explanation,' said Oliver, who had sniffed mystery and was unhappy being fobbed off with tedious old business executives. 'What's the other one?'

'It's the ghost of the Roman legion that used to be stationed at the top of the hill.'

Mrs Robson offered her two theories with equal weight and conviction.

'Which do you believe?' said Diane.

'I make up all the stories myself, honey, so I can believe whatever I fancy.'

After breakfast, Oliver and Diane went for a walk along Hadrian's Wall. Diane's theory was that it would counter the effects of the cholesterol. Oliver's theory was that it would bring them closer to the ghosts.

'This landscape is haunted,' he said, looking around at the gaunt hills, bisected by the Emperor Hadrian's Maginot Line, craggy, crumbling and, on a cold morning out of the tourist season, totally deserted.

'By Roman legions?' said Diane, taking his arm.

'It's nothing to be frightened of.'

'It's a bit weird.'

'We're all haunted. It's all right. It's healthy.'

'Really, truly?'

She needed reassurance. Ghosts were all very well in their place, like Christmas. But border ghosts were a special breed: a reluctant peace-keeping force thousands of miles away from home, defending the imperial dream against passionate rebels with a cause. These ghosts had blood on their hands, much of it innocent. These ghosts made her shudder.

Oliver pulled his cap down, tight against the wind.

'We all have ghosts. It's a fact of life and a fact of death. You're haunted by a farmer called Griffiths and a moneylender called Walsh, and the murderers you want to bring to justice. I'm haunted by Jimmy James and Lester Young and George Farquhar. Your father's haunted by the stonemasons who built the great cathedrals, yes, and this wall, too. And we're all haunted by our parents and grandparents. It's good for us, most of the time. Made a mess of poor old Hamlet but that's Scandinavia for you.'

She was temporarily comforted. Both in and out of bed, Oliver radiated warmth. He was a hot-water bottle *and* a teddy bear: a rare and precious combination.

It was the other man who frightened her. He was walking along the wall towards them. He walked at a slow and even pace, to the beat of a silent drum. His hands were thrust deep into the pockets of a long, dark, heavy coat. His face was totally concealed by a black Balaclava helmet with eye slits. From Beirut to Belfast, it was the international uniform of the intimidator, the hoodlum, the hired assassin.

'Is that someone come to haunt us?' she said.

'Just a moment. I need my distance glasses.' Oliver put on his other spectacles, then focused on the approaching figure. 'I don't recognize him.'

'I don't like the look of him.'

'He's probably lost his legion.'

'I'd go so far as to say . . . I'm scared.'

'But you're a policeperson.'

'Speaking as a policeperson, I'm scared.'

'Speaking as a retired lecturer in comparative religion, I find him a little menacing, but that's because I can't see his face. I don't like Greek drama. I twitch at the sight of a mask.'

But he took her hand and, grasping it tight, led her firmly towards the man. It occurred to him that the scene was like a

Celtic remake of *High Noon*. He even wondered how Fred
Zinnemann would have shot the scene in this setting, and what
music he would have used. 'Do Not Forsake Me, O My Darling'?
But who would sing it? Moira Anderson? Surely not. Lindisfarne?
Or maybe an instrumental version? Ian Carr on a cool jazz trumpet? Katherine Tickell on her Northumbrian pipes? Oliver's
stream of thought was running wild, out of control, in silly directions, as the hooded man approached them. That was a sure sign.
Oliver was scared. He would confess it later. For the moment, he
tried to be big and grown-up.

Diane was scared too, delving into her memory for street-
fighting wisdom. The man had both hands in his pockets. One of
them would be holding the gun. But which one? Was he left-
handed or right-handed? There was a way of telling she'd read
about in Raymond Chandler. You looked at the man's sideboards
to see which side he'd shaved most neatly. She couldn't remember
what Chandler said about men in black Balaclavas.

When the man was ten yards away, he stopped. He appeared to
look towards them. He kept his hands in his pockets. He mumbled something.

'I'm sorry,' said Oliver, 'but we can't hear a word. Either you
must speak up or take off your Balaclava.'

The man took his right hand out of his pocket. There was no
gun. Therefore left-handed? He was wearing woollen gloves.
Therefore no fingerprints? He raised the bottom of the Balaclava
to reveal his mouth.

'I said . . . I'm here to give you a warning.'

'Thank you,' said Oliver. 'We deeply appreciate your concern.
Are you from the Outward Bound place? Relieving your executive stress?'

'Oh, shit!' said the man. 'This is ridiculous!'

He ripped off the Balaclava and stuffed it in his pocket.

'Michael!' said Diane.

'Michael?' said Oliver.

Diane introduced them. 'This is my son, Michael. Michael,
this is my friend, Oliver.'

The two men shook hands and Oliver, touching the peak of his cap, said: 'Delighted to meet you, Michael. I should explain that I'm deeply in love with your mother.'

'I see. Good. Hi, Mum.'

Mother and son embraced and then Diane yelled at him:

'What the hell are you playing at?'

'It's a bit complicated.'

'Your mother thought you were a centurion, looking for your phalanx.'

'What?'

'Ignore him,' said Diane.

'OK.'

Diane, flanked by two of the three main men in her life, began to relax.

'Let's go and ask Mrs Robson for a cup of tea. I'm sure there's a perfectly lunatic explanation for all of this,' she said, and then started to giggle.

'What's funny?' said Michael.

'Why did we eat the frogs?' said Diane.

'Huh?'

'You must forgive your mother. She's had a lot of excitement,' said Oliver.

They made their way down the hill towards Mrs Robson's brown teapot. Diane laughed about the frogs, and Oliver reflected: we have climbed the wall, looked over the border and we are no longer afraid.

10

The Farquhar Connection

Later that day, in the privacy of a Scottish bathroom, Oliver would write in his secret diary: 'My travels are becoming more and more fascinating by the minute. Consider. Having found the woman of my dreams, I then win the approval of her father, pledge eternal love and fidelity in a great cathedral and meet her son on Hadrian's Wall, all in the space of twenty-four hours. He is not precisely a long-lost son. I gather from Diane he's been temporarily mislaid. But the whole situation has a pleasing elegance and symmetry. I can hardly wait to see what happens next.'

What happened immediately was a cheerful greeting from Mrs Robson to Michael, from the doorway of the farmhouse, as the trio returned from walking the wall.

'So you found them, then?'

'Yes, thank you.'

'He's a big lad for his age,' Mrs Robson said to Diane.

'He's a big lad for anybody's age,' agreed the proud mother.

'Kettle's boiling,' said Mrs Robson, holding the door open for Michael, Diane and Oliver, who hesitated in the porch.

'It's Friday, isn't it?' he said.

'That's right, pet,' said Mrs Robson. 'The weekend starts here.'

'*Ready, Steady, Go*!,' said Oliver, spotting the reference instantaneously.

'If you remember *Ready, Steady. Go*! you must be as old as you look,' said Mrs Robson.

'Alas, I think I probably am. World-weary yet curiously beguiling, wouldn't you say?'

Mrs Robson shook her head but not so Oliver would notice, then closed the door on the chill morning.

She gave them coffee as they sat around the table in the living-room, then, after a return trip to the kitchen, produced a gigantic cooked breakfast for Michael. It was large enough to satisfy the massed bands of the Brigade of Guards after a heavy night on the John Philip Sousa.

'He's a big lad but a bit skinny. He needs building up,' said Mrs Robson, as she left the room on her way to slaughter more sausages.

Oliver inspected Michael across the table. This, after all, was a *de facto* stepson, the first he'd ever had. He was tall, dark and scrawny, with stubble on his chin that could be style, or could equally be sloth – it was difficult to tell with the young. But Oliver recognized the symptoms of the recently graduated: the calculated relaxation riddled with angst. The young man had a head stuffed with sixteen years of accumulated schooling, a deep fear that none of it would be of any use in a hostile world, and a keen determination not to be caught out. Oliver had seen hundreds like him: all in their early twenties, juggling ineptly with doubt, debt and despair, while trying to appear resolutely cool.

Overtly, Diane was much less concerned about her son's physical and spiritual well-being than Mrs Robson and Oliver, but that was maternal privilege. Besides, it was interrogation time.

'So what do you think you were doing on Hadrian's Wall in a big coat and a Balaclava helmet?'

'Like I said, I was supposed to give you a warning.'

'*You*? Give *me* a warning?'

'I didn't know it was going to be my mother, did I?'

'Forgive my interfering in family matters,' said Oliver, 'but I understood you had a degree in geology and were selling hot dogs in Macclesfield, rather than giving warnings to people.'

'I quit the hot dogs last month.'

'You didn't tell me,' said Diane.

'I didn't want to worry you.'

'I'm your mother. It's my duty to worry. I read it on the wrapper when you came out of the womb.'

'The caterpillar on the leaf

'Repeats to thee thy mother's grief,' said Oliver.

'Huh?' said Michael and Diane in unison.

'William Blake. It sprang unbidden to my mind.'

Diane explained:

'A lot of stuff springs unbidden to his mind. You get used to it after a while. Take your coat off. You must be roasting.'

Michael was still wearing the long, dark overcoat, despite the roaring fire and the body heat generated by the sausage, bacon and fried eggs.

'I'm all right,' he said, sticking out his lower lip in a gesture of defiance she first remembered his using when he was three weeks old.

Diane decided not to pursue the matter. It was part of motherhood's familiar themes, variations and contradictions. For the first eighteen years of his life her main task had been to persuade him to wear a warm coat when he was going out. To insist on his removing a warm coat when he was staying in seemed perverse.

'All right. Forget the coat. Tell me about the new job.'

'I'm based in Newcastle and the rest is confidential.'

'Confidential? Nothing is confidential from your mother apart from your sex life. And that's negotiable.'

Michael shuffled and muttered:

'It's not the sort of work you boast about. It's the last resort. The job you always warned me about. I'm working for a security firm.'

'You're working for Cosmos Security PLC,' said Oliver.

'How do you know?' Michael said sharply.

'Sorry. Same old problem. It sprang unbidden to my mind.'

'It's a fair cop,' said Michael, standing up.

Diane realized with a shock that, apart from a residual egg stain, his plate was now empty. Not only was he working for a security firm, he wasn't eating properly. Was this his first decent meal since he was home at Christmas?

Probably.

Then she looked up as Michael took off the coat to reveal the uniform of a Cosmos Security PLC operative. It was pale brown with the texture of a moulting hamster. There was a peeling badge on the breast pocket with the same designer logo they had seen on Baxter's business card. Her son looked like a cross between a plumber come to unblock the toilet and a guerrilla taking over the radio station in an underfunded Maoist revolution. He was a long way from the womb.

'Now you can see why I kept the coat on.'

'I can also see how you frighten people,' said Diane.

'But mostly I'm just a night-watchman. Wear the uniform and spend the night at supermarkets. Keeping an eye open for footpads and ne'er-do-wells. Cash in hand, no questions asked, a pound an hour, plus all you can steal.'

He caught the look in Diane's face.

'That's a joke. Just something the guys say.'

'But I think your mother would like some reassurance. Is the work dangerous?' said Oliver.

'No. Mostly it's a doddle, providing you keep out of the way of the guard dogs. Anything serious happens, you ring the police. You get your own mobile, look . . .'

He unzipped the breast pocket, further displacing the logo, and pulled out a small mobile telephone.

'Thank you,' said Diane. 'I've seen a mobile before and I'm not impressed. I still want to know what the hell you were doing on Hadrian's Wall? It isn't a supermarket.'

'Unofficial overtime. For one of the guys.'

'Tell me about this guy.'

Michael draped the coat over his chair and sat down. There was clearly a tale to be told.

'Well. He's just a guy I work with. We call him Psycho.'

'Another geology graduate?' said Oliver.

'No. He got thrown out of the SAS for being violent and unstable.'

'Is he?' said Diane.

'Only when he's on the meths. He's been in mental homes, but now he's getting care in the community. That's me, mostly. I'm his community. Clinically speaking, he's probably schizophrenic. The other guys won't work with him. We play draughts a lot. He likes that, providing I let him win.'

Michael was frightened of Psycho, but also proud to be regarded by him as a friend. It was like knowing a footballer or a rock star. Above all, he was the sort of friend your mother had always warned you about, so that was a plus.

Diane concentrated hard on the facts of the case, and saved the panic attacks for later.

'So your friend Psycho offers you some overtime? Have I got that right?'

'Yes. He tells me he's been given a hundred quid to put the frighteners on these two people who are staying near Hadrian's Wall.'

'Us.'

'Yes. Except I don't know it's you. Psycho doesn't fancy the job because it's Thursday night and every Thursday he goes to Gateshead and gets pissed and puts the frighteners on people for the fun of it. He calls it his encounter group therapy.'

'Every Thursday, I buy the *Guardian*,' said Oliver. 'Chacun a son therapy.'

'So we split the cash, fifty for me, fifty for Psycho's commission. He goes off to Gateshead's Latin Quarter to do a bit of trashing. I come here. Check out the digs. Mrs Robson tells me you're on the wall. End of story. Now read on.'

The room was silent. Diane was chilled by the glimpse into Michael's life-style, while Oliver grappled with the question: who would pay a hundred pounds in cash to frighten them, and why?

He was also mildly irritated by Michael's mangling of the tenses while telling them his story: Oliver called it soccer syntax. He loved football but was moved to rage regularly during the season by balding, bejewelled soccer managers saying: 'So Big

Arnie's took him on and he sticks it in the back of the net, doesn't he?' If he and Michael were to have what his old campus friends used to call a meaningful relationship, this problem would have to be addressed.

But not today.

For the moment, he contented himself with a mild enquiry.

'Is all this making the best use of your geology degree?'

'Save that for another time,' said Michael. 'My turn for some questions. I need to speak to my mother.'

'Well, there she is,' said Oliver.

'Alone.'

'But yesterday, she and I swore some very solemn vows. In Durham Cathedral. No man shall put us asunder. That was one of them.' He looked to Diane for confirmation and support.

'That's true,' she said, 'but would you mind being asunder for a little while. Fifteen, twenty minutes?'

Oliver realized instantly that mother and son needed to talk about him behind his back. That was reasonable.

'I'll walk into the village. I need to buy a *Telegraph*.'

'You said you bought the *Guardian*,' said Michael.

'On Thursday. This is Friday. On a Friday I buy the *Telegraph*.'

'Because of Aristotle,' said Diane.

Oliver stood up and crossed to the door. As he passed the piano he pinged middle C. After he had left, Michael said:

'What was that about?'

'What?'

'The piano routine.'

'He always pings middle C when he passes a piano. It's a homage to Beethoven.'

They watched from the window as Oliver meandered down the path, paused to pat a dog and smell a flower, both of them strays, then continued on his way to the village.

It was Michael's turn to interrogate.

'You've always been terrible at men, haven't you?'

'I don't mean to be. I do try.'

'My dad's a waster. Then you got married to a wimp. And now . . .'

'Oliver?'

'Oliver.'

'What's wrong with him?'

'Well . . . he's a bit naff, isn't he?'

'Naff.'

'Yes.'

'I don't know what that word means.'

'Well, it's sort of . . . like . . . naff.'

She was confronted by the eternal, deadpan ability of the young to invent a flabby vocabulary and beat their elders over the head with it. She had been there and done it, but now she had changed sides.

She had been young, according to the Gregorian calendar, in the Swinging Sixties though the Swinging seemed to have happened the previous Thursday and in the next street. Diane had never swung. But she had learned the words. Her favourite was 'gear' and it used to drive her parents crazy, mainly because she refused to tell them what it meant. It was obvious. Couldn't they understand? Gear was good. Gear was Julie Christie, Albert Finney and the Beatles. Gear was the opposite of naff. And now she realized that gearness, like naffness, was strictly in the eye of the beholder. She sprang to Oliver's defence.

'He's twice been a specialist question-setter for *Mastermind*.'

'Isn't that a bit naff?'

'Not in the slightest. I think it's very impressive. The life and work of Lester Young. And the life and work of George Farquhar.'

'Farquhar?'

'Playwright. He wrote *The Recruiting Officer* and *The Beaux Stratagem*.'

'All right. So the guy's set a few questions for a naff television programme. Is that enough reason to run away with him? You are running away with him, aren't you?'

'We're not running away. We are running *towards*. We have a direction.'

She caught a glimpse of herself in the mirror above Mrs Robson's piano. Her lower lip was sticking out. She retracted it immediately, as Michael said:

'A direction?'

'Yes. A direction. We're going to the Orkneys.'

'Why the Orkneys?'

O God, she thought, here we go, into the depths of naff.

'We're going to the Orkneys to find Aristotle.'

Super-naff.

'Aristotle is the world's greatest crossword compiler.'

Mega-naff.

'It's all because the words "Diane Not Priest" are an anagram of "Predestination".'

Terminal, guilty-but-insane, put-the-cuffs-on-guvnor-I'll-come-quietly, I'm-not-fit-to-be-a-mother naff.

'Mum.'

He said it with genuine parental concern. He understood. She had been a silly girl, but if she told the truth he was prepared to listen, forgive and offer mature guidance about her forward emotional arrangements.

'Do you want the full story?' she said.

'Yes. But only because you're my mother.'

'Are you sitting comfortably?'

It was a little joke, intended to ease the situation, but it fell on stony ground. Didn't he remember *Listen with Mother*? Didn't anybody? No, not under the age of forty.

'I'll begin. It all started when Oliver walked into the police station in Brecon to report a missing person. This is before I was suspended from duty.'

Michael settled down for what he clearly expected to be a long and incomprehensible story, confirming all his prejudices about adolescence revisited in middle age.

He was not disappointed.

Oliver enjoyed his walk. The village was genial and chunky, built out of stone looted over the centuries from the nearby wall: wilful vandalism or responsible recycling, according to the changing ideologies of the times. There was a take-away called Little Bobby's Chop Suey Palace – an oblique homage to a great Tyneside comedian called Bobby Thompson. It had a sign in the window reading 'CLOSED FOR LUNCH' – a pleasingly cryptic message to find at ten o'clock in the morning, thought Oliver.

Opposite the take-away was a pub called the Centurion's Arms. The inn sign depicted crossed spears, but local legend was that the Roman in question was more famous for carnal conquests than military ones.

Oliver learned this, and more, from the newsagent, a large man, also quarried from the local stone. 'Prop.: James Frampton', it said over the door. Oliver pointed out that he shared his name with one of the Tolpuddle Martyrs. Mr Frampton apologized. He had never been to Tolpuddle, but had a lot of respect for martyrs. He himself was a retired wrestler, once famous throughout the Northern circuit as the Masked Vampire. He had hung up his mask and invested his career earnings in the shop. He stocked all the quality papers for the retired bankers and accountants who had invested their career earnings in buying up farmhouses and cottages in the village.

Leaving the shop, the *Telegraph* tucked under his arm, Oliver pondered the wondrous diversity and whimsicality of fame. Here, in a modest village High Street, were celebrated a brilliant comedian, a trade union hero, an illustrious wrestler and a reluctant Roman warrior with a rampant libido. Truly remarkable. He was yanked from his harmless reverie by an abrupt question.

'Are you still here?'

He turned to see Baxter looking up from his car, parked near the take-away.

'I am carrying my morning newspaper, therefore I am still here,' said Oliver. 'Where would you like me to be?'

Baxter got out of the car and fell into step with Oliver as he strolled along the road towards Mrs Robson's farmhouse.

'I was told you'd gone to Macclesfield.'

'Who told you that?'

'A stonemason in Hutton Conyers.'

'I know him well. What we romantics refer to as the girl's father.'

'So I believe.'

'He probably *thought* we were going to Macclesfield. It's an easy misunderstanding. They have family in Macclesfield. By the by, was that one of your men we met on Hadrian's Wall this morning? Raincoat, Balaclava helmet and a concealed logo?'

'Possibly,' said Baxter, keeping his guard up.

'He was supposed to put the frighteners on us. Doing a favour for a friend called Psycho. Do you know anybody called Psycho?'

'I don't know anyone who bears that name legally. But many of the people I work with would qualify. If you take my point.'

'Oh yes,' said Oliver. 'I take your point. It's a threat, isn't it?'

'It is.'

It was obvious that Baxter was trying to put the frighteners on, too. They were approaching the final shop in the street. Beyond it lay a short straggle of cottages and, after that, bleak and open country.

The shop had an unpretentious Victorian façade which had been preserved from improvement. The words on the fascia were 'T. Bewick and Sons – Family Butchers', without a logo. In normal circumstances Oliver would have rejoiced at the sight. It simultaneously honoured the memory of the great Northumbrian wood-engraver, and triggered a cherished fantasy born in undergraduate days, which was to go into such a shop and say: 'Good morning, Mr Bewick. If you and your sons are available, I'd like you to butcher my family. Are you free on Monday?'

But Oliver had no time for these idle fancies; he was too busy being threatened. He considered his options:

Escape. He could run away, galloping towards Mrs Robson's house as fast as his average-sized legs would carry him; but Baxter had a car.

Conflict. He could stand his ground, if the threat became physical, and fight back; but he had never hit anybody in his life and was so obsessively non-violent he kept a patent plastic box on a stick at home to capture and release free-range spiders and other insects who wandered innocently into his living quarters.

Dialectic. He could discuss the situation with Baxter, addressing their mutual fears sensibly and calmly, with appropriate references to Gandhi and the doctrine of non-violence; but Baxter seemed like a man short on philosophy and social niceties, and licensed, trained and eager to kill, probably by a single discreet blow to a little-known vulnerable area of the ear lobe, thus leaving no incriminating marks.

These, Oliver decided, were his main options and they had one quality in common: they were of no help.

The fourth option arrived unexpectedly.

'Now isn't that canny? A bonny lad to carry my shopping and walk me home.'

Mrs Robson came out of the butchers, with two bulging carrier-bags in each hand, and caught up with Oliver, who took the bags from her graciously and eagerly.

'My pleasure.'

Then she saw Baxter. She sniffed the tension in the space between the two men.

'Friend of yours?'

'Not a friend as such. He follows us everywhere we go.'

'Jealous husband?'

Oliver shook his head.

'No. There is a jealous husband but we shook him off in Shrewsbury.'

'Serves him right.'

Then she turned on Baxter with unexpected ferocity.

'Why can't you leave people alone? There's enough misery in the world without you adding to it!'

A face appeared at the butchers' shop window, attracted by the volume and outrage in Mrs Robson's voice. She implied unambiguously that with a single snap of her fingers she would have support from a battalion of Bewicks carrying meat cleavers, with the Masked Vampire on the substitutes' bench and a handful of lost legionnaires on stand-by. It was no longer Baxter versus Oliver, but Baxter versus the village, with more than his ear lobe under threat.

The man was village streetwise. He turned away from Mrs Robson and set off towards his car, saying to Oliver:

'I'll keep in touch.'

Oliver should have let him go quietly but, now that Mrs

Robson had released the tension, his curiosity was out of the traps and running free.

'You didn't actually *go* to Macclesfield, did you?'

'Shut your face!' yelled Baxter, getting into his car and slamming the door. He realized he had trapped his coat. He opened the door. He released the coat. He closed the door again, quietly this time. Oliver and Mrs Robson watched the performance, as did many of the village population. It gave them pleasure. It did not give pleasure to Baxter.

'What a mess, the world, eh?' said Mrs Robson. 'I blame convenience food. What do you blame?'

'I think it started to go wrong with Bill Haley and the Comets,' said Oliver.

While Oliver and Mrs Robson escorted each other home, Diane was completing an almost full and frank confession of her recent activities to her son. She focused on the investigative strand, which was convoluted enough, but easier to handle than the emotional one. She decided to ignore the sexual element until they were both a bit older.

'Everywhere we go,' she said, 'there seem to be unsolved murders. A Welsh farmer called Griffiths floating face-down in a river. A local moneylender called Walsh shot dead. Plus the odd bit of arson. All apparently relating to property deals and all, according to Oliver, part of a huge criminal conspiracy. Complete with the shady businessmen and corrupt police officers.'

'Does Oliver have any evidence?'

'No. He doesn't believe in evidence. He believes in anagrams and crossword clues and jokes and lateral thinking.'

'Like I said . . .'

'He is *not* naff!'

'Anybody can invent a conspiracy plot. Proving it, that's the hard bit.'

'He got it dead right about Superintendent Butler of the Mid-Glamorgan Crime Squad. Right enough for me to be suspended from the police force.'

She decided not to tell Michael the details of her suspension:

that it had come about because of Oliver's belief that in any unsolved murder, the butler was always the prime suspect. It sounded silly. It *was* silly. It was also true, and all of a piece with Oliver's view of the world as a cosmic joke without a tag. In judicial terms, the logical conclusion was to round up the usual emperors and charge them with indecent exposure. That, according to Oliver, was why the emperors made sure they wrote the laws.

'Do you have any evidence?' said Michael, playing the cool professional.

'The evidence might be hiding in here,' said Diane, with no intention of being outplayed in the cool professional stakes. She reached into the bag slung on the chair arm and hauled out the mini-marathon length of computer printout. She spread it on the table between them.

'Where did this come from?' Michael asked.

'It was a present from the Durham police.'

'Of course. That's how we knew about you.'

'Huh?'

'According to Pyscho. A tip-off from the Durham police. This weird middle-aged couple, asking awkward questions, need to be warned off.'

It may have been accurate reportage but it was not a smart thing to say. Michael realized it immediately. Oliver walked in on Diane's outrage, carrying his newspaper open at the crossword.

'Is it safe for me to return?'

'Would you describe us as a weird middle-aged couple?' Diane said indignantly.

'I was only quoting Psycho. I'm not saying it's my opinion,' said Michael, as Oliver assembled his thoughts on the subject, before concluding:

'Let us consider the elements of the concept – a weird middle-aged couple – in reverse order. We are a couple, yes. We swore our vows in the cathedral yesterday and consummated them exuberantly overnight. I am certainly middle-aged and quite possibly weird. Your mother is neither.'

He turned to Diane, addressing her directly.

'You are ripe and mature, nay, luscious, indeed, with more than a hint, as I well know to my infinite joy, of the nubile . . .'

It was too much for Michael.

'Listen to all that stuff, Mum. He *is*.'

'I am what?'

'Michael thinks you're a bit . . .'

'No, don't tell him what I said . . .'

'A bit naff,' said Diane.

Michael tried to dematerialize, but failed. Then he was hit by anxiety. What if he were wrong about Oliver? He might not be as naff as all that. Or he might be even naffer – one of those terminally naff people who turn out to have black belts in obscure but lethal branches of Oriental martial arts.

He need not have worried. Oliver sat down, placid as ever, in one of the large, all-embracing armchairs that leaked their stuffing either side of the fireplace.

'It's a very reasonable assessment,' he said, taking out his fountain-pen and scanning Aristotle's clues.

'Is it?' said Diane.

'For this reason. Naff. Nobody really knows what the word means, since it lacks either a Latin, Greek or Anglo-Saxon root. Even the *Oxford English Dictionary* hedges its bets. Colloquial. Origin disputed. Therefore I am an unknown quantity. The X factor in the mysterious equation we call life. I find that totally acceptable.'

He unscrewed the cap of his fountain-pen.

'Now, I can see you're both very busy with your information. I'll attend to my crossword. I'll try not to make too much noise.'

Diane looked across the table at Michael. They were separated by the old incurable problem: a generation. She could see how Oliver appeared to her son. For all practical purposes she agreed with his assessment. So did Oliver, for that matter. All three of them were in total accord, but the triangle of their relationship was unresolved, simmering on a low light. There was only one thing to do.

Leave it.

'Let's talk information,' she said.

Michael seemed relieved. He wanted to leave it, too.

'OK,' he said, scanning the printout. 'What's all this about?'

'It's what the Durham police have got on the murder of Adrian Walsh.'

'Moneylender of this parish.'

'Quite so.'

'Bullock,' said Oliver.

'Bullock?' said Diane.

'Bullock. Seven across. In my crossword.' Oliver wrote in the word 'BULLOCK'.

Michael spotted an item of interest on the printout.

'There's our company name. Cosmos Security PLC.'

'That's another reason why you shouldn't be working for them. Like they say on my favourite cop show, Cosmos Security PLC are distinctly pear-shaped.'

'I'm very lucky to be working for anybody.'

'Everywhere you look in this conspiracy, you find PLCs. What Oliver would call the X factor.'

'Brazen,' said Oliver.

Diane turned to him.

'Mature, I'll accept. Nubile, maybe. Brazen, I don't think so.'

Oliver peered at her over the top of his reading spectacles.

'You have your moments. But I'm actually talking about nine down. Brazen.' He wrote in the word 'BRAZEN'.

'Here's another PLC,' said Michael, leafing through the information with the assurance of a generation as confident with computer technology as Oliver was with his fountain-pen. 'Look. Adrian Walsh was negotiating with Universal Megamarkets PLC and they're in the same group as Cosmos Security PLC.'

'Also,' said Diane, 'the same group as Nineteenth Hole Developments PLC who probably knocked off Farmer Griffiths in Wales.'

Diane was making notes on a large pad. She had written in big bold letters: 'NINETEENTH HOLE DEVELOPMENTS PLC = UNIVERSAL MEGAMARKETS PLC = COSMOS SECURITY PLC.'

'Ah, now I see it all,' said Oliver. 'It's Farquhar.'

At precisely the same moment, Michael said: 'It's Farquhar.'

Diane looked from one to the other.

'Why are the two men in my life both saying: "It's Farquhar"?'

'Perhaps your son is also naff?' suggested Oliver.

Michael ignored him and explained:

'I said it because all these companies . . . all these PLCs . . . they're all in the Farquhar Group.'

And Oliver explained:

'I said it because the answers to today's crossword are all characters from Farquhar's play *The Recruiting Officer*. Bullock, Brazen, Balance, Pluck . . . no Kite. That's odd. Kite's the one who usually gets the laughs.'

'So you're actually talking about two different people?' said Diane.

'Probably,' said Oliver. 'George Farquhar died in 1707. So I don't suppose he has any companies extant.'

'What about yours?' Diane asked Michael.

'No idea. But I've seen it on our letterhead. Cosmos Security PLC is part of the Farquhar Group of companies. I don't know his first name. I don't even know if there is a Farquhar. He might be like Woolworth.'

'Or British Home Stores,' said Oliver.

Michael's chest made a bleeping sound.

'Poor child,' said Oliver. 'A pacemaker at his age.'

Michael ignored Oliver again. It could become habitual, Diane thought; perhaps it was the psychological breakthrough they needed, if the triple relationship were to prosper. Michael pulled the mobile phone from his pocket and extended the aerial.

'Yes?'

He listened. His end of the conversation continued:

'Yes . . . yes . . . yes . . . OK . . . ten minutes.'

Michael retracted the aerial, switched off the mobile and replaced it in his pocket.

'Who was that?' said Diane.

'My boss.'

'Psycho?'

'Psycho's not my boss.'

'Psycho's his little friend from work,' said Oliver.

Before Michael had time to ignore him a third time, Diane said: 'I think your boss is a man called Baxter.'

Her son was diverted, startled and impressed.

'How do you know about Baxter?'

'He follows us around the country. He's been with us all the way from Wales.'

'I saw him in the village this morning, when I was buying my paper,' Oliver said casually, as he wrote 'THOMAS' and 'APPLE-TREE' in the spaces eight down and thirteen across.

'Why didn't you tell me?' said Diane.

'You were busy with your information. I think he might have been to Macclesfield.'

'Macclesfield?'

'Macclesfield?' said Michael, on his way to the door.

'A private joke,' said Oliver. 'Don't worry about it.'

'I'll try not to.'

After Michael left, to keep his appointment with Baxter, Oliver said:

'I like your son very much.'

'Even though he thinks you're naff?'

'He's young. Young people are supposed to think older people are naff. That's how you identify them as young.'

Baxter had driven his car to a secluded spot half-way between Mrs Robson's house and the village. Strategically it was to maintain his security cover. During the ten minutes he was waiting for Michael, he was spotted by a bearded postman: a mobile librarian spreading culture along the border; and one of the younger Bewicks, doing a delivery round on an old-fashioned errand boy's bicycle. All three wished him an ebullient Northumbrian good morning, together with a silent message that said: watch yourself, bonny lad, or we'll have your ear lobes for garters.

Baxter's opening words to Michael, when he arrived at the car, were:

'Cosmos Security PLC! God help us! What an organization!'

'It's more interesting than selling hot dogs.'

'Let's send in the heavy mob to put the frighteners on, they say. And who do they send? The only begotten son.'

'It wasn't anybody's fault. I didn't know it was going to be my mother, did I? It was just bad luck it happened to be a Thursday. Psycho's night to go to Gateshead.'

'I don't want to know about Psycho! I don't want to know about Gateshead!'

'Sorry.'

They lapsed into silence. Baxter's was surly, Michael's was indecisive. He trawled through his head for cool, professional observations, but the cupboard was bare.

Eventually the older man said:

'Now let us rake through the ashes of this disaster and see what we can discern in the form of a phoenix.'

'Right,' said Michael, vague about the imagery. Oliver would know about that stuff.

'Recapitulating. Your instructions were to put the frighteners on but I assume, in the family circumstances, they are not very frightened?'

'Not very.'

'But they are still asking questions?'

'A bit.'

'About Farquhar?'

That name again.

'Yes. But that's really interesting.'

'Go on,' Baxter said flatly. 'Really interest me.'

'Oliver. You know, the bloke . . .'

'Your mother's paramour.'

'What? Well. Yes. Anyway. Though,' said Michael, putting paramour to one side to be checked later, along with the phoenix and the ashes. 'The Farquhar *he's* interested in is *George* Farquhar.'

'George?'

'A playwright. He died in 1707. Oliver was a specialist question-setter for *Mastermind*. The life and work of George Farquhar.'

'So when he was in Shrewsbury, asking questions about Farquhar . . .?'

'That was about George. He wrote a play called *The Recruiting Officer*. It's set in Shrewsbury.'

'Jesus Wolfgang Amadeus Christ,' said Baxter, a man miserable with his world and its tendency to crumble at a touch.

'What's a paramour?' said Michael, hoping it might ease the tension.

'You're a graduate.'

'In geology. There aren't any paramours in geology.'

'I will offer you another morsel of wisdom, young man,' said Baxter. 'There are no longer any graduates working for Cosmos Security PLC. Burn the uniform. Remember to take it off first.'

Michael was once more an unemployed graduate. It was like going home.

11

Beyond Hadrian

Mrs Robson stood in the doorway watching Diane and Oliver as they loaded their suitcases into the boot of the car.

'Is that lad of yours going with you?'

'I sincerely hope not,' said Diane, preoccupied with teaching Oliver a more constructive approach to packing than hurl and hope.

'Did Michael say anything to you?' she asked him.

'About his onward journeying? No. Nothing.'

'I'll make a few extra sandwiches. Just in case, like,' said Mrs Robson, before disappearing in the direction of her beloved kitchen.

'Why are you so hopeless at packing?' said Diane.

'Am I?'

'This boot. It's disgusting. It looks like a recycling centre before anything's been recycled. And what's that little black box?'

A little black box, square and squat, was preventing the snug and rational placement of her bag between Oliver's matching suitcases.

'Oh, that. It's only a little black box. Were you serious?' said Oliver, keen to change the subject.

'What about?'

'When you said you sincerely hope your son isn't coming with us?'

'You don't take your son on a honeymoon. Especially a large one.'

'Honeymoon?' The word took Oliver by surprise. He had been drifting along romantically on a cloud nine edged with gold but hadn't realized that Diane took the same elevated and gilded view of the situation. Was she soppy too, underneath the policeperson's cool?

'It's the next best thing to a honeymoon, isn't it?'

'No,' said Oliver. 'From my point of view it's an even better thing. Not that I've been on many honeymoons, you understand, but . . .'

'Yes, I understand,' said Diane, 'and I agree.'

'You do?'

'This journey is a better thing than anything I have ever done before.'

'Thank you.'

'Thank *you*.'

Wonderful, thought Oliver, she really is as soppy as I am. And they gazed at each other, in a prelude to a kiss, an overture to a dream sequence, Fred and Ginger dancing cheek to cheek, he in top hat, white tie and tails, she in a blue gown twenty times more daring than Alice's, flying down to Rio in a beautiful balloon with flights of chorus girls on the wings – and so what if balloons didn't have wings? Busby Berkeley would sort all that out when he arrived on their daydream set.

In the event, Busby Berkeley didn't show up. Michael turned up instead.

'Please can I come with you?' He was standing beside the car. Neither of them had noticed his arrival.

'Come with us?' said Diane.

'Where do you want to go?' said Oliver, his head still aglow with Rio and Acapulco Bay.

'Wherever you're going. The Orkneys, isn't it? That'll do for me.'

'You wouldn't like the Orkneys,' Diane said firmly. 'It rains all the time and there's very little for young people to do in the evenings.'

'But I've just been sacked.'

'Sacked?'

'I have to burn my uniform.'

'Why have they sacked you?' said Oliver. 'Is it because you didn't frighten us properly?'

'More or less. I mean, you don't look very frightened, do you?'

No, thought Diane, we look shuffly and adolescent, like a couple of fifth formers found snogging in the chemistry lab at a school dance. She was grateful to Oliver, who came to the rescue with an explanation.

'You caught us as we were totally free from fear, marooned in a little oasis of bliss and tranquillity.'

'I thought it must be something like that,' said Michael, clearly embarrassed by mothers who got tangled up with subversive notions like tranquillity.

'Well, that's what it was. Bliss and tranquillity,' Diane said defiantly. After all, she had a half share in the oasis. 'Couldn't you go back to the hot dogs in Macclesfield?'

'I think that would be a backward step career-wise.'

Oliver adjusted his spectacles, a sure sign that it was his turn to disapprove.

'If you insist on using management jargon like "career-wise", I shall find it difficult to look upon you as a son.'

Michael was still weighing up the starting prices of this latest proposition – Oliver as father – when Mrs Robson came out of the house with two large carrier-bags.

'I made enough sandwiches for the three of you. Are you going with them, pet?'

'Yes,' said Michael.

'No,' said Diane.

'Possibly,' said Oliver.

Michael went with them.

They stopped in Hexham to buy clothing to replace his

Cosmos Security PLC uniform, which they stuffed in the boot. They would burn it later.

The sun was shining as they drove high into the Cheviots. Oliver parked in a lay-by with a sign in four languages to say this was a good view and an officially recommended photo opportunity. But the place was deserted: the photographers had taken both their cameras and their opportunism somewhere warmer.

The three of them sat in big coats on a simulated rustic bench erected to the memory of someone whose name had been worn away by the weather. They looked at the hills and ate Mrs Robson's sandwiches and Oliver said to Michael:

'Did Baxter make you hand in your mobile telephone?'

'He didn't mention it so I kept it.'

'May I borrow it, please?'

'Sure,' said Michael, handing the mobile to Oliver.

'What do you want with a mobile telephone?' said Diane.

'I need to talk to somebody who is not here.'

'Why?'

Diane was a little hurt that Oliver had some unspecified need he could not satisfy within the territorial boundaries of their tranquil oasis. He read her unease exactly.

'Am I correct in thinking that you still want to solve all those murder mysteries?' he said. 'See the guilty men brought to book? In the highest traditions of British justice?'

'Yes, please.'

'In that case, I shall need to use the telephone.'

'I see.'

Oliver stood up.

'You don't mind if I go into a corner? I get very self-conscious when I'm on the telephone and people can hear me. I seem to end up saying things that sound exceedingly silly, even if they're very sensible really.' He started to move away. Diane called after him.

'Who are you telephoning?'

'I wish to fly a kite. With a friend of a friend who works at the British Library.' Oliver walked to the end of the lay-by and round a slow bend in the road until he was out of earshot and out of sight beyond a dry-stone wall.

'I wonder which it is,' said Diane.

'What?'

'Does the friend work at the British Library? Or the friend of the friend? And can you fly kites indoors?'

'Does it matter?'

'No. But if you're going to travel with the two of us, it's the kind of conversation you'll have to get used to.'

'I'm sorry. I didn't mean to be a gooseberry.'

Diane shrugged but said nothing. If Michael wanted maternal reassurance, he would have to earn it. He did his best.

'It's just that I screwed up on the job and I hated it anyway. And Psycho scared me shitless even if I pretended he didn't. And I hated the hot dogs even more. And I wasn't crazy about Macclesfield. And Baxter fired me and I didn't know what to do next and that's why I asked to come with you. And I got good grades in my lousy O levels and A levels and I did all right in my lousy finals. And I even went to lousy graduation in those lousy stupid clothes. And I'm totally pissed off with this lousy country and all the lousy people running it that can't make a few lousy jobs for people like me any more!'

He shed the years at the rate of six months per syllable, accelerating downhill from a mature assessment of his career prospects to simple, foot-stamping rage.

'I know.' She put an arm around his shoulder. Rage was fair comment. Rage was the only thing likely to shift the lousy people who had betrayed him. Rage, like Gough Whitlam said, should be maintained.

'But I don't want to cramp your style,' he said. 'You will tell me if I'm in the way, won't you?'

'Yes.'

'Promise?'

'Promise.'

'Thanks, Mum.'

They sat in silence for a while. A large bird circled overhead. Kite? Hawk? Kestrel? Eagle? Condor? Vulture? Auk? Emu? Dodo? Concorde? And what was the difference anyway? She had once bought an *Observer Book of Birds* but it was never open at the right page and the damn things wouldn't keep still and always flew away before she could match up the tail feathers with the ones in the picture.

The bird flew away. They always did. The hell with them. All that ornithology was strictly for the birds.

'Michael,' she said.

'Yes?'

'You're in the way.'

Oh heck, thought Michael. Does she mean it? Or is it a new style of humour she's learned from Oliver? Either way, she had changed. It wasn't fair. Mothers were supposed to stay the same. What had happened? Before he could ask her, Oliver returned with the mobile.

'Excellent,' he said, handing the telephone to Michael.

'British Library came up trumps again?' said Diane.

'Yes.'

'It's always been awfully good for me too.'

Michael realized. That was it. Sex. Everything she said was charged with sexual innuendo. Even the British Library. He looked at the two of them. They must be doing it. At their age. It was appalling.

They were totally unaware of his discomfort.

'Our major national institutions are there for that very purpose,' said Oliver. 'To be good for us.'

'What are you talking about?' said Diane.

'The Farquhar group.'

'Farquhar wrote *The Recruiting Officer*,' said Michael, mainly to remind them he was with them on the hill.

'The Chairman of the Board. I know who he is and where he lives.'

'You do?'

'I'm not given to making reckless claims where the aristocracy is concerned.'

'So who is he and where does he live?' Diane had her notebook open and pen poised.

'The 13th Baron Kite. He lives on a large estate about a hundred miles to the north of where we are now.'

'And this Baron Kite lives in the Highlands?'

'Sort of high in the Lowlands or low in the Highlands, according to where you set off from. A place called Kirkleven.'

Diane wrote it all down. It was her police training. Write it down and it could be used in evidence. Oliver rarely wrote anything down, apart from his secret diary, and that was a recent development, celebrating the new phase in his life. And his diary would never be used in evidence, except for his own benefit. He was laying it down for his old age, like vintage wine, so that one day he could read it and remember a time when he was happy.

'And you got all this from your friend at the British Library?'

'The friend of the friend.'

'All right. The friend of the friend.'

'Yes. Except for Kirkleven. I suggested Kirkleven and my friend was able to confirm it as the correct address.'

'Why did you suggest Kirkleven? Is it an anagram of Hutton Conyers? Why did you suggest anything?'

'Kirkleven was an answer in Aristotle's crossword this morning. Look.'

He brought out the newspaper and opened it to the crossword.

'Here, you see? Twelve down. Kirkleven. It's an interesting clue. You need to know that "kirk" is a Scottish word for "church" and leaven is what makes bread rise, but you also have to omit the letter "a". But I was also puzzled that the name Kite didn't appear anywhere. It seemed deliberate. Then I remembered. A minor aristocrat called Kite with an estate at Kirkleven. I don't know why I remembered but I think it's a jazz connection.'

Diane interrupted him.

'Can we go back three spaces?'

'We're free spirits. We can go anywhere we like. Why settle for the moon?'

'Hush.'

'I'll do some silent whistling.'

She put her fingers to her lips, studied the newspaper, then flicked through the pages of her notebook.

Oliver silently whistled a theme from Beethoven.

Michael felt more than ever an intruder: a guest celebrity appearing with Eric and Ernie in their prime, and unable to stand the pace: a scene shifter caught accidentally centre stage in Wagner's Ring Cycle, the only person not dressed like a Valkyrie; an umpire who had strayed on to Centre Court at Wimbledon without understanding what those white lines were for.

At least he always knew where he was with Psycho.

Petrified.

'All right,' said Diane. 'Stop your silent whistling and listen to me.'

'Can I listen too?' said Michael.

'Yes, but don't interrupt.'

She turned to Oliver.

'Cast your mind back a few days. You left home to visit your friend Aristotle in South Wales and what did you find?'

'Sheep.'

'And his house was a burnt-out shell.'

'Yes.'

'Conclusion?'

'Nationalism is not enough?'

Diane shook her head.

'Aristotle found out what was going on and was persuaded to run away to the Orkneys. But he's planting clues in his cross-words. He is directing us towards the 13th Baron Kite and Kirkleven.'

'That is an amazing piece of lateral thinking,' said Oliver, 'and you are peerless. A totally remarkable woman.'

'I know I am.'

They gazed at each other in mutual adoration mode, seven steps from heaven. The angel choirs propped up their music. Fred, Ginger and Busby braced themselves for an encore.

Michael was bound to crack eventually. This was the moment.

'Are you two always like this?'

'Like what?' said Diane.

He wanted to say nauseating, but settled for a gentler shade of perplexity.

'When I was little, I'd be in a room full of grown-ups and they'd all be talking and I'd understand some of the words they were using but nothing they said ever made sense. This . . . is like that.'

'A word,' said Oliver, 'if I may, as your temporary, acting, putative stepfather figure. There is no such thing as grown-up and nothing ever makes sense. We are living proof. Shall we go to Kirkleven?'

They drove north towards Kirkleven. Michael, sitting in the centre of the back seat, leaned forward between them and examined Oliver's dashboard.

'Have you got a cassette player?'

'Yes, but we prefer to make our own amusement.'

'What sort of amusement?'

'Sometimes I put my hand on Oliver's thigh.'

'But not if we have company,' Oliver said quickly, sensing Michael's embarrassment.

'Thank you. I appreciate that,' said Michael.

'Let's play famous Scottish names,' said Oliver, with the eager inventiveness of an ageing hipster who had glimpsed the words Marky Mark on the cassette in Michael's hand.

'How do you play famous Scottish names?' said Diane.

'You think of famous Scottish names and say them out loud.'

'Could you give us an example?'

'Sir Walter Scott.'

'Oh, I say, well played.'

Michael was lost again, a bewildered gooseberry marooned at Wimbledon and tripping over those peculiar white lines.

'What is the point of the game?' he said.

'I don't suppose there is one,' said Diane; then, turning to Oliver: 'Is there?'

'Oh yes. The point of the game is to keep on thinking of famous Scottish names until we arrive at Kirkleven.'

'What if we run out?'

'We lose.'

'But who wins?' said Michael, a brainwashed child of

Thatcher's '80s, and the corrosive lunacy that said the strong should take over the earth and the meek could go screw themselves: the gospel according to Canary Wharf. A confused but kindly young man, well on the road to ideological recovery, he still found the idea of a game without winners and losers a concept without handles.

'I suppose, philosophically speaking, Scotland wins,' said Oliver.

'It's an international match,' said Diane, suddenly enthusiastic. 'I've never played in an international match. Shall I go first?'

'By all means.'

'Sir Walter Scott.'

Michael protested.

'Objection. Oliver already said Sir Walter Scott.'

'That was just an example. We hadn't started the game proper,' said Oliver. 'I'm happy to accept Sir Walter Scott. And I'll counter it with Robbie Burns.'

'Robbie Coltrane,' said Michael.

'He's a good player, isn't he?' said Oliver.

Twenty miles later, they were going strong.

'Harry Lauder,' said Oliver.

'Will Fyffe,' said Diane.

'Moira Anderson,' said Michael, who had never heard of Harry Lauder or Will Fyffe, and had forgotten he remembered Moira Anderson. Had he seen her on *Blue Peter*? Later, Oliver would explain to him that this was the real point of the game: to remember things you thought you had forgotten.

'Charles Rennie Mackintosh,' said Oliver.

'George Chisholm,' said Diane.

'Ally MacLeod and his tartan army,' said Michael, thinking: I can keep going for ages with footballers.

'Keir Hardie,' said Oliver, thinking: politics, that's a productive area, all those comrades from the Red Clyde, plus the new model Labour Party's front bench, if the game goes into extra time.

'Tommy Smith,' said Diane, thinking: I'll hit them with a few jazz musicians to prove how hip I am.

'Grandpa Delaney,' said Michael, thinking: I'll save the footballers – there's still a long way to go.'

'Your grandfather's Irish, not Scottish,' said Diane.

'It's the same sort of thing. He's still a Celt. And he's a really nice old guy.'

'And a fine stonemason,' said Oliver.

'All right. We'll accept your grandfather. But no more Irish after that.'

They became so engulfed in the debate about qualifying status that they forgot whose turn it was next. Oliver, in a display of instant recall that passed their understanding, ran through all the names played so far in the game, and decided it was Diane's turn next.

'Bonny Prince Charlie,' she said, unable to think of any more jazz musicians.

'Flora Macdonald,' said Oliver, aware that it was a bit of a soft option.

'Dougal,' said Michael.

'Dougal?' said Diane.

'In the *Magic Roundabout*. It's a Scottish name, isn't it? Can you prove he isn't Scottish?'

They accepted Dougal, though Oliver felt it was a sentimental decision.

By the time they had driven a further twenty miles, Diane was beginning to struggle.

'Isn't there a weatherman? Or a newsreader? Yes. Got him. Jimmy Logan!'

'There's no newsreader called Jimmy Logan,' said Michael.

'I changed my tactics, to confuse you.'

'Hugh McDiarmid,' said Oliver.

'George Burns,' said Michael.

'You can't have George Burns. He's American,' said Diane. She was a little truculent, still smarting over the fuss about Jimmy Logan.

'Not *that* George Burns. This one's a mate. He was at university with me. He got a first in mechanical engineering. And he comes from Aberdeen.'

'But he's not famous.'

'Yes, he is. He was in all the tabloids. And he was on *News at Ten*.'

'Why?'

'He hacked into Pepsi's computer system. Got a year's supply of Diet Coke for the Students' Union. Free.'

'What did he get?'

'Two years in Strangeways. Your turn, Mum.'

'Annie Laurie,' said Diane, yawning and beginning to lose her competitive zest. It was like playing silly games at Christmas: it was an amazingly short step — half a pace, no more — from Scrabble and charades to guilty revelations, and a year's supply of anxiety neurosis. Had it not been for famous Scottish names she would never have known that Michael's best friend was a gaol-bird.

George Burns had probably shared a cell with Psycho. She decided she would rather not know about Michael's little friends. She took the coward's way out and went to sleep.

Twenty miles further north, and deep into glen-ridden postcard scenery, with the smell of tartan and heather in the air, the game continued. The players had agreed to call it the Men's Singles Final. Oliver was as strong as ever. Michael was feeling the pace.

'Mike Denness,' said Oliver.

'Never heard of him,' said Michael. 'Is he famous?'

'Probably, and I would have to check this in Wisden, but probably the only Scotsman ever to captain the England cricket team.'

'Was he any good?'

'As bad as most of the others. Your turn.'

'The Bay City Rollers.'

'If we're talking music, may I offer you . . . Jimmy Shand.'

'Who he?'

'Accordion-playing Scottish country band leader. Specialist in eightsome reels and the like.'

'Amazing.'

'Your turn.'

'Pass.'

'Pass?'

'You must have known I was desperate when I said the Bay City Rollers.'

'You're dropping out?'

'You've lived longer than I have. You're bound to know more people.'

'Alas, yes,' said Oliver, 'I've lived longer than practically everybody.'

'So you'll have to play the game on your own, pops,' said Michael, without realizing what he'd said until he'd said it. Whatever the intention, his casual but affectionate form of address rejuvenated Oliver. He launched into a litany of Scottish heroism embracing the entire forward line of the 1928 Wembley Wizards who humiliated England 5–1: the Glasgow school of whisky-propelled novelists and playwrights, with special emphasis on the magic realism of the Gorbals: the political activists of the twentieth century, restricting himself to those who had been sent to prison for subversion – this to give zest to the challenge; all with brief biographies, critical analyses and lateral footnotes. He finished, as was right and proper in matters heroic, with the comedians.

'And the greatest of them all, Chic Murray, born in Greenock on the Clyde.'

'Never heard of him,' said Michael.

'Chic Murray who, according to legend, was walking down Sauchiehall Street in Glasgow one day and, seeing a drunk rolling on his back in the gutter, remarked: "The poor wee man, he's trying to break the bar of chocolate in his back pocket."'

Michael let out a yell of triumph.

'Yeah!'

'You're supposed to laugh, not shout.'

'You've done it!'

Michael's cries woke Diane, who blinked and said:

'Who has done what? Is it a criminal offence or a civil offence?'

'That was really brilliant!'

'Who or what was really brilliant?'

'Your bloke.'

'I thought he was a bit naff?'

Then she realized the car had stopped. She peered through the windscreen. She saw a road sign that read 'KIRKLEVEN'. The word was surmounted by a thistle, and beneath it a subtitle in one language asked drivers to respect local flora, fauna, lives and limbs.

'He's been thinking of famous Scottish names for the last twenty miles, alone and unaided. You went to sleep and I quit. But he kept going. I think that's really brilliant.'

'He probably invented them,' said Diane.

'That would be even more really brilliant than ever.'

'I appreciate his appreciation,' said Oliver to Diane, 'but I shall have to have a serious talk to our boy about his grammar and syntax.'

Our boy? She wondered where all this paternal stuff had come from? Had Michael discovered there was more than naffness to her paramour? Had something changed while she was asleep?

A little bit. Yes.

12

The Hall of the Mountain King

The family seat of the 13th Baron Kite lay a couple of miles outside the village of Kirkleven. The present house had been in the family for three and a half generations, built towards the end of the nineteenth century on the site of an earlier insurance job. In style it was constipated Gothic owing a little to St Pancras Station and rather more to Count Dracula. The arrow slits had never been used, except as an excuse for a contemptuous one-liner in Pevsner.

From the road the façade was almost totally masked by fir trees, proving that conifers, as well as attracting a useful subsidy, could be socially responsible elements in the environment. Beyond the house there were hills bisected by the silver slash of Loch Leven. The landscape redeemed some of the mess dumped on it by the English landed gentry.

The grounds were surrounded by a high stone wall, tidily trimmed with barbed wire. Oliver manoeuvred the car close to the wall. Then, by climbing on to its roof, the three of them were able to peer into the dark secrets of the estate.

'Homely little spot,' said Diane.

'If all this belongs to him, he must have got a job,' said Michael.

'He's never needed one,' said Oliver. 'This is called inheritance.'

'Shall I go look for some evidence?' said Michael.

'What sort of evidence?' said Diane.

'I don't know. You're the suspended policewoman.'

'Policeperson,' said Oliver.

Michael ignored him and continued:

'Buried bodies. Murder weapons. Blunt instruments. Wine glasses that smell of bitter almonds. You know. Incriminating stuff.' Michael scrambled up on to the top of the wall.

'Careful,' said Diane and Oliver in unison, aware that barbed wire and reproductive organs were mutually exclusive items in the human pageant.

'It's all right. Somebody's made a space, look.' Michael had found a short stretch on top of the wall where the barbed wire, by act of God, climate or local initiative, had been removed.

'A safe haven,' he said, sitting astride the wall and contemplating the ten-foot drop into the grounds below.

'Don't do it, laddy,' came a voice from the undergrowth.

They looked in the direction of the voice. The man who emerged resembled a clump of undergrowth with supplementary limbs. He wore brown corduroy trousers retrieved from the battlefield of Culloden tucked into elderly wellingtons, a skilful assembly of pockets and hidden compartments disguised as an anorak, and a beard of recycled heather.

He was carrying a shotgun.

'All right,' said Michael. 'I won't do it.'

'Are you hinting that this is private property?' said Oliver.

'Not just private but heavily fortified.'

'In that case, we do beg your pardon. We didn't spot the battlements.'

'You know how it is with boys,' said Diane. 'They all love climbing.'

'The Tourist Board keeps mountains on the horizon specially for climbing. Also for winter sports, in season. But stay out of here. This place is swarming with gamekeepers and guard dogs and security men and cameras. And a few geese for good measure.'

'Which are you?' said Oliver.

'Me, I'm a gamekeeper . . .'

'I did wonder, when I saw the uniform.'

'. . . turned poacher. I turned poacher when I was made redundant.'

'You too?' said Oliver, who knew the feeling.

'Is it wise?' said Diane. 'Telling everybody who looks over the wall that you're a poacher?'

The heathery wee man smiled and explained:

'I help maintain the balance of nature. I'm also a colourful survivor of an old tradition. Willy the Poacher. The Tourist Board quite likes me, in moderation.'

'You're a token stereotype,' said Oliver, who knew that feeling, too.

'Quite so.'

'That's all very well,' said Diane, 'but isn't there a danger you'll be seen and identified by that token stereotypical security camera?'

She pointed up into the trees. Mounted on a high branch was a remote-control camera familiar to all users of urban supermarkets, post offices, football grounds and corner shops. It didn't belong up a tree in the Highlands but there it was. Big Brother, like dog shit, could land anywhere.

Willy looked up at the camera, without affection.

'Ah. The celebrated electronic gamekeeper. That is what they replaced me with, a year ago. However . . .' He took a knife from his pocket, opened out the blade, and used it as a pointer. He showed them where the camera cable ran down into the leaves and foliage at the base of the tree, and continued: '. . . the cable is no longer fully operative. It appears to have been chewed by some wee beastie with no love of electronic technology.'

There was a gap in the cable. It had been cut, cleanly, with a knife.

'Oh dear. What a shame,' said Oliver.

'Indeed,' said Willy, closing the knife and slipping it back into his pocket. 'We are all adrift in a sea of uncooperative beasties.'

'What do you think of the 13th Baron Kite?' said Diane, keen
to restore precision to the investigation. It had grown a bit metaphysical for her taste.

'He's English,' said Willy. That was apparently the sum of the
matter.

'We're English,' said Michael.

'You're not English like he's English.'

They suddenly became aware of the distant sound of bagpipes.
Oliver wondered whether the Baron had inherited a token piper
along with his vast acreage, then realized the noise was coming
from behind them.

'Is that another colourful survivor of an old tradition?' he asked
Willy, who shook his head.

'Muzak. Happy hour at the motel. If you hurry they'll sell
you a wee dram at half-price.'

A motel? In the low Highlands? Was nothing sacred?

No.

'Are you going?' said Diane. 'Perhaps we could buy you a
drink?'

'Thank you, but certainly not. I make my own. Besides, it's
getting dark and I have to maintain the balance of his Lordship's
salmon.'

A respectful nod of the head and he was gone, as quietly and
discreetly as when he had first appeared: a Willy-o'-the-Wisp,
thought Oliver.

Then, after a brief discussion, the three English people climbed
down from the wall, got into the car and drove towards the sound
of the bagpipes.

The Bonny Wee Dram Motel had been built after a ferocious
public debate.

Those against argued that it would disinherit three tenant
farmers; corrupt an ancient, Arcadian landscape: cause traffic con-
gestion where historically there wasn't even traffic: clutter the
place up with tourists; enrich a few fat gents in the City of London
without benefit to the local economy; and leave the indigenous
wild life in terminal despair, crying: 'If not here, where?'

Those in favour argued that it would create jobs; spread sweetness and light over all the earth; and besides, they had the money, and those against, including the wildlife, could go screw themselves.

So it came to pass that the Bonny Wee Dram Motel was built. It sprawled across Glen Leven, one storey high – as a concession to the planners and a sop to the protesters – like a disembowelled and flattened-out Tesco's. The architect was of the post-modernist Lego school. He had thrown in a few hi-tech fripperies: some stainless steel plumbing hung on the outside in the hope of picking up a Civic Trust Award from a flabby-minded jury. He had failed, and the villagers looked at what he had made and immediately renamed it Amazing Disgrace.

The motel had created thirty-seven jobs, thirty-six of them part-time – sweaty and underpaid, carried out if possible by young unemployed people on schemes designed by the government as a cringe to the international bankers. The only full-time job was that of chief executive. He was paid £100,000 a year plus all he could embezzle. He commuted by helicopter from Essex.

The sign beside the main entrance was a shrine to thrusting marketing. In large letters it read 'THE BONNY WEE DRAM MOTEL'. Demurely, in one corner, it admitted to being 'PART OF THE FARQUHAR GROUP', with a tiny logo in the shape of a kite, so small it could be mistaken for a full stop. Dominating the lot was a mega-logo, another triumph for the designers of the Heritage Age. The concept was a person in a kilt – sexy but androgynous, thus preserving ideological correctness – relaxing in a Jacuzzi. It looked like a Jacuzzi being ravished by a sergeant of the Black Watch.

Oliver parked the car and they checked in. The receptionist wore a badge saying her name was Fiona. She wore the uniform of the Bonny Wee Dram motel chain: a cream blouse with a matching skirt and beret in a specially commissioned tartan – the Clan Basildon, according to the staff. They had refused to wear the official sporran on the basis that, if people were supposed to wear their pubic hair on the outside, clothes would have been designed with suitable apertures from the beginning.

Fiona was an unemployed school-leaver who wanted to go to art school but couldn't get a grant. She had been on a weekend course to learn how to be a hotel receptionist.

She said what she had been taught to say, robotically, with neither love nor conviction, as she passed a succession of small items across the counter.

'Your room keys. One double room, one single room. Your minibar keys. Please be sure to complete the form provided should you consume any of the contents of your minibars. Your complimentary shortbread. Your complimentary wee drams. Your concessionary tickets for the dry-ski slope.'

'Is that a raffle?' said Oliver.

'No. It's a dry-ski slope,' she said, on the edge of a return to the conventions of normal conversation; but two telephones rang simultaneously, putting a stop to that sort of nonsense. She picked up the first.

'Bonny Wee Dram, can you hold, please?'

She picked up the second.

'Bonny Wee Dram, can you hold, please?'

She left both telephones unattended and turned to Oliver, Diane and Michael.

'Have a nice wee stay.'

'We'll try our wee hardest,' said Oliver.

'What time do you finish work?' said Michael, who thought Fiona was pretty and deserved more from life than doling out miniature bottles of Scotch and being polite to strangers on the telephone.

'December of next year,' said Fiona, who had been asked the question many times; but this time at least she sounded like a fully formed human being. Michael knew how she was feeling. File under Pending, he decided.

The double room was identical with the single room, and both were identical with a million motel rooms across the good earth: from the soft-porn movies available on the in-house video channel at a small but significant extra charge to the complimentary shower-caps in the bathroom. Did anyone ever wear these shower-caps? Where did they come from? Where did they go to? What crazed executive had loosed them on the world in such volume? What had been his reward? A knighthood? A safe parliamentary seat?

Both, probably.

Michael was wearing his shower-cap when he joined Oliver and Diane in their room. It seemed a pity to waste it. Diane took no notice. It was attention-seeking behaviour, she decided. The *Guardian* said you should ignore it.

Michael had worked out a plan of action.

'We've got to break in,' he said.

'Oh yes?' said Diane.

'Climb over the wall. Break into the house. Simple.'

'What about the security men and the hidden cameras and the guard dogs?'

'Not a problem. It'll all be run by Cosmos Security PLC and we know they're a bunch of idiots. They employ people like me.'

'And the geese? That poacher, he said there were geese as well.'

'Sorry. I'd forgotten about the geese.'

Michael was terrified of geese. He looked to Oliver for guidance, hoping he would have an answer to the problem. The life and work of Mother Goose. It sounded like one of Oliver's specialities.

Oliver was otherwise absorbed. He was sitting on the queen-sized bed with the telephone directory open on his knee, studying the intricacies of the push-button phone on the bedside table.

'Why are you playing with the telephone?' said Diane. 'We're supposed to be working out a way of tackling the wicked Baron.'

'I've solved that. It's the telephone I'm having trouble with.'

He picked up the receiver and hit a button, seemingly at random.

'Hello,' he said, as somebody answered.

'How do you mean, you've solved it?' said Diane.

Oliver covered the mouthpiece and said to Diane: 'I'm talking to the Tam O'Shanter Discothèque by the pool.'

'Why?' said Diane, as Oliver resumed his telephone conversation.

'Forgive me. I wasn't aware of the existence of your institution.

It certainly sounds highly animated. I was trying to get an outside line. I see. Dial nine. Thank you very much, Mr O'Shanter.'

He hung up.

'What are you doing?' said Diane.

'We require access to the baronial mansion?' said Oliver.

'Obviously.'

'The best way to do it is by invitation, via the front door.'

'You've got family connections? You and the Baron both went to Sandhurst? His father and your father worked down the pit together?'

'I thought we could use psychology,' said Oliver, with the benign patience of a prophet dealing with two promising but slow-witted disciples.

'Psychology?' said Michael. 'We were thinking Balaclavas and baseball bats.'

'We were thinking nothing of the sort!' Diane said sharply.

'Consider it psychologically,' said Oliver. 'What does every man have?'

'A willy?' said Michael.

'Michael!' said Diane.

'A large ego,' said Oliver.

All three nodded, in total agreement. It was a self-evident truth, right up there in the Top Twenty with Newton's law of gravity, Archimedes' principle and boring Arsenal. Oliver elaborated on his thesis:

'The male ego generally expands in proportion to the size of the house he inhabits and the amount of property he owns.'

'Where do you live?' said Michael. 'When you're not on the road. Nothing personal. Purely as a matter of interest?'

'A small artisan cottage,' said Oliver, as he dialled nine followed by a number he had underlined in the directory with his complimentary Bonny Wee Dram Motel ball-point pen. Diane realized what he was doing and rehearsed his lines for him:

'Good evening, we are total strangers, but we'd like to visit you tomorrow and accuse you of murder, arson, intimidation and criminal conspiracy.'

By the time she had finished, Oliver was speaking on the telephone.

'Good evening, may I speak to Baron Kite, please?'

Oliver smiled. He had obviously found his man at the first attempt.

'Good. You don't know me, and please forgive my interrupting your evening, but my name's Oliver and I'm speaking on behalf of the BBC. Do you ever watch a programme called *Mastermind?*'

Diane nodded approval as she suddenly understood Oliver's game plan.

'I've been asked to set questions for a competitor whose chosen specialist subject is your family history. I understand it goes back thirteen generations.' Oliver listened, making notes on the pad provided by a benevolent management.

'This is the man you thought was naff,' Diane said to Michael.

'I changed my mind. He isn't naff. But he *is* crazy.'

'Also very sexy. Especially in his socks.'

'Mum!'

Oliver, oblivious to the discussions about his sanity and sexuality, reassured the Baron:

'I realize this may have come as a surprise, but we've had much more peculiar specialist subjects in our time. But doesn't that reflect life itself, which is frequently peculiar in my experience?'

No question, thought Diane, my bloke is brilliant. My bloke? Cor!

'We are from the BBC. We have an appointment,' said Oliver into the Entryphone mounted on the wall beside the great entrance to the Kite estate. It remained the most reliable 'Open Sesame' line since 'Would you like to accept this horse with our compliments?' The mighty wrought-iron gates swung open, their remote-control electronics apparently immune to attack from wee beasties, unless the beasties had declared a truce for unspecified reasons of their own.

The gates clanged shut behind them as Oliver drove carefully over the potholes of the long and winding road leading to the big house. Trees and shrubs closed in on them from all sides. There was a powerful stench of neglect, most of it green, a colour Diane associated with legless creatures that crept, crawled or slithered. It was an irrational fear. She agreed with William Blake about the holiness of all living things, just as long as they kept away from her salad.

She shuddered and said to Oliver:

'Are you sure this is a good idea?'

'The Baron seemed very happy about it. Men love to be told they're important. Coffee and biscuits were mentioned.'

'He might be lying.'

'Well, what's the worst thing that could happen?'

'We could wind up face-down in the loch. That's the worst thing that could happen. Death.'

'I can live with that,' said Oliver.

They drove on in silence. Michael lay very still on the back seat, huddled beneath the travel rug.

Willy the designated poacher and tourist attraction watched, unseen, as the car passed by. So did a pair of deer, a brace of partridges, a couple of squirrels and a delegation of assorted beasties, on the run from the Bonny Wee Dram site, still trying to find out who was in charge so they could apply for refugee status.

Oliver parked the car at the side of the house, between an old Fordson tractor and a jeep that looked as if it had been at Culloden with Willy's trousers.

The Baron was waiting for Oliver and Diane at the front door. They did not immediately identify him as an aristo. He was not what they expected. They had discussed it over breakfast. The residual peasant prejudice in Oliver had predicted ceremonial robes and a battery of butlers; he had then planned to refuse to touch his forelock as an egalitarian gesture. Diane had expected a tweed suit and vowel sounds strangled at birth; she had planned to behave exactly as she normally did.

Instead, the man in the doorway wore jeans, a Bob Marley T-shirt, a pigtail and an ear-ring. He was about forty but, in trying to look younger, looked older. He greeted them with a relaxed:

'Hi.'

'Er . . . hi,' said Oliver. 'We are from the BBC.'

'Like the man said . . . nobody's perfect.'

On a simple comparative scale, Oliver sounded the posher of the two, like a senior BBC executive of the old buffer school; while the Baron sounded like a lesser DJ operating in the middle of the night on a commercial pop-and-prattle radio station.

'We have an appointment with the 13th Baron Kite,' said Oliver.

'I am he,' said Kite, 'and I know exactly what you're thinking. Not your regular Baron.'

'It's impossible for me to say,' said Oliver. 'I rarely dally with the aristocracy. My roots are strictly proletarian.'

'That's cool,' said the Baron.

'This is Diane, my PA.'

'Hi, Diane.'

'Hi.'

'Come into the shack.' He led them into the grand entrance hall.

As Oliver and Diane were conducted through the great oak doors, Michael peered out from beneath his travel rug. He was still hidden in the back of the car. He looked around at the yard where Oliver had parked. It was silent and deserted. He double-checked for geese. Not a goose in sight. Good. That was the first step. A goose step. He laughed inside: Aarf Aarf.

The baronial hallway was large, brown and chilly, with a central staircase poised for the arrival at the ball of Queen Victoria or Cinderella, but sick of waiting. The panelled walls were hung with family portraits, most of them portly, bearded gents who looked like W. G. Grace, and not a Bob Marley T-shirt from start to finish. There was less furniture than Oliver had expected. The odd armchair and occasional occasional table seemed to have been spread out to make them look a lot, like stately home *nouvelle cuisine*; but perhaps that was the fashion in aristocratic circles.

'You say you've done this Mastermind gig before?' said the Baron.

'Oh yes,' said Oliver.

'The life and work of George Farquhar,' said Diane, who had grown quite proud of her bloke's achievements in matters of trivia.

'And the life and work of Lester Young,' said Diane.

'Hey, man, that is something else!'

The Baron's self-consciously youthful persona suddenly fell to the ground to reveal genuine enthusiasm. Diane was a bit put out that he'd called her 'man' but maybe some Geordie genes had slipped into the blue bloodstream somewhere in those thirteen generations. They got everywhere if you didn't keep an eye on them.

'So you're a jazz freak?' said the Baron to Oliver, who nodded. 'I once organized a jazz festival here. I've still got the letter from the bank manager.'

'I knew there was a jazz connection,' said Oliver.

'Ask me some of the questions and I'll show you something as a reward,' said the Baron, hauling two large armchairs into a Mastermind configuration. He sat in one. Oliver sat in the other.

'Baron Kite, you have two minutes on the life and work of Lester Young.'

'Hey, this is really cool,' said the Baron.

It was cold in the hall. Diane decided to keep moving and look at some of the family portraits while the boys enjoyed their fun. She would check the ancestral beards for frost.

'Starting . . . now!' said Oliver. 'What was Lester Young's nickname?'

'Prez. Short for the President.'

'Correct. Given to him by whom?'

'Billie Holiday.'

'Correct. What was the name of Lester Young's younger brother who was also a musician?'

'Lee Young.'

'Correct. What instrument did Lee Young play?'

'Drums.'

The Baron scored maximum points, which puzzled Oliver. If the man carried such love and knowledge of the true music, he must be at least forty years old. If that was the case, what was he doing in a Bob Marley T-shirt? It must be either a sop to a younger generation, a praiseworthy gesture towards racial equality or a souvenir of a Caribbean holiday. None of these made him an evil or a stupid man; on the contrary. But they were far removed from the usual expectations when tangling with the landed gentry.

'Baron Kite. You have scored twenty points and no passes!' said Oliver.

'And you shall have your reward,' said the Baron, standing up and heading towards the gloomiest corner of the hall.

He led them along a dark corridor. It was like a special offer from a closing-down sale at the Château D'If. Diane was feeling the cold and hoped the reward might be a cup of coffee. So far life with the upper crust seemed to add up to the boys playing silly games above stairs, like Test Match commentators on Radio 3, with supplementary frostbite. Were these the qualities that built the empire? Or the qualities that lost it?

A bit of each, probably.

The Baron opened a door at the end of the corridor.

'Let there be light!' he cried.

And there was light. They entered a large, dazzling room with floor-to-ceiling French windows at either end, white-painted walls and ceiling, and a white carpet with abstract splashes of colour which, on closer examination, looked like wine, beer and other good-time stains.

'Welcome to the baronial music-room,' said Kite.

There was no furniture. There were musical instruments: a Bechstein grand with the lid open, a piano stool, a drum kit, a few stray amplifiers and a guitar lying on the floor by the window, as if Eric Clapton had left in a hurry.

'What sort of music happens here?' said Oliver.

'We had the festival way back when. Would you believe Dizzy blew in this very room? But these days it's mostly charity gigs for worthy causes. And I have a bit of a jam with some of the cats when we give parties. This is my kit.'

He was standing beside the drums. He picked up the brushes and played a short, rhythmic solo on snare-drum and cymbals.

'I try to play like Jo Jones. You know the guy I mean?'

'Drummer with the Count Basie band. They said Jo Jones played like the wind.'

But Oliver thought: the Baron plays as if he's got the wind. And he uses too many words like 'gig' and 'cat' and 'jam' and he uses them too often. Methinks he doth protest too much his coolness.

'Why don't you ask the Baron if you can play his piano?' said Diane.

'You play piano?'

'No, but I would very much like to ping your middle C, if that's all right.'

'It's a homage to Beethoven,' said Diane.

'Help yourself.'

Oliver walked across to the piano, pinged middle C, then said: 'Thank you.'

'In what way is that a homage to Beethoven? I realize the cat was a serious muso but . . .'

'Let me explain. Apparently Beethoven was a phenomenal pianist with an extraordinary gift for improvisation. But he could rarely be persuaded to play. No point in saying: "Give us a tune, Ludwig." The only way was to ping a note in passing, like this . . .'

Oliver pinged the middle C.

' . . . and then say: "I do believe this piano is slightly out of tune." Then Beethoven, who naturally had perfect pitch, would try it himself . . .'

Again Oliver pinged the middle C.

' . . . and having played one note, he couldn't stop. He would play a thousand dazzling notes, never heard before or since. All this was, of course, before he became deaf. Can you imagine? Not being able to hear this?'

He pinged the middle C for a third and final time. It echoed around the white walls longer than seemed possible, acoustically speaking. Diane imagined not being able to hear it. Poor Beethoven.

Michael was upstairs in what he guessed must be a bedroom wing. He had found his way there by way of a back door of the sort traditionally used by servants, coal or garbage, and a winding staircase provided for the benefit of sexual adventurers seeking to dismantle class boundaries, if only on a sweaty and temporary basis.

It had been his idea. Oliver and his mother would detain the

Baron in Mastermind discussions downstairs, while he searched for incriminating evidence upstairs. What did clues look like? And where did you find them?

No idea.

Downstairs, the Baron gave Oliver and Diane a brief conducted tour of the family portraits.

'These, presumably, are your ancestors?' said Oliver, making notes in what he hoped was a proper BBC manner.

'All the wicked Barons. One to twelve inclusive.'

'Were they wicked?'

'It's kind of interesting. The even numbers weren't bad. Two, six and eight, they were pretty cool cats, by the standards of the day. It's the odd numbers who tend to be the evil bastards.'

'But aren't you number thirteen?' said Diane.

'Unlucky for some,' said the Baron.

'And do they haunt you?' said Oliver.

'I don't believe in ghosts.'

'We spent a night beside Hadrian's Wall,' said Oliver, 'and at the witching hour we heard the marching feet of a Roman legion.'

'We're also preparing a set of questions about the life and work of the Emperor Hadrian,' said Diane, thinking: Oliver didn't tell me he heard the marching feet. Or is he just saying this for effect?

'Sorry, man, I'm not into marching feet. But OK, I cannot tell a lie. I sometimes fancy some of these old guys are keeping a beady eye on me. They're not into the music I play.'

The Baron looked up at a portrait of his great-great-grandfather. It showed an austere, Victorian face with all the gaiety of a chapel in mid-winter.

'Your ancestors look down. My ancestors look up,' said Oliver.

'Sorry, man, you'll have to explain.'

'Let me show you my socks.'

'Is that really necessary?' said Diane, who regarded Oliver's socks as an intimate and sacred component of their sex life, for their eyes only. Consenting adults should keep their socks to themselves.

Oliver rolled up his trouser legs to reveal his socks.

'I don't dig Masonic rituals,' said the Baron, as Oliver explained:

'My mother knitted all my father's socks. She never bought them from a shop. Her pride wouldn't allow it. When he died there were dozens of pairs of socks he had never worn. Including these. My inheritance.'

It was a touching tale and, as Diane knew, a pack of lies. The socks were M&S like everybody else's. She wondered whether the Baron might identify them as such. Maybe not. He wore no socks himself, only a pair of sloppy sandals made from recycled string – the sort of item you saw in Third World charity catalogues that fell out of the *Radio Times* at Christmas. They were probably made by endangered peasant tribes in the Amazon Basin.

But the Baron was impressed.

'Crazy socks, man.'

'Thank you,' said Oliver.

'What did he do, your father?'

'He was a miner.'

'Fantastic!'

'I'm glad you think so.'

'I've been a socialist all my life.'

Oliver rolled his trouser legs down, straightened up, looking around the hallway and said:

'To each according to his needs.'

'That's enough about socks,' said Diane. 'We need to get on with our research.' She was brisk even by her standards, but with good cause. During the great sock debate she had glanced up and seen Michael staring down from the head of the stairs. Her response was a brief maternal gesture meaning: get the hell out of sight or there'll be no pocket money at the weekend and you can say goodbye to the bicycle for your birthday.

Michael got the hell out of sight.

Upstairs he had found a maze of interlocking confusion. The bedroom wings had wings, the annexes had annexes and the whole place felt crusted and abandoned, as if recently excavated a thousand years after an earthquake. The visible evidence was that the human species could no longer survive up here and had given up trying.

The gurgling of bathwater was a surprise. The woman was a surprise, too. He almost bumped into her as he turned a corner, in a hurry to get the hell out of sight.

'Oh. Hi,' she said.

'Hi,' said Michael.

She was fresh out of the bathroom, wearing a quilted dressing-gown and a towel around her head. But this was not Ted Willis's *Woman in a Dressing-Gown*. Even by the standards of a liberated age, Michael recognized her as one of nature's bimbettes. She was a reluctant thirty, trying to look twenty. Half a GCSE pass in home economics was her father's reward for a mammoth cash investment in her education. The face, albeit Identikit – Michael had seen hundreds like it when watching Royal Ascot on television – was distantly familiar. Had she been briefly punted by the tabloids as a possible marriage contender for the House of Windsor?

Yes. But she never came under orders.

She frowned, grappling with a difficult thought, and asked Michael:

'Am I supposed to know you? Are you a cousin or something?'

Michael shook his head.

'No. Nothing like that.'

She relaxed. What a relief.

Michael had a story, one he had prepared earlier.

'I'm here to fix the photocopier. I'm looking for the Baron's study.'

'The study.'

It was another demanding intellectual concept.

'Or his office. Whatever he calls it.'

'He's got a den. Will that do?'

'That sounds really brilliant.'

'I think it's along here.' She led the way along a dusty corridor and opened a door. 'I'm not actually allowed in his den,' she said, then added with a giggle: 'Forbidden fruit.'

'My favourite. I never eat anything else,' said Michael,

deciding that flirtation was probably the best policy. It seemed to work. She giggled again as he peered into the room. Silly, really: older women didn't interest him.

In contrast to the rest of the house, the Baron's den was a modern, hi-tech office with a desk — probably described as a workstation in the manufacturer's catalogue — a swivel chair, filing cabinets and the inevitable computer. The place must be chock-a-block with incriminating evidence.

'Thank you,' said Michael, hoping the woman would go away and leave him to trawl for clues in peace and quiet.

'I . . . have to dry my hair.'

'Sure. Feel free. This . . . won't take long.'

'Good.'

She wandered off down the corridor, a little preoccupied. She had another conceptual challenge to deal with, in addition to drying her hair. Two things at once. Serious co-ordination. It was turning into a tough day.

Michael closed the door, crossed to the desk, sat down on the chair, switched on the computer and swivelled in anticipation.

This was more like country house living, thought Diane, sitting by the log fire in the drawing-room, sipping her coffee. There were biscuits too, some with chocolate on. The only surprise was that the Baron had made the coffee himself, freshly ground from politically correct South American beans. Where were the butlers and the cooks? Had they gone the way of the gamekeepers? Was it totally deserted below stairs? Or was it all part of the Baron's ideological purity?

She lay back in her armchair and thought of Oliver's socks while the two men studied a hefty typescript the Baron had taken from a shelf.

'This is the official family history. From the Act of Union until 1983.'

'Why 1983?' Oliver asked.

'My father was writing this when he died. In '83. I'm supposed to finish it and have it published but I haven't got around to it yet.'

'May I borrow this?'

'Keep it. I ran it off for you. It's all on the computer.'

'Thank you,' said Oliver, passing the manuscript to Diane, who put it in the briefcase she had brought along as proof of her authenticity. 'Could you tell me about the name Kite?'

'Originally it was Kyle, which turned out to be Scots for a long streak of wetness, so the third Baron changed it to Kyte, with a "y", which turned out to be Scots for a fat belly, so my great-grandfather changed it to Kite, which is a bird of prey. Appropriate.'

'But you still need to fill the gap from 1983 to the present,' said Diane, thinking: that's the period when the Farquhar Group started bumping people off, and I for one am not going to be diverted from the pursuit of truth by log fires and chocolate biscuits.

'What would you like to know?'

'Well,' said Oliver, proceeding sideways as usual, 'I wasn't aware, from my researches so far, that you were a socialist.'

'Liberty, equality, fraternity. I go along with all that shit.'

'What about, if you'll pardon the impertinence, redistribution of wealth?'

'That's not down to me, comrade.'

'No?'

'My family's been up here for three hundred years, screwing the peasants into the ground. When the great day dawns and the proletariat march down the drive with the red flag and say: "The game's up, give it all back", I'll go out with my hands in the air. I'll say: "It's a fair cop, I'll come quietly. Lead me to Madame Guillotine."'

He raised his hands high, in the attitude of guilt and surrender. Then he lowered them.

'But it's down to the proletariat, comrade. I'm not going to do it for them.'

The telephone rang. Oliver decided it must be the neighbourhood Soviet-in-exile, saying: we're on our way, citizen, we're on our way, so wear something a bit off the shoulder, and by the way is it all right if we chop down some of your trees to build barricades?

The Baron picked up the phone, listened briefly, then said:

'Sure. Go ahead. In your own time.'

Then he hung up, turned to Oliver and said:

'Next question?'

'I'm not sure how relevant it is to *Mastermind*, but it might give us a spot of light relief from the more medieval aspects of your family history . . . What can you tell us about the Farquhar Group?'

That's my boy, thought Diane.

'The Farquhar Group? It's a lousy, capitalist conspiracy, every bit as corrupt and ruthless as all the others of its kind. I'm the Chairman of the Board. I look good on the letterhead.'

'I see,' said Oliver.

'Next question?'

Before Oliver could ask his next question they heard the sound of piano-playing. It was coming from the music-room.

'Beethoven,' said Oliver.

'Not in person,' said the Baron.

'Sonata number 23, Opus 57. The *Appassionata*.'

'They don't write them like that any more.'

Oliver was in no mood for aristocratic cuteness. He was transfixed by the music. It was the real thing. In the words of Max Miller, a beautiful song, beautifully sung. The playing was crisp and clean around the edges.

'Would you like to meet the piano player?' the Baron said quietly.

'Yes, please.'

Oliver led the way as they hurried to the music-room. He opened the door and looked in. Diane and the Baron stood behind him.

The piano stood, blackly isolated, in the centre of the white room, as if locked into a polar ice-cap. The pianist's face was obscured by the piano lid. Oliver edged around so he could see who was playing. He recognized him immediately.

'Do you remember?' he said to Diane. 'I said to you, I'm sure Mr Baxter would rather be a concert pianist than . . .'

' . . .than whatever he is now,' said Diane, finishing the thought for both of them.

Baxter continued playing and said:

'Now you know my secret. That's very hard to forgive.'

'And we also know your secret,' said the Baron to Oliver and Diane.

'Which secret had you in mind?' said Diane.

'I checked you out with an old school chum at the Beeb.'

'Oh. That secret.'

While they were still juggling with each other's secrets and revelations, a woman in a dressing-gown came into the room.

'I'm horribly sorry to interrupt you, darling,' she said to the Baron, adding, with a big effort of will, 'but do you have a photocopier?'

'Of course I don't have a photocopier. You know I don't.'

'Well, there's a man upstairs repairing your photocopier.'

Later, Oliver would write in his diary: 'I have never expected the world to make sense. But there are times when it makes so little sense, it almost makes sense.'

13

What's the Opposite of Chinese Boxes?

Out of respect for Beethoven, Baxter finished the first movement of the *Appassionata* before getting up from the piano and leading Oliver, Diane, the Baron and the woman in the dressing-gown out of the music-room. As a senior executive of Cosmos Security PLC, Baxter took charge of the proceedings, but he did so calmly and courteously. It was all of a piece with a country house mystery involving a socialist aristocrat, his glamorous girlfriend and three amateur detectives disguised as a chap from the BBC, his personal assistant and a maintenance man come to fix the photocopier.

The Baron even introduced the woman in the dressing-gown to the visitors.

'This is Sara,' he said.

'Without an "H",' she said. It was obviously important to her.

'I call her my spousal monologue or my insignificant other,' said the Baron. It was a long-practised one-liner, designed to impress the sophisticated. Apart from Sara, who giggled dutifully in accordance with standing orders, nobody smiled. Diane decided: we'll have you, you chauvinist bastard.

As they arrived in the hallway Sara said:

'That's him.'

'That is *he*,' Oliver said quietly.

Michael stood at the top of the stairs, wishing he was in Macclesfield selling hot dogs. It was a long time since he'd wished that.

'Hi, everybody.'

'You're here to fix the photocopier?' said Baxter.

'Yes. Sort of.'

'Even though there isn't a photocopier anywhere on the premises?'

Michael shrugged.

'We all make mistakes.'

'You'd better come down the stairs and join us, Sonny Jim.'

As Michael walked down the stairs, Oliver said:

'Sonny Jim? He used to be on cornflake packets when I was little. Or was it porridge? Does anybody remember?'

Nobody seemed to hear. He might ask again later.

Michael reached the foot of the stairs. He found himself face to face and T-shirt to T-shirt with the Baron. Michael's was cheap and purpose-made, an embarrassing hangover from his student days. It read: 'MY PARENTS WENT ON HOLIDAY TO SKEGNESS SO I MADE MY OWN LOUSY T-SHIRT'. It should have given him some sort of kinship with a self-proclaimed Bob Marley freak, but the Baron was unimpressed.

'Does anybody know this guy?'

They took it in turns to stake their claims.

'I saw him upstairs. He was looking for the photocopier,' said Sara.

'He used to work for the firm,' said Baxter.

'He's my son. Has been for many years,' said Diane.

'And he's my *de facto* stepson,' said Oliver. 'A geologist of some distinction. We're very proud of him.'

Michael felt better. He still couldn't tell when Oliver was joking, but apart from his mum and his grandparents, he couldn't remember anyone being proud of him, and nobody ever said so out loud, in company. He was a good guy, Oliver.

The Baron remained unimpressed.

'I expect that in your spare time you're also a specialist question-setter for *Mastermind*,' he said to Michael.

'No. But I play a really mean game of famous Scottish names.'

'How do you play that?' said Sara.

'You have to think of famous Scottish names. Bonny Prince Charlie, Keir Hardie, Denis Law, Chic Murray . . .'

'Shut up!' yelled the Baron, as he saw Sara's interest quicken.

Michael eased back on the famous Scottish names. A pity. He was just warming up. Also, Oliver noted, a quick learner.

'I want to know what the hell is going on here,' said the Baron, losing his cool and starting to simmer. There would be no midnight jamming in the music-room with this bunch of cats: too many strays.

'May I offer a suggestion?' Oliver said quietly. 'Totally without obligation, of course?'

'Go ahead.'

'What we have here is obviously a traditional, old-fashioned, country house mystery. The normal procedure is for all the suspects to assemble in the drawing-room, so the detective can question them and deduce from the available evidence what is going on.'

'But who is the detective and who are the suspects?' said Diane.

'That's the first mystery.'

'Super!' said Sara. 'I love this game. Let's all go to the drawing-room!'

She led the way to the drawing-room, followed by Michael, Oliver and Diane who murmured:

'At least there's a fire in the drawing-room.'

Baxter and the Baron allowed the others to go on ahead.

'Are you in control of this situation, Mr Baxter?' said the Baron.

'Totally. Never confuse silence with inactivity.'

Diane found the armchair closest to the fire. The others arranged themselves neatly around the room, in accordance with all the Miss Marple episodes they had seen. Oliver assumed the detective role, pacing up and down, relishing the situation. Baxter did not intervene. He sat quietly beside the door.

'First of all, may I thank you all for coming here today,' said

Oliver. 'I'm sure, with a little patience and goodwill on all sides, we'll soon get to the bottom of this matter.'

'This is fun, isn't it?' said Sara.

'Are you a detective?' said the Baron, accustomed to being centre stage in his own baronial mansion, even in his cooler moments.

'No. I was a lecturer in comparative religion until I was made redundant. I wasn't cost-effective. The market forces. You must be familiar with them.'

'He may not be cost-effective but he knows something very funny about sex,' said Diane.

'Mum!'

'Do tell!' said Sara.

Diane ignored her. Most of the time people ignored her. She seemed used to it.

'But as I look around, I cannot help but reflect . . . isn't that why the world is such an unhappy place?' said Oliver.

His reflection was so oblique that Baxter broke his vow of silence to ask:

'Why?'

'Why? Because we are none of us doing what we really want to do. I am a redundant lecturer, cast aside on the slag-heap of academe. You, Mr Baxter, appear to be working for Cosmos Security PLC, when your heart says you should be a concert pianist. Michael has a degree in geology but he was selling hot dogs in Macclesfield until he became a temporary and totally miserable night-watchman. The 13th Baron Kite is an aristocrat and a landowner, yet spiritually he is a swing drummer and a revolutionary socialist.'

'You? A socialist?' said Michael to the Baron.

'Peace and love, comrade.'

Michael smiled.

'The Red Baron.'

'That's really brilliant,' said Sara, giggling, before turning to Oliver with a pouting lower lip to ask: 'What about me? Don't I get a turn at reasons to be miserable?'

The pout, which had served her well across two decades of

gymkhanas and ski slopes, said: I'm the only one in the room who hasn't had a lollipop. She wasn't, of course, but that's what the pout said. It had been saying it for thirty years. Most of the time she wound up with a lollipop, which served her right.

'Forgive me,' said Oliver, polite as ever. 'I can offer no thoughts, since we've only just met . . .'

'I always wanted to travel the world and help poor people, but basically I've wound up as his bimbo. He's nice, though, most of the time.'

'I try,' said the Baron.

Oliver approached the end of his sermon. What a preacher he would make, thought Diane, and what a pity he doesn't believe in any of the religions he used to compare. He could make a fortune. She knew that wasn't the point, but it was true all the same.

'So you see, brothers and sisters, we are all alienated and frustrated. We live in a sick and unhappy society. We have travelled hundreds of miles, almost the length of the country, and we have met only one man who is totally happy and fulfilled. And what does he do? He makes tombstones.'

'Grandpa Delaney?' said Michael.

'The same.'

Diane wondered what Oliver would do next. Ask them to get up out of their seats, come on down front and pledge their lives henceforth to the holy ghosts of Beethoven, Lester Young and Chic Murray?

She was wrong.

'So if the world is so unhappy, is it any wonder a Welsh farmer called Griffiths ends up dead, floating face-down in a river?'

Wow.

The temperature in the room dropped by twenty degrees. Baxter remained silent. The Baron said:

'What have Welsh farmers got to do with alienation and frustration?'

'It must be a bit alienating, floating face-down in a river,' said Diane, hoping a touch of dark humour might break the ice that had formed over the room, deflect Oliver in his sudden swerve from philosophical reflections to criminal accusations, and save the three of them from swift immersion in the Baron's personal loch.

'Not to mention Adrian L. Walsh,' said Oliver, just as Diane was hoping he wouldn't mention Adrian L. Walsh. 'In addition to being an anagram of Hadrian's Wall, Mr Walsh was murdered in County Durham. Killed with a shotgun. We have also heard tales of assorted bits and pieces of arson and intimidation, all products of our sickness and greed. Heigh-ho.'

'So it goes,' said Michael, a true believer in all the gospels according to Vonnegut. Good lad, thought Oliver.

'Thank you,' said Baxter. 'Now it's my turn to be the ace detective.' He stood up and crossed to the centre of the room until he faced Oliver.

'Good luck,' said Oliver, adding, as he sat down on the arm of Diane's chair: 'This should be fascinating.'

Baxter waited for silence and stillness before he began. He spoke quietly with the authority of a man who expected people to listen. He reminded Oliver of Bob Paisley, a quiet-spoken former manager of Liverpool Football Club, who used to say: if you want people to listen, speak quietly.

'When you psycho-analysed each of us, you made no reference to your travelling companion. Who is Diane? What is she?'

'She's my mum,' said Michael.

'And the only person in the room who can genuinely claim to be a detective, if I'm not mistaken,' said Baxter.

'I'm in the police force, yes.'

'But currently under suspension, I think?'

'My reward for suggesting that the Chief Constable might have some connection with Welsh farmers floating face-down in rivers.'

Diane stood up.

'My turn,' she said.

'I haven't finished,' said Baxter.

'But you've blown my cover.'

'Have your say by all means, but I will remain standing.'

Baxter stood with his back to the fire, arms folded. He would listen but he would not be moved.

'If you try to make a run for it,' said Oliver, 'we'll regard it as a guilty plea. It's a well-known convention in country house thrillers.'

'Hush,' said Diane to Oliver, before addressing the room: 'The reason we're here is that every crime we've investigated is apparently linked to a series of companies. A property company called Nineteenth Hole Developments PLC. A security firm called Cosmos Security PLC. Both of them part of the Farquhar Group. Chairman of the Board, the Baron Kite.'

'That's you, isn't it, darling?' said Sara.

The Baron ignored Sara, which she expected, and looked hard at Diane, which she expected.

'And you would like to know whether I carried out these murders and these various bits of arson and intimidation?'

'Frankly, I'd expect you to deny it.'

'And I do.' The Baron stood up. 'My turn,' he said.

'Does everybody get a turn at being the detective?' Sara asked Michael.

'No, I think it's voluntary.'

'Gosh. What a relief. I'm seriously embarrassing at charades and stuff like that. It's fun watching other people though, isn't it?'

'Hysterical,' said Michael, unsmiling. He shared his mother's reluctance to be dumped in the loch.

The Baron had identified Oliver as his main antagonist. Michael had clearly come along for the ride and Diane, though bright and resourceful, was equally clearly a woman. It was to Oliver that he said: 'You don't know much about capitalism, do you?'

'I think that's because I've never been overburdened with capital,' said Oliver.

'If you bothered to read your financial pages, you'd know that the Farquhar Group hasn't belonged to me for five years or more. We were taken over.'

'By whom?'

'An international conglomerate. They don't have names. They have initials. They keep moving. The firm changes hands, sometimes twice a day. They merge and mingle like amoebas. In case you haven't noticed, these are the people who now run the world. Americans, Japanese, Germans, Italians. And I believe there's funny money from Eastern Europe arriving by the truck-load these days.'

'But you still have a nominal shareholding?'

'About as nominal as you can get,' said the Baron.

'I could use a few nominal shareholdings,' said Michael. 'Sit on my nominal backside and get a few nominal grand for doing nominal sod all.'

'Michael!' said his mother, recalling a nominal fragment of her upbringing which forbade you to discuss money, sex, politics or religion in polite company.

'He's the one who started talking about capitalism.'

It was a fair point but, before she could respond, Oliver re-entered the debate from the outer limits of left field. Staring into the flames of the log fire he suddenly said:

'What's the opposite of Chinese boxes?'

The room was numbed into silence. Diane, who had run out of steam and questions, returned to her chair.

'I think these people are entitled to a translation,' she said.

'Do we all know Chinese boxes?' said Oliver.

Sara was delighted. At last she could join in.

'I know Chinese boxes. You open a box and inside there's a smaller box and you open that box and inside there's a smaller box and you open that box and inside there's a smaller box and you open that box and . . .'

'For God's sake,' said the Baron, 'we *all* know Chinese boxes.'

'Well, this is the opposite,' said Oliver. 'We start with a little box in the middle. Two murdered men: Mr Griffiths, a farmer, Mr Walsh, a property developer. They're in a box called Nineteenth Hole Developments PLC. And Nineteenth Hole Developments PLC are in a box called the Farquhar Group.'

Oliver stood up and walked across to the Baron, with no hint of aggression; but with honest curiosity, like a tourist wanting to have a closer look at an obscure but interesting relic of a forgotten dynasty.

'Which leads me to the conclusion that the Farquhar Group is in yet another box called . . .?'

'The box with no name,' said the Baron.

Baxter stepped between them and said to Oliver:

'You would be well advised to keep your distance from the box with no name,' then, turning to the Baron, he added: 'Tell them the story you told me, about you and your father.'

'Is it a joke?' said Oliver. 'I collect jokes.'

'No. It isn't a joke. My father was an old-fashioned Tory. I am a revolutionary socialist. He said to me one day: "What will happen when the revolution comes and we confront each other across the barricades? Will you shoot me?" And I said: "I will aim to miss, but I can't speak for my friends." So you see, it isn't really a joke.'

Oliver nodded agreement.

'Yes. I can see that it isn't really a joke.'

Neither Oliver nor Diane asked the question: who were the Baron's friends? Or the question: who would fire the bullets? Or the question: who would dump the bodies in the loch? Was Baxter a good enough friend to carry out these tasks? Or did he too have good and loyal friends?

As they pondered these questions, Baxter said:

'You can feel just as alienated floating face-down in a Scottish loch as you can in a Welsh river.'

'Perhaps a little more chilly, being further north?' Oliver suggested.

'Undoubtedly,' said Baxter. His message was clear. Baxter was the man with the friends; or, worse still, a friendless man with access to the hit squad. And he might love Beethoven but he couldn't speak for his hired assassins.

The telephone rang.

'That'll be Mummy about nail-polish,' said Sara, who always sat close to the telephone. It was her best friend: her rod, staff and security blanket.

She picked up the receiver. It was an old-fashioned black model, a reproduction of the sort the GPO used to make, and therefore in keeping with a medieval mansion; besides, old-fashioned phones were the very latest thing.

'Hi. Yes? Just a minute.' She looked across the room at Diane. 'Is your name Diane Priest?'

'Yes.'

'It's your father.'

Diane crossed the room to the telephone. Her path carried her between Baxter and the Baron. As she passed them she explained:

'He rings me every day. He *always* knows where I am and what I'm doing.'

'He sounds really nice,' said Sara, handing over the phone.

'He is.'

'They have a very good relationship,' said Oliver.

'He's the one who makes the tombstones,' said Michael. 'He's built like a brick shit-house.'

'Michael!' said Oliver.

And on the telephone, Diane said, very loudly so that everyone in the room could hear:

'Dad? We're fine. We've had a lovely time. Coffee and biscuits and a big log fire. And we're just leaving.'

When she had finished talking to her father, they left.

'That went well, didn't it?' Michael said cheerfully, as they stood in the yard at the side of the house.

'Just get in the car,' said Diane.

'I've never met a Baron before. I didn't expect a Bob Marley freak. He's a bit of a dude, isn't he?'

'But he can't speak for his friends.'

'He's very knowledgeable about Lester Young,' said Oliver.

Diane lost patience with the men in her life.

'You heard what they said about floating face-down. The man has his own loch, remember!'

They remembered.

'Let's get in the car,' said Oliver.

As the car made its way along the drive, the Baron, Sara and Baxter watched it from the drawing-room window.

'Nice people,' said the Baron.

'I like Michael,' said Sara.

'The boy?'

'The one who came to fix the photocopier.'

'It's natural to like people nearer your own age.'

The Baron spoke with a sharpness that might have been venom or might have been yearning – probably a little of each.

'They all three have a deceptive quality of innocence,' said Baxter. 'But innocence, whatever the preachers say, is no protection. The meek have never inherited a damn thing.'

Oliver's car moved out of sight, obscured by the trees flanking the drive. The men left the drawing-room. Sara decided to telephone Mummy.

In the car, Michael leaned forward between Oliver and Diane.

'I found some really amazing stuff in the Red Baron's den.'

'Tell us later,' said Diane. 'There are probably hidden microphones in the trees.'

'I spy with my little eye something beginning with CSH,' said Oliver.

'I'm not playing,' said Diane, in no mood for I-spy. It brought back memories of interminable trips to and from rain-bedraggled seaside towns, playing silly games to divert little Michael and persuade him that he couldn't possibly need to go to the toilet again, already.

'CSH?' said Michael, who didn't remember any of that.

'Colourful Scottish Heritage.'

On the driveway ahead of them stood Willy the Poacher, in the shelter of the trees. His pockets were bulging, and he was carrying two heavily laden sacks, in addition to his shotgun. He held out his hand, as if stopping a bus.

Oliver pulled up beside him and wound his window down.

'Good afternoon,' he said.

'Good afternoon,' said Willy. 'Would you be gracious enough to grant me a small favour?'

'By all means.'

'A wee lift? I'm heavily burdened as you can see, and the walls grow higher for the climbing as you get older.'

'You're more than welcome.' Michael opened the rear door so Willy could climb in.

Diane was less beguiled than the others by the colourful

qualities of the local heritage. He was a security risk and he didn't smell so good.

'I hope you all realize we are being watched,' she said coldly, pointing at a surveillance camera mounted high in a tree and looking down at them.

'Please don't worry yourself, ma'am. The wee beasties have been about their business again.'

He indicated where the cable had been cut, neatly and cleanly, at the base of the tree.

'Citizens are entitled to their privacy, I say. Isn't it in our Charter?' said Willy, as Oliver drove towards the gates.

There were twenty-four television monitors mounted in rows on the wall of the basement room. Only five were operational. The other nineteen were blank. Baxter and the Baron were not impressed.

'It says Cosmos Security PLC on our letterhead,' said the Baron. 'Global? Look at that. We can't even make my back garden secure.'

'Private security firms,' said Baxter. 'The fastest growth rate of any activity in the last two decades. Along with bankruptcy, repossession, lunacy and suicide. Conclusion?'

'Tell me.'

'Most security firms are run by idiots, drop-outs and psychopaths. That's why we prefer to rely on cameras. However, your head gamekeeper tells me that wild animals chew the cables.'

'He could be lying.'

'I forgot about lying. That has the fastest growth rate of all. Starting at the top. The spin doctor as high priest.'

'Conclusion?'

'If I tell you, you won't believe me,' said Baxter.

Willy lived just outside the village of Kirkleven. It was, he explained, a tied cottage: 'But not tied so tightly as to become oppressive, you understand?'

Michael helped him with his sacks as he climbed out of the car.

'I'm grateful for your kindness. May I offer you something in return?'

'Totally unnecessary,' said Oliver. 'We never accept gratuities. It offends our dignity. We're just nice.'

'That being so, you would be most welcome to browse in our freezer cabinet. Salmon, partridge, venison, pheasant?'

'We're four hundred miles from our nearest domestic kitchen,' said Diane.

The wee man nodded.

'That would seem to be a limiting factor, I understand.'

'But you could possibly share some information with us.'

'I thought we had enough information,' said Oliver. 'The bedroom's full of it.'

Diane ignored Oliver. Now they were a safe distance from the Kite estate, she was once more in full investigative flow.

'Does the Baron ever entertain hunting, shooting and fishing parties on his estate?'

'According to season, yes. I would estimate it to be a major part of the estate's income.'

'Gentlemen from abroad?'

'As a rule, yes, from abroad. It is very expensive, you see.'

Oliver caught the drift of Diane's questions and decided to join in, though mainly because he enjoyed Willy's use of the English language. He spoke it with a subtle blend of the pedantic and the musical, as if it were his second tongue, which, historically and spiritually, it was.

'I think we would like to know which foreign countries these well-breeched foreign gentlemen claim allegiance to? Would that be the case?' Oliver turned to Diane for support.

'Yes. That would be the case.'

Oliver realized they were both talking like Willy but he seemed not to mind.

'To be sure,' said the wee poacher, 'for the most part we are talking about the old colonial powers. Germany and Italy. And the newer colonial powers. America and Japan. And a few Englishmen, though not so many as, if you'll pardon me, in England's days of yore. Then, more recently, there have been one or two Russians.'

'All businessmen?' said Diane.

Willy gave this question serious thought before answering.

'The truthful answer, according to my observation, would be yes. But if you believe the rumours in and around the village, some of them are also gangsters.'

'Gangsters?' said Diane.

'Gangsters, yes. Though, to be sure, that might come to the same thing as businessmen, according to where your loyalties and convictions lie in these matters.' He turned to go into his cottage, hesitated, then asked them: 'Would you be staying at the motel?'

'Yes,' said Oliver. 'But we're not likely to use our dry-ski slope tokens. Would you like them?'

'Thank you, no, but if you decide to eat in the restaurant this evening, I can whole-heartedly recommend the pheasant.'

14

A Friend of a Friend

The motel offered two choices of eating: the Bonny Prince Charlie coffee-shop or a theme restaurant called Flora Macdonald's, with uniforms and décor to match. Oliver and Diane agreed it looked more like a tribute to Jeanette MacDonald, but it was the obvious place to find Willy's pheasant.

'Keep your head down,' said Oliver, 'Nelson Eddy might come galloping in any minute.'

'Even worse, he could be singing,' said Diane.

They spent ten minutes explaining to Michael what they were talking about, and were into the second chorus of the famous duet when a young woman arrived at their table.

'Good evening, my name's Moira and I shall be your waitress this evening.'

'I'd guessed you weren't a gynaecologist,' said Diane, growing weary of heritage in general and themes in particular, especially children who were otherwise innocent dressed up like clowns and talking like idiots. They were probably paid in bags of toffees and colouring books.

'Will you stop saying embarrassing things,' said Michael, who was strictly on the side of the staff. He had been dressed like a clown by Cosmos Security PLC and the humiliation still lingered.

'I doubt it,' said Diane.

Moira stood, unmoved and unconcerned, until the generational spat was over, then announced:

'I'd like to tell you about the Flora Macdonald special for this evening, which is locally born and bred free-range pheasant.'

'Poached?' said Michael.

'No. I believe they roast it in the oven.'

'I think we'd all like the pheasant, wouldn't we?' said Oliver, looking at the others, who nodded their approval. 'It's a friend of a friend.'

'And we'd also like three wee drams,' said Diane.

Wee drams, they had all three decided, were the acceptable face of Scottish heritage – maybe the only one, apart from Willy the Poacher.

'Your wine waiter for the evening is called Peter and he'll be here to take your order directly.' Moira collected the huge tartan menus and headed for the kitchen, like a Glaswegian galleon under full sail. The Muzak played Harry Lauder's greatest hits, recycled by the James Last Orchestra. There was ambience all around and a pseudo-Celtic numbness pained Oliver's senses.

'If I eat all my pheasant and leave a clean plate, please may we leave here and go to the Orkneys tomorrow?'

'Of course,' said Diane. 'Why not?'

'I've been trying to go to the Orkneys for some considerable time, and I keep stumbling over unsolved murders and falling in love, as indeed you know.'

'Yes. I know.'

'The Orkneys. That's north from here, isn't it?' said Michael.

'Approximately,' said Oliver. He demonstrated the geography of the situation with the salt and pepper pots. These were in the shape of toy soldiers with holes in their heads, dressed in the uniforms of famous old Scottish regiments.

'We are the salt, here, represented by the King's Own Scottish Borderers. The Orkneys are the pepper, here, represented by the Seaforth Highlanders. The one is due north of the other, as you can see.'

'Can you drop me in Aberdeen on the way?'

'Aberdeen is miles away,' said Diane.

'Is it?'

She took the mustard pot, a soldier of the Black Watch with a lid instead of a hole. She placed it on the edge of the table, well away from the salt and pepper.

'You see? Aberdeen. On the east coast.'

'That's west,' said Oliver and moved the mustard to the opposite side of the table.

'I always have trouble with east and west,' said Diane.

'Either way, it's the same message, right? It's miles out of your way, and it's a nuisance.'

'A little,' said Oliver.

'A lot,' said Diane.

'Well, drop me somewhere handy and I'll hitch a lift.'

'Why do you want to go to Aberdeen?' said Diane.

'To see George Burns.'

'Your little computer friend? I thought he was in prison.'

'He'll be out by now.'

'I hate to sound like a concerned mother and policeperson but why do you want to see George Burns? He's a convicted criminal.'

'I told you. I found this really amazing stuff, upstairs at the big house, in the Red Baron's den.'

'What sort of amazing stuff?'

He dipped into the back pocket of his jeans and brought out a notebook. He opened it and said:

'I'm not an expert but I think it's all their computer codes.'

'You stole this?' said Oliver, browsing through the book, which contained handwritten lists of totally incomprehensible names and numbers.

'Obviously.'

'That's theft, isn't it?'

'Technically, I suppose. I couldn't think of any other way of getting it.'

Oliver returned the book. He was a lifelong specialist in the cryptic but this material was beyond his ken and it was welcome to stay there. He found computer languages hostile, graceless and devoid of jokes.

The young had no such fear.

'Give George twenty minutes hacking time, he'll solve the whole thing.'

'Michael, these are heavy-duty villains,' said Diane. 'They have people killed.'

Unconcerned, Michael stuck the book in his back pocket.

'And I wish you wouldn't keep things in that pocket. You're bound to lose them.'

'I never lost anything yet from that pocket.'

It was true. Since Michael first started wearing jeans, he had always stuffed his intimate personal possessions in the back pocket. From day one Diane had advised against it sensibly, tediously and maternally. And he had never lost a thing, damn him. She had even contemplated snitching his wallet to teach him a lesson, but even she could see the pathetic hypocrisy of such a measure.

'I know,' she said. 'Sorry to go on.'

'I think it would be very sensible of me to leave you and go to Aberdeen,' said Michael. 'George will crack the system and solve the mystery. And anyway, you two want rid of me, don't you?'

'Rid of you?' said Diane. 'No. Yes. Possibly.'

O God, she thought, my son is so mature and grown-up. Where did I go wrong?

Oliver, who had sat quietly during the jeans discussion, with nothing useful to contribute, intervened:

'Michael did place it on record that he considers me a bit naff. Indeed, I thought he made out a very good case for the proposition.'

Michael immediately shook his head.

'No. I was wrong about that. I thought you were a bit naff at first. But you're not. You're really good news. But Mum's turning a bit naff. I think that's probably down to you. But you're all right. You're cool.'

'In what way am I turning a bit naff?' said Diane.

'Saying embarrassing things in public, mostly.'

'I don't say embarrassing things in public.'

The family row was already galloping to first base when the young man approached the table and said:

'Good evening. My name's Peter and I shall be your wine waiter this evening.'

'I'd guessed you weren't a gynaecologist,' said Michael, quickly.

'Correct. I failed the oral.'

Diane glared, first at Peter, then at Michael.

'That settles it,' she said. 'First thing tomorrow. Aberdeen.'

Game, set and match to the younger generation, but it was a mother's privilege to be a bad loser.

While Oliver was in the bathroom brushing his teeth, Diane lay in bed with the road-map, brushing up on her east and west. It was easier if she held the map upside down. She picked up their complimentary Bonny Wee Dram ball-point pen and drew a ring around a point where the A9 met the A95 south of Inverness. Geographically it seemed a good place to drop Michael. They would wait until he got his lift before driving north; truck and trucker would need to be vetted.

Oliver took ages to clean his teeth. When he eventually emerged she said:

'What have you been doing?'

'Cleaning my teeth.'

'You were a long time. How many teeth have you got?'

'I was doing something else as well.'

'You should be ashamed of yourself.'

He climbed into bed.

'I have a deeply intimate secret.'

'We don't have deeply intimate secrets. Predestination means no deeply intimate secrets.'

'My secret is I keep a secret diary.'

'What's in it?'

He looked at her over his glasses. She answered her own question.

'Secrets? Deeply intimate?' He nodded. 'As in socks?'

'Yes. As in socks.'

'Any other secrets?'

'Only one. But that's a secret.'

Then they embraced and Oliver said: 'Though we cannot make our Sun.

'Stand still, yet we will make him run.'

'Huh?'

'It's a quotation. From the greatest love poem in the English language. Andrew Marvell's "To his Coy Mistress".'

'Me? Coy? Is *that* coy?' She performed a subtly erotic miracle with his pyjama cord.

'Hardly at all,' said Oliver.

Under her influence, he went into a free-form improvisation on the erotic possibilities of theme motels. The D. H. Lawrence Motel where you could ring room service for a daisy-chain; the To Have and Have Not Motel where the management organized whistling workshops; the John Donne Motel where on arrival you were given a licence for your roving hands; the Carry On Motel where you could send out for a younger man and a set of jump-leads.

He was like John Coltrane on Newcastle Brown Ale. Diane, even in mid-erotica, wondered what sort of stuff was going into the deeply intimate secret diary. But she knew a secret, too. It was bad manners to talk with your mouth full. She knew a hundred ways guaranteed to stop him talking, especially now they had overcome their initial shyness.

She stopped him talking. Then they shared the greatest secret on the stall and soon, in his single room next door, Michael turned up the volume on CNN.

It was an empty fish lorry. You could tell by the smell. The word 'Aberdeen' was written on the side beneath the name of a family firm, 'SHEARER AND SONS', and no sign of the dread initials PLC. The driver, as far as they could discern through an accent thicker than the walls of Durham Cathedral, was of sound mind and noble intentions. The vehicle's brakes appeared to be well maintained. And Michael seemed happy and relaxed, smiling down at them from the cab.

'See you, guys. Mind how you go.'

'Take care,' said Diane.

'Stay cool,' said Oliver.

The driver shouted something cheerful and incoherent, then the lorry drove off towards Aberdeen. Diane watched until it was out of sight. It was like seeing your child go to school for the first time. You worried whether he would be able to manage without you, and, even more, that he almost certainly would. Then the guilt galloped up like a wolf on the fold. She was sad that he was leaving them; and, simultaneously, she was thrilled to bits.

'Alone at last,' she said to Oliver.

'Thank you for reminding me.'

'What?'

He handed her the keys and climbed into the car without replying. She was driving so he could concentrate on the *Observer* crossword. Apparently Aristotle always set a few special traps on a Sunday and these would require Oliver's total concentration.

She drove north, through Carrbridge, Moybeg and Daviot, and past a road sign to Cawdor.

'Where the thanes come from,' said Oliver, without looking up from his newspaper.

'What?'

They wound their way around the Cromarty Firth and then along the coast by way of Invergordon towards the Dornoch Firth, and Diane said:

'I thought we'd be playing a game.'

'What sort of game?'

'Famous Orkney persons? Orkneyians?'

'Orcadians.'

'Orcadians.'

'I only know four famous Orcadians so it might be quite a short game.'

'I don't know any. Unless I've been wrong all these years about Sophie Tucker.'

Oliver threw his newspaper into the back of the car. He hadn't finished the crossword but he knew the line of Aristotle's thinking for the sabbath, and was confident that if he followed it he would find his way to the depot.

'The four famous Orcadians I know are the Old Man of Hoy, who's made out of stone, Magnus the Martyr, Margaret the Martyr . . .'

'They're a bit heavy on martyrs. Are the islands safe?'

'And the great George Mackay Brown.'

'George Mackay Brown?'

'Storyteller and poet. He writes like an angel. It was by reading his books that I found out about the other three.'

There was rain in the air and beyond Dornoch, where the road hugged tight to the coast, by Golspie and Brora, they drove beneath the two rainbows. According to their naked eyes, the rainbows were a hundred yards apart, each one spanning the road, springing out of the dark hills high to the left, soaring overhead, then diving in a great arc down into the sea on the right.

'Look,' she said. 'Rainbows.'

'Lawrence's.'

'And Finian's.'

'Both.'

'No. Ours.'

Every rainbow Diane had ever seen disappeared when you came closer, but these were made of sterner stuff. She drove beneath them and then, checking in her rear-view mirror, saw they were still there, behind the car and shining bright.

'Was that magic?' she said.

'Wherever we are is magic.'

'Yuck. Yuck. Vomit. Vomit.'

'That's the game. It's called Alone at Last. You reminded me about it earlier.'

'Alone at Last? How do you play? Will you have to change your socks?'

'It's a talking game. You have to talk as if you're in a soap opera.'

'What's the point of the game?'

'It doesn't have one.'

'I see. Like cricket.'

'And if you can't think of anything to say, you say: what's that supposed to mean?'

Diane was totally baffled. The game seemed totally devoid of all meaning and purpose; but since meeting Oliver and especially here, somewhere beyond the rainbows, all things were possible and perhaps even compulsory.

'You'd better start,' she said.

'Right.' Oliver took a deep breath, whistled a few bars of music combining the worst bits of the themes from *Brookside* and *Neighbours*, then said: 'Alone at last. Wherever we are is magic. But darling, we have to talk.'

Diane hesitated, then, playing for time, said:

'What's that supposed to mean?'

'You know what it means. The first time I saw you, I knew.'

'You mean,' she said, getting the idea, 'when I walked into the room?'

'When you walked into the room, I saw you and I saw myself clearly for the first time. I saw what I had become. A man running away.'

'I sometimes think we're all running away in this God-forsaken world.'

'But what have we been running away from?'

'I guess what we've been running away from is . . . ourselves.'

'I guess so,' said Oliver.

The ball was in her court, but she was on top of the game now and played the classic return shot.

'And I guess this is when the running has to stop.'

'What's that supposed to mean?'

'You know what it means.' She glanced across at him. He was smiling. She smiled back. He tried to sing the theme music from *Dallas*. She tried to sing the theme music from *Dynasty*. They failed, simultaneously, making a joyful noise and a terrible sound.

Diane almost forgot to make the left turn at Helmsdale. It was Oliver's idea that they should travel by the narrow road through the Strath of Kildonan and Strath Halladale, overland to the North coast and eventually to the ferry terminal at Scrabster. The names along the way promised Celtic mystery: Kinbrace, Forsinard, Dalhalvaig.

The road was narrow, flanked on either side by bleak

moorland. It was the sort of road where witches were advised to walk in threes. A fine rain was falling as if it had done so since the beginning of recorded time. There were no rainbows.

On such a day as this, it was a cheerless and forbidding landscape. Totally unspoilt, it said in the guidebook. Spoil it, somebody, thought Diane: taint it with a Little Chef or Happy Eater; if this is the promised land, God should be sued for false pretences. She needed cheering up.

'Can we play another game?' she said.

'American cops and robbers?'

'All right. You start.'

Oliver slipped into a strange mid-Atlantic accent: a Yorkshire-born Al Pacino with overtones of Brando in the days when he could have been a contender, battle-scarred and weary from the Hill Street war zone in the 87th Precinct of Sheffield.

'Say, lady,' he said, 'when you picked me up way back there, I never took you for a law enforcement officer.'

'It's my job. It's what I do,' said Diane, trying to sound like Cagney or Lacey – one of the two. She always mixed them up.

'Sure. I get the picture. You hang out on the mean streets.'

'Yeah. The way I figure it, this world is full of crap. I'm the crazy kid with the bucket and spade, figuring I can clean the place up. I figure you gotta be crazy to believe that.'

Oliver turned, gazed at her, dazzled by her performance. She was brilliant at games. She was brilliant in bed. She was brilliant. What a woman! She deserved Humphrey Bogart. He snarled with charm:

'You win a hill of beans, you lose a hill of beans? Right?'

'We're being followed,' she said.

'That's the way it goes, kid. You're the crazy guy with the bucket and spade, some crazy son of a bitch is gonna follow you.'

'I mean it!' she yelled. She had to raise her voice above the sound of the helicopter as it roared over the top of the car, missing it, seemingly, by inches. It raced on ahead of them.

'Scotland is full of helicopters,' said Oliver, playing the rational man. 'They take supplies out to the oil rigs.'

'We are not an oil rig. We do not need supplies. He is not bringing supplies.' She was a policeperson and she knew about helicopters. They operated under strict rules. They were obliged to carry clear identification markings. This one carried none. It was painted in battleship grey, it was totally anonymous and she figured it was trying to kill them, right?

Right.

It hovered above the road half a mile ahead of them, then turned and flew towards the car, head to head.

'I think you're right,' said Oliver. 'He is not bringing supplies.'

When the helicopter and car were a hundred yards apart, Diane accelerated, swerved almost at right angles and pulled up on to the grass verge. She had seen the man sitting beside the helicopter pilot. He had a machine-gun.

The bullets spattered along the surface of the road where they had been, seconds earlier, as the car bumped to a halt.

Diane opened the car door.

'Come on!' she said, and ran.

Oliver opened his door as he saw her running, fast, towards an abandoned crofter's cottage twenty yards from the road. He followed her. They crouched down in its shelter.

'This is ludicrous,' he said.

'Are you all right?'

'No. I'm cross.'

'Cross is better than dead.'

'I've seen all this before. *North by Northwest*. Alfred Hitchcock. 1959.'

The cottage walls were intact, as was part of the old slate roof, enough to conceal them from the air as the helicopter hovered. They crouched low as it circled and zoomed back along the road. This time the bullets sliced across the car, shattering the windows and scoring the tyres.

'It was an aeroplane in *North by Northwest*,' said Diane.

'In 1959 helicopter technology was still in its infancy.'

He peered out of the doorway.

'Don't go out,' she said.

'I think they've gone into the next street.'

They listened hard. It was quiet, apart from the unending
noise of moorland wind and rain, and the occasional cries of
unseen birds and beasts, the hunters and the hunted. Nature was
suddenly very comforting.

'Right,' said Oliver.

'What are you doing?'

'I'm going to check the car.'

They looked at it. The tyres were flattened, the windows shattered.

'What is there to check?' said Diane. 'It's shot at.'

'As it were.'

Again they fell silent. They listened. Nothing.

'I need my newspaper,' said Oliver, taking a few wary paces
towards the car. 'I haven't finished the crossword.'

She knew it was pointless to argue with Oliver *and* Aristotle.

'In that case, you might as well collect the luggage while it's
still in three pieces.'

She watched, keeping a lookout in all directions as he hurried
to the car and rescued his newspaper from the back seat. Then he
opened the boot and took out the luggage: the matching suitcases, her holdall and the little square black box that seemed to
go with him everywhere.

'Hurry,' she said.

It was quiet but it felt more like a lull than a cease-fire.

'I am hurrying.'

She met him half-way to help him.

'What's in the black box?' she said.

'My other secret.'

'I have ways of making you talk.'

'Not out here. It's too cold.'

They had almost reached the shelter of the cottage and the
comfort of their playfulness when the roar came. This time the
helicopter approached from the side, across the valley.

They dived headlong into the cottage, throwing themselves
face-down. They never knew what caused the explosion. It might
have been a bullet hitting the petrol tank. It might have been an
air-to-ground missile of the sort international arms dealers give

away as special offers at trade shows. It might have been spontaneous combustion.

They heard the explosion and the noise of the helicopter flying off into the distance. They stood up cautiously, counted their limbs, discovered two full sets, all intact. Then they turned to look at the car. For all practical purposes, there was no longer a car, only a pillar of flames and smoke. It was extinct: as deceased as Python's parrot.

'Will I lose my no-claims bonus?' said Oliver.

'You need his registration number and the name of his insurance company,' said Diane, and then she began to shake.

He put his arms around her.

'I'm sorry,' she said, 'I may be a law enforcement officer but I'm . . .'

'Shit scared?'

'Yes.'

'Me too. I only joke when I'm frightened and, as you must have noticed, I joke almost all the time.'

'I noticed.'

They huddled close, wrapped up in each other, sharing what they knew to be a false sense of security; but it was the only sort available.

'On the other hand,' said Oliver, 'had I been destined to die this afternoon, it would have been a very good time to go.'

She had never seen him so serious. She needed a little lightness and said, with an earnest attempt at a smile:

'What's that supposed to mean?'

'It means I would have died at a time of maximum contentment. I am very happy being with you. That is what that is supposed to mean. If you see what I mean.'

'I see what that is supposed to mean.' She kissed him gently, twice on each cheek, and said: 'Thank you.'

The lorry driver was an honourable man. Once he had learned to understand Michael's English, he had done a minor, uncomplaining detour and dropped Michael at the end of the street where George Burns lived.

It was Michael's first time in Aberdeen but he had been here before. The street was part of a familiar pattern: elegant town houses built in the nineteenth century for prosperous merchant adventurers, their families and servants. They were now chopped up into bits and pieces of flats and bedsitters, ideal for the upper crust of the urban poor, those few, those happy few, with a few bob in their pocket to rent a temporary roof: the disinherited, disenchanted and disenfranchised; people on the run from parents, partners and tax collectors: clowns, balladeers and strolling players; poets and peasants: nomadic dreamers of dreams, dreamers of nightmares, looking for care in the community: hustlers, pedlars and vagabonds; paid-up members of the lesser lunacy and lower banditry.

And, of course, students. Michael was at home here. He was on his own turf.

He scanned a bank of bells with names beside them. Most of the names seemed false: Mary Poppins sharing a flat with Charlie Parker? In Aberdeen? The bells looked like they hadn't rung since Victoria's coronation. But there, half-way down the list, was the name 'BURNS'.

He pushed the bell and pressed his ear to the door. He heard an upstairs door open, a burst of music, footsteps on the staircase.

A girl of about his age opened the front door. She had dark hair, cropped sensibly short, wore jeans with a faded T-shirt designed to save the blue whale from extinction. She had the slim build of an athlete and a pre-Raphaelite face: the Christina Rossetti of the four hundred metres hurdles.

'Hi.'

'Hi. I'm looking for George Burns.'

'Who are you from?' she said, a little nervously.

'I'm not from anybody. I'm just me. My name's Michael. I was at university with George.'

'You're Michael?'

'Yes.'

She relaxed.

'That's great. He talks about you a lot. I'm Cathy.'

'Is he around?'

'He's inside.'

'Can I come in?'

'Not inside. Inside.'

'I thought he'd be out by now.'

'He was out. Now he's in again.'

'That's tough.'

'You'd better come in.'

'Thanks.'

The bedsitter had been inhabited by a succession of students and was a messy history of good causes bravely fought and generally lost, from the Peterloo Massacre to the Miners' Strike. It was the sort of room that looks like it's been burgled when it hasn't. The floor was knee-deep in empty beer cans, last year's newspapers, forgotten garments and old regrets. It needed cleaning but the archaeologists would have to move in first.

The walls were a shrine to the flexible iconography of the young: Will Hay, Lenin, Toni Morrison, Harrison Ford, the Blues Brothers, the Beverley Sisters.

'The Beverley Sisters?' said Michael.

Cathy explained that she and two friends had briefly formed an a cappella group who wore their oldest clothes to sing the Beverleys' greatest hits. The group was called Kitsch in Sync. It had folded after one gig.

They sat on leaking floor cushions and drank instant black coffee from chipped glass tankards, nicked from the pub on the corner.

'What's George gone down for this time?' said Michael.

'Income tax rebates.'

'Income tax rebates?'

'He had a word with the Inland Revenue computer, organized one or two payments into his account.'

'He's never paid tax in his life. He's never had a job. How could he claim tax rebates?'

'That was the prosecution case.'

'The swine.'

'George's defence was why shouldn't he have his rebates now? He'd pay the tax later. He said he was planning to become a millionaire executive computer consultant.'

'Did they believe him?'

Cathy shook her head.

'Hardly at all. He got six months.'

'Heigh-ho.'

They sipped their coffee in silence, brooding on the grotesque injustice of justice.

'It's a pity,' said Michael. 'I had a job for him.'

'Hacking?'

'Yes.'

'Who are you trying to stitch up?'

'It's a multinational business conglomerate, run by some sort of Baron-type guy.'

'I can do that.'

'Can you?'

'Piece of piss. George wouldn't leave me to look after his flat if I couldn't feed the cat and handle the information technology, would he?'

She added, by way of evidence: 'I was talking to NATO head-quarters last night.'

'What did you say to them?'

'Told them to launch a missile attack on Westminster.'

'Did they do it? I haven't heard any news today.'

'No. They thought I was joking.'

They agreed it was a bad outlook for the Western World if NATO couldn't be relied upon to carry out a simple order. What price national security?

Cathy made some more coffee, apologized she was out of milk and sugar, and then they watched a video of *The Commitments*.

A deep depression had settled over Oliver and Diane. The scattered showers were now persistent, and aimed directly at them with a venom that seemed personal. The wind had freshened and was contemplating a career move up to gale force. Diane opened one of the matching suitcases and unpacked their scarves, pullovers and big coats. She had taken over responsibility for packing and unpacking. They put on the additional layers of clothing but they were still cold, wet and, in Diane's case, miserable. The remains of the cottage gave little shelter. No wonder the crofters had moved out.

Diane looked up and down the road. There was no sign of life, no promise of life later in the day or even in the hereafter.

'I'm trying to remember the name of the man who said: "Let's take the B road, it'll be more interesting."'

'You have to admit, it wasn't dull,' said Oliver.

'I spy with my little eye, something beginning with SA.'

'Scottish ambience?'

'Sod all.' She looked up and over her shoulder. 'And I still expect that thing to come back any minute.'

'When you feel you're in danger, do you know the safest place to be?'

'Tell me.'

'In a crowd.' Oliver was trying to be cheerful, supportive and loving: he struck Diane as avuncular, patronizing and stupid.

'So all we need is a crowd.' She looked up and down the road and said: 'We're more likely to meet King Lear.'

'Don't despair. That's the real enemy. Despair.'

She exploded at him.

'Stop talking like a Christmas cracker! I'm sick of it!'

Oliver smiled beatifically.

'Oh ye of little faith.'

'You're doing it again!'

'Look.' He pointed along the road. A single-decker country bus was trundling towards them at a steady and secure twenty miles an hour.

'It's very odd,' he said. 'The sequence in *North by Northwest* begins with a bus.'

'So there's a bus,' said Diane, unimpressed. 'Terrific. Show me the nearest bus-stop.'

Oliver had already picked up the matching suitcases and the little black box and was running to the road, keeping well clear of the smouldering wreck of the car. Diane collected her holdall and followed him.

He held out his hand. It was a well-known fact that buses stopped by request. It was written on bus-stops the length and breadth of the land. The bus stopped. The destination board read: 'SPECIAL'. The windows were covered in stickers reading 'GOD IS LOVE'.

The automatic door opened. Oliver held out his hand to help Diane climb into the bus, saying: 'What a friend we have in Jesus.'

15

A Sermon on the Mount

Mrs McCall stood just inside the door of the bus, alongside the driver. She was in charge of the bus and was fully prepared to accept responsibility for the sabbath and the rest of Christendom, too. If, after her threescore years and ten, the good earth was going to hell, it wasn't her fault. Her bus always travelled along the paths of righteousness.

She was a gentle woman, with cheeks she hadn't even turned yet. She believed in strength through peace, and talked with the polite precision of the Gaelic races. If you were looking after someone else's language, you were obliged to take proper care of it, were you not?

'This isn't a regular service bus, I'm afraid. There will, therefore, be no charge, but I fear our destinations may not coincide.'

'What time is the next service bus?' said Diane.

'Thursday, I believe.'

'Could you possibly give us a lift?' said Oliver. 'We seem to have fallen by the wayside. On stony ground.'

'We're only travelling as far as the kirk.'

'That's the church,' said Oliver to Diane.

'I know what a kirk is.'

'And as you can see, it's standing room only.' Mrs McCall

directed their attention to the assembly of God-fearing passengers. Most of them were gentle women, dressed in black and of an age with Mrs McCall. They could all have been her sisters, with the odd stray brother thrown in – which, spiritually speaking, was near enough the truth.

'My word,' said Oliver. 'Your bus runneth over.'

'Quite so.'

'Security in a crowd,' said Oliver to Diane, before turning to Mrs McCall: 'We would be honoured to come to your kirk. We have travelled many miles for that very purpose.'

Mrs McCall's eyes lit up.

'Would you be our visiting preacher, by any chance?'

'If necessary,' said Oliver.

'God bless you, my son,' said Mrs McCall.

God help us, thought Diane, before thinking: sorry, sisters and brothers, perhaps I should rephrase that, no offence meant.

Mrs McCall glanced at the driver; her glance had the power of a commandment. He closed the automatic door by hauling on a piece of string, then shifted into first gear and set off. He was very loyal to first gear and rarely, if ever, left it: he thought acceleration was aggressive and pagan.

It was natural that he should react with pained disapproval as a police car, blue light flashing and siren blaring, raced past them in the opposite direction. Diane watched through a space between the slogans in the rear window of the bus as the police car pulled up beside the wreckage of Oliver's car. Two eager young coppers jumped out. It was probably the first major incident of their career, excluding sheep-stealing in bulk, and they were excited to be first on the scene with the pretty coloured tape. They had got it and, sabbath or no sabbath, they were going to flaunt it.

They already had the area taped off as the bus trundled around a slow, heathery bend and the site of their trauma was lost from Diane's view. She was pleased to be rid of it.

'Where did you get this?' said Cathy.

'I nicked it from head office,' said Michael.

She had the Farquhar Group's code-book open on the draining board, beside the computer. The kitchen was the nerve centre of the absentee George Burns's well-intentioned but reckless activities among the institutional giants of the age.

George's kitchen was in good hands. Michael stared in awe and wonder at the entanglement of wires leading from the computer, all plugged, eventually, into various mystic sockets. It looked majestically illegal. The VDU glowed with the promise of rich pickings. Cathy's fingers danced across the keyboard with the careless audacity of an Art Tatum.

'Makes it dead easy, having this book.'

Names and numbers scrolled across the screen.

'These are seriously weird people,' said Cathy. 'Filthy foreigners even.'

'Well, according to Willy the Poacher, our mole, there are American and German and Japanese and Italian and maybe Russian gangsters and . . .' He hoped to impress her, but she was swallowed up in the world revealed on screen: it was the biggest game in town.

'What about the Vatican?'

'Nobody's mentioned the Vatican so far.'

'I keep coming up with the word Priest.'

She highlighted the words for him on the screen: PRIEST. S & D.

'S & D?' said Michael.

'Sid and Doris?' Cathy suggested.

'Hang on,' said Michael. 'That's my mum's name. Priest. My name as well, now I come to think.'

'Where is your mum?'

'Somewhere between here and the Orkneys.'

'Is she involved in all this crap?'

'I think she started it.'

'Can you get in touch with her?'

'No. She's on the road with her bloke. I gave her this number. Is your phone working?'

'It's disconnected.'

'That figures.'

'But it's still working, if you see what I mean. We've privatized it.'

'So what's the problem?' He could tell something was wrong. Cathy stared at the screen, her fingers momentarily in neutral.

'S & D. These people generally use it as computer shorthand for Search and Destroy.'

'They can't search and destroy my mum!' said Michael, horrified. 'Can they?'

Cathy stayed calm.

'They probably can. But take it easy. I can stop them. All we have to do is find the magic button marked: Abort.'

Her fingers skipped into overdrive. Michael watched, his admiration now tempered with anxiety and rage. Nobody had the right to search and destroy his mum. She had paid her dues and found Oliver along with something that looked to him very much like true happiness, even if they were a bit daft and sometimes noisy with it. Anybody who was out to search and destroy that would be answerable to him. He wasn't above a little freelance searching and destruction on his own account, if provoked. He wasn't sure how to do it but he had a tongue in his head. He could ask Cathy about the searching and Psycho about the destruction. They would know; what's more, they would enjoy it.

The bus chugged and slithered its way up a mountainous cart track running along the edge of a barren field. At times it went so slowly Oliver thought it might speed things up if the driver changed into reverse.

Diane bumped against him and whispered:

'Are you serious?'

'Except when I'm frightened.'

'About preaching the sermon I mean?'

He kept his voice down, aware that his congregation was already taking a keen but polite interest in the new preacher found wandering in the wilderness.

'I taught comparative religion for several centuries.'

'Did you teach their kind of religion?'

'I'm prepared to gamble that we're travelling with the pacifist wing of primitive Methodism. I can handle that.'

He was reminded of the scene in *The Third Man* where Joseph Cotten had to give a public lecture to protect himself from the heavy mob. He had also been brooding about Robert Donat and Madeleine Carroll in *The Thirty-Nine Steps*, pursued across the Highlands, while handcuffed, and finding sanctuary of a kind in a croft run by a belligerent John Laurie and a kindly Peggy Ashcroft. Perhaps the very same cottage where they had found shelter from the helicopter? Except that Hitchcock generally worked in the studio. Wise man, if the weather was always like this.

Oliver decided not to share these doodling thoughts with Diane; it wasn't the time for a discussion about life's tendency to imitate art and get it all slightly wrong. Instead, he simply placed a reassuring hand on her arm and said:

'Put your trust in me, sister.'

'Amen.'

'Bingo!' said Cathy.

'You've stopped them?'

'Not only have I aborted their Search and Destroy programme, I calculate their entire empire is now knee-deep in noxious substances. Plus a few rude words.'

'You're brilliant,' said Michael, passing her a can of lager. This had been his contribution to the work in hand: a trip to the off-licence for a six-pack and some Bennies. She took a swig from the can and said:

'I didn't get my Ph.D. for being a stand-up comedian.'

'You've got a Ph.D.?'

'Sure. Hasn't everybody?'

'Job prospects?'

'I made the short list at the car wash but they said I was overqualified.'

The 13th Baron Kite sat in his den. He was not happy. His computer screen had gone crazy. Instead of a cogent and comprehensive account of his business affairs, he was staring at one word, reaching out to infinity, vertically and horizontally:

BOLLOX BOLLOX BOLLOX BOLLOX BOLLOX BOLLOX
BOLLOX BOLLOX BOLLOX BOLLOX BOLLOX BOLLOX
BOLLOX BOLLOX BOLLOX BOLLOX BOLLOX BOLLOX
BOLLOX BOLLOX BOLLOX BOLLOX BOLLOX BOLLOX

It was like reading a huge roller towel designed by a pimpled adolescent.

He had called Mandy at the computer helpline. She had promised to solve his problem as soon as she managed to stop giggling. He had hung up angrily and was now on the phone to his head of security.

'It's just rows of bollox, in every direction, as far as the eye can see.'

'Relax,' said Baxter. 'It's when you get the red mist you really start to worry. Call the computer helpline.' Baxter switched off his mobile. There was nothing in his job description about computers and he had problems of his own, though he was coping with them phlegmatically. He was in his car on a tiny B road in the Highlands, caught up in what, by local standards, was a major traffic jam. The police had cordoned off the road ahead.

He was third in a line of six vehicles: immediately ahead of him was a holiday caravan bearing a family who had agreed it would be a fine adventure to explore the Highlands out of season; in front of the caravan was an old and fragile Ford Cortina – it looked like the original prototype.

Baxter got out of his car and strolled to the front of the queue. The man in the Cortina was complaining to the young policeman on duty with the frustration of the righteous.

'I'm a lay preacher. I'm due to deliver a sermon in five minutes time.'

'I'm sure heaven will wait, sir.'

'God is a person of infinite mercy and patience,' added Baxter supportively as he looked at the scene beyond the taped barrier: the burnt-out wreck of the car, the leisurely men in plain clothes taking measurements and photographs, the breakdown truck waiting patiently to clear up the mess. It was a big deal for the emergency services. They were going to make it last.

'Anybody hurt?' Baxter asked the policeman, who was keen to help a member of the public, especially one who had come to his aid when dealing with a recalcitrant preacher.

'Apparently not. No casualties. No sign of anyone.'

'Good.' Baxter returned to his car, pausing by the Cortina to say to the lay preacher: 'You see? Nobody was hurt. You may add infinite mercy to God's qualities.'

'But I shouldn't be here at all.'

'If we are ordained to be here, then that must be part of his purpose,' said Baxter, reflecting to himself that you could say the same about the infinite bollox on the Baron's computer system.

He returned to his car and switched on Radio 3.

The little stone chapel stood high on a hill. There was no human habitation for miles around. The building was at least two hundred years old. Oliver decided it must have been built by people who needed to keep their convictions well out of sight of the judges and militia. It was a strong point in their favour.

Inside, there were half a dozen rows of pews, packed with the faithful, and a simple altar. Mrs McCall played the harmonium as the congregation sang a fine old Nonconformist hymn called 'Sound, Sound Your Instruments of Joy'.

Oliver recognized it. He had it at home on a record by the Watersons, a Yorkshire folk group. The hymn had fallen out of *Hymns Ancient and Modern* in the middle of the nineteenth century, probably because it made a joyful noise and might have done permanent damage to Victorian values. But these worshippers were made of sterner stuff; they were wide awake and singing with their mouths open.

They finished with a grand 'Amen', then fell silent. Mrs McCall looked at Oliver. It was his moment. He stood up and crossed to the small wooden lectern. Then, speaking without notes, he opened his mouth and taught them, saying:

'First, may I thank you for the warmth of your welcome and the shelter of your temple. We were strangers and you took us in.'

He nodded to Diane, who half-turned and smiled nicely at the people.

'I would like to take as my theme two well-known texts. The first is: "Thou shalt not kill." The second is: "What's that supposed to mean?"'

Mrs McCall raised an eyebrow.

' "Thou shalt not kill" is, of course, the popular variation of the Sixth Commandment which actually says, according to the *Book of Common Prayer*, "Thou shalt do no murder." But "Thou shalt not kill", is good enough for me.'

Mrs McCall lowered the eyebrow.

' "What's that supposed to mean?" is a text from a television soap opera. Any old television soap opera. Any night of the week. It is a trite and lazy line, indicating the writer couldn't think of anything more interesting for the character to say at that moment. But it is a very good question.

'Put our two questions together and what do we have. "Thou shalt not kill. What's that supposed to mean?" I've been thinking about this question a great deal for the last couple of hours because a couple of hours ago somebody tried to kill us.'

Mrs McCall raised both eyebrows.

Diane peered round at the congregation. There was no way of telling whether this was what they wanted to hear, but as sure as the morning after followed the night before they were listening.

Oliver raised his hands, as if to reassure them that he was alive and well and free of stigmata.

'They failed to kill us, as you can see, but as a wise man once pointed out, it does focus the mind something remarkable. You ask questions like: who are these people? Answer: no idea. Never met them in my life. Why are they doing it? Answer: because they're carrying out orders. Is that a good enough reason? Answer: no, it's the oldest excuse in the history of mass murder. Who is responsible and who should bear the guilt? Well, as an even wiser man once pointed out, that *is* the question.

'The easy answer is that the true responsibility rests with the man who gives the order to fire. Alas, and I speak as a male of the species, it is usually a man, though not always. But who is this man? Does he have a name? Our world is full of men without names. I could even tell you a story about a box with no name but that might confuse you. It certainly confuses me. Let me tell you instead about my pension fund.'

This time it was Diane who raised her eyebrows. Pension fund? She didn't know he had a pension fund. They had never talked about it. It wasn't important. Frankly, my dear, she didn't give a damn. So what was it doing in the middle of a sermon? She found out.

'Recently, though it seems much longer, I was made redundant. I am one of the mighty army of the dispossessed and displaced. Perhaps some of you are, too. But I have a pension and once a year the company writes me a letter to let me know that my money is safely invested for my old age. In the letter there is a list of companies where the pension money, including my few pence, is invested.'

What *is* my man going on about? thought Diane.

'One of those companies where my pennies reside is part of a company that is operated by the men who, I believe, gave the orders for today's attempt on our lives. Those orders were issued in the interests of the company. I ask you to think about that. Think hard.'

Diane thought about it. She thought hard. What *was* he going to say next? If he mentioned socks, there'd be tears before bedtime – also during and after.

'It means that the company with no name has decided that my investment is best protected by having me murdered. It is in my own interest that I should be killed. It's for my own good. Naturally, I do not agree with this point of view. And you may decide: none of this makes sense anyway.

'True. It does not make sense. But then, I have never expected the world to make sense. I suppose that is why we have religions and I certainly wish you comfort and joy in yours. For my own part I find comfort in the love of a good woman, and joy in music and in old jokes. My favourite joke is about frogs. My second favourite joke is about a horse that liked to sit on eggs. My third

favourite joke concerns religious faith and it's about a man in a
bowler hat. May I tell it?'

There was a murmur of assent, resembling the response Oliver
had heard from the people earlier, when Mrs McCall had led
them in prayer. Instead of 'Lord, hear our prayer,' the thrust of the
murmur was, 'Let's hear the joke, brother.'

He told his third favourite joke.

'A man was walking through a forest one day and in a clearing
met a second man. The second man was stark naked apart from a
bowler hat. "Excuse me," said the first man, "you haven't got any
clothes on." "I know," said the second man, "nobody ever walks
through this part of the forest." "So why are you wearing the bowler
hat, if nobody ever walks through this part of the forest?" "Well,"
said the second man, "you never know – somebody might."'

Nobody laughed. Oliver was used to it. People rarely laughed
at his jokes immediately. Diane had laughed at the frogs the day
after he told her the story. An old school friend had once written,
to say he had just laughed at one of Oliver's jokes, thirty years
after hearing it behind the cycle sheds.

So the silence in the church was not a matter of concern. He
was preoccupied with his message to the congregation.

'Religion is, I suggest, a bowler hat we choose to wear – or not,
according to our convictions – in case it turns out that we are not
alone in the depths of the forest.

'I also think "Thou shalt not kill" is an excellent commandment
and a sound basis for a decent life. It's very difficult to shoot
someone with a ploughshare. We thank you for your charity.'

Oliver sat down. There was a long silence with some muted
but audible shuffling. Then Mrs McCall stood up and said:

'We will sing hymn number 205.'

She played the introductory chords on the harmonium and
the people stood up.

'All right?' said Oliver to Diane.

'Brace yourself.'

'For what?'

'Thunderbolts. Frogs. Locusts.'

*

Michael opened the last two cans of lager, while Cathy tapped reflectively on the keyboard, as if juggling with fifty-seven varieties of possible subversion.

'These people who've been bothering your mum. They're not only weird but dangerous. Right?'

'Right.'

'Thing is, I've screwed up their systems. It'll take them a couple of days to get on track again but we could go a little further if you like.'

'Like what?'

'Finger the people in high places. They're in there. I've spotted them. We could dig them out. Names and addresses. Who got paid off. Who did the paying and why. All the incriminating shit.'

'What happens when you've dug it out?'

'Find a doorstep. Dump it. Sit back and laugh.'

'Great. Shall I make some coffee?'

'No. You've got some more shopping to do. Another six-pack and some kebabs from the carry-out. We're talking a double night shift here.'

'Sure.'

He hesitated, then added:

'I'll go as soon as my mum's telephoned.'

'Sure.'

He didn't have to explain. She was a woman.

The emergency services had cleared the debris and traffic was on the move again. Baxter was driving north. He had used his ID card to impress the friendly young policeman and now had a clear picture of what had happened. He was conveying the gist of it to the Baron on his mobile.

'Listen. No more cowboys in helicopters. No more cowboys with shotguns. No more cowboys with blunt instruments. That sort of behaviour attracts attention, would you believe? Got that? Give that message to your leader with the compliments of your head of security.

'From now on, it's me against them. I am the cowboy. The sole agent of retribution. It's what I'm best at. It's what I'm paid for.

It's also, though I never make a production number out of it, what I deeply and sincerely enjoy.'

He switched off the mobile and stuck it in the glove compartment, then continued, talking to himself:

'I am the cowboy. Listen to yourself. The Lone Ranger rides again. Vanity of vanities. Hi-ho Silver.'

He whistled the *William Tell* overture which all right-thinking citizens knew was the theme music of *The Lone Ranger*. Baxter was feeling good. He was in control. He even pulled up, a knight of the road, to give a totally unnecessary right of way to a single-decker bus driving out of a field and heading south. The bus was covered with mud and slogans extolling the greater glory of God.

Mrs McCall had found seats on the bus for Oliver and Diane, even though it involved her standing, and wedging an elderly man up against his walking-stick.

'I'm very happy to stand,' said Oliver.

Mrs McCall was insistent.

'Did you not earn a seat with your sermon?

'I don't know. Did I?'

'We are a Nonconformist sect. Why should we object to a sermon which does not conform? It would be a betrayal of our own principles. My concern is about these attempts on your life. What are we going to do about them?'

'As long as we remember to duck, we should be all right,' said Diane, feeling they'd caused these people quite enough trouble already today.

'We can't allow you to be murdered in our parish. Would it not reflect on the entire community? What are you planning to do tomorrow?'

'We were hoping to go to Orkney,' said Diane.

'On the ferry?'

They had explained to Mrs McCall that, while in the early part of the day they had been in possession of their own car, this was no longer the case. They had not been too specific about how they had lost it: it seemed unkind to sully her charity with melodramatic tales of aerial attacks, helicopters and machine-guns.

She sensed the nature of their problem and said:

'I will take you to the ferry.'

'Do you have transport?' said Diane.

'Mondays to Fridays I have access to transport,' said Mrs McCall, 'which only leaves the problem of overnight accommodation.'

'There's a hotel in Thurso, handy for the ferry terminal, and guaranteed free of theme restaurants,' said Oliver. But he was ignored.

'I have two spare rooms at my house,' said Mrs McCall. 'Or will one be sufficient?'

'Thank you,' said Diane. 'One will be sufficient. Do you also have a telephone?'

The telephone rang. Michael looked around the kitchen.

'In the bread bin,' said Cathy.

He slid open the cover of a roll-top bread bin and there, in a tangle of wires and illicit connections, Michael found the telephone. He picked up the receiver.

'Hi . . . Mum! . . . You all right? . . . You haven't been searched and destroyed? . . . What? . . . The Samaritans?'

'The Samaritans?' said Cathy.

Michael covered the mouthpiece and explained to Cathy.

'Not *the* Samaritans. Just a bunch of regular, everyday Samaritans.'

'Sure. You get quite a few in the North.'

Cathy found access to another secret cell brimming over with the great, the good and the gorblimey, as Michael lectured his mother on the phone.

'Listen. Stop trying to reassure me. Tell me the truth. If you don't give me something to worry about, I'll worry about what you're not telling me.'

'Are you Jewish?' said Cathy.

It was midnight. The Baron had given up on his computer and gone to bed. Then he had given up on sleep and come downstairs into the drawing-room. He had settled in an armchair with a bottle of single malt.

That was where Sara found him.

'I lost you,' she said.

'Couldn't sleep. Kept dreaming.'

'You must have been asleep. How else can you dream?'

He was in no mood for logic, especially hers.

'In my dream, there's an army of peasants with pitchforks and red flags marching up the drive.'

'That's nice. It's what you've always wanted, isn't it?'

He drained his glass, topped it up from the bottle and said:

'Do you fancy a few days' holiday?'

'Where?'

'Skiing?'

'There isn't any snow.'

'We'll tell them we were misinformed.'

'What?'

'It's a reference,' said the Baron.

'Oh.'

'Casablanca.'

Sara frowned and said:

'There's never any snow in Casablanca.'

The Baron drained his glass, topped it up again from the bottle and said:

'You know what I am? I am the classic example of the man who could not make up his mind.'

'I know that one,' said Sara, smiling with relief. 'That's Hamlet, isn't it?'

The Baron raised his glass and drank a toast:

'I give you flights of angels. Absent friends. The Kite dynasty. Revolting peasants. Comrade Baxter.'

'Are you pissed, darling?'

'Pissed, perchance to dream.'

He drained his glass. The bottle was empty.

When Mrs McCall told Oliver and Diane that she had access to transport, Monday to Friday, they had not expected a mobile library. She explained it was her job. It was what she did: touring outlying areas of the Highlands with weekly deliveries of literature, and ferocious advice to the borrowers. It was her turn to preach a sermon as she drove them to the ferry terminal at Scrabster.

'I tell them, you'll get no Archers or Coopers from me. There are station bookstalls for that class of writing. Read your heritage. George Mackay Brown, Edwin Muir, Eric Linklater, Hugh Marwick. You'll thank me for it one day. That's heritage with a small "h". I have no time for those people who put capital letters on words and believe that gives them dignity and importance.'

On the quayside, they parted with two pledges. Oliver promised to read all the books on the reading list Mrs McCall had given him, and Diane promised to stay out of trouble and stop worrying her son.

'God bless you both,' said Mrs McCall.

Her blessing was almost drowned out by a cacophony of car horns. There were two long lines of traffic: one leaving the ferry, the other waiting to go aboard. The mobile library straddled both lines.

'It's the tourists who get cross,' said Mrs McCall. 'The locals are a gentle tribe.'

She made a short speech to the fretting drivers.

'You must please be patient with me. I learned to drive during the war. I was a motorcycle dispatch rider. I have a strong sense of priorities but I never truly mastered reverse gear.'

Oliver and Diane boarded the ferry. They leaned on the rail and watched as Mrs McCall turned her mobile library around in the midst of the two-way traffic. The gearbox sounded like a cross between an iron foundry and early Bartók.

'I've never seen a three-point turn with so many points,' said Diane, 'and I used to be a policeperson.'

Oliver had learned the map by heart.

'We are in Thurso Bay and that's Dunnet Head, and once we're out of its shelter we'll be in the Pentland Firth. It might get rough. Do you suffer from seasickness? We've never discussed it.'

'No. But I sometimes get sick of people wittering in my ear about why I should be having a good time.'

'I'll be quiet.'

He stayed quiet for five minutes, then said:

'I haven't finished yesterday's crossword. All that excitement. Aerial bombardment and sermons.'

'You can do your crossword in bed tonight.'

'Being very careful not to get ink on the pillow.'

'So that's two things for you to look forward to.'

'Two things? Will there be complimentary shortbread as well?'

She looked at him. He stayed quiet for half an hour. The boat sailed along the coast of the island of Hoy. Oliver identified Tor Ness, Green Heads, the Red Hill of Sneuk and Rackwick, but stayed quiet until they rounded Rora Head. Then all he said was:

'Look.'

'What am I looking at?'

'The Old Man of Hoy. They call it that because it looks like an old man. Geologically speaking, it's a rock stack.'

She remembered a television programme, years ago, with a bunch of loonies climbing up it and a bunch of even bigger loonies filming them. Why was it she remembered old television programmes but forgot last week's as soon as they finished?

'Yes,' she said. 'Impressive. And it does look like an old man.'

It was all the encouragement he needed.

'The remarkable thing is, he used to have two legs, but one of them disappeared.'

'Recently?'

'Early in the nineteenth century. Nobody saw it go. It just disappeared overnight. Here today, gone tomorrow.'

'Just like life,' said Diane.

'So people tell me.'

16

Do We Look Like That?

The cathedral was modest as cathedrals go, but towered humanely over the town of Kirkwall, population five thousand, capital of Orkney.

Oliver and Diane sat inside. They agreed that the Durham masons had done a fine job, and cathedrals were built to last in those days. Then Oliver told her the legend of Magnus the Martyr.

'In the twelfth century, Magnus was joint Earl of the Orkneys.'

'Joint Earl?'

'He and his cousin, Haakon. They were both Norwegians. But Magnus was a good Norwegian. Haakon was a bad one.'

'I thought all Norwegians were nice. Like Canadians. Isn't that why they get no votes in the Eurovision Song Contest? Because they're nice.'

'Not in this instance. Magnus, good guy. Haakon, bad guy. And they fell out.'

'Power-sharing. It never works. My dad's Irish. I know.'

'Magnus, being a good guy, tried to negotiate a settlement.'

'Don't tell me. He made Haakon an offer he couldn't refuse?'

'Except Haakon refused it and put an axe through Magnus's head.'

Diane made a face. She had liked the story so far, but now it had turned into another yard and a half of peace through violence.

'That's a bit tasteless. Also, I don't believe it.'

'Alas,' said Oliver, 'it's true. "Cleft in twain" is the Biblical expression.'

'What I mean is, I bet he didn't do it himself. I bet he got somebody else to do the clefting for him. The arm's-length approach. There must have been a hatchet man.'

Oliver nodded.

'His cook.'

'His cook?'

'Haakon ordered his standard-bearer, a man called Ofeig, to kill Magnus, but he refused. He knew a good guy when he saw one. So up stepped Lifolf the cook. He was probably thinking about his pension rights and I imagine he had easy access to a suitable axe.'

'And he clefted Magnus's head in twain?'

'Yes.'

'It's a tough life, being a martyr.'

'It's the job. It's what martyrs do. And look, you get your own cathedral.'

'And it keeps my dad's union in work.'

As they left, they looked up in homage to the vaulted ambition of the nave. They walked out across a small yard into the main street. Cloistered precincts had never caught on.

'Are there any happy Orcadian stories?' said Diane.

'Magnus is a happy story. When he was buried, a heavenly light shone across his grave.'

'A heavenly light?'

'Celestial. With healing properties.'

'You don't believe that stuff.'

'If I'd lived here in 1115, I might easily have believed that stuff.'

'Especially if the alternative was an axe through your head.'

They had hired a car. Mrs McCall had organized it from the mainland with one phone call to a friend of a friend. It had automatic transmission. Oliver enjoyed driving it, once he came to terms with the missing pedal. Diane explained that it was quite simple if you strapped one leg behind your back. Oliver said that sounded like a sexual deviation of no interest whatsoever. Socks were his absolute limit.

They drove south from Kirkwall, across the Churchill Barrier, the causeway leading to the islands of Burray and South Ronaldsay, and to another legend. The islands were low in the water, like green-backed whales taking their leisure. There were no trees.

Oliver explained that the wind, unrelenting and sometimes at gale force, made it impossible for trees to grow on the islands. They had given up long ago, and moved to more hospitable territory on the mainland.

'I'm sorry,' said Diane. 'I wasn't listening. I was brooding.'

'There's a lot of that goes on too. Brooding. Sometimes leading to depression. Because of the wind.'

'I was brooding about Magnus. When was he killed?'

'AD 1115'

'Nothing changes.'

'Since AD 1115? I must respectfully disagree. Consider the giant steps humanity has taken since then. We've had jazz and the Football League and the hula hoop and cornflakes and . . .'

Diane interrupted him. She was serious.

'Nothing changes. The bad guys always get somebody else to do the dirty work for them. Whoever was flying that helicopter that tried to kill us, it wasn't the chairman of the board. It wasn't Haakon. It was the cook.'

'The police should round up all the usual cooks.' He reached out a hand, placed it on hers. 'Forget about helicopters. Stay cool. We're on holiday.'

She took his hand, replaced it on the steering-wheel.

'On holiday? I thought we were supposed to be looking for Aristotle?'

'All in good time. Besides, you don't find things if you look for them. They've done research at several American universities. It's called the underpants syndrome. Relax.'

She relaxed. Relaxation was still a strange phenomenon, but with Oliver's tuition and support, she was improving. Anxieties arrived one at a time, instead of by the bushel. Most of them were code-named Michael.

They parked the car at St Margaret's Hope, a tiny village on South Ronaldsay, nestling in a bay. It was a cloudy day but the grey light shone brightly across the harbour.

'A healing light,' said Oliver.

'I feel better already.'

'*Brigadoon* syndrome.'

If you closed your eyes you could imagine Gene Kelly in a kilt, skipping along the street, singing about heather and hills in a Scottish accent fresh out of LA. It was a good argument for keeping your eyes open.

They sat on the harbour wall and Oliver told another story.

'Once upon a time there was a little girl called Margaret. She was seven years old and lived in Norway. On the death of her grandfather, Alexander III, she was proclaimed Queen of Scotland and betrothed to Prince Edward, who later became Edward II of England. She set sail from Norway to claim her inheritance but was taken ill on the ship. She died here in November 1290. That is why the village is called St Margaret's Hope.'

'She died in 1290?'

'Yes.'

'And Magnus died in 1115?'

'Yes.'

Diane did a quick sum in her head.

'A hundred and seventy-five years apart. So I doubt whether the deaths were connected.'

'Relax. Please stop being a policeperson.' He was very firm by his standards. By mainland rat-race standards he was demure and apologetic.

'I'm sorry,' said Diane. 'Thank you for the story. It's very sad, isn't it? Did she get a celestial light?'

'We're looking at it.'

They looked at the healing light for a while. It changed minute by minute. Then Oliver said:

'Did you ever want to marry a prince?'

'No. I wanted to marry Sean Connery.'

'I wanted to marry Jeanne Moreau.'

'And look at us.'

'I have no complaints,' said Oliver. 'Indeed, I am basking in a predestined tranquillity.'

He waited for Diane to cast her vote and make their tranquillity unanimous, but she said nothing.

'You're not basking today?' he said.

'I'm thinking.'

'Not basking but thinking. Well. Better than brooding.'

She stood up and said:

'Walk this way.'

It was an old music-hall gag Oliver had taught her. You said 'Walk this way' and set off walking with a limp or some other peculiarity, and the other person was supposed to follow, imitating your movements as exactly as possible. This time Diane cheated. She walked briskly and smartly, in the style of the police force on parade for inspection. Oliver found it difficult to walk that way: limps and other eccentricities were much easier. Normality was tough.

She led him to the main street and to a souvenir shop overflowing on to a small courtyard. It sold postcards, knitwear, pottery and a variety of memorabilia devoted to St Margaret and her shattered hope.

Diane found the postcards and Oliver the books by local authors. A woman came out of the shop.

'Can I help you?' she said.

She was about thirty, dressed in universal-style jeans with a logo on the right buttock, and a chunky sweater decorated with runic writing. Her question was genuine. She really wanted to help. It was unlike those big city shops on the mainland where the question arrived with instant innuendo: can I help you to carry all that stuff you've nicked and put in your plastic carrier, or shall I wait until you step outside and then call the police, and should I remind you about the hidden cameras, and by the way our policy is to prosecute all shoplifters, and, all that being so, can I help you?

This was a small offshore island and it was different.

'Thank you,' said Diane. 'I shall need a postcard for my son but I don't like to rush these things. You might be able to help my companion.'

'I'm very tranquil as I am,' said Oliver. 'I don't need any help.'

'Yes you do.'

'Do I?'

Diane explained to the woman.

'He's trying to find an old friend who moved up here about a year ago. But he's too shy to ask.'

'Do you know the name and address?'

'If I did,' said Oliver, 'I would go to the address, knock on the door and say: "Hello, old friend." Besides, we've never actually met, face to face.'

'But if you know his name . . .' said the woman, still determined to be of assistance.

'We only know him by his pseudonym,' said Diane.

'Which is . . .?'

'Aristotle.'

'I see.'

'He's a crossword compiler,' said Oliver, sensing a switch in roles: it was now their job to help the shop assistant. Besides, it was polite and the further north they travelled the more prominent the role politeness apparently played in everyone's daily round.

'Aristotle is also a living legend,' added Diane.

'It can be tricky, finding people in the Orkneys. Especially if you don't know which island he's living on. He could be on any of twenty. Seventy, if he doesn't mind living rough. Basically, your best plan's to ask around.'

'That was the advice we were given at the hotel,' said Diane. 'Ask around the locals. I think we thought that was what we were doing. Asking around you.'

'Sorry. You picked a wrong 'un, asking me.'

'I do hope you're not a cook,' said Oliver.

'What?'

'Ignore him,' said Diane.

The woman ignored Oliver and explained:

'What I mean is, basically, I've only been here a couple of months myself.'

'An incomer?' said Oliver, who had spotted a Home Counties accent but didn't like to say so out loud in case he seemed to be flaunting his Northern roots. He was proud of his background but had never made a profession out of it.

'Where did you income from?' said Diane.

'Basildon in Essex.'

'You're a long way from home.'

'No. This is home. I'm a long way from Basildon in Essex.'

'Why did you leave?'

'I'm running away.'

'So are we,' said Oliver. 'It's nothing to be ashamed of. On the contrary, it's very sensible. Though, strictly speaking, we're no longer running *away* but running *towards* something finer.'

'What are you running away from?' said Diane, determined not to be sucked down into Oliver's metaphysics.

'People ask me where I'm from. I tell them. Basildon in Essex. They look at me. That's what I'm running away from. The look that people give me.'

Oliver and Diane traded glances. They were trying to spread the guilt because they had both looked at the woman in the way she had run away from. It might have been one of the more trivial human tragedies of the century, but was none the less real: pain in the soul of the beholder.

Diane drove the car back to Kirkwall. She was growing weary of Oliver trying to put his foot on an imaginary pedal. Scapa Flow and the islands were drifting into dusk and she concentrated on the road ahead. She caught a sideways glimpse of a building set back from the road: small, painted white, semicircular with a tower.

'What was that?' she said.

'The Italian Chapel,' said Oliver.

'What is it?'

'A chapel. It was built during the war by Italian prisoners.'

'I can probably guess how it got its name.'

'I love an educated woman.'

'Maybe you should send out for one.'

There was nothing thematic about the Scapa Flow Hotel (proprietors: George and Eileen Davidson). It was a simple two-storey building. Apart from the cathedral, all buildings on Orkney obeyed the natural law of the island: anything taller than two storeys would go the way of the trees.

The hotel overlooked Scapa Flow, so the Davidsons had given it the obvious name. The facilities had simple names too: reception, dining-room, bar and bedrooms, and not a theme, logo or dry-ski slope anywhere in sight.

George Davidson, a courteous mainland Scot in his fifties, was on the desk when Oliver and Diane collected their key. He already knew their names and their room number.

'Did you have a pleasant day?'

'We paid our respects to St Magnus and St Margaret,' said Oliver.

'Oh. You like the modern stuff?'

'Modern?' said Diane.

'Oh yes. Anything that has happened since the birth of Christ we regard as a bit newfangled. It's a peculiarity of the islands.'

Oliver nodded agreement; he enjoyed this man's serenity. It carried a hint of scholarship, of books read, marked and understood.

'There's much to be said for your peculiarity.'

Diane was handed the key and had taken three modest steps towards the staircase when Davidson said:

'Now you mustn't go without your messages.'

'Messages?'

He was too polite to say so, but clearly thought her three modest steps betrayed unbecoming haste verging on headstrong abandon. Diane returned to the desk. Davidson referred to his pad.

'Mrs Priest. Your father telephoned, as you said he might, and I told him you were well and happy, as you instructed. I've written it all down.' He tore off the sheet and handed it to her. His handwriting was neat and the message set out in paragraphs, carefully and correctly punctuated.

'Thank you, Mr Davidson.'

'And your son telephoned. He would like you to telephone him this evening. He said it was in connection with corruption in high places and that you would understand. I've written it all down.' He tore off the sheet and handed it to her.

'Thank you, Mr Davidson.'

'And Mr Baxter telephoned.'

'Baxter?'

'He left no message, but I have written down his name.'

Davidson tore off the sheet, bearing the word 'BAXTER', and handed it to her.

'Thank you, Mr Davidson.'

'I think those are all your messages.'

Then he turned to Oliver.

'Did you have any luck with your enquiries? Concerning your friend?'

'We consulted the locals, as you suggested. All of the people we spoke to were from Basildon in Essex.'

'I'm sure you will find him. It's another peculiarity of the islands. Progress may be slow, but it's also inevitable. And don't be surprised by Basildon. Many of us came here from the mainland.'

'I don't think you're from Basildon,' said Oliver, whose ears had placed Davidson within a fifty-mile radius of Glasgow.

'Correct. I came here from the Clyde. A long time ago. I wanted to be near my father.'

'Does he live here?' said Diane, but realized by the look in the man's eyes that the story was not as simple as that.

'Are you in a hurry? Or may I show you?'

'We are not in a hurry,' said Oliver who had assumed the gentle pace of the island the moment he had stepped off the ferry the previous day. It was pure and healthy nostalgia. It reminded him of the benign pace of his old training college, before it became the New University of the Rhondda Valley. After the arrival of the dreaded go-getting Vice-Chancellor, it had accelerated to the speed of light, in several wrong directions simultaneously. That was the problem with go-getters. They became so obsessed with high-velocity going and getting they forgot what they had gone to get.

Davidson knew precisely what he was about. He led them into the bar, saying:

'This won't take many minutes.'

They crossed to the window and looked out at the dark water.

'Scapa Flow.'

'Yes,' said Diane.

Oliver remained silent. He had half guessed what was coming.

'You see the buoy?' said Davidson.

They saw the buoy floating on the water, its light blinking at regular intervals.

'Yes.'

'The buoy marks the position of the *Royal Oak*. The *Royal Oak*?' He waited to see whether the name had significance for them.

'The *Royal Oak*,' said Oliver. 'British battleship. Sunk by a German submarine during the Second World War.'

'On 13 October 1939, with the loss of 833 men,' said Davidson, leaving the rest of the story hanging on the air.

'Your father . . .?' said Diane.

'He was one of the men.'

'Your islands are haunted,' said Oliver.

'But we live very comfortably with our ghosts.'

'Quite so. Didn't we pay homage to Magnus and Margaret this afternoon?' said Oliver.

'And when I go to bed, I look out of my window and say good night to my father. I think that's a nice thing to do, don't you?'

'Yes,' said Diane. 'It's a nice thing to do.'

'Do you hear him answer?' said Oliver.

'Oh yes.'

'Another peculiarity of the island?'

'I imagine so.'

They stared at the marker buoy for a long time and then Oliver said:

'Thank you, Mr Davidson.'

Oliver and Diane ate supper in the dining-room: fresh trout, caught locally and legitimately. They had a wee dram of Highland Park in the bar. Then they went to their room. Oliver lay on the bed and switched on the television set, hoping there might be football. Diane sat by the telephone.

'What are you doing?' said Oliver.

'Telephoning my son.'

'We're not here to investigate crime and corruption in high places. You are under suspension from the police force and you are also off duty and on holiday with your chosen male companion.'

'I am telephoning my son to tell him that I love him.'

'I have nothing against love,' said Oliver, hitting the Mute button on the remote.

Oliver zapped around the channels in silence. There was no football. He was too late. The least bad television in the world was marooned in the Never Never Land of late-night movies: otherwise forgotten films only fit to be dumped on boozers, shift-workers and insomniacs. Three of them were about lantern-jawed Americans hunting down the killer; the Channel 4 film had subtitles and Oliver couldn't tell what it was about, if indeed it was about anything.

The telephone rang in George Burns's kitchen. Cathy opened the bread bin, picked up the receiver and said:

'Hi . . . just a minute . . .'

She called to Michael.

'It's for you.'

Michael wandered into the kitchen, eating a bag of chips. He wiped his hands on his trousers before taking the receiver from Cathy.

'Hi . . . Oh, Hi Mum . . . What? . . . Yes, thank you, I love you as well . . . Listen, is there a fax number for that place you're staying? . . . Yes, sure, I'll hang on . . .'

While he was hanging on he said to Cathy:

'She says she loves me.'

'That's parents for you.'

Diane hurried to the lobby of the Scapa Flow Hotel. Eileen Davidson was behind the desk, doing her VAT returns. She looked up, delighted by the distraction.

'Can I help you, dear?'

'Do you have a fax machine, Mrs Davidson?'

'Indeed we do, and you'd be amazed at some of the things we learn from it.'

'I'm sure. May I have the number please?'

'My pleasure.'

Diane hurried back to the bedroom, picked up the phone and gave Michael the number. In the Aberdeen kitchen Michael repeated the number to Cathy, who tapped it into the computer.

'Now brace yourself,' said Michael to his mother.

In the office to the rear of the reception desk, the fax machine rang twice then clicked into action.

In the bedroom Oliver said:

'Good heavens.'

Diane was pacing up and down, waiting for a call from reception to say the fax had arrived.

'What's wrong?'

'Buttocks.'

'What?' She looked at the television screen. It was full of buttocks, heaving enthusiastically: buttocks with attitude.

'What *are* you watching?'

'I imagine it's simulated sexual intercourse.'

'What's the programme called?'

'I don't know. It's difficult to tell without sound. It's probably a film. Or do you suppose it's *Wild Life on One*? Or *World in Action*? *Two-Way Family Favourites*? *Match of the Day*? *The Week in Westminster*? *Your Hundred Best Tunes*?'

'You should be ashamed of yourself,' said Diane, refusing to be drawn into the titles game. 'No wonder you wear glasses.'

Oliver peered at her over the top of his spectacles, and said:

'Do we look like that?'

'Of course not. You're lying on the bed watching television and I'm walking up and down waiting for a fax from my son.'

'I don't mean now. I mean when we're doing what they're doing.' He indicated the screen. They were still doing it. These buttocks had stamina as well as attitude. Diane had a look.

'I expect so. We have four buttocks between us and I imagine they heave in the regulation way. I've never watched. Obviously.'

He switched off the television set and said:

'I liked sex better the way it used to be.'

'Has there been some change I wasn't informed about?'

'I liked it best when the boy kissed the girl and the next thing you saw was waves lapping on the seashore, or smoke belching forth from a chimney or a train rushing into a tunnel.'

'You sweet old-fashioned thing.'

'Well, my dear, you know what lips were made for, don't you?'

She walked across to the bed and looked down at him. He started to chuckle.

'I shall live to regret this. What were lips made for?'

'To stop our mouths from fraying at the edges. Arthur Askey, *circa* 1948.'

She leaned over and kissed him, to stop him telling any more old jokes. She sat down on the edge of the bed, to give greater ease of access. The telephone rang. She sat up.

'That used to happen as well,' said Oliver.

'What?'

'The boy would kiss the girl and the telephone would ring. It would be the other boy or the other girl or the parents to say they were coming home early. Apparently in Hollywood they call it UST.'

'UST?' said Diane, picking up the phone.

'Unresolved sexual tension. Though mostly these days they just get heaving with the buttocks and resolve it.'

'Shut up, I can't hear properly.'

She listened briefly, then said:

'Right. I'll tell them.'

She hung up, then walked across to the door.

'It was Michael to say the fax machine has run out of paper.'

'It's more original than "Sorry, I've got a headache" but it must take a great deal of organizing.'

'If I'm not back in five minutes, start without me,' said Diane at the door, before making a Groucho-style exit.

Sometimes, thought Oliver, she behaves exactly like I do.

Inexplicable.

The length and lateness of the fax were unique in the history of the hotel, even when BBC news teams were in residence. Both Davidsons had emerged to handle the situation. Eileen was at the desk and George stood by the machine.

'You must remember to put all this on our bill,' said Diane as she collected up the first two rolls of paper.

'We'll make a wee adjustment,' said George.

'But don't fret,' said Eileen. 'We enjoy little moments of excitement. In due moderation, of course.'

'We're the same,' said Diane, thinking: I hope we haven't got to the moderation yet.

'Ah, it seems to have stopped.'

George tore the final roll of paper from the machine and brought it to the desk, saying:

'A little more bedtime reading.'

'Thank you, Mr Davidson, Mrs Davidson. I'm deeply grateful. Good night.'

They wished her good night. She gathered up the three rolls and left the lobby. Then they went into the dining-room.

'Did you happen to glance at any of those pages?' said Eileen Davidson to her husband, as they were preparing the tables for breakfast.

'Certainly not.'

'Nor did I. But I couldn't help but notice that they seem to know some very famous people.'

'They do indeed,' agreed George Davidson.

In George Burns's kitchen in Aberdeen, Cathy switched off the computer, with the contented smile of a woman who has done a good day's work and demolished several carefully constructed, male-dominated empires.

'That'll fix the bastards,' she said.

'You're a genius,' said Michael.

'Probably.'

She pulled the plugs from those sockets she knew to be fire risks and said:

'Fancy watching a video?'

'Yes. Great.'

'*Dumbo?*'

'Brilliant.'

Oliver decided to start his book. He had bought it that morning in Stromness. It was called *Greenvoe* and it was by the great George Mackay Brown who lived around the corner from the bookshop. It ran to 261 pages plus a glossary of Orcadian words.

Oliver was no mathematician but he had made two calculations. The first was that he would finish the book, including the glossary, before Diane worked her way through the information from Aberdeen. The second was that the fax paper, stretched end to end, would measure seventy-five metres, or eighty-two yards in old money, or the length of a football pitch minus one penalty area. He pointed this out to Diane, who said:

'Read your book, there's a good boy.'

She checked through the first ten metres of information, making marginal notes as she did so, then said:

'This is amazing stuff.'

'I'm reading my book.'

'Oh, come on. Don't you want to know about it?'

Oliver lowered the book.

'Only because you are my chosen and predestined female companion. Therefore I take a keen interest in everything you do. Failure to do so could be disastrous. Our relationship can only flourish on the basis of shared passions.'

'Is this likely to be a long speech?'

'It's over. Tell me about your stuff and why it is amazing.'

'The kids have hacked into all the Farquhar Group's computer systems. Details of all the scams and how they operate. Names and addresses.'

'You can find names and addresses in a telephone directory.'

'Not these names and addresses. These are strictly ex-directory names. Heavy-duty business tycoons. Government ministers and civil servants. Men with knighthoods. Masters of foxhounds. Merchant bankers. Household names.'

'Like Harpic or dustbin?'

'And it's international.'

'Crowned heads of Europe?'

He was relentlessly facetious. It was beginning to irritate her. Here she was with a Holy Grail, fully kosher, guaranteed to make the sky fall, and he was saying, very nice, dear, but it's not as funny as my revolving bow-tie and big daft boots.

'You're not taking this seriously,' she said.

'These are people in high places. They're bound to be crooked. Power corrupts. Absolute power corrupts absolutely. You heard what happened to Magnus.'

'Don't you believe in justice?'

'Yes. I think it's an excellent idea. But I don't expect to see it put into practice in my lifetime. The judges and lawyers get in the way.'

She got up from the table, walked to the bed and showed him the names she had listed in her notebook.

'Does that mean you're happy for these people to get away with it?'

He glanced at the names, then looked up at her, no longer facetious.

'No. I'm deeply unhappy about it. I'm also deeply unhappy that Baxter knows where we are. I'm deeply unhappy that he might send in the helicopters tomorrow. I'm deeply unhappy that our concern for justice might result in our death when I am deeply happier than I've ever been in my entire life. I don't want us to be cleft in twain when we're happy. And since there are two of us we'd be cleft in quatrain. Though that's a four-line stanza and probably the wrong word.'

She waited for him to finish, then said:

'Is that true?'

'It was a long speech but I expect I meant most of it. Which bit had you in mind?'

'Deeply happier than you've ever been in your life.'

'Oh yes, I meant that bit. I think I said as much the day the helicopter attacked us.'

'I thought that was the stress of the moment.'

'Here and now, at this moment, in our little room on this tranquil island, I am deeply happier than I have ever been.'

'Thank you.'

He was deeply serious. Then he added:

'I've had other good moments, of course. My O level results. Learning the reverse turn in the quickstep. Scoring for the second eleven. My first Duke Ellington LP. Getting Spike Milligan's autograph. The 1973 Cup Final. I could go on but . . .'

'Don't.' She put her fingers to his lips, and said: 'I'll forget about incriminating evidence for a while, clean my teeth and see whether we can summon up the waves on the seashore and the express trains racing into the tunnel. How's that?'

'I could tell you about my first train set, if you like.'

Later that night, he did.

17

The Ultimate Mystery
of the Cornflake

In Scapa Flow the water lapped gently around the shore. In the dining-room the milk lapped gently around Oliver's cornflakes. He had asked, as usual, for semi-skimmed and for the first time during their travels it had been available, delivered to their table with speed and grace. Semi-skimmed was good for you.

'Do you ever think about cornflakes?' said Oliver.

'Hardly ever. Do you?' said Diane; then, seeing the look on his face, she added: 'Yes, I expect you do. I expect you're going to tell me about it.'

'I've been eating cornflakes since I was a little boy and they've always tasted *exactly* the same. Imagine. Every cornflake in the world is identical in size, shape, texture and flavour.' He picked up a single cornflake on his spoon and held it out for her inspection.

'Thank you,' she said. 'I know what a cornflake looks like.'

'But the question, the ultimate mystery, is this. Is it wonderful or is it sad? It is a triumph of technology over the world's natural resources? Or is it a dismal failure of the imagination?'

'It could be both.'

'Both. I'd never considered that.'

'You can't expect the world to make sense.'

'You really do have a remarkable mind.'

'Eat your cornflakes.'

He ate his cornflakes. Diane ate her toast: it was made from locally baked bread, sliced by hand from the loaf. She had checked it for holes made by a toasting-fork, but Oliver said that would have been expecting too much: Arcadian rather than Orcadian.

When George Davidson came to the table to clear away, he said:

'There's a gentleman would like to speak to you.'

'Is his name Baxter?' said Diane.

'No. I am quite sure his name is not Baxter.'

She consulted Oliver:

'Would you like to meet a gentleman who isn't called Baxter?'

'Very much. Especially if he isn't called Baxter. Perhaps he'd like to join us for a cup of coffee?'

'I will ask him.' Davidson left the dining-room.

'Are we expecting company?' said Diane.

'Probably a man from the cornflake company, here to share their ultimate mystery.'

'He doesn't *look* like a man from the cornflake company.'

Diane's chair was facing the door and she saw him first. He was a tall, thin man, dressed in a black suit, tie and overcoat, and carrying a black hat. He was aged between thirty and sixty-five. Oliver wrote later in his diary that he looked as if he had come to audition for Ingmar Bergman.

He walked across to their table and said:

'Hallo.'

It was a vital ethnic clue. The man was a genuine Orcadian. Walking in the streets of Kirkwall and Stromness, total strangers had greeted Oliver and Diane this way: not 'Hello', not 'Hullo', and certainly not 'Yo' or 'Hi' – but a simple, friendly, unobtrusive 'Hallo' spoken with a short 'a' and totally without guile. They had learned to respond in kind. It was the proper courtesy of way-faring strangers: you ate the food, drank the wine and spoke the language of the country.

'Hallo,' said Oliver.

'Hallo,' said Diane.

'My name is Mr Gunn. I think I might be able to help you. I called on my way to work, which is why I am in my working clothes. Here is my card.'

He handed his business card to Oliver, who read it, then said to Diane:

'Mr Gunn is an undertaker.'

Diane nodded and thought: yes, I'd guessed he wasn't an Elvis impersonator or Mr Wacky-and-Zany 1993.

Mr Gunn explained:

'I was going about my business in St Margaret's Hope last evening and was told you had been enquiring about a man called Aristotle.'

'That is so,' said Oliver, echoing Mr Gunn's cadences and precision of speech.

'Do you have half an hour you might be able to spare?'

'We do.'

'Because I believe my best plan is to show you what I know and let you be the judge of whether it is pertinent to your enquiries.'

'Thank you,' said Oliver.

Mr Gunn declined to drink coffee with them. It would, he indicated, be inappropriate during working hours. They were left with the feeling that for Mr Gunn, coffee-drinking in general would be a giant step into areas of flippancy with no part in his philosophy.

He suggested they put on their warmest coats. It was likely to be windy where they were going. He led them out of the hotel and across the car park to a large hearse. It was the same colour as his clothing.

'Do you mind travelling in my car?' he said. 'I know where we are going, you see. You could follow my car in your car, but that might cause misunderstanding and possible embarrassment.'

'I'm sure we'd be happy to travel in your car,' said Diane.

'It will be a new experience for us both,' said Oliver, intrigued to see whether this would make the undertaker smile. It did not.

He opened the door of the hearse, saying:

'There is ample room for the three of us.'

Mr Gunn sat in the driving seat, with Diane and Oliver alongside. There was, as he said, ample room for all three. He drove at a stately pace in the middle of the road. Such traffic as there was gave way to him, perhaps influenced by the coffin in the back of the hearse. He was at pains to assure them that it was empty. It was required for his next appointment but they were not to concern themselves as he had allowed himself plenty of time.

The cemetery was on a green hill not far away. It sloped gently towards the sea, which gave the illusion that all the headstones were tilted. Oliver wondered, idly, whether they were placed in position ready-tilted, so that the prevailing winds would blow them into a true vertical position.

Mr Gunn led them along a grassy path. The turf was soft and gentle to the feet. He stopped beside one of the newer stones.

'This is what I thought you should see.'

They looked at the stone. It bore the inscription:

MARY SCOTT

1919–1994

RIP

'POETRY IS OF GRAVER IMPORT THAN HISTORY' — ARISTOTLE

'Mary Scott? A woman?' said Oliver.

'Indeed,' said Mr Gunn. 'And a fine-looking lady, too.'

'You knew her?'

'Only in my professional capacity.'

'Do you know anything about her?'

'A little. I know that she arrived on the island about a year ago. She lived alone in a house off the Street in Stromness. She died three months ago and left instructions in her will that her headstone should carry only her name, dates and the quotation from Aristotle, in English of course. Exactly as you see written here. It was an unusual request, unique in my experience. That is why I thought it proper to contact you.'

'Does she have family on the island?' said Oliver.

'No. Two children came from the mainland. They were here for the funeral.'

'She was an incomer.'

'Like so many of us,' said Mr Gunn.

'You too?' said Diane, surprised.

'My family came here from Scotland during the Highland clearances. However, we are beginning to settle in now.'

Something that might easily have been mistaken for a smile ghosted across his face, then disappeared as swiftly as it had arrived. It could have been an optical illusion, a trick of the Orcadian light or the echo of a joke first told several centuries earlier.

Oliver made a note of the quotation on the margin of his morning newspaper.

' "Poetry is of graver import than history." I shall have to think about that and check the source. T. S. Eliot had very much the same idea, but he was a classical scholar, of course.'

Then he looked at his paper. It was, according to the cryptic rota, Aristotle's day in the *Independent* and Oliver had already opened it to the crossword page.

'Heigh-ho,' he said.

'I'm sorry,' said Diane.

'That is all I have to show you,' said Mr Gunn. 'I hope it has been of help.'

'Thank you, Mr Gunn, it has,' said Oliver.

'I will drive you to your hotel and then I must go about my daily business.'

They drove in silence for a while and then Oliver said:

'May I ask you another small favour?'

'We are always happy to perform small favours.'

'We've noticed that,' said Diane. 'Is it a peculiarity of the island?'

'I have no way of telling. I have never left the island. Is it not like that in London?'

'We don't live in London,' said Diane. 'We've never lived in London.'

'Forgive me. But we rely on the television for our information. According to the television, the mainland of England appears to be London.' Then, turning to Oliver, Mr Gunn said: 'What is the small favour?'

'You say that Mary Scott had a house in Stromness. Would it be a breach of professional confidentiality if you told us the address?'

Mr Gunn gave it serious thought before answering:

'On balance, I think not. The house is empty and for sale. There would be no harm in your looking upon it. You wish to pay homage, no doubt?'

'Yes. We wish to pay homage.'

'So you shall.'

The main street in Stromness was called, with characteristic directness, the Street. It was narrow and meandered almost parallel with the harbour. It had the intimate security of a pedestrian precinct, without any legal compulsion. The traffic flowed lightly and politely, at a brisk but careful walking pace.

Oliver and Diane made their way along the Street in casual spurts. He had never walked past a bookshop in his life and she was on the lookout for a runic pullover like the one worn by the runaway girl from Basildon.

She held his arm and repeated what she had said at the cemetery.

'I'm very sorry.'

'Sorry?'

'You travel all this way and Aristotle is dead.'

'I came to pay homage. I can still pay homage. That's what we're doing.' He stopped to look at books.

'Assuming Mary Scott *was* your Aristotle,' said Diane.

'I agree there's still a question mark,' said Oliver.

'I mean, where are the crosswords coming from? There's one in the paper today. How come, if she died three months ago?'

'She probably left a stockpile.'

'A stockpile?'

Oliver noted two books and a newspaper to check on the way back. They moved on, and he explained about stockpiles.

'In my desk at home I have several sets of purely speculative

Mastermind questions on specialist subjects that nobody has yet wanted to answer.'

'Like what?'

'Three sets of questions on different aspects of Beethoven, then there's the footballing career of Horatio Stratton Carter, the development of bebop, 1945–55, the life and work of Wilson, Keppel and Betty . . .'

'You do all that for fun?' she said, stopping to look at runic pullovers.

'Of course. People like Aristotle and myself, we do tend to become a little obsessive.'

'You surprise me.'

She noted a jumper to check on the way back. They moved on and Oliver spotted a street sign reading Khyber Pass. It was their turning. It led into a tiny close of stone-built terrace houses leading directly on to the narrow pavement.

They found Mary Scott's house. It had 'For Sale' signs in the window. The woodwork had been painted within the year and the windows cleaned within the week. It was a reticent house where a civilized woman could lead a civilized life and not be a nuisance to anyone.

'Imagine,' said Oliver. 'The greatest crossword compiler of our time lived in that little house.'

Diane corrected him, saying:

'In that *wee* house.'

'Peedie, to be precise.'

'What?'

'The Scots say "wee". The Orcadians say "peedie".'

He was pedantic, even when paying homage; but she had begun to understand the nature of his pedantry. He was passionate with it. He needed to know everything, he needed to know it, if possible, by yesterday and he often did. He knew all about Magnus the Martyr and St Margaret's Hope and the Italian Chapel and now he knew about 'peedie', and she had no idea how he did it. He seemed to arrive at a place, take a deep breath and be on immediate first-name terms with the ebb and the flow, the quick and the dead, the grammar and the syntax. He would have made a wonderful detective. What a shame he had so little faith in the judiciary.

Though maybe not.

'All right,' she said. 'I stand corrected. Aristotle lived in that peedie house. *If* we are assuming that Mary Scott was Aristotle.'

'Having seen the house, I am in no doubt.'

He crossed the narrow street and placed the flat of his hand on the stonework. He had done so twice before: once at D. H. Lawrence's birthplace in Eastwood, once at the Keats house on the Spanish Steps in Rome.

'This is the place,' said Oliver.

Diane watched in silence, respecting the moment, but thinking: keep your distance, folks, my man's communing with ghosts again, stand well back, there's nothing to see.

Oliver broke his own spell.

'There's a note pinned to the door,' he said.

'I don't want to spoil the beauty of the moment,' said Diane, 'but it probably says "No milk today". Or even "No milk ever again. Have gone to the great six-letter word beginning with "H" in the sky."'

'Do you think it could be for us?'

'Don't be ridiculous. We're not the milkman.'

But she was intrigued too. They looked up and down the peedie side-street. Nobody was watching. Oliver edged closer to the door and said:

'We could peep, then put it back, neatly and carefully, leaving it exactly as we would wish to find it.'

'I spot an obsession coming on.'

'It could be a final, tantalizing anagram.'

Diane hesitated. She felt a recurrence of her old law-and-order symptoms. Then she decided the hell with it, it's only a note for an unknown milkman.

'Go on then.'

Oliver pulled out the drawing-pin holding the note to the door, unfolded the paper and read the message.

'I think it might be for us. It certainly has nothing to do with milk.'

He passed it to Diane. The message read:

ITALIAN CHAPEL, 2 P.M. – BAXTER

She returned the note to him, saying:

'What do you think?'

'I'd like to see the Italian Chapel. It's a very interesting story.'

'What do you think about Baxter?'

'We could take the usual precautions.'

'Like staying well away?'

'Tell the people at the hotel where we're going. Say if we're not back by three o'clock, would they please inform your father and the UN Security Council?'

Diane was uncertain. She knew Oliver was convinced the island had its own built-in security. Orcadians left their doors unlocked, like people used to in Olde Englande. They were a law-abiding race. But she knew, by experience and in her bones, that the Baxters of the world wrote their own laws as they went along and had access to their own militia.

'I thought you were sick and tired of me being a policeperson?'

'I came here on a quest. My quest is at an end.' He placed his hand on the house, then moved it on to her shoulder.

'And I want you to pursue your quest. If it makes you happy.'

'Thank you.'

She had become so absorbed in Oliver's quest she had almost forgotten her own. In any case, Oliver's quests seemed more fun and less lethal than hers, but just as satisfying.

He tried to reassure her:

'We'll be very careful. We'll make sure your quest doesn't render us both cleft in twain and thereby deceased.'

'Terrific. I feel a lot better.'

'We have to share each other's quests. Your quest is mine and mine is yours.'

She realized that if he had taken a half-share in her quest she might as well swim with the tide of his obsession. Her bloke was like Bugs Bunny: a time-served zealot who trebled the effort when he had forgotten the point.

She compromised. She agreed to keep the appointment with

Baxter, taking the precautions Oliver had suggested; but first they returned to the Street. Oliver bought her a runic sweater and she bought him two slim volumes of local verses and a copy of the weekly newspaper, the *Orcadian*. It contained an article on the annual general meeting of an accordion and fiddle society, a police report of a broken window in Kirkwall, and no crossword.

They parked the car in the piazza of the Italian Chapel, close to a statue of St George killing the Dragon. There were two other cars parked nearby.

Oliver said the presence of the cars was a guarantee of security: there was safety in a crowd. Diane said that was nonsense. Baxter had obviously turned up with a mob and his battle plan was clear: one body would go in each boot. They would be spirited away via the roll-on/roll-off and the peaceful, neighbourly, law-abiding Orcadians would be none the wiser. It wouldn't even make the local paper.

They were arguing quietly in the shelter of St George when the chapel door opened and Baxter came out and stood in the door-way. He reminded Oliver of the little man who used to pop out of the weather-house his mother kept on the mantelpiece. He only popped out when it was going to rain.

'Is something wrong?' Baxter called to them.

Diane called back: 'We don't know whether you're going to call up your helicopters.'

'Don't worry. I'm alone and unarmed. I'm also a devout Catholic and this is holy ground.'

He remained in the doorway.

Oliver and Diane hesitated. The man could be lying: about being alone, about being unarmed, about being a Catholic. This was the age of liars. Baxter held up his hands, half-way to an atti-tude of surrender.

They walked towards the chapel. This is a bit like *High Noon*, thought Oliver, but Gary Cooper won that one and he was the good guy. His mind refused to keep still. It leapt sideways from the Wild West to the South Side of Chicago, and he said:

'Wasn't Al Capone a devout Catholic?'

'Shut up,' said Diane.

Baxter greeted them with a smile.

'There's nothing to be frightened of,' he said.

'We were dive-bombed in Scotland,' said Diane.

'I'm afraid things got a little out of control. They are now under control. *My* control.'

'Is that good?' said Oliver.

'You two are my sole responsibility.'

'You haven't answered the question,' said Diane. 'Is your control good?'

Baxter held the door open for them.

'Do come in. The frescos are lovely and warm.'

Diane tried very hard not to think about spiders, flies and parlours. Oliver tried very hard not to think about the Norman Bates motel. They went in. Baxter welcomed them, enthusing about the interior of the chapel like a devout Roman Catholic.

'Isn't this a gem? All the work of a remarkable man called Domenico Chiochetti.'

Baxter was right. The place was a gem, dominated by the altar with a holy picture of the Madonna and Child, the sanctuary separated from the more austere body of the chapel by a delicate wrought-iron screen. Colonel P. N. Nissen, 1871–1930, could never have anticipated his corrugated semicircular invention finding such an elegant state of grace.

'Chiochetti was an Italian prisoner of war,' said Oliver.

'You know the story?' said Baxter.

My man knows all the stories, thought Diane. He knows stories that haven't been invented yet. He'll make them up for you if you don't stop him.

'During the war,' said Oliver, 'Italian prisoners of war built the causeway from Orkney to Burray. They were devout Catholics and the military authorities gave them two Nissen huts to use as a chapel. Chiochetti supervised the work, and painted the frescos himself. The ironwork and the rood-screen are by a metalworker called Palumbo.'

Stop him, thought Diane. She wanted to hear the story, but another time, another day.

'What about the sequel?' said Baxter.

'Is that the bit where we disappear without trace?' said Diane.

Baxter seemed hurt by her suggestion.

'Please. We are trying to tell you a story.'

He was like a primary school teacher reprimanding a naughty seven-year-old: no Plasticine for her today.

'I'm sorry,' she said, thinking: this man tried to have us killed so why am I apologizing? But she listened. She didn't want to stay behind after school.

'In 1960 the chapel had fallen into disrepair. Chiochetti was tracked down in Italy via, would you believe, the BBC World Service. He returned to the island and restored his work. As you see it now.'

They stood still as Baxter walked the bounds of the chapel, admiring the restoration work and celebrating the purity of the conception: a good deed emerging from a wicked war. He finished his walk and, moving close to them, said:

'Now I need you two to help restore my work.'

'You're not a painter,' said Diane. 'You're a piano player.'

'My security work.'

'Is there something wrong with your security work?' said Oliver.

'It has sprung a leak. I believe you two are the leak. I believe you have acquired information, probably by illegal access to our computer systems . . . information which from my point of view . . . and from the point of view of the people I work for . . . and most of all from your point of view . . . is lethal.'

'Lethal?' said Oliver.

'Lethal. In its precise dictionary meaning. Causing death.'

'You don't mind my questioning you?' said Oliver. 'I hate people who use the English language carelessly.'

'I am never careless in my choice of words.'

Baxter approached the altar.

'Consider, if you will, this exquisite altar. It is made out of concrete. The rood-screen was made from scrap-metal. They used wood from a wrecked ship for the tabernacle. The good Chiochetti supervised the work but he had people to help him.

Palumbo, the smith, as you mentioned. Primavera and Micheloni, the electricians. Bruttapasta, the cement worker. And the honest labourers. Barcaglioni, Battato, Devitto, Fornasier. It was a co-operative effort.'

He gazed at the work of the Italians, then turned to face Oliver and Diane.

'So shall we follow their excellent example? Shall we co-operate?'

'What form of co-operation had you in mind?' said Diane.

'Give me your lethal information.'

'And what do we get?'

'I hate to sound like a second-rate gangster but, lady, you get to live.'

Then, turning to Oliver:

'You too.'

'It does sound a little second-rate,' said Oliver, 'when you hear it spoken like that. In real life, I mean.'

'It's deceptive,' said Baxter, 'because whatever else I am, I am not second-rate.'

'Do you know the legend of Haakon and Magnus?' said Oliver.

'I do.'

God help us, thought Diane, now it's the Eurovision Tale-Telling Contest. I bet my legend can beat your legend. Not only that, I bet my dad's got a taller story than your dad, and if I ask him, he'll come and bash you with it.

Men.

'If we are Magnus,' said Oliver to Baxter, 'who are you? Are you Haakon, who orders the execution? Or are you the loyal standard-bearer, who refuses to carry out the order? Or are you the cook, who does as he is told?'

'For all practical purposes, I am all three.'

Diane decided to quit. She was fed up with the whole business. In future she would stick with Oliver's quests. They were trivial, without apparent meaning or purpose, but everybody got to live.

'As far as I'm concerned, you can have your lethal information. I'm sick of it.'

As they left the chapel, Baxter looked at his watch.

'Two thirty. I imagine your father is telephoning your hotel at three? To make sure you're safe and well?'

'Yes.'

'So shall we meet at four o'clock? Beside the Barbara Hepworth?'

'We'll be there.'

There was a Barbara Hepworth piece in the courtyard of the Pier Arts Centre in Stromness. They had planned a visit later in the afternoon. How did Baxter know that? Did he know everything? Was he bugging their lives?

In a way, yes.

He walked them to the car, pausing to admire the statue of St George and the Dragon.

'This is an interesting piece. Also made out of concrete.'

'Fascinating,' said Diane, who had never been less fascinated in her life. She just wanted to be back in her little hotel room listening to her father's voice on the telephone.

'Concrete, on a framework of barbed wire,' said Baxter.

'I imagine,' said Oliver, 'that you're about to tell us there's a moral to that. True beauty is impossible without strength?'

'I wouldn't dream of suggesting such a thing.'

'Can we drop you anywhere,' said Diane. 'Or are you being air-lifted out?'

'Thank you. I am self-sufficient.'

'Lucky old you,' said Diane.

'Four o'clock,' said Baxter.

They drove back to Orkney across the causeway built by Chiochetti and his fellow prisoners. In the water on either side were the spiky remains of old ships, scuttled as ballast for the enterprise. There was a long tradition of sinking and scuttling in Scapa Flow. You could go on a conducted tour of famous wrecks.

Diane found the idea of sunken ships eerie and chilling. She preferred Oliver's ghosts. They were weird, some of them, but he made them live and they knew a few good jokes.

Sensing her gloom, he tried to cheer her.

'Mr Baxter is very unusual, as gangsters go.'

He seemed to imply that gangsters were ten-a-penny in his past life: from the gin joints of Yorkshire's South Side to the mean streets of the campus.

'In what way is he unusual?'

'Do you suppose Al Capone knew about Barbara Hepworth?'

'They spoke of little else in Chicago,' said Diane.

Oliver said no more. He understood her need for a period of silence.

Her father telephoned at three. Diane assured him she was well and as happy as could be expected.

'How happy is that?' said her father.

'Surprisingly,' she said.

Mrs Davidson brought tea and home-made shortbread, which restored their souls. After she had gone, Diane opened the wardrobe and took out the three rolls of fax paper. She had hidden them inside their dirty laundry.

'We'll need a bag,' she said.

'I found this in the car,' said Oliver, holding-out a large plastic carrier bearing the word 'DOBELL'S'. 'It's wasted on Baxter, of course.'

'Wasted?'

'Famous jazz record shop. That's why the bag is LP-shaped. Dobell's. Now closed. An innocent victim of the recession.'

She loaded the paper into the carrier, saying:

'The bag is another homage?'

'What else is there?'

'Why do you think I'm doing this?'

'Because we're a bit frightened of that nasty man?'

It was the wrong answer. She explained why.

'All this information represents the pinnacle of my professional career. A major triumph. I could win medals and promotion. And we are about to hand it over to Baxter. What we are handing over is the life and work of WPC Priest.'

'You have two minutes on the life and work of WPC Priest. Starting now.'

She was not playing games, nor did she need two minutes.

'The work is less important than the life. The work is in the bag. The life is in this room.'

'You mean me?'

He pointed at himself, to be sure there was no misunderstanding.

'Call it predestination. I am paying homage, you daft pillock! To you!'

'Gosh.'

For the second time that day they walked along the Street in Stromness. Oliver was carrying the bag because it was heavy.

'Let me be the man,' he had said.

'How long have you done impressions?' she had said.

They already had well-oiled routines, which they sometimes flaunted: it took most people years. Some people never achieved it.

They turned left from the Street into a narrow passageway.

'In the West Riding of Yorkshire they'd call this a ginnel,' said Oliver.

'Thank you, I know a ginnel when I see one.'

It led them into a small, rectangular courtyard overlooking the harbour. Flanking the courtyard was the gallery, formerly a coal store, now housing an art collection brought to Orkney by an incomer with a generous eye and a sensitive cheque-book for the St Ives school.

The Barbara Hepworth was called *Curved Form*. It was a small abstract, stood on a plinth and dominated its surroundings eloquently, without trying: like a solo by Johnny Hodges.

Baxter was waiting, as promised.

Oliver handed him the carrier.

'Thank you.'

'You may keep the bag.'

'What?'

'It's a homage,' said Diane.

Baxter did not react. He gave the impression that he wished the whole transaction to be completed in monosyllables or better still in silence: like those cold war movies when spies came in from the cold.

He was turning to leave when Oliver said:

'Have you noticed something, Mr Baxter?'

'What?'

Oliver caressed the surface of the *Curved Form*.

'No barbed wire.'

'I hate to sully your innocence,' said Baxter, 'but there is barbed wire everywhere. The invisible kind is easily the worst.'

They watched him leave the courtyard. Then Oliver said:

'Shall I tell you something nice?'

'What?'

'I've got another of those bags at home. A better one, that doesn't have a hole in the bottom.'

'Good.'

'I wouldn't allow my best one to fall into evil hands.'

'Obviously.'

Then they went into the gallery where Oliver had arranged for them to meet Barbara Hepworth, Ben Nicholson and Terry Frost.

18

The Ring of Brodgar

It was a familiar big city sound: a police siren. It seemed to stop outside the house.

Michael removed the headphones. He had been listening to a tape of Freddie and the Dreamers, on loan from a friend of Cathy's who thought 'You Were Made for Me' represented a turning point in twentieth-century culture. Michael was unconvinced.

The flashing blue light reflected on the ceiling of the bedsitter. Combined with the music the place looked like a 1960s theme disco fallen into receivership.

Cathy wandered through from the small back room to look out of the window.

'They're a bit late,' she said.

'The police are coming here?'

Michael, alarmed, stopped the tape, dumped the headphones and crossed to the window. Cathy, as usual, stayed cool.

'They usually search the place the first Tuesday in the month. Relax. Sit in your chair and play dumb.'

'Piece of piss,' said Michael.

Cathy recognized the two policemen standing on the doorstep. They were called Sergeant Lynch and Police Constable Weir.

They had no idea they shared their names with illustrious fictional predecessors. Weir was too young and Lynch was too dim. The sergeant was vaguely aware that the younger coppers called him Bet behind his back, in honour of the celebrated *Coronation Street* barmaid. Weir was equally vaguely aware that he shared his name with a dam on a river. But overall they were dour men, reluctant to share anything with anyone, including their names.

'Hi,' said Cathy.

'Is George at home?' said Lynch.

'He's inside. It should be on the police computer.'

'It's down again,' said Lynch. 'So we'll just take a look around if that's all right.'

She held the door open for them. It was an ancient, well-honed ritual.

'You know where everything is. I'll make a pot of tea,' she said, as they made their way up the stairs; then, as an afterthought she said: 'Hey, George hasn't escaped, has he?'

'No idea,' said Weir. 'The computer's down.'

'He can't have escaped,' said Cathy. 'He'd have telephoned.'

She led the policemen into the bedsitter. Lynch saw Michael slumped in the armchair and said:

'Who's the comedian?'

'This is Michael. He's crashing here for a few days.'

'Another computer whizz-kid?'

'No. I'm a geologist. And my mother's in the police force.'

'Is that right? Well I'm the Secretary of State for Scotland,' said Lynch. As the senior partner he carried the joker's licence.

He turned to Cathy.

'You still keep the stuff in the usual place?'

'I'm looking after it for George. I keep it dusted and such like.'

'You check around in here,' said Lynch to his companion. before going into the kitchen with Cathy.

Cathy had tidied up the back room in anticipation of the visit.

'Our information is you've been up to your tricks again,' said Lynch.

'Impossible. Michael's a geologist and I can't even change a fuse.'

'So what's this?'

The computer was switched on. It showed a combination of words running vertically and horizontally.

'Computer Scrabble.'

'Is that a word?'

He pointed to the word in question: ZO.

'Himalayan cattle,' said Cathy. 'A cross between a cow and a yak.'

'Is that a fact?'

'You can also spell it with an "H".'

'ZOH?'

'ZHO.'

'We're not here to discuss Himalayan cattle.'

'Sorry, Sergeant. But you did ask.'

He sighed. This was not his scene. Dockside tavern brawls: they were his chosen specialist subject: comforting the wounded with homespun wisdom like: 'I wouldn't like to see the other feller'; and intimidating the usual suspects with amiable threats to their intimate anatomy, behind closed doors, where proper justice could be meted out.

Paradise.

All gone. The docksides. The taverns. The brawls.

He looked around the back room for hints of malfeasance and skulduggery. What did they call those things? Floppy discs? If he could take a floppy disc back to the station it would look good on the record. Where would the kiddies hide a floppy disc?

'What's in the bread bin?'

'Half a sliced loaf and a packet of oat cakes.'

Lynch slid open the bread bin. He found half a sliced loaf and a packet of oat cakes.

Police Constable Weir had a little learning in these matters. He knew a floppy disc could be hidden among records, compact discs and tapes. He did a thorough check of the shelves. He picked up an audio-cassette.

'Freddie and the Dreamers?'

'Friend of Cathy's says they're a turning-point in twentieth-century culture.'

'Bollocks.'

'Yeah.'

The policemen had a cup of tea then left the house, frustrated and empty-handed. In the car, Lynch said to his partner:

'Why is it those bairns make me feel so old?'

Weir opened his mouth to reply.

'Don't tell me. I don't want to know,' said Lynch.

Cathy watched from the window as the police car left the street.

'You were brilliant,' said Michael.

'It's a bit sad really.'

'Sad?'

'Women got the vote, when? Seventy years ago? And I can still fool the cops with a fluffy female routine.'

She moved into self-parody mode.

'Me, Sergeant, I can't even change a fuse. I need George to do all that. Let me make you a nice cup of tea while you get on with your man's work.'

She moved back into Cathy mode.

'I'll tell you this for nothing. If I was running their computer, I'd have people like me locked up in no time.'

'Do you think they suspect something?'

'What about?'

'All your hacking and faxing and such? About the Red Baron?'

'It's their job to suspect things. Proving it, that's the tough bit. You realize, they've probably got satellites up there in the sky recording everything we do? But the pictures get a bit blurred by the time they're transmitted back to Aberdeen. And the guys down the station, they'll be watching football or a dirty video.'

Michael stood up.

'Still. I'd better ring my mum, tell her we've had a police raid.'

'I'll re-rig the telephone and the rest of the crap.'

She lifted up the cushion from Michael's armchair. Beneath it

lay three rolls of computer printout, a dozen floppy discs, a telephone and a hundred yards of assorted wires and cables, coiled up
and looking like an emu's nest.

'Bit uncomfortable, sitting on that lot,' said Michael, stretching.

'Your arse must look like a waffle.'

He laughed. Cathy was crazy but he really, really liked her.
George was a lucky guy.

It was midnight at the Scapa Flow Hotel. Diane lay on the bed,
fully dressed, trying to finish the *Independent* crossword. Oliver
stood beside the bathroom door.

'I am going to clean my teeth. I may be some time.'

'You don't have to keep your secret diary secret from me.'

'I've done my diary. It isn't that. It's something else.'

She realized he was hiding something behind his back.

'What are you hiding?'

'Nothing. Well. Something. It's my other secret.'

'It's your black box, isn't it?'

He nodded, a guilty plea, like the day he was caught reading
Men Only in class when the others were reading Thomas Hardy's
The Trumpet Major.

'You can tell me all your secrets.'

'I'm learning to play the flute.'

He mumbled the confession, in an uncharacteristic burble, as
if hoping that it would be too quick to be detected by the naked
ear.

'So?'

'I'm not very good. I'm tempted to quote that line of Danny
Kaye's from *Tubby the Tuba*. An ill wind that nobody blows good.
And I have trouble with my *embouchure*.'

'Your what?'

'My *embouchure*.'

'I love your *embouchure*,' she said, with a dirty laugh. 'It makes
the seagulls cry and the waves lash against the shore.'

He gave her a serious, ten-minute lecture about *embouchure*. It
was vital to the beauty of the music. It was the formation of the

lips used when blowing across the aperture of the instrument.

'Well, it works for me, kid,' she said.

He continued the lecture. *Embouchure* required a precise and controlled configuration of lips and teeth, resembling that when pronouncing the French word '*tu*'. The hardest part was increasing the intensity of the breath expelled when moving into the upper registers, without losing tonal continuity.

'The higher the notes the harder you blow?' she said.

'Exactly.'

She remembered now. She had seen him, in off-moments, blowing silently through his teeth in an abstracted way. He reminded her of a silent whistler back at the police station, an Inspector who used to whistle 'Seventy-Six Trombones' through his teeth at times of stress. It was always the same tune: 'Seventy-Six Trombones'. It drove her potty. She had wanted to kill the Inspector in a deranged frenzy but it would have been a breach of the regulations concerning respect for rank.

Oliver was different. He was her shy, shuffly, obsessive bloke who had confessed his final secret.

'Play me a tune,' she said.

'I can't play if anyone's watching,' he said.

'Go into the bathroom and play me a tune.'

He thought long and hard about the proposition before saying: 'All right.'

He took the black box into the bathroom. There was a long silence. He opened the door and peered out.

'Sorry about the delay. It's a little tricky to assemble and it has to be just right.'

'In your own time.'

'I'll play "Body and Soul", but I might fluff the middle eight.'

He closed the bathroom door.

She heard a couple of false starts, like the *Flying Scotsman* warming up. Then she heard the tune: 'Body and Soul'. He was as good as his word. He fluffed the middle eight and was uncertain when moving into the upper register.

It was lovely.

When he finished, she applauded. He stayed in the bathroom.

She timed him. He stayed there for nine minutes. When he eventually emerged she said:

'Thank you.'

'I'm sorry I was such a long time. I had to pack it away and then I decided to floss my teeth.'

'It was beautiful.'

'Did you think so? There's a very difficult key change in the mid-section. And of course I haven't been practising while we've been away.'

'The music was beautiful and you are beautiful and I am beautiful and we are beautiful and the island is beautiful and now I think we should slake our lust.'

'All right.'

The tide turned and the seagulls braced themselves in readiness.

By the time Cathy had reassembled the telephone in the bread bin it was midnight. Michael decided it was too late to ring his mother. He was wrong and he was right. He was wrong in that she was still awake; he was right in that she was not accepting incoming phone calls.

He rang the following morning.

Oliver was in his pyjamas, lying on the bed watching breakfast television, waiting for the previous evening's football results. Diane was commuting to and from the bathroom, washing and drying her hair. When the telephone rang she said:

'You take it.'

Oliver switched off the television sound, picked up the phone, listened and said:

'No, this is not she. This is her lifelong companion.'

He said to Diane:

'It's your son.'

She had a hair-drier in one hand, a towel in the other and was trying to pick up a comb with her knee.

'You talk to him.'

'She says I have to talk to you. I imagine in my *de facto* capacity. I should explain that I'm not allowed to make any arrangements but I am allowed to take messages.'

He picked up a pen and prepared himself for messages.

While he was doing so Diane caught a glimpse of a familiar scene on television. A news reporter wearing a designer raincoat and a well-planned but wind-blown haircut was standing on the bridge overlooking the Welsh river where Griffiths, the farmer, had been found floating face-down a year previously.

She found the remote and switched up the sound in time to hear:

'The killing of Mr Griffiths, a local farmer, has baffled the police for almost a year. Today's arrest of two men, stated to be employees of a security organization, was, according to a police spokesperson, the result of a tip-off.'

Simultaneously, Oliver said:

'I've written all that down and will pass it on to your mother at the first opportunity.'

And Diane said:

'Shut up.'

On screen the reporter handed the viewers back to the news-room in London where a presenter wearing a calculated suit and a studio-controlled haircut continued the story:

'Scotland Yard confirmed that there could be a connection with the arrest, earlier today, of a security official in Gateshead. The man is assisting with inquiries into the murder of Adrian Walsh, a property developer in the North-East. And now over to Julia for the sport. Julia.'

He swivelled towards Julia with a smile full of crowns, caps and bridgework that Thomas Telford would have been proud of.

Simultaneously, Oliver said:

'Freddie and the Dreamers? Definitely a turning-point in twentieth-century culture. The only question is which direction was it turning? Love you madly. Stay cool.'

He hung up, then turned to see Diane turning off the set.

'I wanted to see the sport.'

'Never mind the sport. Did you hear what they were saying on the news?'

'I got the gist.'

'And?'

'Murder suspects are being arrested. Society is being cleansed. We believe in that.'

'What did Michael want?'

'The police raided the flat last night. But all they found was half a sliced loaf and a packet of oat cakes.'

Diane sat down in front of the mirror and attacked her hair. It had resented being ignored in favour of the news. It was fighting back.

'Do you really believe that?' she said to Oliver.

'What?'

'Society is being cleansed?'

'It could be the cultural turning-point of the twentieth century. Better than Michael's suggestion.'

'What?'

But he was watching the fag-end of the sport.

Before breakfast, they settled a small domestic problem. Diane had decided she wanted to do Aristotle's crossword on a daily basis, instead of filling in the odd easy clues left on the side by Oliver, which was patronizing and sexist. Oliver agreed and suggested a compromise. If he did the Across clues, she could do the Down clues. Diane said that was stupid. Oliver agreed and suggested an alternative. If he did the clues with even numbers, she could do the clues with odd numbers. Diane said that was even more stupid. Oliver agreed and Eileen Davidson, who was on the desk in the lobby, said it would be her pleasure to photocopy the crossword so they could have one each.

They sat in the dining-room and did the crossword over breakfast. Oliver finished his at the same time as he finished his porridge.

'Extraordinary,' he said.

'Is it?' said Diane, staring at the clues as if they were written in Sanskrit.

'You'll see why.'

'Why?' she said. 'It's all gobbledegook. One across. Perimeter of Scottish church. What's that supposed to mean?'

'Think about Scottish churches. And think about where we are.'

She thought hard about both, then said triumphantly:

'Kirkwall!'

'Correct.'

'That's near here, isn't it? On the island? By Jove, I think I've got it! Are they all near here? Are they all Orcadian?'

'I said it was extraordinary.'

She wrote in some of the easier landmarks: the Old Man of Hoy, Scapa Flow, Shapinsay and Stronsay.

'Brilliant,' said Oliver.

Eleven down gave her trouble. The clue was: 'Frog with broad grin. Stoned? (4, 2, 7).'

'I need another clue,' she said.

'It's an anagram.'

'It can't all be an anagram. There are too many letters.'

'Some of it's an anagram.'

'Thanks a bunch, lover man.'

She stared at the clue and at what she had written so far. The first part of the answer began with 'R' and had an 'N' for the third letter.

'Is the first word "ring"?'

'Ring of bright water. Ring of inner cleanliness. Ring-a-ring o' roses. Ring at the end of his nose. Ring-a-ding-ding.'

'Telephone,' said Eileen Davidson to Oliver. She had approached the table quietly as ever, while they were absorbed in their problem-solving. 'A gentleman on the phone would like to speak to you.'

'Did he give a name?' said Oliver.

'He says his name is Aristotle,' said Eileen before departing about her business.

'Aristotle?' said Diane.

'I wonder what he wants.'

'Since Aristotle is a dead woman called Mary Scott, I imagine he wants mouth-to-mouth resuscitation and a sex-change operation.'

'I'll ask him,' said Oliver.

Diane stared at the crossword while Oliver went into the lobby to deal with the phone call. She was staring at the crossword when he returned.

'Who was it?'

'Aristotle.'

'That's impossible. Aristotle's dead. Both of them.'

'We shall see. We're meeting him in an hour. Finish your crossword.'

'I can't do it! It's too hard!'

'Bring it with you,' Oliver said calmly.

They drove inland from Scapa Flow, the road flanked by Loch Stenness to the left, Loch Harray to the right. Oliver was driving so Diane could carry on with her crossword. It was his idea to switch on the radio for the news. This is weird, she thought: we've swopped places.

They came in half-way as the newsreader said:

'Baron Kite was arrested as he was leaving Heathrow Airport with a female companion. Also assisting the police with their inquiries are a Chief Constable from Wales, two former civil servants from the Ministry of Defence and several City bankers. No names have been released. Westminster sources have denied rumours that senior Cabinet Ministers are implicated in what some sections of the media are now calling Farquhargate.'

Diane switched off the radio, saying:

'I can't concentrate with that on.'

'Comprehensive cleansing of society is going on and you'd rather do a crossword?'

She looked out of the window.

'Where are we?'

'Almost there.'

'Almost where?'

'The Ring of Brodgar.'

'Good.'

She pondered this briefly, then looked down at her crossword. It was the slowest burn since the graceful, simmering days of Stan and Ollie, but eventually a bright light shone through her consciousness, and there was great rejoicing.

'That's it, isn't it? That's the answer! Ring of Brodgar! "Frog with broad grin. Stoned?" It's an anagram of "frog", "broad" and "grin". What has "Stoned?" got to do with it?'

'You'll see.'

Minutes later they stood on the perimeter of the great Ring of Brodgar.

'It's a stone circle,' said Oliver, patting one of the great flat stones. 'Your dad would appreciate this.'

'What place is this?'

'The Ring of Brodgar.'

'How old?'

'Five thousand years.'

She stared. The circle was over a hundred yards across. The surviving stones stood equidistant around the perimeter, some taller than others, craggy and uneven, weathered by five thousand years of prevailing winds and worship. The ground beneath was soft, like a peat bog. Either side of the ring lay the two lochs and beyond them low green hills and beyond them grey infinity.

'Does anybody know what it was for?' she said.

'Homage, I expect.'

'Religious?'

'If you make anything this big, it's bound to turn out religious. Think of Lord's or Headingley or Wembley.'

'But nobody really knows.'

'It's a mystery. Perhaps they knew that too. Perhaps they were celebrating the mystery of not knowing.'

Oliver and Diane walked slowly around the edge of the circle. The ground was wet. They had been warned to wear sensible shoes. They had done their best, wearing sneakers of substance but free of logos. The sneakers were not sensible but if they ended up ruined, it was a modest sacrifice at such a shrine.

The sun came out, low and harsh, striking long shadows, like a message from the gods.

'Wow,' said Diane.

'Yes,' said Oliver. 'That's how we're supposed to feel.'

'Awesome, yes?' said Baxter, stepping out from behind the stone column immediately ahead of them.

They stared at him in silence. Diane noticed he was wearing walking boots. Oliver spoke first:

'Yes, it is awesome but . . . why aren't you under arrest? Or assisting the police with their inquiries?'

'Why should I be?'

'Everybody else is. We heard it on the news.'

Baxter smiled.

'I *am* the police. I *am* the inquiries.'

'You're the police?' said Diane.

He nodded and brought out an ID card. Diane checked it. Yes. He *was* the police, and from a high and mighty branch in the heart of the metropolis.

'Your carrier-bag had a hole in it, but your information was crucial. It helped us spring the trap. I'm deeply indebted.'

'You've been one of the good guys all along?' said Oliver.

'Relatively speaking. Relatively good. Though I had to pretend to be relatively bad, for the look of the thing.'

Oliver was impressed.

'The honest cop working under cover for the villains. I've always wanted to meet one of those. And now I have.'

'You remember the legend of Haakon and Magnus? You asked me which one I was. I'm Ofeig, the honest standard-bearer who refused to strike the fatal blow.'

'What about the helicopter?' said Diane, unwilling to let Baxter off the hook, simply on the basis of an ID card, a grateful smile and a senior rank.

'Too many cooks.'

'We could have been cleft in twain,' said Oliver.

'It's the company I was keeping. The market's awash with cowboy security men. Refugees from Eastern Europe. Good old boys from the KGB and the like. Eager to prove their credentials in the democratic West.'

'What if we'd been killed?' said Diane.

'I'd have sent flowers.'

It was an honest and chilling assessment. Diane felt cold. She needed circulation. She started walking. They walked together around the circle of stones.

Oliver was the first to speak:

'I'm told that you can't cleanse society of all evil without breaking a few eggs. I suppose we would have been a couple of broken eggs on the road to the Isles.'

'Quite so.'

'And is your Farquhargate going to cleanse society?'

'The odd gutter, no more. We won't touch the grey men in their tall towers. We'll put away the hoodlums. Perhaps one or two medium-range fall guys. The poor old Baron, he'll get a nominal year in a soft nick. He'll end up running liberal studies classes in the prison library. When he comes out he'll write a book and sell the serial rights to a posh newspaper.'

'But the grey men in the tall towers?' said Oliver.

'Their towers are too tall. Remember Haakon. He inherited the earth.'

'He stole the earth,' said Diane.

'Inheritance? Theft? They look very similar to the naked eye.'

They walked on together, apparently in silent accord concerning the myth of temporal justice. Again Oliver was the one to speak:

'We're very grateful for your full and frank explanation, and for your world-view but . . .'

He hesitated, then continued, with sudden sharpness:

'How dare you pretend to be Aristotle!'

Baxter stopped, stared at Oliver in hurt disbelief.

'I'm not pretending. I *am* Aristotle. I inherited the name from my mother. I believe you visited her grave.'

'Mary Scott was your mother?' said Oliver.

Baxter nodded, then looked away, eyes cast down, and walked on.

'But I used to write to her. I went to her cottage in Wales and it was in ruins.'

'I know.'

The sun disappeared. There was a sudden shower of rain, scudding hard and horizontal. They had been warned the climate offered four seasons in a day. This was the third so far in one short walk. Winter lay in wait.

They found shelter beside a tall tower of stone, and Baxter continued.

'The cottage was set on fire. It was arson. My mother was like you,' he said, looking at Oliver. 'She had an inventive and lateral mind. No use in a straight line, but brilliant sideways. She stumbled on what was happening in Wales . . . the Griffiths murder . . . the corrupt Chief Constable . . . so they set her house on fire. I was angry about that. I decided to do something instead of sitting in my tall tower waiting for my pension. Don Quixote. Take out a couple of windmills. But it was nothing to do with cleansing society. It was purely personal and vindictive.'

'And the crosswords?' said Oliver. 'Are they hers or yours?'

'She left a stockpile, but I'm taking over, slowly and with respect. I dropped in the odd clue, to tempt you up here.'

'We noticed,' said Diane.

'It was when I met you in Shrewsbury, I decided you could be useful to my cause.' Baxter smiled. 'You could say I was your recruiting officer.' Then the smile faded and he continued: 'But I was really paying homage to my mother.'

Diane noticed Baxter's eyes were wet, but it could have been the wind and the rain.

'It's all about paying homage,' said Oliver. 'Hearing what the ghosts are saying.'

'What are they saying? said Diane.

'They're saying . . . please listen.'

They listened.

Warner now offers an exciting range of quality titles by both established and new authors. All of the books in this series are available from:
Little, Brown and Company (UK),
P.O. Box 11,
Falmouth,
Cornwall TR10 9EN.

Alternatively you may fax your order to the above address. Fax No. 0326 376423.

Payments can be made as follows: Cheque, postal order (payable to Little, Brown and Company) or by credit cards, Visa/Access. Do not send cash or currency. UK customers: and B.F.P.O.: please send a cheque or postal order (no currency) and allow £1.00 for postage and packing for the first book, plus 50p for the second book, plus 30p for each additional book up to a maximum charge of £3.00 (7 books plus).

Overseas customers including Ireland, please allow £2.00 for postage and packing for the first book, plus £1.00 for the second book, plus 50p for each additional book.

NAME (Block Letters) ....

ADDRESS..

....

☐ I enclose my remittance for _____

☐ I wish to pay by Access/Visa Card

Number ⬚⬚⬚⬚⬚⬚⬚⬚⬚⬚⬚⬚⬚⬚⬚⬚

Card Expiry Date ⬚⬚⬚⬚